the Briar Crown

HRP
PUBLISHING

The Briar Crown

Copyright © 2023 by Helen Rygh-Pedersen

Published by HRP Publishing
eBook ISBN: 978-82-93831-10-5
Paperback ISBN: 978-82-93831-11-2
Cover Design: AK Westerman
@akorganicabstracts
First edition: January 2023

Also by
Helen Rygh-Pedersen

Series

Riverda Rising:
Waking Ursa Minor

Picture Books
A Whiff in the Woods

**Short Stories writing as
H. Rygh-Pedersen**
Heifer

In loving memory of
Elizabeth 'Betty' Gibson

the Briar Crown

ZEMKOSKA

Eredhza

Bergam

Domovina

Kesktee

Tokaveror

Bergam

Domovnia

Keshtee

okavdor

Hadku

Novledia

Kojiba Chutka

Oscanbad

Dumba

Yobisz

Chapter 1

The sound of the whip ripping at naked flesh echoed around the square. The hissed intake of breath that accompanied the strikes of the metal cord soon turned to spittle and blood-laced expulsions of pain as their owner lost his battle to remain silent.

Roslyn wanted to close her eyes, to look away from the face contorted in pain, but she dared not. There were too many soldiers—too many of the Oderberg bulldogs staring into the crowd, making sure each and every one of them understood the cost of disobeying the crown. Sour saliva filled her mouth and she wanted to spit. She swallowed her feelings down in revulsion and leant back into the muscular chest that was propping her up as the scene seared her eyes. She risked a quick look up at Eik and saw his bearded chin set squarely, brown eyes staring straight ahead. His heart was pounding with rage; she could feel it through her bodice. He gave her arm a tight squeeze and she lowered her gaze back to the stage just as a soldier shifted his spear in his hand at her lack of attention.

4

Finally, when the sentenced number of lashes had been administered, the leader of the troop of soldiers stepped forward. He grimaced slightly as the young man's blood blotted the edge of his polished steel boot.

"Let this man's punishment of twenty lashes be a reminder to all Domovnians: use of magic will not be tolerated. The next man, woman or child to be found practising any form of hexery will be executed before his majesty, the king, at Novlada."

A hushed murmuring spread around the crowd that had been forcefully gathered that morning. The soldiers had arrived, all polished steel, red capes and feathers in their metal helmets, before most people had made it out of bed to start the day. They'd near beaten down the doors of anyone who failed to answer and dragged the inhabitants of the small woodland village into the streets in various states of dress. Roslyn had been dressing, ready to sneak out of her lover's house when they'd arrived. Eik had put his arm around her protectively as they followed the crowds of confused villagers into the square, an unusual but much appreciated gesture of public affection.

"All hail King Casimir!"

"HAIL!" the soldiers barked back at their commanding officer, striking the butts of their pikes into the dust, drowning out the half-hearted echo of the townsfolk.

Roslyn looked around as, now the punishment was over, people began drifting back to their daily lives, sending worried backwards glances to the bleeding figure on the scaffold. She followed their gaze, gripped her satchel tightly and made to step towards him, but a firm hand grabbed her elbow.

"Ros, I know you want to help Dmitri…" Eik turned her around so that her face was level with his chest and wrapped his trunk-like arms around her. "We all want to help him, but we can't. Not until they've gone."

There was a rustle in the crowd and a small woman, grey hair flying out from under the folds of her barely tied kerchief, hurtled towards the troop leader.

"I demand you let me tend to this man!"

The guard towered above her and folded his arms over his chest. "And just why would we do that, Domovnian?"

"Because if you do not, he will die."

The guard shrugged. "What's that to me? Perhaps you would like to join him? If you even so much as think of using your powers—"

"I have none!" the small woman shouted back. Roslyn's heart swelled with pride at the sight of her mentor, Hedda, scolding the Oderberg soldier like a schoolboy. "I am one of the many humans who just so happen to live in this land that you have tramped all over with your big steel boots! I am also a healer, so if you wouldn't mind…"

The guard, somewhat taken aback, looked around for confirmation. A few of his men who were permanently stationed in the ghetto nodded their heads. Hedda pushed past him and flew up the steps to the scaffold and Roslyn breathed a sigh of relief that her friend would be well tended. She turned her attention back to the man who held her in his arms.

Bowing her head, Roslyn felt the warmth of him through his cotton shirt and scratchy woollen tunic. "They are always here! The blood from one victim hasn't had chance to dry before they pull someone else up there for punishment! What did he even do, Eik? We've known

6

Dmitri since he was a boy. He wouldn't hurt a fly!" She paused and then raised a hand to her mouth, muffling her words. "You don't think... He'd never be so foolish as to join the rebellion, would he?"

Eik pulled her into the crook of his arm and manoeuvred her away from any potentially prying ears. She couldn't have resisted even if she'd tried. He steered her out of the main square and down a side alley between the bakery and the church.

"No, he wasn't a rebel. Dmitri didn't mean anyone any harm, but he was a fool. He's been obsessed with some Oderberg girl two villages over. Last night he thought he could woo her by turning her lawn into a bed of—"

Roslyn's mouth fell open as she remembered the young Bloomer's affinity with flowers. "Daffodils. And they whipped him for it? For being in love?"

The clomp of boots silenced their hushed words and prompted Eik to lean down from his enormous height, scooping Roslyn into a loving embrace. His lips pressed against hers, whiskers scratching her chin as a couple of soldiers traipsed past the entrance to the alleyway. One of them made a crude "Oi, oi" as they passed, but other than that, they were left to themselves.

Roslyn's heart was pounding from the fright of the soldiers, but the man looking down at her mistook it for something else. He smiled sadly and stroked her cheek with his thumb. "Some people aren't as lucky as we are, falling in love with someone we're supposed to."

Heat flushed her cheeks pink and she looked away, untangling herself from the young man and trying to lighten the moment.

"Who says we are in love?"

7

Eik opened his mouth and tried to look offended, but couldn't help smiling when she grinned back up at him.

"Ah, yes, that's it. You are just using me for your own selfish pleasures." He slung a heavy arm around her shoulders and they made their way along the alley into the street. "Talking of which… When can you use me for your pleasure again?" He looked up and down the street as she bit her lip in a wince.

"Look, about that—" She started to let him down gently when he cut her off, oblivious to her sudden shyness. Although she enjoyed the attention and the way his kisses usually made her feel, she wasn't really in the mood. Not when a young man was near bleeding out because he had dared express his own affection.

"Anyway, Ros."

"Roslyn."

"Yeah, that's what I said. I have to…" He looked around again somewhat nervously. "I have to do something."

"What?"

"I'll come by later, and we can finish this properly." His lopsided grin and the bulge in his britches, which he pressed her hand to, left her with no illusions of precisely what he meant to finish later.

"Where are you going?"

He ducked down and planted a kiss on her unsuspecting lips, silencing her before rushing off down the street, weaving in and out of the crowds. He gave a wide berth to any Oderbergs lurking on corners.

Roslyn scoffed. She'd known Eik all her life, and they'd grown even closer the last year, but never had he left her standing in the middle of the street to go on a

8

mysterious—not to mention suspicious—quest. He was up to something, and she was determined to find out what.

Shifting her satchel on her shoulder, she set off, following the immense form of Eik as he tried to disappear into the hubbub of the crowd which, for such a large man, she had to admit he was doing extremely well. She almost lost him several times, but then caught a flash of his brown curly hair by a thatched roof or glimpsed the blue tails of his tunic trailing him around a corner.

He was leading her in a merry dance around the village. He occasionally doubled back on himself, forcing her to press herself into a doorway or behind a water barrel so that he wouldn't see her. His face was etched with concern and, Roslyn noted, a new sense of determination she hadn't noticed before. What was he up to?

Finally, Eik turned into a ginnel toward the edge of town. The narrow alleyway that sat between a row of cottages and the wall that the invaders had wrapped around the entire settlement to keep them in, was filled with piles of rubbish. Roslyn followed and crinkled her nose. The stench that wafted up made her gag. Tearing her eyes away from her prey, she looked down to pick a path through the unidentifiable, stinking brown globs that covered the dirt floor and was dismayed to find that when she looked up again, he had vanished.

"Oh, bugger," she swore, not entirely under her breath. Roslyn screwed her hands into fists and placed them on her hips. Where was he? There was nowhere he could have gone as the ginnel stretched on far into the distance, running almost the entire circumference of the village wall. She should still be able to see him.

Sighing and picking up her pale green skirts, she wandered further into the rubbish, looking around for any sign of an entrance. There was nothing, only a wizened old man curled up on a potato sack; it looked like he had crumpled in on himself. He hid his legs beneath layers of hessian, but even the disguise could not hide the fact that they were not of average stature. Her heart went out to him. Sitting up, he leant against a splintered apple crate and squinted up at her with rheumy eyes. He had folds of dirty fabric wrapped around his head in lieu of a cap.

"Are you lost?" His voice croaked with age or lack of water, or perhaps both.

"No, but my friend is. Have you seen a tall young man with curly brown hair and a beard come this way in the last few minutes?"

The old man looked up and down the ginnel and shook his head. Then he laughed with a toothless grin.

"Not here now, is he, apple seed? Must've disappeared." He leered at her in a sing-song way. Roslyn rolled her eyes and was about to turn away when the old man's tone changed. "Seen lots of young men disappearing round here of late. They don't notice me, of course, just think of me as a sack o' spuds in their rush of rebellion."

Roslyn tucked a strand of her mousy brown hair back into her kerchief and shook her head. "No, no… Eik wouldn't join the rebellion." But even as the words left her lips, a kernel of doubt took root within her.

The beggar cackled. "Are you sure about that, little apple seed?"

She sniffed and crossed her arms under her chest. "Of course, I've known him forever. And wrong Affinity, by the way." She motioned to her embroidered sleeves.

The old man shrugged. "But how well do you know him? Things—and more importantly, people—aren't

10

always what they seem." He reached out a greyish, gnarled finger and pointed to another crate on the other side of the alley.

As Roslyn approached, she noticed it was crooked, not flush against the wall as she had assumed it to be at first glance. She scooped her skirts up around her knees and crouched to get a better look. A soft breath of musty air came from the crack, wafting up a dark staircase and carrying with it dust motes that sparkled in the morning light. There was a distant burble of voices, muffled and indistinct, as if the speakers were in another room further away. She turned to the beggar again, who inclined his head a little to the left. Forgetting the grime that lined the ginnel, she tiptoed further along the wall, the voices getting clearer with each step. Before long, she stood above a grate that curved from the rubbish-laden ground part way up the once whitewashed village wall, now stained green with the passage of time.

As she peered into the gloom between the bars, it startled Roslyn to see a meeting hall filled to the brim with people huddled together, glancing around furtively as they spoke. Completely forgetting her previous concern about the muck, she knelt on the ground beside the grate, trying to get the best view possible whilst at the same time staying out of sight.

The ceiling was low, the ancient mortar barely holding the bricks in place above the heads of those in attendance. They were mostly men, dressed in work clothes, practical but still proudly traditional: sleeves embroidered with their Affinity plant, denoting their status in society; bell-bottomed trousers fastened just below the knee; leg wraps fastened in place by a bronze pin of their plants. A few of the older men wore thick capes, the spring morning still chilly.

Several women were scattered within the haphazard rows of seats, dressed much as she herself was, their plants noted on their sleeve and skirts, heads scarfed; however, the cut of their cloth set them apart. Roslyn was limited to the roughest of homespun linens and wooden clogs, but not these women. The number of velvet strips sewn on their skirts betrayed their status, as did the fine leather of their shoes and the twinkle of their sparse but much-prized jewellery.

One woman laughed a little too loudly and Roslyn furrowed her brow at the dark-haired beauty. Her olive skin glinted with the powdery sheen passed down from the Ancestors, the dryads and naiads from whom their powers came. Rose Troyand was a literal thorn in Roslyn's side and had been since childhood—prettier, smarter and one of the most powerful Bloomers, to boot. The only thing Roslyn had managed to best her in was gaining Eik's attentions, but how long that would last was anyone's guess.

The noise of someone clearing their throat sounded and all the heads turned to stare up at a man at the front of the hall who was speaking. Roslyn's eyes followed their gaze past the smoking tallow lanterns and her jaw dropped.

The young man who had just been teasing her about their nocturnal activities paced the floorboards. The boy from her childhood was gone, replaced by a man whose eyes blazed with passion and fury. He slammed his fist into the palm of his other hand as he spoke to hammer home his points.

"Too long has this gone on, too long!" The assembly nodded as he spoke, murmuring agreement, scowls etched into the faces of the villagers she knew so well. The effect transformed them into something else, something dangerous.

"Another Domovnian whipped, and for what? For professing his love for a girl with flowers! Since when was courting a crime?"

"Since twenty-five years ago, if it involves the Affinity! They can't stand the magic the Ancestors blessed us with," a voice from the darkness shouted back at him. Roslyn didn't recognise it, but it had the croak of an older man about it—a man who had been there at the time of the invasion, a man who had survived and remembered.

"And we will stand for their cruelty no more!" Eik's voice rang loud and clear over the hubbub. "Now is the time to strike. Now is the time to join forces with the rebels, to unite under the Domonov banner once more!"

A hush fell, the gathering looking at each other with worry. The croaky voice sounded again. It became louder as the speaker moved towards the leader of the meeting, and Roslyn realised it was Old Voloshka, his cornflower blue eyes heavy with sorrow in the gloom.

"Young master Devero, the Domonovs are dead. Every last one of them was killed that night at Eluha. I was there. I saw them slaughtered before my very eyes, heard their cries, their screams…" The hunched figure closed his eyes and shook his head with the subtlest of movements to banish the memories. "There is no one to carry their banner; no one for us to rally behind."

"Poor ol' bugger." Roslyn jumped at the voice in her ear. Unbeknownst to her, the beggar had crawled from his

13

hiding spot to perch at her shoulder. He ignored her fright. "Did you know he used to be a servant of the Domonovs? Yes! They say he only survived because a stone from the ramparts fell on his leg as the palace burned around him, and he passed out with pain, so they thought he was dead!"

Roslyn shuddered.

"He crawled over the rotting corpses days later and told everyone what had happened, or at least the parts of it he can speak of…" the beggar paused, and she noticed his eyes had wandered into a dark place of memory, his voice lowering to a bass rumble. "No doubt there are many more horrors we shall never learn of, for they are too terrible to live again, no words enough to convey them."

She stretched out a tentative hand to comfort the beggar , but as soon as it had come, the shadow passed, and he pointed back into the basement.

"You are right, old friend." Eik placed a paddle-sized hand on the man's shoulder and led him to a nearby seat. "The king and queen of Domovnia are indeed dead, but they did not find their child."

The crowd rumbled in a chorus of incredulity and faith as its members debated the myth.

"The princess is dead!"

"The body was never found!"

"Even if she is alive, no one knows where or who she is!"

Eik waited patiently for the hubbub to quieten down.

"You're right. She may be dead; we don't know for sure, but none of that matters. We can still raise the banner in her name, in the name of all Domovnians. Just the whisper of the Domonov Princess gives us hope, and the Oderbergs fear. This is our land, a land that was once full of plenty, but since the invaders from Bergam have claimed it, it has grown as barren and lifeless as their own.

"I will not stand for that! I will not hide the power of the Affinity anymore! I will not suppress my nature and neither should you, because in doing that, we are suppressing nature itself. Look around! The harvest yields have diminished each year since the fall of Eluha. The streams are running dry, and it is all because of the Oderbergs and their fear of the Affinity. So, I will fight them, in the name of the Domonov Princess, in the name of the Affinity! The only question is, are you with me?"

Something stirred in Roslyn at the image of her countrymen rising beneath a banner of the Domonovs, the entwined cycle of the Sea and the Tree, proclaiming the name of the lost princess. The hush that leaked out of the grate was so heavy, Roslyn could almost taste it. Were they seeing the same vision she was, or were they remembering the carnage, terror and repression of the last twenty-five years?

"I will not ask you to decide now, but think of what we could achieve if every Domovnian, every Arbor, every Bloomer—and even Hedgie, if it came to it, rose up together to take back what is rightfully ours. Not everyone can fight, I know this," he gestured towards Voloshka. "You gave your strength and youth trying to defend our land, and for that we are grateful, but the rebels and I will need help from the townsfolk. We will need supplies, places to hide; we will welcome anyone with open arms. Those who want to fight…" he let his statement hang momentarily. "We meet at the last moon of spring to ride south. There, we will join with the others and prepare for the offensive. By Tree and Sea…"

"May it be!" came the chorused reply, its solemnity sending a shiver down her spine.

Roslyn sat back and let Eik's voice return to a mumbled drone. Her heart was pounding in her chest. He was leaving. Eik, her Eik, was heading up a rebel contingent in her own village. Why would he do something so stupid? Where had this recklessness come from? Why hadn't he told her and asked her to join them? She sighed, knowing the answer to the last question.

She was a Hedgie, the least skilled of all Domovnians with the Affinity, and she was the lowest of them all, only able to stir a handful of weeds. She wouldn't be much use in a fight. Not like Eik, the son of one of the Arbor nobles who had fought and died at Eluha. By rights, he was the nearest thing to royalty they had. His Affinity was with the mighty oak, bending the impressive trees to his will when he wanted it. Even Bloomers, whose Affinity lay with flowers, could command vines and thorned plants into weapons.

She stood slowly and brushed the gunk from her skirts. Raising her eyes, she caught those of the beggar.

"See, not everything or everyone is what they seem."

Roslyn snorted. She was exactly what she seemed— all but powerless and next to useless. That was why he hadn't told her. That was why Rose fucking Troyand sat there instead of her. Anger stirred within her as Eik's lies and disregard for her bit to her core.

Suddenly, the wooden crate scraped along the ground and she pressed herself flat against the wall. Her eyes went wide with the thought of being discovered, so she grabbed one of the moth-eaten potato sacks the beggar threw at her and hid beneath it, hoping between that and her green skirts she would blend into the mould on the wall.

16

Luckily, her disguise worked and the crowd of would-be rebels crept out in twos and threes, making sure no one, especially an Oderberg, was around. Finally, as her calves burned from her half crouch, she heard two familiar voices ascending the steps. Eik helped the limping Voloshka out into the sunlight.

"Do you really think we can do this?" The old man's voice was wavy with worry.

"I don't know, but I do know that if we don't try, we will die. Domovnia will die. Listen," he lowered his voice further still, so that Roslyn had to crane her neck to hear, "there have been sightings of our former countrymen, our allies, the centaurs and fauns, even satyrs in the forests. If they are coming back, then the Ancestors are on our side. It's now or never."

"Stuff and nonsense!" Voloshka grumbled. "Those Bergam scum hunted them for sport! There is no way they will bless this land with their presence while the Oderbergs rule."

Roslyn didn't catch the rest of the old man's mumbled reply, but she was fairly certain it wasn't particularly kind to the brashness of youth and likely contained a few expletives. He waved his hand dismissively at Eik before tutting in surprise. "Silen? What're you doing here?"

The beggar grinned up at Voloshka, his snub nose red with merriment. "Apple picking."

The old man shook his head and held out a hand. "Come on, you old fool. Let's away before someone accuses you of mischief."

She waited a few more moments, listening to the groans of the beggar Silen as Eik hoisted him to his feet, until the *tap, tap, tap* of Voloshka's cane faded down the ginnel. As Eik turned to follow, Roslyn threw off the sack and jumped up with a loud, "Ha!"

"Fuck me!" Eik gasped. The hand that had reached for the knife at his waist rose to his pounding heart once he saw his attacker was Roslyn. "Don't ever sneak up on me like that! I could have killed you! What were you doing?"

Roslyn crossed her arms under her bosom, a scowl across her lips. "That's funny. I was about to ask you the very same thing."

Chapter 2

Eik scuffed his feet in the detritus of the ginnel, looking abashed for only a split second before he raised his eyebrows.

"I don't know what you're talking about," he pouted.

Roslyn raised her own eyebrow back at him and pointed to the hole from which he had just emerged.

"Oh, I don't know, perhaps the super-secret meeting you've just hosted, in an unknown basement below the village. What could it have been about? I wonder... Could it have been about this year's flower festival? Or was it about joining the rebellion?" Her voice was loud, and she knew it, but she didn't care even when he shushed her.

"Will you be quiet?" Eik rushed forward and clapped his hand over her mouth with force. The side of his palm pressed up against her nose and she smelt not only the familiar smell of him but also dirt, soil and something she couldn't put a name to. Perhaps it was his deceit. She shrugged him off and pushed him away while he continued to chastise her.

"Do you want to bring the guards down on us?"

"Do *you*? You are the one entertaining ideas of rebellion, not me." Roslyn let her shoulders droop and then in a quieter voice, said, "Why didn't you tell me? Why didn't you let me come with you?"

Did he not trust her? Disappointment crushed her and she tried her best not to let it show, but Eik had already noticed. He reached out to her with his large hands and rubbed her upper arms.

"Ros, I was trying to keep you safe. The less you know, the safer it is for you; the safer it is for all of us. Just imagine if one of the guards catches you and makes you talk, then you'll give us all away."

Roslyn grimaced at the marks he left on her blouse's cream sleeves, and at the backhanded insult he'd hit her with. "You know I wouldn't. I'd never give anyone away; I wouldn't tell them anything."

Eik sighed and dropped his hands, looking frustrated. "You don't know that, not under torture. You'd tell them anything, anyone would."

Roslyn scowled. "I know how to hold my tongue to protect those I love." She sighed and pressed on with her next point of enquiry. "And what about letting me join you? Why won't you let me help? I'm sure there's lots I could do. I want to fight with you, Eik, to fight for our people, for our freedom."

He looked around nervously and then gestured that they should make their way back into town. He placed his hand on the small of her back with a little too much pressure, making her roll her ankle. He was silent for a few minutes, obviously thinking about what he wanted to say. Finally, when he did speak, his voice was full of pity and condescension.

"Ros, honey, it's not that we don't want you to fight. We know you could if you had to. But, well…"

Roslyn knew why, but she wanted to hear him say it. For once, she actually wanted to hear someone say the words. "Well?"

Eik made a strange, gargled coughing sound and the lump in his throat bobbed up and down nervously. "Well, we just think you'd be better off here, tending the sick as you do. That's how you can help."

She wasn't going to let him off the hook so easily. She needed to hear him say it. "But why would you want me just tending the sick when I could actually come with you and attend the fighters if they get injured in the field?"

He stopped and turned round to face her. A vein pulsed in his temple and his nostrils flared. "You know why, Ros. We need people whose Affinity is strong, pure. We need fighters who can *use* their magic, bend nature to their will. Can you do that?"

Even though she had wanted him to say it, say that she was next to powerless because it was the truth, it still hurt her more than she thought it would. Eik was on a roll now, the words spewing from his mouth as if he couldn't stop them.

"I mean, come on. You're a Hedgie, and one that can only influence dandelions and nettles. You don't even have Affinity with something useful and edible like—oh, I don't know—blackberries or gooseberries, something that can feed the people who are, as I'm sure you're aware, starving. Ros!"

Roslyn bit the inside of her cheek hard to stop the tears from forming. Eik had just voiced all the thoughts that plagued her every day when she saw the Affinity within others and wondered what was wrong with her. Nettles could have been useful for food and fibre, or would have been, if she'd had enough power to increase their yield.

Eik suddenly ran out of steam and, sighing, wrapped his arms around Roslyn's neck and pulled her into his chest. She took a deep breath and smelt the sourness of his woollen jerkin, felt its fibres itch against her cheek. She wanted to pull away but he held on too tightly, rocking her slightly as if she were a child that had to be consoled.

"I'm sorry, Ros, I didn't mean for it come out quite like that."

But he *did*; Roslyn knew that Eik thought her beneath him. He was a son of one of the last Domovnian nobles, and she was only a hair's breadth away from being human. He had only taken an interest in her as she blossomed into a young woman. Not that it stopped his eyes wandering, of course.

"Look, I meant what I said about you healing people. You've learned well from that herbalist woman."

"Her name is Hedda," Roslyn snapped, finally managing to push herself out of his grip. They walked along the ginnel and back to the street that would lead them into the centre of town.

"Yes, yes, I know, I'm sorry. I know she's like a mother to you. She raised you well and taught you everything she knows. And that's what we need from you, that's how you can help. You are of more use to us collecting your herbs, making your potions and poultices that can help us if we get injured. All your equipment is here, all your foraging grounds are here." The bullish young man grabbed her wrist, swirled her around and took her face in his hands, forcing her to look up into his eyes. She saw sincerity there, but with an undeniable trace of

22

pity. She felt his breath on her face, warm and laced with the faintest hint of ale as he whispered in her ear.

"You are part of the rebellion, if you want to be, but your task will be different. You can busy yourself here and we'll send someone regularly to collect your wares. And you can know that you're helping us, that you are helping all the Domovnians fighting for our freedom. How does that sound?"

She felt her lips curling out in a pout and knew she was being childish. Of course, she was a better help to people by healing them. Besides, she barely knew one end of a sword from the other. Finally, she looked him in the eye and nodded.

Eik smiled and clapped a hand on her back, pushing her out of the alley and back into village life.

"Good girl! I knew I could count on you. Now, you go get your baskets and get going. We're going to need all the help we can get."

✳

Roslyn was fuming.

"Good girl? Good girl! How dare he? What a selfish, pompous prick!" She stomped through the undergrowth with her empty baskets, woven from last year's willow, banging against her legs. She gripped the strap across her chest, her knuckles white with fury. She had been planning on going out to forage anyway, but now that Eik had said that was the only way she could join the rebellion, she was incensed and didn't want to go any more. But there were people in the village who needed her. Hedda was relying on her. So, she'd stomped home to the little cottage she shared with the herbalist for her baskets and her cloak.

Just before she stormed out again, a movement by the hearth stopped her. She looked back over her shoulder and saw the familiar shape of Hedda bent over a steaming pot of broth. The old woman looked around, saw her, and raised a finger to her lips, pointing to the ceiling.

"Dmitri's upstairs," she whispered.

Roslyn's anger abated and guilt took its place. She'd almost forgotten the horrors of the morning and her childhood friend who had suffered them. "How is he?" Her voice was hushed and trembling.

Hedda shook her head. "Not good. As much as he held his nerve under the whip, his body tells a different story. Five lashes too many, if you ask me."

"*One* too many, you mean!" Roslyn interrupted bitterly. Hedda nodded her agreement.

"He'll be lucky to make it through the next sunrise."

The old woman's face was etched with fatigue, sorrow and something else, something that all Domovnians shared—hate. She visibly shook it away and looked down at Roslyn's attire. "You're going out... good." She walked over to the sideboard, its tall shelves stacked with bottles and jars. Drying plants hung from the rafters above it. She reached up high, and fumbled around for the jar she needed, then lowered herself back to the rush-strewn floor.

"I need you to pick some more feverfew. I've enough left to help him when the fever starts, which it will anytime now, but if we are to keep him alive through the night, I need more." She waggled the dusty jar under Roslyn's nose so that the remaining dried flower heads and leaves pinged against the glass.

Roslyn nodded. "Of course." She leant over and gave Hedda a tight hug, breathing in her soothing scent of lavender and knocking her kerchief askew. "Take care of him."

Hedda pushed her back and smiled sadly, leading her to the doorway. "You know I will. Now, go and get that feverfew." She paused. "And burn off whatever had you charging in here in such a rage. We'll have no place for that kind of temper when you get back. We've got work to do."

In a soft, familiar movement, she stroked and then patted Roslyn's face before pushing her out into the street and hurrying back inside to her patient.

As she made her way out of the village, Roslyn passed the soldiers manning the entrance, having to stop, show them her empty baskets, and explain her reason for leaving. Her rage and hatred stirred again. She was angry; with the soldiers who had whipped her friend for naught, leaving him on death's door, with Eik for joining the rebellion, but most of all, she was angry with the Oderbergs and their king for forcing him to do so.

She was so incensed, she tore at the plants she was foraging, ripping them roots and all from the ground. She was sorry for that, but it couldn't be helped. They were, like her, weeds of no importance; they would grow back soon enough. As she stewed in her bad mood, Roslyn's feet led her off the path and before long she was blundering blindly through an unknown part of the forest. At first, the trees grew thicker, the light from above being blotted out as the canopy closed in above her. She couldn't see any shrubs or weeds on the ground that she needed for her poultices, so she carried on until the trees thinned again. By now, her fury had quelled to a disgruntled fizz, leaving a cold sweat underneath the cotton of her blouse.

Roslyn stopped tramping and pulled out her waterskin, sloshing its contents greedily into her mouth. A channel of water ran down her neck. She made a sputtering sound and jerked forward in an attempt to stop the rivulets running down in between her breasts, but it was too late. She was soaked. She sighed and looked around for a leaf to blot away most of the liquid. It was while doing this that she noticed a large, lush spread of yarrow peeping out from the shrubbery of the forest. The spindle-thin stalks bobbed under the weight of their umbral white flowers. Flurries of feather brush leaves reached up from the ground towards her. She had never seen such a wealth of it. In her delight, she forgot all of her disappointment and anger and knelt on the forest floor to harvest the woodland weed. This would help Dmitri far more than the feverfew could, slowing the bleeding and healing his wounds.

Enveloped in its crisp pine scent, Roslyn clipped as many leaves and petals as she thought she could use before they went bad. Unfurling a scrap of cotton, which she wet with water from her skin, she dug up one of the plants to take home with her. She hoped she might cultivate a patch as glorious as this.

Roslyn wondered why she had never seen it before, and then she looked up and realised she had no idea where she was.

"Oh, for fuck's sake, Roslyn!" she chided herself. One of the first things Hedda had taught her was to always be aware of one's surroundings. With a sigh, she began to pack up her belongings, placing the clippings carefully into the baskets and arranging the dug-up plant in amongst

26

the bottles and jars and bandages in her satchel. She was just about ready to stand up and sling them over her shoulder when the hairs on the back of her neck stood up.

There was something or someone nearby—she could feel them. Her imagination roared in her head. Was it one of the fabled fauns or centaurs Eik had whispered about? She wasn't sure she was ready to meet one. Were they dangerous?

The breeze bent the trees around her, causing them to groan and creak ominously. Not for the first time did she wish she was an Arbor, able to understand what the great trunks were saying to her. With a sense of foreboding, Roslyn picked up her satchel and turned back the way she had come, just as the bush in front of her was crushed under the hooves of an enormous wild boar.

Chapter 3

Panic rose in her throat like bile, its sour sting making her mouth water, but when she tried to swallow, she found she couldn't. Her throat was completely and utterly dry.

The world seemed to slow down for an instant as the beast crashed through the undergrowth and into her clearing, and in that moment, she saw her own fear mirrored in its wide glassy eyes. It was frothing at the mouth and the very tips of its tusks were tinted with blood. Barely a heartbeat passed before time sped up again and the angry, frightened animal squealed and continued to crash on through the undergrowth, oblivious to her presence. As the world began to move again, Roslyn's heart pounded in her chest, her breathing loud and desperate in her own ears. It was then that she heard screaming.

The spine-tingling cries pulled her back to her senses and her duty as a healer. Snatching up her belongings, she followed the gut-wrenching sound, ploughing through shrubs and batting away branches as if they were no more than flies. Someone was hurt; she had to help them.

When she finally found the person responsible for the caterwauling, a scene of gore stopped her in her tracks. A man lay on the ground clutching his leg, or what should have been his leg, but all Roslyn could see was a bloody, gouged mass of flesh. It was a mess. The fact that he wasn't already dead meant the boar's tusk hadn't perforated his major artery. If she acted quickly, she could stop him from bleeding out here and now on the mulch of the forest floor. It was in that moment that he looked up and saw her.

His fair hair was plastered to his scalp with sweat. Tear tracks ran down his grubby cheeks, exposing the fair flesh beneath the grime, and his sky-blue eyes widened as he took her in.

"Help me! For the love of the Mountain, you have to help me."

The man's voice was shrill with panic. His life was ebbing away before his very eyes, shooting out through the wound in bloody spurts.

Roslyn rushed forward and threw her bags on the floor, not caring for the samples she'd previously arranged with such care. With trembling fingers, she unlatched her satchel, pulled out a glass jar and wrenched the cork out with her teeth. She poured the amber liquid over her hands and the wound of the man before her. If his screams had been loud before, they were nothing compared to what came out of his mouth now; the alcohol burning his already damaged flesh.

"Will you stop wasting all your energy on screaming!" Roslyn chastised. If she was going to get any work done and save his life, she needed him to be quiet, or at the very least, not deafening her. The man before her tried to steady himself while she carefully pulled back the torn and saturated fabric of his leggings. He hissed with pain, but she was glad to see that he was following her advice. As the bloody cloth folded back in her hands, she felt him tense and wince underneath her.

The muscle and sinew in his leg gaped, giving her a wider view of the damage. His thigh had been ripped almost from top to bottom, narrowly missing the artery that would have ended his life had the boar touched it. Still, she needed to work fast. There was a lot of blood, and he was in a lot of pain. However, she couldn't stop the faintest of smiles creeping onto her lips. "I can fix this!"

Heavily perspiring, the man scoffed and nodded his head sarcastically. "Oh! That's great! Now get the fuck on with it!"

"Alright, alright!" Roslyn exhaled.

"Look, I don't know who you are, but please, for the love of Hoff, just do what you have to do." His voice was coming out in ragged breaths, now, and Roslyn knew she didn't have much time. She looked into his crystal clear, blue eyes and for a second, her heart stopped. But then she saw the colour drain from his cheeks. She knew she had to hurry and turned back to the wound. Without thinking, she took the man's arm, grabbed his sleeve and pulled. The ripping sound in the forest's quietness was deafening.

Roslyn wrapped the sleeve tight around the man's leg above the wound. He swore as she pulled as tight as she could, spinning the ends around each other and tying them into a knot. The blood slowed enough that she could see what she was doing. She fumbled in her satchel as the man slid back onto his elbows, faint with blood loss. The wound had to be sewn up.

As she was looking for her needle and thread, her eyes fell on the small white heads of the yarrow she had just

30

foraged. It was exactly what she needed to help the blood coagulate. She retrieved a piece of bark and leant back towards the man's face. "Here, chew on this. It will help with the pain, because trust me, this is going to hurt, and I'm sorry."

He didn't say anything, but looked up at her, nodded and opened his mouth to receive the bark. His breath was warm on her hands as she inserted it gently. Time seemed to slow down again as he looked up into her eyes and received her offering, his lips closing slightly on her finger and sending a dart of lightning to the pit of her stomach. Time sped up once more, only now, it seemed to go twice as fast.

Pulling a length of waxed thread from a bobbin, she threaded the needle and plunged it into the man's muscle. He screamed again and this time, she didn't blame him. At his cries, the bushes came alive with the sound of rustling and several heavily armed Oderberg soldiers crashed through the undergrowth towards her.

"Take your hands off him!" the tallest of the guards shouted, pointing his heavy broadsword right under her nose. "Remove your hands from his person at once, and you may yet be allowed to live!"

Roslyn ignored him. In fact, she ignored all of them and concentrated only on the precise placement of her needle as she pressed it into the hot, sticky muscle at her fingertips. Each stitch she made pulled the two sides of rent flesh closer together so that it could eventually heal. She glanced hastily up at the invalid and saw that he had stopped chewing on the bark. His eyes were shut and his lips hung open, the bark resting gently between his teeth. He had passed out from the pain.

The Oderberg soldier took another step towards her and this time raised her chin with the tip of his blade so that she had nowhere else to look but up into his moustachioed face. His eyes glowed black as coals with some sort of protective anger.

"I said," he hissed slowly and deliberately, "step away if you value your life."

Roslyn matched his steely gaze with one of her own. "If I stop what I am doing, if I remove my hands from your colleague's leg, he will bleed out and die. Is that what you want?"

The group of soldiers looked at each other in fear. A couple at the back, younger ones by the looks of them, shook their heads urgently. The one with his blade under her chin sighed and pulled it back from her face. However, he did not sheath it and kept the weapon at the ready.

"You do what you have to do, you fix him up. You better be damn sure that he lives."

Roslyn scoffed and returned her gaze back to her work, which she took up again at thrice the speed. "That's what I'm trying to do, and it would go a lot faster if you'd stop bothering me." The Oderberg grunted and clasped his sword tighter. He glared at the younger soldiers in his band who dared to smile at his being rebuked by a simple peasant girl.

The Oderbergs' presence slipped away from her consciousness as she focused on her task. The world vanished, and it was just Roslyn and her healing. Nothing else existed, nothing but her needle, thread, and the man that she tended. Now and then she glanced up at him to check on his progress, but he was still unconscious, his chest rising and falling slowly with the steady breaths that accompany oblivion.

When she dared to look at his face, she was amazed to see how beautiful it was. If he hadn't been bleeding out before her very eyes only moments ago, she would have sworn that he was something from the heavens. So perfect was his skin, so lovely were his damp, blonde curls that framed his expertly crafted face.

Once the wound was closed, Roslyn reached for her satchel again and picked up a bunch of the wispy yarrow leaves. She fumbled with one hand, searching for her mortar and pestle, but cursed when she remembered she'd taken it out to clean it. Roslyn shrugged and raised the leaves to her lips and chewed. She chewed until her jaws ached and her tongue tingled from the numbing properties within.

Finally, she spat the gooey, green concoction into her hands and spread it up and down the new stitching. Having no bandages to hand, she ripped off her own sleeve, a shame as it had taken such a long time to embroider, and tore it into strips to bind the mess to his leg.

"What do you think you're doing?" The moustachioed soldier stepped forward again. His hand was tight around the hilt of his sword, ready to run her through with it.

"I am putting a dressing on to help the wound heal and to keep away infection," Roslyn said as if this were the most obvious thing in the world, especially to a soldier who had no doubt seen many injuries in his time. "Surely you recognise this." She held up another stem of yarrow. "What is it you soldiers call it, 'woundwort', I believe?"

"I do, but never have I seen it mixed in the mouth."

Roslyn glared at him. "No, normally it is prepared in a tincture or cream, but time was rather of the essence, so I had to resort to more... primitive measures. His blood needed to be stopped, and besides," she grinned, "saliva is a known antibacterial. It can only help."

The Oderberg looked at her suspiciously and then said, "Who are you? What are you? You'd better not be one of those Isapf-damned Domovnians with their flower magic. If I find out that you are and you've used magic here…"

Roslyn stopped him with a glance that could curdle milk. "You'll what? I have just saved your friend's life." She gestured up at the sleeping man's face, now smooth and free from pain. "If I had not been here to administer my poultices and sew him up, he would have bled out into the very ground we stand on. Does it matter who I am? Does it matter if I am a Domovnian or not?"

Her blood was boiling after everything that had happened today and she couldn't take it anymore. She didn't know if she could stand to be punished for saving an Oderberg, for that was what she had done, and she dreaded to think what Eik would say when he found out. Oh, Roslyn knew what he would say—that she should have left him to die. But that was not her way. She had to help those who were injured, no matter who they were. It was part of a healer's law. She stood and squared up to the Oderberg with the brown moustache that hovered over her. "For your information, I *am* Domovnian."

At this revelation, all the soldiers drew their swords and pointed them at her, taking out ready stances and awaiting their commander's order.

"Yes, that's right. You heard me. I am a Domovnian, but it will please you to know I'm a rather defunct one. I am classified as a Hedgie, but it would turn out that I'm pretty useless at that and all I can do is make weeds wave in the breeze. So, I have taken my knowledge of plants

34

and I have learned from one of your kind, a human herbalist. That is the only magic I have used here today."

Her heart was pounding and she could feel the flush of rage in her cheeks. She was almost willing the brute to spar with her in this verbal battle, but he didn't. To everyone's surprise, the commanding Oderberg sheathed his sword.

"And what, Hedgie-who-is-practically-defunct, is your name?" The calmness with which he uttered it pierced a hole in Roslyn's balloon of defiance. Her buoyed-up bravado hissed through it and she felt herself deflate under his calm scrutiny.

"My name is Roslyn Pleveli. I live in Koliba."

The commander nodded and turned back towards his men. "Get a stretcher built immediately. We need to get the prince back to the palace as soon as we can, so that *proper* healers can attend to him."

The man's comment hit Roslyn's chest like a battering ram. The prince? Did he just say *prince*? She felt her jaw drop at this news and heard the commander's dry chuckle.

"The prince?" she breathed.

"Yes. You, Roslyn Pleveli, have had the pleasure of attending to his Royal Highness Prince Frederik von Oderberg. Now, you will gather your things and take yourself back to your filthy little village, and there you will wait. And you will pray. You will pray for the prince's survival and that what you have done here today did in fact save his life, because if his Royal Highness dies, then the king's fury will know no bounds."

Roslyn's mouth went dry. She stumbled backwards and tripped over a half-hidden root, landing on her buttocks and staring up at the approaching man. "But... but it was a boar!"

The commanding Oderberg gave that dry, brittle laugh again and rocked on the hilt of his sword with confidence as he swayed over her. "It may have been a boar that wounded him, but what's to say that you, little Hedgie, didn't kill him with your subpar medical practice? So, like I said, get yourself back to your little village and pray on your knees." The tone of his voice changed suddenly into something slimy, as did the glare in his eyes as it roamed over her bare arm. Roslyn shivered as he continued. "On your knees, bent over, like the whore that you no doubt are."

Fear of a new kind rippled through her as she suddenly realised what kind of situation she was in. She was a young woman, alone, with an entire troop of red-blooded, cruel soldiers. As quickly as she could, she shoved all of her belongings back into her satchel and slung it over her shoulder. She fumbled with her baskets and fled from the clearing, the cackles and guffaws of the Oderbergs spurring her on her way.

Chapter 4

Roslyn's heart was beating against her ribcage. As the wooden door pounded against the wall, a chunk of the yellowing plaster fell off and crashed to the floor where it shattered into a fine dust. Hedda looked up at the bloodstained and bedraggled girl that burst into her sanctuary and gave a small cry of alarm.

"Oh, my goodness gracious me!" She bustled to the doorway, pulled Roslyn inside, and slammed the door shut again. "What on earth has happened to you? Are you alright? Why is your dress torn?"

So many questions came tumbling out of her mouth it was hard for Roslyn, who was still catching her breath, to know which one to answer first.

"I… I…" her breaths were coming out as gasps and none of the words that she tried to form made any sense. Hedda ushered her into the seat by the fire. As Roslyn sat and tried to calm her breathing and her pounding heart, her matronly protector looked down at her with widened eyes.

"Roslyn?" The woman's voice was low, and she raised an eyebrow. "Whose blood is that?"

Roslyn was shaking as she tried to grip her hands and stop them quivering, but failed utterly.

"I—there was a man, in the woods, he…" How on earth was she going to explain what she had done?

Hedda walked over to the sink, grabbed a bowl, a pitcher of water and a clean cloth. She placed the cracked blue and white porcelain dish on the table beside Roslyn and patted her gently on the arm.

"There, you just think about what you need to say while I get you cleaned up. Whatever happened, you know I am here for you. Now let's get this blood away before somebody comes in and thinks you murdered someone."

She was trying to make light of the situation, trying to ease Roslyn's discomfort, but it didn't work. It only made Roslyn more agitated. Instead of trying to form words, she let the old herbalist wipe away the blood, dirt, tears and snot that caked her arms and face. She let the woman drag up her torn, bloodstained blouse and cast it into the laundry pile. There was blood on her skirt too, but short of leaving her standing there in her slip, which was also bloodstained, she left it on.

By the time Hedda came back with a blanket and wrapped it around Roslyn's shoulders, she could breathe normally again.

"I was foraging in the forest, and I strayed too far. I know what you've always taught me, to stay in the areas I'm familiar with and to make sure where I'm going, but I was just so angry. Angry at what happened with Dmitri, angry with Eik…"

Hedda looked up at her sharply. "Angry with Eik? What's he done? Did he do this to you? Roslyn, did he force himself—"

"No!" Roslyn exclaimed. Then she lowered her voice again, hoping she hadn't woken Dmitri. "No, this wasn't Eik. I was angry at him for… something else and wasn't paying attention, so I wandered off the path. Then a boar ran into the clearing, but it didn't hurt me. I don't think it even saw me; it was running away from somebody."

As the memories flashed before her eyes, she realised her luck in that moment that the boar didn't even see her as it ran past. She could be lying dead in the forest now. Everyone knew wild boar could rip you from navel to nose; she saw the same relief pass over Hedda's wrinkled brow. Roslyn was on a roll now. She needed to finish her story.

"And then I heard screaming. A man was screaming. The boar had attacked him. It'd ripped his leg to shreds. So, I did what you have taught me, Hedda. I did what anyone would have done. I helped him."

Her voice trailed off, so that only the crackling of the fire could be heard. Hedda placed a hand on her knee.

"So, this is his blood?"

Roslyn nodded, her words deserting her again.

"And where is this man now? Did he—" but Hedda didn't get to finish her question. The door opened and in stormed Eik. He did a quick turnabout, peered out of the doorway again, checking for anyone following and then shut the door. The two puzzled women stared at him as he made his way on silenced feet towards them.

"What is this I hear, Roslyn? You just saved Prince Frederik von Oderberg's life? It's all the Watch are talking about!"

Roslyn looked up at him with wide, apologetic eyes. She all but felt Hedda's mouth drop open beside her, the woman's piercing eyes looking at her for confirmation.

"I didn't know it was him," Roslyn protested.

"But you must have noticed his uniform? His fine clothes? The dryad-damned Oderberg emblem on his chest?" Eik roared down at her. There was a creak of the floorboards above them, and Hedda whacked him with the back of her hand.

"Shush! Will you be quiet!" It wasn't a question. "I have an injured man upstairs who is trying to recover, and I have a very traumatised young lady here. So sit yourself down so that we may hear what actually happened!"

Eik looked down at the fearsome little woman, her chin jutted upwards, her kerchief skew-whiff and her eyes blazing with the authority of age. The bearlike man looked around for another chair, but finding none in the vicinity, folded his enormous frame down onto a small stool. He looked almost comical as he tried to nudge the stool further away from the fire. Hedda turned back to Roslyn.

"Now then, let's get this straight. Was the man you saved the Oderberg prince?"

Roslyn nodded. "But I didn't know that. I didn't see his clothes or his emblem or anything else. I just saw a man who needed my help." But looking back now, she should have noticed, should have baulked at his crude Oderberg curses.

Hedda nodded. "And then what happened?"

Roslyn drew a deep breath and refused to look either of them in the eye as she told the rest of her story. When it was over, she peeped out from under lowered lashes and awaited their scrutiny.

Neither of them said anything for a moment, taking it all in.

"You gave them your name? You told them where you live?" Eik wasn't shouting, but his quiet incredulity was almost more terrifying.

"What would you have me do? What else could I have done? If I had refused to tell them who I was, they would have killed me there and then. You know it, Eik."

Hedda nodded to the side of her.

"And if he dies?" Eik turned to her, clasped his hands over his knees, and cocked his head, his eyebrows raised.

"If the prince dies," Roslyn swallowed, "then the king will have his men arrest me and kill me." She said it calmly; she was just stating the facts. There was no other way about it. If the prince died, that was her fate—she may as well accept it now.

"Now, just wait a minute," Hedda interjected, shaking her head and waving a hand between the quarrelling couple. "Tell me exactly what you did. Tell me which stitch you used to sew up the wound. Tell me what you used in the dressing."

Roslyn told her mentor everything that she had done in excruciating detail, as if she were doing it that very second, as if she were reading out of the textbook.

The old woman nodded. "Good, good. Well, if you did all that, and you did it in a timely enough manner, then there should be absolutely no reason the prince shouldn't live. You are very good at what you do, and I have every faith in your skills. So, I doubt we will receive a visit from the king's guards." She sighed and stood up quickly, as if to end the matter.

Eik looked at Hedda and then back at Roslyn. "Ros, you need to run. Even if the prince lives, they know who

41

you are and they know what you did. It isn't allowed to be within ten yards of the royal family, you know that."

Roslyn sighed. "I know, I know. But this is my home. I don't want to leave. Where would I go?"

Hedda bustled over to the kettle which was now bubbling away over the fire, threatening to sing, and pulled it off the hook. She took the steaming pot over to the workbench and poured a measure into a wobbly, handmade clay mug. Roslyn recognised it immediately. It was one she'd made for Hedda when she was at the local village school. She smiled at the memory of how the woman's eyes had lit up with sheer delight as she'd freed it from its linen wrappings.

Hedda brought it back to her, thin wisps of steam rising from it and the heady scent of a sleeping tisane inside. "No one is going anywhere tonight. Now take this up to your room, Roslyn, get into your night things, and then go to bed. Everything will look clearer in the morning."

Roslyn took the offered brew and nodded. Hedda was right—she should never make decisions in the heat of the moment. Things were always clearer after time had passed. She stood to walk up the stairs when Eik patted her arm. The gesture was suddenly strange from someone who had shared her bed.

"I'm glad you're alright," he said. Roslyn almost snorted. It had taken that long to ask if she was physically harmed from her ordeal, but he didn't pull her close or plant a kiss on her forehead as she had expected him to. Instead, he ran his hands through his thick, dark hair and shrugged. "I don't know if I can do this, Ros."

"Roslyn," she hissed automatically. "What are you talking about? Do what?"

Eik scoffed and threw his hands up. "You and me. I don't know where your loyalties lie anymore. I need to think."

Roslyn took a step towards him and tried to take his hand, but he pulled it away. "Eik, I am still me..." she lowered her voice. "I am still on the rebels' side."

The young man bit his lip and shook his head, giving in to the small smile that crept to the furthest corners of his lips before whispering. "Well then, if you get near to the prince again, do us all a favour and kill him, next time."

✳

Roslyn spent the next day in a nervous fury. Not wanting to draw more attention to herself, she kept busy by tidying Hedda's ingredient cabinet, dusting and polishing, cataloguing, and making lists of everything they would need to forage for over the summer. Not that she wanted to go out foraging for anything now, of course—not until she at least knew what her fate was going to be. But she wanted to be prepared, or at least leave Hedda prepared should the Oderbergs turn up on her doorstep.

During that first day, she caught herself staring at the door, piercing it with her gaze as if daring it to open. But it never did, not even to admit entry to Eik or any of the other villagers. The only time it opened was when Hedda accompanied Dmitri down the stairs and out into the streets. He was well enough to go to his own home to convalesce. The feverfew had worked, and his wounds

43

were bound. If she was still here in a few days' time, Roslyn would visit him to change the bandages.

No one came that first day. Nor the second. Nor the third. And so, Roslyn's shoulders straightened with relief, and she gave up on notions of running away. It would appear as if Prince Frederik was still alive and healing in the comfort of his own castle.

❋

Chapter 5

On the fourth day after the incident, a knock sounded at the door. Roslyn, who was elbow deep in the washing up basin, snapped her neck towards it.

"I'll get it," Hedda mumbled, wiping her green-stained fingers on her apron. As the old woman unhooked the latch and opened the door a crack, Roslyn shrank back against the whitewashed wall, hiding herself but obscuring her own vision in the process. She heard hushed voices, a good sign—soldiers weren't usually so quiet—followed by a laugh.

"Come in, my dear, come in! Roslyn? Your friend has come to see you."

The young woman wiped her hands on a towel and stepped away from the sink. Curiosity crinkled her brow as she looked at the figure pulling down the hood of her cloak. Long tresses of dark silken hair hung over the woman's shoulders, held in place by a red velvet ribbon that lay just above the perfectly smooth olive forehead.

"Rose? What are you doing here?" Short of the Oderberg guards, this was the last person Roslyn wanted to see. No, in fact, she'd rather have that ridiculously moustachioed soldier standing in her living room than the *perfect* Rose Troyand.

Hedda looked at her sharply as she took the young woman's cloak, sending a waft of fragrant perfume towards Roslyn. Her nose itched as she breathed it in. Rose oil, of course. What else?

"Roslyn, is that anyway to speak to a guest?"

She forced a smile and raised her head to meet their visitor's eye. "Do come in, Rose. What can we help you with?"

Those perfectly plump, pink lips spread into a smile and a tinkling laugh sounded as Rose took Roslyn's hands and led her to the chairs by the fire. "Why, I've come to see you, you silly thing."

Her voice was light but Roslyn was near smothered by its insincerity. Never in her life had Rose deigned to talk to the poor little orphaned Hedgie unless she needed something. She'd teased her mercilessly at school for not only being the lowliest of Domovnians, but also for living with a simple human. She'd once crowned all the girls with wreaths of roses, but when it was Roslyn's turn, she had smirked and settled the crown forcefully so that Roslyn's scalp bled. No, Rose was not here for friendship.

Hedda knew none of this. Roslyn had never spoken of it, never admitted it was she who had made her school days a misery, pretending instead to be clumsy. The old woman smiled. "It'll do you good to have some company Roslyn, you've been ever so down since the... incident. I'll leave you two to chat for a while, then. I must go and check on poor Silen, he's been hobbling around worse than usual lately. No doubt his stump is infected." She mumbled more to herself than the young ladies as she

46

threw on her cloak and picked up her basket. She didn't see Rose's grimace of disgust at the mention of the beggar's stump, but Roslyn did. *Heartless bitch.*

"Shall I put some tea on?" she muttered half-heartedly.

Rose nodded, that fake, innocent smile sliding into a snide and cunning one. "Yes please, and if you wouldn't mind infusing some thistle into it, I'd be most grateful."

"Thistle?" Roslyn raised an eyebrow. The ingredient was infused in teas when one was anticipating a fun-filled night between the sheets and wanted none of the consequences that came with it.

Rose tilted her head down modestly as if blushing but her cheeks betrayed her performance, shining only with the glow of the Ancestors.

"Why, yes. There's a small gathering tonight, just a small group of us from school, you know the usual crowd, and well..." She looked up from her position of mock humility and raised her eyebrow. "I just want to be prepared. You know how things can get after a few flagons of ale." Her eyes widened and her fingertips shot to cover her rounded mouth. "Oh, but of course you don't! You've never been invited."

Roslyn stomped over to the supplies and pulled out the thistle jar. On the verge of shoving one of the dried, spiky barbs into those perfectly rounded lips, she instead plopped it into the steaming water in the kettle and swirled it around angrily with a copper spoon.

"And who do you intend on... having fun with? Klen? Neven?"

A soft chuckle sounded. "Why, Eik of course."

Roslyn nearly dropped the kettle as she poured the infusion into a cup.

"Eik?" she breathed incredulously. "But, he—I—we…"

Rose pointed to the steaming mug with a dismissive finger. "A drop of cold water in that, if you don't mind." She leant back in her chair and fixed her adversary with an icy stare. "Yes, Eik. You are finished, aren't you?"

Her hand shot up to her mouth again in fake shock, and Roslyn had to physically berate herself for the overpowering desire to throw the scalding tea into her perfect face. "I'd never approach him if I thought he was still sowing his wild oats in your furrow, but he told me it was over."

Roslyn bit her lip to stop the tears as she held the cup out to Rose. Since when had "I need time" meant "it's over", with no further discussion?

Rose raised the cup to her lips and blew on the steam before taking a cautious sip. She pulled a face and held it up to her again. "Haven't you got any honey to sweeten it with? It's rather bitter. Besides…" She cocked her head as Roslyn fetched the honeypot from the kitchen table and dribbled in a generous dollop. "You can't expect the new rebel leader to consort with a woman who just saved the Oderberg heir, do you?"

She looked at Roslyn over the rim as she took another sip and nodded, the taste much more to her liking. Her gaze drifted. "I've never seen him so angry. It was…" She gave a theatrical shiver and bit her lip. "Thrilling."

Roslyn's knees went weak and she found herself sitting in the chair opposite Rose, the velvet-striped hem of the latter's black skirt brushing her own water spattered apron. Had he really left her that night, full of rage, and gone straight to Rose? Had they started seeing each other then, or whilst they were still together? Her stomach

48

clenched and she swallowed down the bile that rose up her throat. She didn't want to know and shook her head, clearing her throat.

"Is that why you are here, Rose? To tell me that my relationship is over?"

Rose patted her knee, a pout on her lips. "Oh, I am sorry to be the one to tell you..." She pulled the cup to her lips once more. "How incredibly awkward."

Roslyn forced her lips into a closed mouth smile. She just wanted her gone. "Not at all. To be perfectly honest, I wish you both happiness. Now..." She stood and tipped the bottom of the cup upwards so that Rose was forced to gulp down its contents. She was pleased to see a rivulet dripping down from each corner of her mouth and splashing sticky honied tea onto her blouse. "You'll need to take another thistle tea tomorrow morning, after your... activities." She almost threw the dried thistle head at her and held out her hand. "That'll be five crowns, please."

Rose narrowed her eyes at the steepness of the fee, but dropped the coins on the boards of the table with a clatter before donning her cloak.

"You always were a filthy, greedy beggar, reaching above your station, weren't you?" She took a step towards Roslyn, scowling. "Well, your time with your betters is over. I hope you had fun while it lasted, because you won't be seeing Eik again."

She turned to storm out of the door but stopped and held a hand out above the table. As she turned her wrist over, a ruby red bloom appeared from nowhere. She dropped the rose and its long-barbed stem on the table. With a final glance over her shoulder, she smirked. "For the smell."

Chapter 6

After a week had gone by, Roslyn had all but forgotten the incident with Frederik, except for the memory of his golden curls and sculpted jawline. The image pushed itself to the forefront of her mind when she was lost in thought, but a swift shake of the head soon saw it on its way again.

＊

When she awoke, the sun was streaming in through the window, blinding her as she tried to open her eyes. She lay for a moment, nestled under the eiderdown and let the warmth of the rays bathe her as she lingered. It was an exquisite luxury, but one that she could ill afford. After all, she had a medicine cabinet to restock and she had wasted enough time worrying about soldiers turning up on her doorstep—and all for nothing. In fact, the Oderbergs had seemed almost bored with the villagers in recent days. There'd been no whippings, no beatings and no advances on any of the young women of the town.

Roslyn stretched languidly before pouring herself out of the bed and onto the floor. Lazily, she walked over to her dresser and pulled out a fresh slip, blouse and a green linen skirt she'd worn the day before. Then she bounded downstairs, pecked Hedda on the cheek, and stole the slice of bread the woman had been toasting in the pan. Two more skips and she picked up her baskets, flung her cloak around her shoulders and with one final hop, she wrenched open the door to greet the day.

But what she greeted instead was the moustachioed soldier from the forest. Roslyn stopped stock-still, her eyes wide and her mouth open, the toast falling from her lips to land buttered side down on the doorstep. The guard twitched one side of his lips into what might have been a smile; she couldn't tell because of his bushy moustache, but the look in his eyes made her feel filthy.

"Miss Roslyn Pleveli," he drawled. "We meet again. My pleasure." He bowed dramatically and then stood up again, ramrod straight, and clicked the heels of his steel boots together as if his facetiousness moments before had been part of her imagination.

Roslyn peered around him and into the street. A crowd was gathering at the sight of a cohort of Oderberg soldiers, all mounted on horseback, and a carriage painted with the emblem of the Chained Mountain. It wasn't a luxurious carriage by any means, but it was a far cry from the prison wagon that usually rolled into the village. Roslyn stepped back in shock. What was going on?

As she moved, the guard pushed his way into her home and two of his colleagues traipsed in after, none of them wiping the mud from their boots. Hedda looked up, alarmed at the sudden intrusion and bustled over, hands on her hips.

51

"What is going on here?" Her voice was shrill.

Moustache looked down his nose at her and snarled. "I am here on the king's business."

He stalked up and down the small room, taking in its worn, tired appearance. At one point, he even reached up and pulled down a cobweb that had taken root in the corner of the ceiling and scowled, flicking it from his fingers with disgust. Roslyn peeked at Hedda and saw her flush with shame. As much as she tried to keep a clean house, insects did have their way of getting in, hardly surprising with all the plant matter they brought inside to dry.

Suddenly, he was back to drawling in that pompous, conceited tone. "You would not be attempting to stall the king's business by any means, would you now?"

Hedda swallowed and shook her head slowly, a thin line appearing where her lips should have been. She knew better than to question the Oderbergs. Even though she wasn't a Descendent of the dryads, she was still used to Oderberg brutality.

"Good. Good, that's just what I thought. Now, Miss Roslyn Pleveli, you have been summoned by his majesty King Casimir von Oderberg. He has requested your presence at court in Novlada."

Roslyn's heart was beating fast, the sound of it almost drowning out the drone of the guard who was still issuing orders.

"You will pack a bag and accompany me to the carriage outside. You may have a moment to say your goodbyes but, if you even so much as think of running, be aware I have men stationed at the back of this hovel, round the sides and at each window. You are surrounded. So, go on then, hurry up."

Roslyn couldn't move. She was numb, her legs jelly. Had the prince died? Had they come to take her to the scaffold? Her mind buzzed with possibilities, and she barely noticed Hedda grab her arm and drag her upstairs back into the room which she had only minutes before vacated. Once inside, the woman closed the door and began rummaging around in Roslyn's things.

"Alright, it's alright. Let's just get our things packed, and then we'll sort it out from there. We have to see the positives in this."

Roslyn suddenly snapped out of her reverie. "Positives? What positives? The Oderbergs are here for me! Eik was right, I should have run!"

The old woman stomped over to her, grabbed her arms and shook her a little. "Don't think like that, Roslyn. Come on now. If they had come to kill you, they would not be telling you to pack a bag. The king wants to talk to you and… I don't know what he wants, but I will be there for you, and we will do this together."

Roslyn nodded along with her words, breathing heavily. That was right, they wouldn't tell her to pack a bag if they were going to kill her; they would just wrench her from her home with no warning at all. But on this occasion, the Oderbergs seemed almost courteous in how they were treating her. True, moustache man was snide and slimy and made her feel like she was standing naked before him, but he had not unsheathed his sword and he was using no physical aggression towards her. Hedda was right, as she always was.

Roslyn nodded and reached under her bed, pulling out her tattered carpet bag. She threw in a couple of changes of clothes, not even looking at the combinations. Then she turned instead to her satchel of herbs, ointments and potions. It hadn't left her side since she had started her training, and it wouldn't now. She was paying so much attention to it she barely noticed Hedda turn back to her garment bag and pick out some offending items, replacing them with better ones. Roslyn was going to be presented to the king, after all. She would need her best clothes, even if a peasant's finest was little better than a palace maid's.

Soon enough, the pair of them trundled downstairs again. They placed their bags at their feet, wrapped their cloaks around their necks and stood waiting for their next instructions. Roslyn reached out and held Hedda's soft, wrinkled hand in hers. The woman squeezed it tightly.

"Where do you think you are going?" The moustached guard loomed over the herbalist. "I have instructions to take, Miss Roslyn Pleveli and no other to the king. You will not be accompanying us."

"But… you can't expect a young lady to be escorted to the palace in the presence of—how many soldiers have you got?—with no chaperone. It is improper, and I will not have it."

The guards laughed and Hedda bristled. Roslyn's heart sank to her boots, and she gripped the old woman's hand tighter. She didn't want to go at all, let alone by herself.

"Oh, fear not, you old hag. We've already thought about that, or at least the king's steward has. If you will accompany me outside?" The guard half bowed and extended his arm towards the door as if he were ushering them through it cordially. They had little choice but to walk through the door.

The crowd that gathered outside the cottage had grown, and people thronged the street. Roslyn saw so many familiar, worried faces amongst them, but couldn't meet any of their eyes. Instead, she looked up and took in the simple carriage. The guard waltzed over and rapped curtly on the door. He stood back as it swung open. A tall, dour-faced old maid descended the kicked-out stairs. Her skirts were long and heavy, rising to a cinched in waist— or what would have been, had the woman indeed had any waist to speak of. The bottom of her bodice was the same girth as the top and gave way to a mound of frilled ruffs that seemed to choke her.

Perhaps that was why her lips were pinched together so tightly. She looked bloody miserable. Roslyn took in everything about the woman and, in that instant, knew they weren't going to get along. But the woman's presence seemed to appease Hedda somewhat.

"Fine. Seeing as the king has demanded it and provided a chaperone, then I suppose I will have to let you go, my dear." Hedda's voice was wavering on the verge of tears. Roslyn felt her own resolve crumbling and dived into the smaller woman's embrace.

"Hedda, I'm scared." Her voice was so thin that only the matronly woman heard her plea for help.

Brushing Roslyn's tears away and sniffing back her own, Hedda nodded to convince both of them that everything was going to be alright. "Come now, come now. You'll be back here before you know it."

Moustache man sighed heavily. "That's enough of the goodbyes, now."

"No!" a deep voice shouted from the back of the crowd. The guards snapped their heads in the voice's direction, hands on their weapons. The throngs of people shifted as Eik pushed his way to the front, some frowning at his intrusion and wayward elbows.

Roslyn's mouth twisted and an ember of hatred burned in her chest. How dare he?

55

"I have not had my goodbye."

"Miss Pleveli has a lover? How quaint." The guard was losing his patience now. "I suggest you give your woman a kiss goodbye, then. It might be the last loving one she gets." He turned away in disgust, not wanting to see the public display of affection that was about to occur.

Eik swept Roslyn into an embrace, almost smothering her with the strength of his arms; her attempts to push him away were futile. He lowered his head and nestled it as close to her ear as he could. His voice was breathy and urgent. "Remember what I said! If you ever get near the prince or the king, kill them. Do it for me."

"Why should I do anything for you, you bastard? Why don't you just get Rose to do it!" she hissed up at him, straining to get free of his grasp but he wrapped his hands around the fleshy part of her arm, digging his nails in hard.

"Then do it for us you pathetic girl, for all Domovnians!"

"Time's up, lovebirds."

Eik had just enough time to grab Roslyn's face roughly between his hands and press his lips into hers. It hurt, and as she opened her mouth to protest, their teeth scraped against each other. Then two of the Oderberg guards pulled him away.

"Get in," ordered the moustached guard. The sour-faced chaperone returned to her seat in the carriage, waited for Roslyn to take hers and then slammed the door shut behind them. The guards took to their mounts again and within seconds Roslyn heard the crack of the whip. The carriage lurched forwards, forcing her to lean out of the window. She tried to hold Hedda's gaze, one which was full of concern as she was pulled away from the people she loved, her home, but all too soon she was out of sight. Roslyn didn't know if she would ever see any of them ever again.

She sank back into the corner of the carriage with tears in her eyes and a flutter in her heart. She glanced up at the woman who sat with hands clasped in her lap and eyes trained on her charge. Well, she could stare all she liked, but at least she couldn't read minds. If she had, Roslyn was pretty sure the carriage would have been stopped immediately. For the only thing that was running through her mind were Eik's final words.

"Remember what I said, if you get near the prince."

He hadn't been serious, surely? Roslyn scoffed and startled the woman in front of her. Typical Eik. He hadn't asked anything about her well-being; he hadn't said that he cared for her and everything was going to be alright. He'd snatched a kiss, if you could even call it that, even though he was fucking another woman. No, he just reminded her that if she met the prince again, she had to do all Domovnia a favour and kill him.

Chapter 7

The carriage rolled on and further away from everything Roslyn knew. The shaded, wooded glades soon gave way to open expanses of farmland that were practically bare. True, it was early in the season, but little seemed to sprout from the crusty ridges of coffee coloured soil. Instead of looking at the monotonous and somewhat disheartening scenery, Roslyn turned her attention inwards to the woman in the carriage. She was an austere woman whose hair was scraped back from her head so severely that her skin shone white at the temples. Only a sliver of grey was visible before the remaining locks were hidden beneath a simple lace scarf.

Her face didn't look much better, either. The woman's eyes were small and set a little too close together. Her nose was thin and crooked, giving the impression of a hawk, a buzzard or some other large bird of prey. She pursed her thin lips together so tightly that they looked like a puckered anal sphincter. The lace ruffs of her collar gave way to a lavish, yet modest gown of dark blue velvet.

Roslyn decided to try to talk to the woman, find out more about where they were going and who she was.

"So, we didn't have an introduction before. My name is Roslyn, and yours is…?" Roslyn proffered. The woman furrowed her brow, pursed her lips even tighter—which Roslyn didn't even think was possible—and nodded.

"That's true. Captain Dietrich neglected his duties of a formal introduction. I am the Lady Margitte, recently widowed of the favoured Lord Magnus von Oderberg, and aunt to his majesty, the king. And to my chagrin, it would appear that my duties include babysitting you." The Lady Margitte then turned her head out the window, but Roslyn wasn't ready for the conversation to be over.

"How long will it take us to get to the castle?" Her voice was shaky and hesitant, and she disliked herself for it, but she didn't want the woman to bark at her again.

"It will take until tomorrow. We shall retire to an inn this evening. On the morrow, you shall rise, wash and dress in your best clothes for your arrival. The king has insisted that I take you to him in immediately and I, for one, will not stand to be embarrassed by you."

She hadn't turned from the window at all while she said this. There was no doubt now that the conversation was indeed over. Suddenly, Lady Margitte shifted in her seat and made a compressed, uncomfortable grunting sound.

"Are you alright?" Roslyn asked in alarm. Lady Margitte did not look at her, but unabashedly lifted one side of her ample buttocks. A loud, rasping sound came from within the folds of her velvet skirt, followed by the most disgusting stench to ever accost Roslyn's nostrils; it smelt like something had died. She tried not to wrinkle her face in abject horror and disgust, but failed to do so. The

Lady Margitte, on the other hand, pretended it had never happened.

✳

The trip was long, dusty and flatulence-filled. Her chaperone frequently and unashamedly released her noxious gases into the confined space. Roslyn had to fight back a gag several times. Once the noblewoman muttered something about travel disrupting her stomach, but it wasn't an apology.

As the sun rose, the heat inside the little wooden box also increased and dust from the dry roads flew up around the carriage. Roslyn peeped out of the window every now and again, but the scenery didn't change from flat, barren fields. Soldiers flanked them, sweat dripping from under their tin hats and down their faces. They seemed to trundle on and on, and Roslyn wondered if they were ever going to stop.

Just when her stomach started to rumble, a call came from beyond the carriage and the vehicle turned off the road and into the shade of a copse of trees. As it rolled to a halt, the door was flung open by the moustached guard, Captain Dietrich.

"Right, ladies. We will pause for one hour to eat and complete our ablutions, then we will be back on the road so that we may make better progress and stop at an inn nearer to the castle." He didn't look at them as he barked the order and disappeared into the rectangle of greenery behind him.

The Lady Margitte jumped up from her seat, ran down the steps which had barely been unfolded, and disappeared into the tiny speck of woodland in which they had sought refuge. The guard turned to shout after her that she should always keep an eye on her charge, but the quick quip from the noblewoman contained so many expletives that he let it rest. He turned to Roslyn and looked at her with a raised eyebrow. "Is she alright?"

Roslyn nodded and frowned. "Alright for someone who has uncontrollable wind." She was pleased to see the captain grimace as she had done.

"Well, you'd better go check on her. Then at least I can say you have been in each other's presence the whole time."

Roslyn descended from the carriage, her legs relishing the sudden movement. As much as she would have preferred to eat first, the captain had given her an order, and it was best to obey it whilst her life still hung in the balance. Following the damaged greenery, the snapped off bits of twig and brush where the noblewoman had rushed through, she soon stopped by a bush that was emitting a strange grunting noise.

"Excuse me, Lady Margitte, are you alright? The captain has sent me to find you."

An exasperated sigh sounded from behind the shrubbery, and after a rustling of skirts, the sour woman's face appeared level with her own.

"No, I am not alright. I have been on the road for two days to come and get your miserable behind and take it to the king. And because of that, my habits have been completely disrupted. Stoppered up like Frier in the Mountain!" She looked about her and sniffed, rearranging the bodice of her dress, suddenly remembering her station. "I suggest you make your ablutions here so that we may eat in peace. I shall stand with my back turned while you get on with it."

Roslyn rolled her eyes but did her business quickly and efficiently. When she was done, she nodded at the noblewoman who traipsed back to the makeshift camp. On the way, Roslyn, as she usually did, looked about the forest floor and up into the trees to see if there was anything she could forage. It was habit and one that had been instilled into her from a very young age, but this time it proved worthwhile. She spied a little spread of peppermint growing by the side of the road. Still walking, she bent down, hoping the Lady Margitte wouldn't see her out of the corner of her eye and scooped up a handful that she stuffed into her satchel.

Their victuals were less than impressive. Well, Roslyn's were. The Lady Margitte produced a bottle of wine and poured it into a fine crystal glass. She had been presented with a beautiful, linen-lined wicker hamper filled with apples, boiled eggs, soft oozing cheeses which she smeared on fresh fluffy bread, a cold meat pie and many other things which Roslyn hadn't even a chance to see before the Lady snapped the lid of the basket shut. However, she could guess that whatever other rich foods were in there, they were a more likely cause of the woman's discomfort that the rocking of the carriage.

The soldiers had their rations: ale from a casket, soft fresh bread rolls and creamy yellow cheese. Roslyn's fare, on the other hand, was yesterday's hardened crust and the putrid rind of the last cheese round. She tapped them together with a clunk. Both could inflict serious damage if she wanted to escape, but her stomach rumbled violently, so she dipped the bread into her beaker of water to make it somewhat less likely to break her teeth.

After they had finished eating, one of the guards called over to her from his reclined position against a tree.

"Oi, flower witch, show us some magic then."

Roslyn shot a glance at Captain Dietrich and shook her head. "You know I can't. It is forbidden."

The captain snorted. "I thought you said your powers are basically defunct. Besides, I do have to ensure you are not a threat to the king. So, it's a pardon. Come on then, Roslyn Pleveli. Show us what you can do… Or not."

The Lady Margitte's mouth was pinched into a flat white line. From the shake of her head, Roslyn couldn't decide if it was in disgust or a warning. However, yet again, she had been given an order.

Roslyn shook her head. "I can't do much. I'm only a Hedgie."

The soldier that had corralled her before smiled in an almost friendly manner and waved his arm dismissively. "Just do it! No concerns or repercussions! Show us."

Once again, the captain gave his confirmation that she would not be punished, nodding his head gently. So, she stood up and looked around her, talking as she went.

"Well, I don't know how much you know about the Affinity, but each Domovnian is linked or paired with certain plants. For example, a Hedgie tends to have Affinity or power with hedgerow plants and—"

"Weeds." The moustachioed captain interjected. "Useless little weeds, isn't that right?"

Roslyn's cheeks flared with heat but she nodded and continued to look around, fearing she would not find the plants she had Affinity with. She walked in wider circles, aware of all the guards' eyes upon her.

"Exactly, hedgerow plants and weeds, but there are others who have Affinity with trees, although mainly one

63

or two types of trees. Not all of them. My friend, he has Affinity with oak trees."

"And this friend's name is…?" Captain Dietrich left the question hanging. Roslyn's heart clenched painfully in her chest. She wouldn't be so stupid. She couldn't give Eik or any of her friends away.

She pretended she hadn't heard him. "Now, when one has Affinity with the plant, you can draw on its natural powers and make it move to your will, or grow… or you can simply enhance its natural abilities, which comes in handy for healers. Many plants have medicinal benefits and you can enhance those to make the remedies more powerful, so the patient will recover quicker."

Lady Margitte sniffed loudly and cleared her throat. "If the plant's abilities can be enhanced for medicinal purposes to make a remedy stronger, does that not also mean that they can be used for harm, such as a plant with a poisonous element?"

Roslyn turned to face her, her hatred of the woman growing even more as she saw the snide smile at the corners of her lips.

"Well, yes, but as a healer, one wouldn't use those properties unless absolutely necessary. One definitely wouldn't enhance them. There are dangerous plants, but some can be used as well-known cures if administered in the right quantities. That is why an herbalist has to be trained to use them. Oh!"

Roslyn had found what she was looking for and pointed to a shadowy part of the clearing. At her sudden movement, the captain and the other soldiers jumped to alertness, but when they saw she was only pointing at the tiny shoot of a newly sprouted nettle, they loosened the

64

grips on their weapons and sank back into their reclined positions.

"There is one of my Affinity plants," Roslyn said with a smile on her face and approached the stinging nettle. She crouched down and whispered quietly, "Hello, my friend."

The nettle before her was young and hadn't reached its full height yet, but it bobbed its spiky leaves from side to side as if waving at her.

"Was that it?" blurted out the guard who had demanded she perform for him, barely hiding his disappointment.

"According to her own admission, she has next to no abilities. It wouldn't surprise me if all she could do was make it wave at us. Or was it merely the breeze, Miss Pleveli?" Captain Dietrich jeered in her direction, knowing very well it hadn't been the wind. There was none to be had. The sun was high in the sky now and the heady perfume of sun-baked pine overwhelmed the copse, making its residents sleepy.

Roslyn bowed her head and blushed. "It's true. I can't do much, but I can do more than that."

"Well, go on then, we are all waiting," insisted Lady Margitte, already bored by this pathetic and permitted act of treason.

Roslyn stood back from the little nettle and planted her feet wide. Then she closed her eyes and reached down into the earth through the balls of her feet. She could feel the fibres of the nettle's roots searching out moisture in the ground and channelled herself into them. Then, with all her might, she pushed up, her hands clenching invisible balls at her sides as she urged the plant upwards. She grunted with the effort and was soon sweating from exertion. Her breathing was heavy and when her head suddenly thudded with pain, she let go, her energy seeping back into her. Then she stepped back and opened her eyes.

When she looked down at the little nettle again, she was pleased to see it wasn't little anymore. The head of the plant was now no longer ankle height, but had stretched up to her shoulder and was heavy with seeds that hung from its tip like tiny green pearls. She couldn't help the smile that broke out on her face and she whispered, "Thank you."

Placing her hands on her hips, she turned round to face her audience, but the smile was wiped off her face and her shoulders sank as she took in the unimpressed faces. Awkward silence reigned for a while and then suddenly Captain Dietrich stood and wiped the dirt off the back of his britches.

"Right, well. If that's all, I think we'd best get on."

The soldiers grumbled as they packed up their lunch things and took Lady Margitte's basket from her, although Roslyn noticed she kept the bottle of wine and her glass when she went to ascend into her carriage again. Roslyn did not want to go. It was hot. She'd just embarrassed herself and showed them how truly powerless she was. How could she sit back in that stifling wooden box to be rolled and jolted around on the dusty roads whilst her companion filled it with foul vapours that smelled like rotten eggs and putrefied meat? She lingered a little while, allowing the others to traipse before her. The guard that had egged her on leant in for a nudge to hurry her along.

"I can see why you trained as an herbalist, then. Give you something to do, seeing as you're such a useless Domovnian."

They left the shadow of the trees where the heat hit them with a blow, pressing the air out of their lungs. Just before he helped her up into the carriage, an improvement on the last time when she'd been all but bundled in, the soldier turned and raised an eyebrow at her. "By the way, what else is your Affinity with?"

Roslyn smiled as she caught a glimpse of the very plant he was talking about. It peeped out of the ditch that separated the road from the forest and waved at her in the brilliant sunshine, its golden, buttery yellow petals reflecting the sun's own brilliance. She reached down to pull it up by the root, spraying dirt everywhere and forcing the soldier to take a step back with a gargled cry. She held it aloft proudly, watching the long, carrot-like root spin in mid-air.

"The dandelion. King of all weeds."

The guard scoffed. "Does that make you their queen? Well then, your majesty," he dipped into a mock bow before kicking her backside up the stairs. "Your carriage awaits."

✳

Roslyn must have fallen asleep, for when she opened her eyes again, it was dark beyond the window frame. Well, not pitch black, but it definitely wasn't sunlight pouring through the rectangle of the carriage door. While the sun had beaten down on Domovnia in the daytime, the moon was full and radiant. It blessed the land in a cool, white glow that lit up passing fields and thatched cottages, betraying the edges of the forests.

As the carriage crested a hill, her breath was forced from her lungs in awe. On a nearby hilltop rose a ghostly castle of shimmering white, bright against the shadowy backdrop of the sea. Its turrets were torn and parapets had tumbled down into the night-time hillside. Despite its destruction, Roslyn saw it had once been the most beautiful palace in the entire kingdom. But beauty didn't necessarily mean safe. The longer she looked at the dilapidated, moon-kissed ruins, the more her skin prickled with unease.

Roslyn looked down at her arm and the hair was standing on end, but more than that, her tan skin held the faintest shimmer, as if the moonlight had dusted her skin with its beauty. Her lips parted, and she breathed a faint sigh. Her skin had never shown the sign of the Ancestors before. Surely it was just a trick of the light? She rubbed her arm quickly and caught the Lady Margitte's eye.

"What is that place?" she couldn't help but ask, even though she knew there was only one place it could be. The noblewoman confirmed her suspicion.

"That, my dear, is all that remains of Eluha, the ancestral home of the Domonovs, the last royals your people ever had." It might have been the light, but Roslyn could have sworn she saw a touch of sadness in the old woman's eyes. But if it had been there, it was wiped away by a tree's shadow cast in the moonlight.

As the carriage wound its way down the hill and the ruin of Eluha began to slip out of sight, Roslyn couldn't help but stare at it again. Her heart sank as she realised that what she was staring at was not just a ruin or historic battlefield, but a tomb. A burial place that pulled at her, called to her, tugging at something inside.

Not long after the ruin was lost from view, the carriage rumbled and jolted along a potholed road and came to an abrupt stop in the well-lit courtyard of a tavern. Stablehands rushed forward to lead the soldiers' and the carriage's horses away. Roslyn and the Lady Margitte found themselves bustled out of the vehicle and into a yard that smelled like pig swill. Dietrich came out of the tavern door and beckoned the two ladies forward.

"I have arranged for your dinner to be sent up to your room and a bath drawn. I suggest you stay out of sight." He glanced at Roslyn snidely. "We don't want to attract any undue attention."

No, Roslyn thought, *you just don't want people to know that you're travelling with a Domovnian*. But she was grateful that she could just follow the noblewoman, who in turn followed a servant girl carrying a pitcher of water for their bath up the rickety staircase that began just short of the inn proper. The wooden floorboards of the narrow upstairs corridor creaked with every step. Roslyn half wondered if they were going to fall through and into the crowded room below where she could hear music playing.

Once the serving girl had left them, Lady Margitte plonked herself on the larger of the two beds. Although, if truth be told, the large, four-poster monstrosity was the only real bed; a small trundle bed, little more than a cot, lay at its base. Roslyn knew where she would spend the night and if it was to be at the base of that flatulent woman's bed, she was going to have to do something about it if she didn't want to be suffocated in her sleep.

Roslyn watched as the old woman sank into the featherbed with a groan.

"Oh, that is good," she exclaimed, closing her eyes in the simple pleasure of sitting down on a non-moving apparatus. Still with her eyes closed, the Lady Margitte continued. "Now, Miss Pleveli, you will arrange the screen for me by the bath, and then you will sit silently whilst I cleanse myself of the road dust. Oh, my poor fragile skin! Then, and only then, may you make use of the water that remains."

Roslyn gritted her teeth. She highly doubted that the water would have any heat left by the time the old woman was finished, but she put on her sweetest smile and bobbed into a half curtsy.

"Of course, my lady, and may I prepare a soothing tisane for you whilst you bathe?"

The old woman opened one eye and stared at her. "What kind of tisane?"

Roslyn shrugged. "Oh, a very simple one that any farmer's wife knows—just a blend of peppermint to ease the stomach, a little sprinkling of aromatic herbs such as lavender and catnip to relax the soul and stevia for a little something sweet."

The Lady Margitte opened both her eyes and crossed her arms under her ample bosom, her voice dripping with sarcasm. "And will you be partaking in this tisane, to soothe your own weary bones after the road?"

Roslyn nodded, clasped her hands before her and rubbed the back of one leg with the foot of another. "Of course, I am unused to travel and I am feeling very worn out. My nerves are somewhat strained."

Lady Margitte sniffed haughtily, placed her own hands in her lap and then nodded. "Very well. You may prepare your herb infused concoction. I have to admit, the peppermint you speak of sounds wonderful before I

70

attempt my dinner." She said no more, but heaved herself from the bed and disappeared behind the screen.

Roslyn busied herself with her ingredients, unloading her pestle and mortar, her brewing pot and the herbs she had shoved down her belt earlier that day. All she needed now was a kettle of boiling water. She rang the bell and requested one when the serving girl came. Then she set about washing the dandelion root and chopping it into tiny pieces. She glanced over her shoulder at the screen as she heard what she assumed to be a sigh of relief as the woman slipped into the warm water, but sounded awfully like a moan of pleasure from another source. Roslyn shook the disturbing image of the Lady Margitte writhing in ecstasy out of her head.

Once the kettle had been brought up to the room, she infused the ingredients. The smell was exquisite, and Roslyn herself was looking forward to a cup. However, she thought it best to brew a cup for herself without the addition of the dandelion. After all, she was not the one who needed to purge her bowels.

A shrill voice called out from behind the screen at the far end of the room. "Girl! Girl, where is that tea you promised me?"

"It just needs a few more moments brewing, my lady," she called back.

The woman sniffed and sat back down, the water audibly sploshing over the sides of the copper tub. "Very well. But I'm getting thirsty."

The tea was ready and strained when the Lady Margitte removed herself from her bath and wrapped a robe of downy velvet around herself, twisted her hair up in a turban and placed golden threaded slippers on her feet.

Roslyn ushered her to the seat by the fire, where she had placed not only the woman's tisane but also the cloched dinner that had been delivered. The old woman looked up at her and narrowed her eyes.

"Is everything alright, Lady Margitte?" Roslyn took a step back, uncomfortable with the sudden attention, but the woman grabbed her wrist in a painful snatch.

"Turn your head to the left, yes, just like that. Hmm…" The noble tilted her head over her shoulder, her voice thin and whispery. "You know, in the firelight just now, you reminded me of someone, but I can't… I can't remember who." A sudden expression, somewhat akin to fear lit the woman's eyes, and she sniffed. When she spoke again, her voice was strong and full of orders.

"You may take your bath now, girl." Lady Margitte waved her away, not looking at her whilst taking a cautious sip of the tisane. She nodded approval before eagerly removing the cloche on the steaming dinner beneath. Roslyn's mouth watered at the sight of the mashed potatoes soaking in butter, the boiled carrots sprinkled with dill and the brilliantly plump and pink fillet of salmon that rested alongside them. There was also fresh bread and more butter to slather on its barely cool surface. The Lady Margitte caught her staring and tutted.

"Well, go on then, before it gets cold. You can eat after."

Roslyn looked sadly at her own, much smaller cloche that she was certain did not contain quite the same dinner as her superior. Her stomach growled in protest and resentment. No doubt that, too, would be cold by the time she got to it. She nodded and made her way behind the screen. The huge, high-backed copper tub was lined with a sheet of linen, but she didn't need it because of the heat.

That had long since gone. She set her clothes neatly on a chair by the side and slipped into the tepid, slightly mucky water. To her delight, a bar of lavender-scented soap sat on the table and she snatched it up and lathered her skin gratefully. Then, once she was clean, she allowed herself to wallow in the water for a few moments longer. Suddenly, a voice disturbed her tranquillity.

"You'd better make sure you scrub yourself carefully. We will see the king first thing tomorrow." The Lady Margitte's voice sounded agitated and Roslyn heard her stand, the chair scraping backwards along the wooden floor in a sudden flurry of movement. As she continued, her voice was more laboured and moved from the fireplace towards the door. "I suggest you wash your hair too… I—I just have to make use of the privy. I'll be back in a moment; don't you go anywhere!"

Roslyn suppressed a giggle as the strained woman ran from the room, her need to relieve herself absolutely overwhelming all sense of propriety. It would appear that the dandelion had done its job.

73

Chapter 8

"Is that really what you are wearing to meet the king?" Lady Margitte scoffed.

Roslyn looked down at her outfit. It was soft, pale green linen of the highest quality that was available to the general populace who didn't happen to be Oderbergs, with a lace-up bodice and matching skirt down to the knee. It flowed beautifully and was embroidered with the spiky green leaves of both her Affinity plants. The yellow dandelion heads were dazzling spots of colour, accompanied by the white, powdery seed puffs that seemingly floated up to the waist. Underneath the well-fitted bust, she wore a thin cotton shirt.

"What's wrong with it? It's… it's all I've got."

The old woman sighed. "Well, it will just have to do then, but mark my words, he will not be impressed."

The drive to the castle was short and uneventful, but as the hills dropped away and the road ran straight towards the high walled citadel before them, the tension in Roslyn's stomach grew. She was suddenly regretting the enormous bowl of porridge laced with cinnamon and sugar that she had wolfed down for breakfast that morning, unsure if it had been her last meal or not.

Where the ruins of Eluha had been majestic and almost moving with fluidity despite its dereliction, the fortified town of Novlada was solid, harsh and imposing. Once she was within those walls, Roslyn knew very well that it would only be with express permission that she would be allowed out again. She craned her neck out of the window as the carriage rolled under the heavily guarded gateway. Lady Margitte snatched at her arm, pinching her, and dragged her back into the carriage.

"What do you think you're doing?" she hissed. "You will remain in this carriage at all times. You must not let anyone see you. No one may know you are even here until I have presented you to his Majesty."

The Lady Margitte stood and snapped the blinds shut but the city was not entirely blocked out. Roslyn still heard the sounds of the metropolis—the hustle and bustle of market stallholders hawking their wares, the cries of children as they pleaded for their parents' attention, pleaded for money or food, or ran around annoying their elders. Soldiers barked at people; men and women laughed raucously as they fell out of taverns and stumbled into the street. She heard the curses of other carriage drivers and the whips that they brought down not only on their horses, but the people around them. What kind of place was this?

The noise soon faded away as the carriage rolled up a finer paved street and towards the castle proper. They were stopped at the entrance where Captain Dietrich was submitted to several checks and the door was wrenched open for a guard to inspect the two women inside. This particular guard looked at Roslyn as if she were something he had pushed out of his arse earlier that morning. He hissed and spat on the ground before slamming the door on her.

"Well, that was most unnecessary," huffed Lady Margitte, and Roslyn couldn't help but agree with her for once.

The carriage made its way around to the stables and was actually driven inside, so afraid were they that anyone should see the Domovnian before the king. Someone bustled Roslyn into a long, heavy cloak with a hood so that only her hands were visible. She was somewhat grateful for this extra level of anonymity as the searing stares of the stable boys tried to pierce the darkness of her hood, wondering who she was. It was in this state of suspicion that she was led through the palace. She received the same curious stares from the servants in the hot, steamy kitchen as she did from the highest nobility in the antechamber to the throne room.

Roslyn could not blame them. It must have been most unusual to see a small cloaked woman escorted, not only by a widowed aunt of the king himself, but by a whole host of Oderberg guards. But as much as they stared at her, she stared back, taking in their ruffs, their heavy velvet court clothes and powdered faces.

The entourage stopped abruptly before two enormous wooden doors, ornately carved and gilded. Roslyn didn't have time to admire the artistry as the cloak was wrenched from her shoulders, causing an intake of breath from those around them. A sudden hiss of whispers echoed around the antechamber. Looking around nervously, Roslyn saw she stuck out like a sore thumb. Her clothes were simple, her skin and hair much darker than the golden-haired, fair skinned Oderbergs. She glanced down at her forearms and, to her horror, saw that the sheen on her skin was still there. Why had she never noticed it amongst her own people? Was theirs so strong she'd always believed she had none?

Lady Margitte ignored the gossipers with impeccable dignity, betraying her elevated position and the breeding that came with it. She turned to Roslyn."Now, you are about to have an audience with his majesty, King Casimir von Oderberg. You will enter, head bowed, as befits your station. He is finishing his morning audience, so you will be silent and, when presented, will speak only when spoken to. You will show the utmost humility before him."

Roslyn was seething inside both with frustration at the way she would have to behave before this boar that had destroyed her country, but also with fear. She knew what he was capable of, she knew what he ordered his guards to do to her people. And now she was about to have an audience with the man himself, and she didn't yet know why. She nodded her head in response to Lady Margitte's command and the woman rapped three times on the massive door. Roslyn tried to swallow in the pause that followed, her throat constricting with a glob of saliva that she couldn't seem to shift. As the doors creaked slowly open, her stomach turned to ice.

The doors shut behind them as Roslyn was ushered into the enormous throne room. At the far end, two men sat side-by-side on gilded thrones. Of the three chairs that stood there, the one in the centre was the largest and the most ornate; the two on either side were modest in comparison, and one remained ominously empty.

Courtiers and advisors lined the sides of the hall, and a group of peasants stood before the dais, blocking her view. They were humans, but dressed in the traditional Domovnian style. Even if they weren't Descendents, they were still her countrymen. She was astonished that they had been permitted entry, but then, they weren't 'tainted' by the Affinity. She leaned in to listen.

"… Snapped my boat clean in two. I only just escaped with my life! Please, your majesty, if you do not send soldiers to join the armada with the Kestians and Tokavors, the sea wyrms will climb out of the waves and claim the coast from Yakir to Dumka. It will be carnage!"

A hush fell on the hall as the fisherman's plea rang in the stillness. Roslyn heard an intake of breath and a low rumbling voice barked. "You dare to tell me what I should do with my men! That I should join those soft Summerlanders and bookworms in fending off sea lizards! See, this is what sort of superstitious nitwittery that comes from letting fairy folk rule you for so long! Guards—"

A heavy sigh and a drawling voice to the right of the dais silenced the order that was about to come. "Do not trouble yourself over this, father. I am due to ride out on patrol soon and it has been some time since we have inspected the coastal regiments. If what this man says is true…" The voice paused and at an unseen signal, the poor fishermen were surrounded, the sharp end of the soldier's pikes pointing their way. "Then you can release these presumptuous upstarts with a firm reminder that they demand nothing of the king."

A low rumble sounded at the other end of the hall. Roslyn strained to hear, but the reply from the nonchalant speaker left her in no doubt what had been asked.

"And if I see no trace of these fabled sea wyrms, then you can use them to send a message to the people about wasting royal time."

Roslyn tried to swallow down the lump in her throat as the pleading men were jostled at spearpoint out of the hall. Lady Margitte gripped her by her wrist and pulled her along the length of the central aisle. It was time for her audience with the king.

Once at the top, she felt a swift kick in the back of her knees from Captain Dietrich, and she buckled into a resentful bow.

"Proceed," sounded a stern voice from the far end of the room. Roslyn didn't need to look up to know that it was the older man on the centre throne. She kept her head down as she walked up the length of the room with Captain Dietrich and Lady Margitte on either side. Their footsteps echoed on the paving slabs, a cold, clipped sound that seemed lost in the vacuum of the high-ceilinged space. They stopped short of the stone steps that led up to the platform on which the thrones sat and, again, Roslyn was forced to curtsy to the man she despised. Though her neck was bent towards the floor, she peered up through the wisps of mousey brown hair that fell into her eyes and took in King Casimir von Oderberg, the man who had stolen her country.

He was not entirely what she'd expected. Though he was not the stalwart, gnarly old warrior she had anticipated, he had evidently been so once— the remnants of his broad form now sat idly in clothes padded to disguise the fact that his muscles had wasted away; his once golden hair was a ghost of what it had been and stuck up in downy tufts from beneath his heavy golden crown. His face was lined with not only the usual wrinkles that appear in later life but also those that come with a perpetual struggle of the self. Roslyn couldn't help but wonder what it was that gnawed this man from within. She hoped it was guilt.

"Rise," the king croaked, and finally she could get a better look at not only him but also the man sat at his side.

This man was what the king should have been, and most likely had been in his youth. He had the same square jaw and solid brow, the same stern and commanding expression, the same bulk. However, the mass on this younger man was very much muscle and Roslyn knew from reports that it had been put to good use in putting down the Domovnian rebels who had dared rise against the Crown.

This was the crown prince, Viktor von Oderberg, named after his father's victory over the magical peasant folk of Domovnia, his birth following only days after. It had been seen as fortuitous and a portent of what he would achieve in his lifetime. He would be a great man, a great King, greater possibly than his father, who had paved the way for him to rule.

The king and crown prince stared down at her with cold calculation and Roslyn couldn't help but turn her gaze back to the floor, fearful lest they were able to sense her thoughts. She was almost certain that the Oderbergs fed on fear like the mythical bloodsuckers in folktales. Why else would they continue to wound, maim and kill the natives?

"Step forward, girl. Raise your head and look at me," the king commanded. He leaned forward in his seat, resting his elbows on the very edges of the armrests, his bushy eyebrows furrowed. "Do you know who I am?"

Roslyn resentfully bobbed yet another curtsy and raised her head to look him in his chilling blue eyes. "I can make the assumption, your majesty."

No sooner had the words left her mouth, she received a quick slap to the back of her head from the Lady Margitte.

"You will speak respectfully when addressed by his majesty."

The king, however, smirked, gave a little chuckle and waved away his aunt's chastisement. "Well, she's definitely a Domovnian. Only they would speak to me with such spirit." He sat back in his chair and laced his fingers over his withered stomach. "Yes, you are correct. I am the king of the Bergams and, by extension and happy military campaigning, of your people too. This is my son, Crown Prince Viktor, who will one day take my place upon this throne." He paused, shifting uncomfortably in his seat. "And it would appear that we are in your debt, an unheard-of occurrence. Had you not been in the right place at the right time—and had you not had such quick thinking and skills with plants, so I am told by my physicians—then my youngest son would be dead. So, you have saved the prince's life and for that I must thank you," He held her gaze and she shivered, feeling his eyes piercing her soul. "Sincerely."

"Is… is that why I'm here, for you to thank me? I'm sure it would have been easier to send a letter." Roslyn received another slap to the head for speaking out of turn, but again the king, to her surprise, laughed.

"Yes, I quite agree with you, that would have been much easier and far more fitting for the occasion. But my son, once he had recovered enough to realise he was not on death's door, was plagued by visions of a young girl in the woods who had chastised him and his men like a fishwife and saved his life. It is he who wants to thank you personally, and it is he who wishes to give you employment."

The crown prince snorted into his hand, which was supporting his chin, but the king continued.

"Frederik would like to offer you the position of his own personal healer and herbalist whilst he is recovering from the boar attack. Indeed, he is most insistent about it, despite everyone's protestations. He is adamant." The king's timbre lowered to that of a fed-up grumble. "Part of this newfangled idea he has of extending an olive branch to the natives of Domovnia."

Roslyn struggled to take it all in. She was to work for the prince of the Oderbergs, just because she has saved his life? She had been uprooted and snatched from her family, and was supposed to believe it was an honour that she had been chosen to perform such a service?

A long, languid sigh came from the crown prince, who stood and stretched before sitting down again in a much more regal position than he had before. "He does have a point, father." His voice was dry and arrogant, laced with the drawl that only nobility seem to accomplish. "It has been twenty-five years and we are still battling with almost weekly rebellions. We should begin to..." He paused and waved his hand nonchalantly. "Explore new possibilities, perhaps in small case studies, in controlled environments so that we may see the results before we give the people any hope." He shrugged and looked down at Roslyn as if she were a scullery maid. "Besides, she will meet none of her kind whilst she's here. She can hatch no plans."

Roslyn shook her head in disbelief and stepped forward before Lady Margitte could give her a third blow to the head.

"So, as a reward for saving my enemy's life, I am to be his captive?" Her voice was shrill and petulant, but there was nothing she could do about it; her emotions were stretched to breaking point. "Is he ill, my lord? Does he need constant care? Do you not have physicians of your own?"

While the king looked baffled that she had dared to speak out of turn and in such a tone, Crown Prince Victor smirked and snorted into his hand again as it found its way under his chin.

"He is ill from the effects of wine often enough that he seems to think having a maid with a knowledge of herbs will help him recover for the next party faster." He rose from his seat and lolloped down the steps with a casual ease towards Roslyn until he towered over her.

"My brother is a dandy, a drunkard and a party prince, despite his protestations of change. Just be sure not to fulfil his wishes for any stronger herbs than those of the restorative kind, because he will most assuredly ask." He was about to turn back when he paused and looked down at Roslyn with a glance that betrayed the filthy thought in his head. Roslyn felt naked and exposed under that gaze and wished she could wrap her arms around herself, but she swallowed and raised her head to meet the prince's eye.

"Oh, and if I were you, I'd stay well away from his bedside while treating him. He has an eye for... pretty things."

The king smacked his hand down on the hand rest and bellowed. "Enough! Sit down, Victor. You, Domovnian— I have been told of your near inability with the Affinity. That is in your favour, and why you were not beheaded as soon as you stepped into this castle. However, you will be watched over by an apothecary whilst concocting your blends and lotions and potions and whatnot, just to ensure you don't do anything you shouldn't. For if I hear that you have even so much as requested anything, any single little weed that could do us harm, you will leave this palace in a box and without that pretty little head of yours. Is that quite clear?"

Roslyn swallowed and did not break eye contact with the enraged King. She curtsied and bowed her head. "Quite, your majesty."

King Casimir sat back in his throne with a nod, as if he had got his way, as usual. Captain Dietrich grabbed her arm, twirled her around and marched her back out of the throne room. Their footsteps echoed on the paving slabs again, faster this time and with each *tap, tap, tap* of their shoes on the stones, Eik's words pounded in her brain.

"If you ever get the chance to kill him—do it."

Not only would she have intimate access to Prince Frederik, but also the entire royal family. Could she do what Eik wanted, could she do all the Domovnians needed her to do? Could she actually kill them?

Chapter 9

Captain Dietrich dragged Roslyn through a plain door that led to the servants' warren. Her wrist chafed as he pulled her down stairs and along corridors until he pushed her through a door into what looked essentially like a broom cupboard. Then he bowed at the old noble woman who had stalked them and left. It was a grey, bare stone room just off the kitchen where someone had plonked a stool, a small table and a simple lunch.

"It is here I will leave you, Miss Pleveli," Lady Margitte said as she clasped her hands over her waist. "I would say it has been a pleasure travelling with you, but I'm not prone to lying. With that same thought in mind, I hope our paths do not cross too often, and should they do so, I would pray that you remember your station."

Roslyn half chuckled in astonishment and nodded her head in agreement. "Likewise, milady, likewise. But what am I to do now?"

Lady Margitte shrugged. "I know not, only that I was to bring you here, where you will be watched over by Captain Dietrich's men. You are to eat lunch and then, I presume, will be taken to Prince Frederik. I will bid you adieu."

True to her word, the noblewoman nodded curtly and turned on her heel, leaving Roslyn alone with her thoughts. Although the door was closed, she could hear two men whispering outside. She briefly wondered where Captain Dietrich was, but then her stomach growled. She forgot all about him entirely, turning to inspect the food on the table.

It was simple fare: bread, cheese, white bean paste and a mug of ale. She nodded her head in appreciation. It was the best meal she'd been given yet. Not long after the food had been demolished, she wiped her mouth on the back of her hand. The door opened and in marched the familiar moustache of Captain Dietrich.

He clipped his steel heels together as he came to a halt before her, ramrod straight and arms clasped behind his back. "Prince Frederik has summoned you. I am to take you there." He looked down at the plate and empty mug on the table and hesitantly asked, "You enjoyed your luncheon, I hope?"

Roslyn was taken aback by his sudden civility. There was no trace of the sleazy brute that she had met in the woods, nor the bullish guard who had just dragged her through the castle like a criminal. The constant sneer was gone and his face seemed softer and younger for it. Had his superiors noted his attitude and given him a dressing down for it? She raised a perplexed eyebrow, but bowed her head gracefully. "Yes, thank you. It was satisfactory after our travels."

"Very good. If you will follow me." Captain Dietrich extended his arm, allowing her to leave the lunch cell first. Then he swept in front of her and led her in a mind-boggling tour of the back passages of the palace, hewn in the same oppressive grey stone, all dark with only slits for windows that let in sparse shards of light. This was more like a fortress than a palace, but then perhaps sunlight was allowed to enter the royal abode and it was just the servants who were forced to live in the shadows.

They climbed up stairs and walked round corners until Roslyn was well and truly lost. Finally, they stepped out of the servants' halls and into the family's living quarters. The corridors expanded not only in size but in light and decoration. Roslyn found herself outside another set of wooden, gilded doors, but these were much smaller than the ones that graced the throne room. She had just enough time to see the letter F carved amongst swirling patterns, disappearing in and out of the golden carved foliage. It was flamboyant, but also artistic, and Roslyn wondered if the prince himself had ordered the decoration.

She didn't really know what to expect after a warning from Prince Viktor. She swallowed, steadied herself and walked into Prince Frederik's quarters, certain that she would not be letting any party prince have a good time with her.

The first room was empty, a large sitting room of sorts with sofas and chairs and games dotted around as if the prince had just had company and the guests had all vanished. Captain Dietrich didn't even blink at his surroundings, nor the wineglasses that were scattered here and there, some upright, others laying drunkenly on their sides. He marched into another chamber, a smaller one where a large green velvet chaise longue was situated, on which sat a shirtless, grinning, golden-haired man.

"Miss Roslyn Pleveli," Captain Dietrich began dryly, "might I formally introduce you to his Royal Highness

Prince Frederik von Oderberg, whom you have already had the pleasure of meeting."

Roslyn gawked at the man on the sofa. She barely recognised him. He was no longer sweating profusely, covered in blood and screaming like a child. Here sat a man who was confident not only in his position in the world but also in his body. He lounged on the sofa with such ease; it was as if he'd been painted upon it. His left arm rested on the back, while his right flowed down the side of his muscled chest, over the thin cotton sheet draped across his waist, coming to rest on his thigh. His blonde hair, not flattened by perspiration, crowned him like a golden halo, framing his smiling and dimpled cheeks. Roslyn wanted to twist those perfect curls around her finger, feel their silkiness, their bounce. She shook her head at the sudden thought and kept her eyes fixed firmly on his glittering blue ones as she curtsied.

"You only hurt your leg, you know. There's no need for you to be naked." She tried to sound confident, but her voice shook a little. Her eyes betrayed her and wandered down to his navel.

"Miss Pleveli, you will talk to the prince with respect," Captain Dietrich snarled.

Prince Frederik burst out laughing. The sound was like crystal clear water bubbling in a brook on a hot summer's day.

"Oh Dietrich, don't you remember how she spoke to us when we first met? This one has the tongue of a fishwife. What she just said was most likely the pinnacle of her politeness. I would expect nothing less from her."

Roslyn shifted uncomfortably at the uncharacteristic description of herself, but raised her nose into the air and crossed her arms under her chest. If this was how they saw her, then that was how she would be. "Well, with the formal introductions out of the way, your highness, I would like to enquire why I have been made a prisoner."

Again, Prince Frederik laughed, although this time not quite so long and loud when he saw the glare in Roslyn's eye. "You aren't a prisoner, Roslyn. May I call you Roslyn? You may leave whenever you like."

Roslyn nodded. What else could she do? He could call her whatever the hell he liked. But now her interest was piqued.

"If I'm not a prisoner, then how should I see it, your highness?"

"As a fantastic opportunity,"

"An opportunity?" Roslyn interrupted. "For what?"

The prince gripped the sheet around his waist, his hand resting somewhere Roslyn was trying very hard not to look, and tried to rise to his feet. However, his injury had other ideas and sent him toppling backwards onto the couch with a muffled grunt. Roslyn, despite herself, rushed forward to help him back into his reclined position, lifting his injured leg up for him, the hot weight of it making her hands shake with something akin to nerves.

"You must keep off this leg until it is healed."

"Yes, yes, I know. That's all the physicians have said since I came home. But, had I not stood just now, you would not have rushed forward so gallantly to come to my aid, and here we are together, side-by-side—Oderberg and Domovnian. This is the opportunity I speak of Roslyn. We have an opportunity to bring our cultures together."

His enthusiasm was ludicrous, and she bit her lip to stop herself from snorting in derision. How strong were the painkillers the healers had given him? Bergams and Domovnians together? He was insane. Roslyn kept her

89

head down and rummaged around in her satchel that Captain Dietrich had placed at her feet. She gave a noncommittal *mm* sound and unwrapped the old bandages on his leg.

Normally, the position of a person's injury didn't interest her at all; it was the wound itself that took all the attention of the moment. Yet as she inspected it, looking for signs of infection or gangrene, Roslyn was all too aware how close it was to the edge of the sheet and the appendage that lay underneath.

"It is healing well. You have been very lucky. Had the tusk gone any further to the left, that boar would have hit your artery, and you'd have bled out before I got to you."

She reached out to the table where she had placed clean bandages when Prince Frederik grabbed her hand. He held it with both of his and the sudden squeeze he gave it made her look up into those sapphire eyes. As he pulled her hand to his chest, and lay it on his beating heart, she found herself pulled towards him. Her breath caught and her own heart pounded in time with his. His voice was low and husky when he spoke again, completely at odds with the boorish joviality it had had a moment ago.

"It was not luck that saved me, Roslyn. It was you. And for that, I am eternally grateful. I owe you a life debt."

Roslyn swallowed and wrenched her hands back. She sat up straight, pulling herself out of his personal space.

"Is that why you've given me a job? Hardly seems enough to fulfil a life debt."

She didn't look at him, focusing instead on rubbing a new salve onto the wound and wrapping the clean bandages around his leg as he talked.

"No, I'm giving you a job so that we can show that Bergams and Domovnians can live and work together. I hope to give not only *you* a life, but all of your people. Unlike my father and brother, I want peace." His voice changed and returned to that of a spoiled, rich boy. "Besides, you have no idea what all these little rebellions are doing to the trade. Getting good wine across the border is nigh on impossible!" He chuckled at his own joke. "No, no, in all seriousness, I want the peoples of this land to forget what has happened and move on."

Roslyn pressed her lips together and breathed out heavily through her nostrils. How could he say such a thing? Was he an idiot or completely naïve? She stood and slammed the soiled bandages onto the decorated tiles with a wet slap.

"We will never forget! You came into this land uninvited. You murdered our king and queen, all of our nobles, and upset the balance of the Tree and Sea—of nature itself! You starve us, beat us and continue to murder us, for what? Tell me, for what?"

Frederik made to rise again, his hands outstretched as if she were a horse about to shy, but she pointed her finger at him and swiped it down, indicating that he should remain in his seat. He relaxed and sat back but didn't lower his hands.

"That… was my father. I want things to change. Look, stay here willingly, and do the job I have asked of you, that's all. Heal me. Heal my…" he paused and Roslyn could see him scrabbling about in his head for an alternate word. What had he been about to say?

"Others, then my father and brother, will be more willing to consider an Assimilation Act that would let your people into the cities, to set up homes and have trades, to reduce taxes, give them the same rights as the citizens of Bergam. Don't you want that for them?"

"That's all?!" Roslyn stormed over to the little table and snatched up her belongings, throwing them back in her satchel without a care, knowing she would regret it later if they smashed. "My people will think I am betraying them if I help you!"

Prince Frederik shrugged.

"Well, it's either heal us or die. Because although I am not keeping you a prisoner, I can't say the same of my father. Besides…" The seriousness on his face disappeared, the threat vanishing instantly as his lips parted, displaying his brilliantly white teeth. Roslyn felt her knees quiver. She was lost around this man. How could he change his expression from one of menace to charm so quickly? It was unnerving. "We could have some fun along the way. What do you say?"

Roslyn scoffed and sidled over to his bedside, swaying her hips alluringly as she did so. His eyes grew misty as he watched them, the smile dropping just a little at the hint of possibility that walked towards him. She leant down and placed her face a hand's breadth from his own. She felt his excited breath upon her face as she lowered her hand and placed it on his leg. Then, with a sudden jab, she dug her thumb into the wound and stood up. Frederik yelped, cursed and glared at her, his charm evaporating instantly.

"Get that Act passed before I even think of healing anyone else. Then you might have a deal." Roslyn snatched up her things and headed for the door. *And when it is done, I will do my duty and kill the lot of you.*

Chapter 10

Captain Dietrich didn't say a word to her once they had left Prince Frederik's rooms. He did glare though. It was a glare that was well practised and laden with loathing. He walked quickly and Roslyn struggled to keep up with him, constantly having to shift her satchel on her hip. He led her back into the servant halls, away from the wider, airy rooms of the nobility and deeper into the warren than she had been before. They went down past the kitchens, the courtyard, and Roslyn was pretty certain after her little display with the prince that he was taking her to the gaol. The corridor they stopped in did seem somewhat dungeon-like. It had an arched stone roof and every couple of metres there were locked doors.

However, she heard no wailings, saw no gaolers. Eventually they made it to the end of the hallway and stepped out into a crypt-like space. The ceiling towered high above them, needing tall columns to support it. Between each pillar was a thick wooden table, littered with various experimental implements, jars and bottles. Some were strewn with paper and books. Bunches of herbs were also strung up between the pillars to dry, and gave the room a heady, overpowering scent that hit Roslyn square between the eyes.

Despite the gloom of the basement, the room was well lit, with braziers and torches evenly spaced. At the far end, Roslyn spied an enormous wall of jars and bottles filled with ointments and potions.

"This is the apothecary." Captain Dietrich looked over his shoulder lazily to see her reaction. She knew her mouth hung open, but she could do little about that. She had never seen such a well-stocked medicine room. It made Hedda's small cottage look infantile in its production. She closed her mouth and tried to remind herself with a smirk that, as with other things, it was not the size that mattered but the results it produced. A flush of heat rose to her cheeks as she caught herself remembering the way the cloth had draped over the prince's crotch, how it had betrayed the bulk of his manhood and wondering what effects he might produce.

A group of elderly men looked up from a table in front of the larder. They all wore dark blue robes, the colour of apothecaries, and stared at her with utmost dislike. One of them stepped down from the raised platform and strode down the aisle, his footsteps ringing.

"This is she? The Domovnian who the prince has favoured over us, with a collective five hundred years of learning?"

Captain Dietrich inclined his head and again stared up indolently at the man who was trying to be so threatening.

"This is Roslyn Pleveli, the Domovnian who saved his Royal Highness's life. And it is his wish she should treat him; therefore, you will aid her in this whilst also

94

ensuring that she does nothing untoward. You being the man with, as you say, five hundred years of knowledge."

The man snarled, his long white beard twitching as he did so. Then he turned to Roslyn. "Empty your satchel."

Roslyn clutched the strap tighter to her chest. "What?"

"I need to inspect every herb, tincture, poultice or powder you have smuggled into the palace to ensure you do not intend to poison the prince. Now, hand it over."

The man reached out and ripped the leather bag from her shoulder, passing it to one of his lackeys who scurried to the other apothecaries at the back of the room.

"Hey!" she cried with a wince, watching as they upended it onto the solid bench, glass bottles clinking together harshly and the simple stone pestle rolling towards the edge. "Be careful!"

An apprentice leapt forward and caught the grinding club as it fell. She gave him a half smile of thanks, a gesture that was not returned by the men rifling through her things. They tore through the wax paper packages and pulled the medicines from their holders. It was going to take her forever to organise everything again. After an agonising wait, one apothecary raised his head and bellowed, "All clear!"

Roslyn sensed the captain's shoulders relax ever so slightly as the apothecary sighed and rolled his eyes.

"Come on then, girl. You've plenty to be doing before nightfall and you're already late." He turned and strode back up to his colleagues, his robe spreading out behind him as he walked, giving him the air of an overgrown indigo bat.

Roslyn gave Captain Dietrich one last glance, as if imploring him to help her, but he just shrugged and walked back down the corridor and out of sight. She scurried to keep up with the apothecary and was soon standing before the assembled group. It was there that she noticed that not all of them were wearing blue robes; two were in black, the robes cinched in with golden belts. These weren't apothecaries, these were the king's own personal healers, and they looked just about as happy to see her as the herbalists. She gave a small curtsy, not knowing what else to do, and clutched her newly returned satchel to her for support. The man who had approached her before turned and crossed his arms.

"My name is Gruber, and I am the head apothecary to the king, and while you are here, you are under my instruction. Finally, the prince may have chosen you to administer his medicines but I, for one, will not let you use your disgusting Domovnian magic on him."

The other men nodded and muttered inane comments like "hear, hear" as he continued. "The prince has been receiving care round the clock since they brought him to us. We were," he admitted begrudgingly, "impressed with your uncture. Primitive though it was, it served the purpose of stopping infection—"

"And her sewing was excellent!" interrupted one of the healers a little too enthusiastically, awarding him a dig in the ribs from the other. "What? There will be no scar. You couldn't have done better yourself."

The apothecary sighed at the interruption and continued. "His dressings are to be changed thrice daily with a tincture of comfrey root. He has also been on pain-relieving medicines comprising willow bark, administered also thrice daily. Therefore, your visits to the prince shall be thrice. However, he requires a sleeping draught upon going to bed, and because the prince keeps such unusual hours, you will be needed at his side to administer it."

Roslyn furrowed her brow. "Why does he need a sleeping draught?"

The elder of the healers stepped forward, looking down at her as if she were a slug or some other such offending creature. "His Royal Highness Prince Frederik has been having recurring nightmares since the attack. He wakes up screaming and sweating profusely. Therefore, we have decided it is best to eliminate those whilst he recovers."

"But nightmares are a malaise of the mind, not the body," Roslyn interjected. "Surely, he needs to talk to someone—a priest perhaps—about the nightmares, not dampen them with sleeping draughts."

There was another hubbub of discontented murmurings from the group of old men. Roslyn rolled her eyes. None of them were going to take her seriously at all, even though she knew from experience that when the mind was healthy, the body recovered faster.

"Young lady, we have decided what is best for his Royal Highness. Just because you have been chosen does not mean you can question our ruling. Here," Gruber held out three pieces of parchment, a recipe scribbled on each. "The remedies you will be required to make. You will make these and none other. You will use none of your Affinity with any of the herbs or plants we have in this apothecary. Is that quite clear?"

Roslyn gritted her teeth and nodded, repeating herself for what felt like the hundredth time since she had arrived at the palace. "Quite clear."

These men had obviously not been briefed about her Affinity, or lack thereof. She was promptly dismissed. An assistant led her over to a workspace and tried to smile kindly at her, but was called away sharply by his superiors. The table had everything she required: a burner, jars, mortar and pestle, beakers, and the herbs needed for the day's set of medicines. These particular remedies were required to be brewed fresh—what a stupid idea. She was already listing ten other remedies in her head using alcohol which could be made in advance batches and would no doubt treat the prince's wound far better. But she set to work and, after what felt like hours, finally finished. She was hungry and tired when she removed her apron and placed the medicines in her satchel.

She was just about to leave when the head apothecary, Gruber, came over to her. He shifted slightly on his feet, as if uncomfortable, and rapped his knuckles nervously on the workbench.

"You have impressed me thus far, Miss Pleveli. You have worked efficiently and quickly today. I am surprised to see such a work ethic from a Domovnian, let alone a woman."

Roslyn seared inwardly. "If you please, Apothecary Gruber, I was just on my way to get something to eat. Then I will make my way to Prince Frederik's rooms to administer his third dressing of the day."

The man nodded, his beard juddering in time with the motion. "Yes, yes, quite. One must keep oneself fuelled if one is to aid others. Off you go, but be on time tomorrow."

Roslyn gave a perplexed bob at the man's softened mood towards her and walked out of the cavernous apothecary. She made her way back up to the noisy, sweaty din of the kitchens, where a platter was already awaiting her. She sat down to eat it at the communal table and tried to ignore the stares and jeers of the servants as she ate. She suddenly felt very lonely, and the food turned to ashes in her mouth.

By the time she had wolfed down her food and subjected herself to enough of the whispers and stares that simmered more than the pots on the stove, she grabbed her things and made her way out of the kitchens and up the narrow servants' stairwell.

It was dark outside and had it not been for the doleful bell that chimed in time with her steps, she would have had no idea just how late it was. She wanted nothing more than to give this pompous Prince his sleeping draught, shut him the hell up and find out where in this maze-like castle she was supposed to lay her own head. Her feet had swollen with the effort of standing on them all day and they throbbed with each step she took.

Finally, Roslyn pushed open the doorway into the royal apartments. The whoops of joy and drunkenness met her first, then she was assaulted by the melody of a crumhorn and the out-of-time stomps of dancers. This cacophony of merrymaking grew louder and louder the nearer she approached Frederik's doors and she scowled. Hoisting her satchel up her shoulder and trying to juggle the medicine bottles and bandages in her other hand, she pushed open one of the heavy doors and gasped at the sight that accosted her.

Prince Frederik's sitting room was no longer abandoned. It was full to the brim of young men, their cravats abandoned, their shirts untucked; they were jeering, laughing and drinking in the company of a group of women. Now, this would not normally have upset Roslyn so much, bar the fact that not one of these women had any more than a silk scarf tied around their waist, leaving nothing to the imagination.

Some of them gyrated to the awful music, if indeed it could be called that—it sounded more like a goat being sat on repeatedly—whilst others draped themselves over the male guests, whose hands did not hesitate to wander. Indeed, the moment she opened the door, a roar of surprise and joy and arousal erupted as two of the nude dancers fell into an erotic embrace. Their hands caressed one other's breasts and buttocks and their mouths sought each other's hungrily. It was only as the men roared their approval that the two women looked around, but as they pulled apart, they saw Roslyn, and so did everybody else.

The music honked to a halt, and she finally spied her patient on a couch much like the one where she had left him, only now wearing clothes. Compared to his companions, he actually looked overdressed, the ruffs around his neck highlighting his frown. She kept her eyes on him as she shook her head with shock and indignation.

"What is going on here?" she asked in a schoolmarmish voice.

A few of the men scowled at her. The one closest to the door ambled up to her unevenly, a glass in one hand, its contents sloshing over the rim as he walked. He grabbed her chin between his thumb and fingers and shook it a little before patting her on the cheek. She wrinkled her nose at the smell of sour wine on his breath as he spoke. "Well, as Freddie here can't come to the party, and we've not seen him since he arrived back from his studies abroad, we decided that the party had to come to him. So, here we are. Now…" He tilted his head to the side and looked at her with sarcastic sweetness. "Who the fuck are you?"

Roslyn could not allow herself to be cowed by his unearned superiority and bullishness.

"I am his healer, and it is well past his bedtime. The prince has suffered an extremely traumatic injury and

100

should be resting. This party, as you so call it, is not helping him to recover."

The drunken man before her swung around unevenly to face the prince, his long blonde hair wafting out behind him. His voice was thick with wine. "So, it's true, Freddie? I had heard the rumours that you'd got yourself a little Domovnian delight? Ah yes, I see how she glows." He glanced down at her chest, her bosom heaving with fury, and grinned. "You devil, you! Wait till your father hears about this!"

Prince Frederik finally cleared his throat and entered the conversation with the most irritable roll of the eyes Roslyn had ever seen. "It's not up to my father. Roslyn here saved my life and I would trust my recovery to no one else. Besides, what she says is true. This party is tiring."

The assembled bachelors of the Oderberg nobility gave a groan of boyish disappointment, but the long-haired fop who stood between Roslyn and the prince, and indeed commanded the floor, walked before them all as if he were on stage, his presence that of the ultimate actor.

"Come now, Freddie," he sang cajolingly. "Just because you're a little under the weather doesn't mean we can't all have a good time. Just like we used to, right? So why don't we just forget about this minor disagreement? I can get Miss Domovnia here a little drink." He sauntered back towards Roslyn and wrapped his arm around her shoulder.

She tightened instinctively. Her flesh crawled at his touch; his arm stroked down her body until his hand had gone well below her waist and was resting on her behind, where he proceeded to give her a slap. She yelped in surprise and tried to wrench herself away from him. "Get off!"

But he held her fast and, in the scuffle, the bottles and bandages flew out of her arms and scattered on the floor, one of them smashing on impact. The lech holding her was still muttering in his entitled manner, shushing her as if she were an upset dog. "Come on now, come on now. Let's just have some fun. Show us how they do it Domovnian style!" He peeled off into laughter and didn't notice when the prince stood suddenly and limped over as fast as he could. He set his hand on the drunkard's shoulder and wrenched him backwards, spinning him round. His face was stony and his eyes cold.

"You do not touch her."

The prince's friend stopped laughing and scoffed, his face creasing in confusion.

"You can't be serious. Freddie, she's just a servant and a Domovnian at that. Where's the harm in having a little fun?" He stroked Roslyn's face, making her recoil, but she found the door in her back and could not retreat further. Prince Frederik snatched the brute's hand away as he went to stroke her again and muttered in a low growl.

"I said, you do not touch her, Yannis. Nobody touches her. She is my guest here at Novlada and she will be treated as such. Is that understood?"

It wasn't a question. Yannis nodded slowly, not blinking, and shrugged his cuff straight as Frederik let it go, the colour in his face draining from a pink flush to a sallow grey. Roslyn rushed past the drunk noble and slipped her arm around the prince's waist as he tottered on his good foot. She looked up at him and saw a sheen of sweat on his forehead.

"Lean on me," she whispered, but then once they were nearly at his couch, she straightened and regained her authority as a healer. "I told you not to walk on it. Do you want to end up with a limp?"

At her last question, Yannis and some others snorted with laughter. Prince Frederik's face scrunched into a scowl as he looked up at Roslyn resentfully.

Yannis waltzed over and clapped Roslyn on the back before quickly holding his hands up in surrender at the prince's glare. "That was a good one, Domovnian. Now that was a good one. Then we'd have to call you Prince Limp! After all," he turned round to his chums who sniggered, already knowing where he was going with this. "Everyone knows you've gone soft on the natives since studying at the coast, and from the way you're not sampling our most generous gift," he waved his hand at the array of naked women before him, casting a glance down at the prince's crotch "it seems you might have in other ways too."

The room erupted into laughter from both the prince's supposed friends and the women paid to please them. The prince rose to his feet once more, despite Roslyn's hand against his chest, and roared, "Get out!"

The immediate silence reeked with awkwardness. Yannis took a swig of wine and almost danced on his feet in an expert way that betrayed how often he imbibed, and bowed facetiously to the prince. "It's alright, we were leaving anyway, Prince Limp. Let's take this party elsewhere."

A few of the others had the decency to look bashful. They picked up their bottles of wine and the women gathered their clothes around them as they were bustled out into the corridor by Yannis. When the door had finally shut and their revelry had vanished down the hallway, Roslyn turned to Frederik and held out both hands.

"Come on. I'll change the dressing in bed. It's sleep you need now more than anything."

The prince didn't disagree with her and placed his hands in hers. They were smooth to the touch, but she could feel the strength in them as he pushed down to lever himself up. He was gripping so tight, combating his own pain so he didn't notice how tightly he was squeezing her fingers. Without needing to be told, he wrapped his arm around her shoulder and used her as a crutch as they hobbled towards the bedroom.

"Thanks for that," he said churlishly. "Now I shall forever be known as Prince Limp, and trust me, reputations in this place are quickly given and not so easily lost."

Roslyn grimaced in apology but didn't say anything. She'd only been trying to help, but could see why a young, red-blooded man such as the prince would not want to be associated with anything limp.

As she plonked him on the bed, he groaned with relief and sank back into the downy pillows. He tried to remove most of his outerwear, this time actually trying to hide his modesty, but Roslyn had to help peel his trousers down his legs and take his heavy black boots off his feet. Then, once he was comfortable, she changed his dressing and pulled the eiderdown over him. He looked so small suddenly, and weak, just like a boy recovering from a fever. Regretfully, she looked back through the doorway into the sitting room and at the smashed vial on the floor.

"I'm… I'm afraid there will be no sleeping draught for you this evening. It's… when Yannis…"

Frederik closed his eyes and waved her apology away. "I don't need one." He looked up at her, his blue eyes proud. "I never needed one. They just want to keep me doped up and in this bed forever."

Roslyn laughed. "Now, why would they want to do that?"

Her voice was full of maternal reproach and it hit the mark as the prince crossed his arms sulkily and mumbled something to himself before opening his mouth. He drank the medicine she spooned into his mouth and recoiled, shaking his head from side to side before sticking his tongue out. "Blurgh! Urgh! Hoff, that is awful. Anyone would think it was the apothecaries trying to kill me, not the Domovnians."

The corners of Roslyn's mouth twitched, just a fraction. "If I'd got my way, it would be made with brandy,"

"Now that I would drink!" the prince laughed and drew out Roslyn's hidden smile out into the open. "Why isn't it?"

Roslyn scoffed. "Have you met Apothecary Gruber?"

Frederik pursed his lips and nodded his head. "Ah yes, I see your point… Well, keep at it. I have no doubt you can wear him down."

It was Roslyn's turn to roll her eyes as she packed up her satchel, slung it over her shoulder and turned to leave.

"Where are you going?" the prince called after her, teasing in his voice. "Your room is right through there."

Roslyn followed his pointed finger in horror. Not far from his bedside was a small, simple wooden door leading to a servant's cell. She scurried into it and found her bag already placed at the foot of the bed. Then she bustled her way back into the royal sleeping chamber and stared at the prince, wide-eyed and shaking. She couldn't decide whether she was more disgusted, frightened or offended.

"This is improper!"

Prince Frederik laughed. "Don't worry, it locks from the inside." Then he gestured to his leg. "Besides, do I look in any condition to come pestering you in the night?"

Roslyn crossed her arms and huffed.

"No, it doesn't... Prince Limp." She narrowed her eyes with glee and returned his sudden glare. "But I'll still be locking it." She walked into the room and slammed the bolt home, shouting through the door, "As an extra precaution!"

Chapter 11

Roslyn's bare feet slid across the cracked cobbles of a dilapidated courtyard. The surrounding walls shone white in the moonlight, glistening like pearl, but they were crumbling and the spires of the twisted towers had long since fallen and smashed upon the ground where she walked. She was in an inner sanctum, where two enormous trees bowed together over a silvery pool. They bore no leaves, and their bark was as white as the stone hall which encased them.

The water in the pool was still for a moment, reflecting the shimmer of the moon. Then it began to quiver, bubbling and roiling the closer Roslyn walked, but when she peered over the rim of the basin, there was no water at all. Suddenly, impossibly, a substance was seeping out through cracks in its enclosure, disappearing through the broken cobbles. Roslyn jumped back in alarm as it touched her toes, fearing her feet would be frozen into lumps of molten silver.

She desperately wanted to leave; she wanted to go back to wherever it was she had been before, but she couldn't remember where that was or how she had come to be here. When she spun towards the arched entrance of the courtyard, she came face to face with a woman.

In shock, Roslyn stumbled and fell to the ground, dousing herself in the freezing, argent liquid that continued to pour from the basin. She scrabbled backwards until she was pressed against it, but the woman didn't move. She, like everything else in this desolate place, was pearlescent and shimmering. Was she a ghost? Roslyn wasn't sure.

Her eyes were kind and her lips smiling. She knelt down so that she was level with Roslyn, and reached out an ethereal hand, palm up, inviting.

Without warning, the woman's smile dropped. She quivered and her eyes rolled back in her skull. Her mouth stretched open so that Roslyn could see the very back of her throat, whence erupted a soul shattering scream.

✳

Roslyn jerked awake with a strangled cry. She was covered in sweat and her heart was racing, but the screaming hadn't stopped. It still rang in her ears. Although, now it sang a different tune; no longer was it the high-pitched shriek of a banshee, but a tortured plea of someone fighting for their life. Its timbre was much lower than that of the ghostly woman's and Roslyn suddenly knew where it was coming from.

She threw back her blanket and shivered as her feet touched the cold stone floor, reminding her for an instant of the vanishing water that had felt like ice under her toes. But she had no time to linger in the land of dreams. She lit a candle and rushed to the door, scrabbling with the bolt. She regretted slamming it shut with so much strength earlier and hurried into the prince's room to find him writhing in the realm of a nightmare.

His sheets were tangled, twisted around him like a serpent intent on smothering its prey, and no matter how hard he kicked and wriggled, the cloth only wound itself tighter around his flailing body. His buoyant curls had been flattened once more with sweat, bucketloads of it plastering it to his head. In this state, he was entirely unrecognisable as the pampered prince she had met earlier that day, but more like the man she had saved in the woods. His cries came out as guttural gulps and curdled cries; he was pleading with something to stop and let him live.

Roslyn now understood why the healers insisted he have a sleeping draught. If he carried on wriggling and writhing in such a manner, he was sure to open his wound up again, pulling the stitches that hadn't yet had time to heal and likely causing permanent damage to the muscle. She had to subdue him, but she had very little on her. The apothecaries had ransacked her satchel, taking out her most prized herbs and leaving her only with the basics, the harmless ones with which she could not concoct a poison nor engineer an overdose.

She had to calm him down. Roslyn drew in a shaky breath and hitched up the skirts of her nightgown. She was on the bed in seconds, untangling the sweat-drenched sheet from the prince's body, not daring to look at his nudity as his nightshirt rose up past his waist. Then she fought past his flapping arms, placed herself against the headboard and pulled him up between her legs. She locked him into a tight embrace, trapping his arms and rocking him from side to side, fast at first and then as he calmed, slower and slower and more rhythmically, all the while stroking his head and shushing him. As the nightmare slipped away, the prince's breath became less ragged and Roslyn felt his heartbeat slowing. He took slow, deep breaths as one who has just entered a deep sleep might, but when she tried to extract herself, he leant his head back on her shoulder and looked up.

His forehead brushed the underside of her chin and she swallowed, suddenly aware of how dry her throat had become. His voice was croaky.

"Do I need to put the lock on my side of the door?"

Roslyn couldn't help but smile and she batted him ever so slightly with her hand. He joined in her laughter, weak though it was, and laid his hand on her arm.

"Thank you," he breathed into the darkness.

Roslyn shook her head. "No, you shouldn't thank me at all. Had I not dropped your sleeping draught, you would never have had these terrors."

She pulled away again and this time Frederik let her, turning his head slightly as she readjusted her nightgown so that she was decent. She hadn't realised how much it had ridden up as she pulled him into her to calm him, leaving her milky white thighs exposed on either side of him. The prince also arranged his own garments, but Roslyn took one look at the soaked nightshirt and shook her head.

"That will have to come off, and so will the sheets. They're drenched. You'll catch a chill on top of everything else if you go back to sleep in those."

Frederik sighed and shook his head. "I doubt there will be any more sleep for me tonight. I'm only sorry that I

110

woke you as well. Hoff knows, you must need your rest after having your world turned upside down."

Roslyn wanted to agree, to shout and ease the pain in her heart, the growing homesickness, but she kept her mouth shut and walked over to an enormous wardrobe on the far side of the room. There she found new linens for the bed, and in another by the dressing screen, she found a new nightshirt for the prince. She flung these in his direction and raised an eyebrow at his perplexed face.

"What am I supposed to do with these?"

Roslyn sighed and placed her hands on her hips, trying to look authoritative, but then remembered that she was standing in front of the fire and the glowing embers probably illuminated everything under her shift. So, she crossed her arms and walked quickly back towards the bed. She withdrew the nightshirt from the pile and held it up for him.

"This, you will change into. Then when I come back, you'll help me as much as you can to change the sheets. Now, I need to find something that might help you sleep. It won't be as powerful as what you're used to, but it might just calm you enough."

She hurried back to her room, where she grabbed not only her satchel but also a shawl. The chill of the night was starting to seep into her bones after the sudden exertion. Back in the room, she tried to ignore the prince as he pulled the fresh nightshirt down over his sculpted chest and made her way to the fire.

It really was down to its last embers, but she fed it another log and blew into its glowing remains. The fire was soon alive again, and she placed the small copper kettle onto the warming hook at the side. Truth be told, it surprised her to see one in the prince's chamber, but then

111

again, princes may require tea at whatever time of night and it was most likely one of the healers that had placed it here for occasions such as this. In the strengthening light of the fire, she opened her satchel and removed leaves of chamomile, lavender and, in a secret compartment, the tiniest shavings of valerian root. Roslyn smiled; at least they hadn't found that in their searches. She put a small amount of each ingredient in the kettle while it simmered and turned to help Prince Frederik with his sheets.

It wasn't easy, changing the largest bed she had ever come across whilst there was still a man lying on it—a very unhelpful one at that, having never changed a bed in his life. But she smiled at his determined grin.

"It's never too late to learn new things," he said cheerfully, reaching over and unhooking one corner of the sheet so that she could pull it out from underneath him. Getting the old sheet off was relatively easy, but applying the new one... Well, that required a little more intimacy than she had anticipated. Whilst Frederik could shift his weight onto his hands, Roslyn still had to pull the sheet up under his buttocks, which she saw through the thin linen of his nightshirt were firm and round, clenched slightly with the efforts of holding himself up. As she pulled the fabric underneath him, it stuck, forcing her to pull harder. Her hand snapped upwards and slapped gently against his arse. She felt the downy hair and taught muscle pressed against the back of her hand as he gave a yelp of surprise.

"I apologise, your highness!" she stammered, blushing so furiously she was sure he must've felt the heat coming off her cheeks as she rearranged the cloth so that he could sit back down.

"No harm done," he laughed, his voice a little croaky as she leant over him to tuck in the last of the linen sheet.

112

As she did this, she was acutely aware of how close they were. Their faces were almost touching as she folded the last corner, their chests an inch away from each other, and she was certain he could hear how hard her heart was hammering in her chest. She raised her eyes and was ensnared in his gaze as it moved over her face. Their breath mingled in the gloaming and she felt an inexplicable pull to set her lips against his. Suddenly, the kettle sang.

With relief, she let go of the sheet. It would do for now. Roslyn ran back over to the fireplace, not wanting the kettle to awaken any of the servants with its song. She used the corner of her shawl around the hot handle and removed it from the hook, pouring some of the tea into the clay cup that was waiting on the hearth. She paused for a moment, then picked up another cup and poured one for herself. She was definitely going to need something to help her relax after these nocturnal activities. She splashed a dash of cold water into the mixture so the prince could sip on it immediately and took it over to him.

As he took the cup in her extended hand, he placed his own around it and looked up at her earnestly. His eyes twinkled in the firelight and she felt the heat rise in her cheeks again, thankful that her back was towards the light so he wouldn't see.

He was the enemy. She shouldn't be behaving like this, shouldn't be reacting like this. It was probably just an Oderberg ploy to get her to let her guard down.

"You know..." she murmured tentatively, "Sleeping draughts cannot cure nightmares, only dampen them. You should talk to someone."

Frederik shook his head and lowered his eyes, his voice a primal growl. "No. I mean... I'm not ready." He adjusted his tone and forced a smile onto his lips, even though his eyes were still haunted by the memory of the nightmare. "Come." He patted the mattress in front of him. "Tell me a story while we drink, then perhaps I'll sleep."

Roslyn picked up her cup and sat, smirking. "Are you telling me that my stories are boring before having heard one? Very well, how about the tale of the Sea and Tree, how we Domovnians came into being?"

"A history lesson?" The prince raised an eyebrow. "Well, I do want to sleep, so…" He grinned as she mocked offense.

"You said you want to know about my people. Then, you need to know where we come from." She leant forward and pulled the coverlet up over his chest. His hand patted hers gently.

"Go on, I'm all ears."

Roslyn sat back, licked her lips and called forth the familiar words.

"Long ago, before the birth of man, the god of the sky flew over the endless sea, alone and adrift, until one day, he looked down and saw a single tree on an island. This was something new to the god, and he marvelled at its beauty and how its leaves swayed in the wind he created, how its branches shaded the land and gave food and protection to the animals who lived in its boughs and roots. In no time at all, he fell in love with the tree…"

"A god fell in love with a tree?" Frederik smirked incredulously.

"Shh and listen." Roslyn frowned, prompting a raise of a surrendering hand. "He was so in love with the tree that he breathed life into it and created the first ancestor, Zemya. Although her roots were sunk deep into the earth

114

and prevented her from moving, she and the god of the air had many children together—dryads—and were happy for a long time, but the god had a wandering eye. Soon, his affections fell on the animals around him and the cousins of the dryads were born: the fauns, the centaurs, the satyrs."

"Randy old bugger..." Frederik interrupted, earning him a mock slap on the leg.

"He was so distracted, he forgot to tend to his lover; he forgot to move the clouds in the sky so that rains fell. Before long, Zemya's children were dying, shrivelling up with lack of water. So, she used the last of her strength to reach her roots out of the ground and into the sea. There, she made a deal with the god of water, that if he gave her his seed, his children would rule over the land alongside her own. They would work together to balance nature and create a paradise on earth where no one would ever hunger or thirst.

"And so, she birthed the naiads, nymphs of the rivers and seas. As their sisters took on the forms of trees and plants, these children took on the form of lakes, rivers and all life that dwelt therein. The first daughter of Zemya was anointed Queen, and the first male descendant of a naiad became her King. Together they would oversee the balance."

Roslyn's voice had gone husky with memory as the words of the Living Church found their way to this most unlikely listener, who was nestled deep into his pillows, fighting the sleep that the tea pushed him into.

"After thousands of years of peace, a new creature came into being. They had heard of the fabled land of the Tree and Sea and wanted this bountiful haven for themselves. They waged war against the ancestors, using their weapons to cut down trees, fire to burn and arrows to pierce." Her voice grew firm and Frederik moved his eyes from hers, the parallels of the story spreading a tinge of red across his cheeks.

"What happened? How did they resolve it?" his voice was thin, almost pleading.

Roslyn snorted. "Well, to skip a few legends and famous battles in the telling, some of Zemya's children fell in love with injured human soldiers. The children they created were human to the eye, give or take a few distinctive features, with the powers of their mothers. Zemya saw she could not turn away her own descendants and called for a truce. The humans could stay, and breed, sharing in the bounty of Zemya's land, so long as they swore to protect it and serve the king and queen, and their descendants, forever."

Silence fell between them, and Roslyn tapped at the clay of her cup in agitation. The story of the Tree and Sea always left her feeling less than adequate. The blood of the Ancestors had been so thinned through breeding with humans that she was almost one of them. How was it that some strains were stronger and had survived the passage of time, but hers was useless? She was pulled back to the present, to the man before her as he spoke.

"Ah… love. Solves everything in stories, doesn't it? If only it could now." Frederik's voice was faint, his eyes closing, but he sat up and took her hand in his. "Time for bed, I think… but I meant what I said." He licked his lips, a movement which Roslyn couldn't tear her eyes from. "I meant it when I said you are my guest in this castle, and you will be treated as such. That includes by myself."

He let go of her hand and raised the cup to his mouth. He blew on the steam with rounded lips. He seemed suddenly wary, and his voice was low and soft.

"Thank you for helping me tonight, and for the tea and the story. But I am afraid I've put you too much at risk of rumour and have not taken propriety into consideration. I must now bid you leave my bedchamber, Miss Pleveli."

His sudden change in demeanour startled her, but she nodded. She knew what he spoke was decent and proper, but she couldn't help notice her heart sinking just a little as she walked back to her cold, barren room alone, visions of long dead deities swirling round her head.

Chapter 12

When Roslyn peeped her head out of her room the following morning, the prince had his back to her and appeared to be asleep. Either that, or he was very good at *pretending* to be asleep. She didn't attempt to rouse him, not then, at least. Everyone knew royalty liked to lounge about in bed, but an injured one should technically spend the whole day ensconced in their satin sheets. She eventually, after many wrong turns, made her way to the apothecary and made up his first batch of medicines, prepping the materials for the midday dressing before hiking all the way back up the stairs to administer it.

He had moved. His back was still towards the door, but his hands were now shoved under the pillow and his breathing had changed. Instead of the slow rhythmic breaths of a sleeper, they were shorter and more uneven. Roslyn knew he was awake this time. She knocked on the threshold from the sitting room to the bedroom and cleared her throat.

Nothing.

"Excuse me, your highness... Prince Frederik?" She sighed. He was, in fact, ignoring her. Fine; if he was going to be sulky about what happened last night, with his friends and then the nightmare, then he could just have at it. She had other things to be getting on with, even though in reality the only other thing she had to be getting on with concerned Prince Frederik. She walked to the bedside table and stared down at his wan face, his eyelids flickering with the effort of remaining shut to uphold his ruse. She sighed and set the medicine on the table with a loud clunk.

"I'll just leave your medicine here, then. I should change the dressing, but I'm pretty sure it's high treason to wake a slumbering royal, so I'll just leave the new dressing, the cloth to wash the old one away, and fresh bandages right here, as well. You can do it yourself. I'll be back at luncheon to give you your next dose and check out your handiwork." Her voice was sickly sweet and judgemental. She smirked as his lips quivered and he fought back a retort. He was certainly keeping to his ploy of being asleep. Roslyn rolled her eyes and stomped back out of the room.

Things didn't get much better the rest of that day. Although awake the next two times she visited him, Frederik refused to meet her eye and only uttered the merest courtesies to her. Had she overstepped some sort of line last night? When she thought about it, she was sure she had, but at the time he had thanked her for her intervention and then he had been the one to withdraw, proclaiming propriety. But it seemed propriety and politeness were no longer bedfellows.

So, Roslyn spent most of the day in the dark, oppressive gloom of the apothecary, trying to ignore Head Apothecary Gruber as he flitted around her, constantly critiquing her work, or suggesting better ways to do something. Ever since she had admitted the incident where the sleeping draught had shattered on the floor, causing the prince nightmares, he had taken back his praise and instead took to shadowing her like an overgrown bat. He was constantly underfoot or peering over her shoulder. She had tried to say that if they use another recipe, the sleeping draught could be made in advance and stored in precise doses in his room, avoiding such incidents. In fact, all his medicine could be stored so, if they would only allow her to make a few simple changes to the ingredients and method of preparation. Apothecary Gruber had turned to her with an icy stare.

"The point is not whether we can prepare the medicines in advance. I know full well that there are some that can be." He took a step closer and stared down his equine nose at her. "The point is that you need to be seen, you need to be watched handling these medicines and if you think for one moment, I am going to let you have your way with some peasant concoction that could very well kill his Royal Highness, then you are most grievously mistaken."

And thus, Roslyn endured the most miserable couple of days of her life. She was ignored by the man she was meant to be healing; she was beaten down by those who were supposed to be helping her, and everyone else just stared and whispered whenever she crossed their path as if she were a malignant omen.

120

＊

By the third day of Frederik's moping, Roslyn was well and truly fed up. Nothing she did was helping, but she was half certain that his attitude was also hindering any attempts at healing. He refused to get out of bed for anything other than the chamber pot; he turned away all his friends and his trays were more or less untouched.

She had just made it to the top of the servant's stairwell after the long climb up from the basement and swung open the door into the royal apartments when she all but collided with Crown Prince Viktor.

She stepped back in fright and bobbed several shaky curtsies, not daring to meet his eye while apologising profusely. He, in turn, berated her.

"Watch where you are going, Domovnian," he spat.

"I am so sorry, your highness, it will not happen again. I wasn't paying attention."

The prince crossed his arms and sneered down at her. "No, just as you haven't been paying attention to my brother—the only reason you are here at all, enjoying the life of an Oderberg healer."

Roslyn felt as if someone had squeezed the air from her lungs. *Enjoying*? Is that what he thought she was doing? Enjoying her time as a captive of the people she loathed the most in the world?

The prince continued. "My brother has shown no signs of improvement since you arrived. In fact, he has done the opposite. He has not left his bed, he is morose, he barely eats. What in the shadow of the Chained Mountain is going on? What have you done to him?"

121

"I… I have done nothing but what I am permitted to do! I have done everything those apothecaries and healers have asked me to, even if I disagree with both their remedies and their methods."

Viktor crossed his arms and shifted his weight over one hip. "What do you mean?"

The momentum of adrenaline buoyed Roslyn as she stepped towards the crown prince, chin jutting upwards with righteous indignation.

"Their medicines are archaic, time-consuming and have little effect. The prince will need to be on them for months to show any signs of improvement, and don't get me started on how they are dealing with his nightmares."

Crown Prince Viktor's brow furrowed. "Nightmares? What are you talking about?"

Roslyn was just about to answer when the doors to Prince Frederik's apartments flew open and there he was, in all his dishevelled, nightgown-trussed glory. His face was flushed with exertion and what seemed to Roslyn like panic. His arms were outstretched, one hand on each side of the door frame, supporting himself as he caught his breath.

"What… What is going on here? I was trying to recuperate… trying to rest and all I can hear is my healer"— he pointed at Roslyn with one hand and took a step forward, wobbling slightly with weakness before pointing with the other at his brother—"and the future king, squabbling like a whore and her punter over rates."

The pair of them balked at his comparison, both exclaiming in indignation that they were nothing of the kind.

"So?" Prince Frederik widened his eyes, jutting his head out and shaking it slightly. "What are you arguing about? I can only assume it has something to do with me and my health."

The crown prince stepped back and straightened himself up to his full height. His muscled girth was certainly impressive and had the desired effect. Now that the adrenaline had somewhat worn off, and she realised just who she was sparring with, Roslyn immediately took a step back, her shoulders tensing as they rose.

"I was just asking your *healer* why you weren't healing and had taken a backwards turn into melancholy. She says she is doing everything she is *allowed* to do." He put so much stress on allowed that he almost sounded facetious.

Frederik turned to look at her, the same quizzical expression as his brother's etched across his fine features. "What do you mean, 'allowed to do'?"

Roslyn explained again that she had more efficient and powerful remedies that would get the prince on his feet in no time. Once she had finished, the three of them stood in uneasy silence.

Suddenly, Prince Frederik sucked in a breath and cocked his head at his brother.

"Get her everything she requires, Viktor. After all, you and father wanted to see if my crazy idea had legs— you wanted to see how fast she could heal, if she was any better than any of our own pompous, brown-nosing apothecaries, but you do not allow her the tools to do so. You do not give her a fair ground to show her skills. So, you will give her everything she asks for, any herbs, any tools, where she wants them. Is that understood, Viktor?"

The sudden steeliness in his voice as he threatened the man who would one day be king sent a shiver down Roslyn's spine and she suddenly saw the part of him she did not want to anger. Her lips parted as she realised that up to now, she had been on his good side.

Viktor smiled, his left nostril rising and dragging the lip below up over a white, pointed canine.

"Fine," he hissed, and then turned to Roslyn. The hope Prince Frederik had just instilled within her was immediately slaughtered by the threat in his voice as he brandished his finger at her face. "If he's not on his feet within three days, you are finished. You hear me? Finished."

Roslyn gulped and nodded, certain that he wasn't simply talking about her state of employment in the royal household.

The tall mountain of muscle turned and walked away as regally as he could, having just lost a verbal battle. Roslyn followed his gait with wide eyes until he was out of sight, and then turned to the other prince at her side. To her amazement, he had a huge pearly white smile plastered onto his gods-favoured face.

"I always know how to get him." He crossed his arms over his chest and tried to put his weight on his bad leg, causing him to curse and hop about on the healthy one like a court tumbler. Roslyn rolled her eyes as he came to a stop, the foppish grin creeping back onto his lips.

"Wipe that smile off your face," she said pointedly. "If I have to get you walking in three days, you are going to have a lot of hard work, too, not just me. Healers and patients work together… which is what you wanted, isn't it? A Domovnian and Oderberg working together? Well, now is your chance. So, have you stopped sulking over whatever reason made you take to your bed?"

Frederik shrugged and pursed his lips. "I can see how my mood these past days has not helped the situation and

124

I apologise for that. I am susceptible to bouts of melancholia, especially when hope seems hard to find." He sighed. "Your tale made me realise how far we have to go." He held out a hand as a peace offering. "Are we friends again?"

Roslyn scoffed and swept past him, calling over her shoulder. "I didn't know we were friends to begin with." She launched into her healer's spiel before he'd even managed so much as to turn around in the door frame. "Now. You are to walk, hobble—or even crawl, for all I care—up and down these apartments with..." she looked around and then spied the object she was searching for tucked away behind the door. "This."

She held up a finely carved and gilded walking stick. It was the finest specimen she'd ever seen, and she knew plenty of elderly gentlemen back in her village that would have given their right arm to have it.

"You cannot be serious?" Prince Frederik groaned as she thrust it into his hands.

Roslyn nodded, eyes wide, expression sweet with a hint of acid. "Yes, up and down these apartments for two hours each day. They don't have to be all at once, but for two hours for the next three days. You will do this, if you don't want to be known as Prince Limp."

The prince glowered and set the stick in his left hand, tapping it pointedly on the stone floor with each step he took. He grumbled and cursed under his breath with each painful step as he started on the new regime.

Chapter 13

Roslyn's back was aching after bending over the bench in the apothecary, preparing the prince's medicines, when Gruber walked in, cloak billowing after him. His eyes scanned the room and narrowed when they rested on her. Her stomach clenched and she swallowed as he made straight for her.

"You," he hissed, his voice twisted in malice.

"Yes, Apothecary Gruber?" She tried to make her voice light as the usual hubbub of the cavern stilled.

"Who gave you the right? Who said you could treat *my* patients?" He leaned in, forcing her to crane her neck backwards or their noses would soon be touching.

"I am only treating the prince, as was commanded. I don't know who else you're talking about?" Her voice wavered slightly under the steeliness of his gaze, but she would not allow herself to be cowed. She took one step back, suddenly thankful the table was between them and placed her hands on her hips.

"You have no idea, do you? Then why is that crackpot old woman refusing to take her medicine, hmm? She says you gave her a tea which did her bowels more good than any of my remedies and she will have nothing else. Curse the Mountain!"

Roslyn pressed her lips together to stop her smirking. "She was indisposed on the road. If you have spent any time in her noxious presence then I'm sure you can understand that giving her a purgative was as much for my benefit as it was hers!" She paused and let her hands fall to her side. "But I am sorry if I overstepped."

Gruber leered. "Damn right you'll be sorry, because you'll be seeing the old crone much more often. She, like her great nephew, will have no other prepare her teas... and just so you know, she hasn't shit in a week."

Roslyn grimaced but nodded. She stepped round the side of the table to fetch the ingredients she needed when the blue-robed man stepped in her way. He was so close, she could smell the stale garlic on his breath as he snarled down at her. "Is it my job you're after, Miss Pleveli? Well, you'll not have it, that I swear on Hoff's hammer... but you will have your comeuppance, that you will."

A shiver ran down her spine at his words. She didn't doubt he would think of some way to discredit her. She snatched her satchel up from the floor; there was no way she would leave it out of her sight now. She raised her chin and met his rheumy eyes with her own bright ones before pushing past him.

"If you'll excuse me then, I have a patient to see."

❋

The Lady Margitte's quarters weren't far from Frederik's own, but they were simpler in comparison. The doors were uncarved and the furniture practical but comfortable, even if there was an overwhelming number of lace doilies on every surface including the edges of the fat, armed sofa. Roslyn waited in the reception room as the middle-aged maid spoke with her mistress.

"She was lucid earlier, but it seems the memory fog has returned. It often does, this late in the day. I tell you, it's a miracle she didn't have an episode while you were on the road. They wouldn't let me come." The woman's tone was curt but not unkind. She sighed and shrugged her shoulders. "We find it's easier to play along and not mind the things she says. If you contradict her, you'll only upset her." She cocked her head and pointed a stern finger, "and I don't want that right before bedtime, you understand."

Roslyn nodded. "How long has she been afflicted with the memory fog?"

The maid, who Roslyn now realised was in fact the old woman's nurse, crossed her hands under her ample bosom. "A couple of years now. It's slow to progress though, thank the Mountain, yet we all know that won't always be the case. Call me when she's drunk the tea. I'll fetch the commode chair."

She said no more and walked into a small backroom, probably her own chambers to rest. Roslyn couldn't blame her; she'd seen those afflicted with memory fog before and the strain it took on their families. She hitched her satchel on her shoulder and walked towards the open door.

Lady Margitte was sat in a cushioned armchair, staring into the crackling fire and ignoring the book in her lap. Roslyn coughed to announce her arrival and the old woman turned to the newcomer. Instead of the sharp, piercing gaze that had scrutinised her on the carriage ride, wide and innocent eyes looked up at her. Then the

128

wrinkled face creased even more as her thin lips rose in a smile.

"Ouna?" The delight in her face was unrestrained. "What are you doing here? School doesn't start up again for another month!" She reached out a frail, liver-spotted hand for Roslyn to take.

Who was Ouna? *Just play along, that's what the nursemaid had said*. Roslyn stepped forward, smiled and took the noblewoman's hand.

"I was told you were sick, and I thought I'd bring you something to make you feel better." She set her satchel by the fire and set about pulling out the ingredients.

"It's only a cold, Ouna, you needn't have come all this way, but I am very glad you did. It's been a dull, cold winter and I can't wait to return south with you. What's that you're making… a tea?"

Roslyn looked over her shoulder and nodded. "Yes, just the thing for a cold."

Lady Margitte made a face and crossed her arms over her chest before a sly smile made her eyes twinkle. "Haven't you got anything stronger?"

Roslyn chuckled. "I'll raid the cellars later."

Margitte clapped her hands in delight. "Have you seen my brother, yet?"

Roslyn shook her head as she set the kettle on the fire hook to boil. "Um… no… not yet."

"Oh, well as soon as he knows you're here, you won't be able to get away. You made quite the impression on him at Dumka…" She left the statement hanging in a way that gossips had, trying to eke out more information.

Roslyn turned away to hide her confusion and embarrassment. "I don't think I did…"

"Well, of course, I told him." Margitte batted her comment away and leaned forward with a sudden renewal of energy. "As a Domonov princess, you must wed a descendant of the naiads, but he wouldn't listen."

Roslyn's heart turned to ice. This Ouna had been a Domonov princess? Lady Margitte thought Roslyn was this woman? The mind fog was obviously worse than she thought. Margitte had most likely seen the shimmer on her skin and her confused brain had made the link. Unless…the fog was unveiling some secret long buried by the conscious mind. The ridiculous notion made her tut at her overactive imagination. She was a nobody.

"Speaking of which, have you met your intended yet? Oh, kettle!"

"What?" Margitte's question roused her from her thoughts.

"The kettle's boiling." She pointed to the copper pot, which did indeed have steam pouring from its spout. Roslyn hurried to take it off the hook and poured it into the teapot to infuse the herbs. They needed to steep awhile, so she sat in the opposite chair. By the Tree, it was soft!

"I said, have you met your intended yet? Is he a Zabim or a Glaucan? I hear they are ever so handsome. The Mountain forbid they've pawned you off on a Krostak!"

Roslyn hadn't the faintest idea what the old woman was talking about, the terms unfamiliar to her, so she shook her head. "No, not yet. What about you?"

Margitte slouched in her seat and pouted with all the vigour of a teenage girl. "It's a toss-up between the Duke of Tetmedlum—"

"A Summerlander? That would be nice!" Roslyn interrupted. Surely a young girl from the frozen wasteland

130

that was Bergam would have been thrilled at the prospect of moving to Tokaveror, the land of eternal summer and plenty?

"A Summerlander who is older than my father!" the old woman hissed. "The other suitor is some distant cousin, Magnus, I think his name is. At least he's young."

The pair fell silent and the old woman returned her gaze to the fire. "Oh what it is to be the daughter of a king…"

Roslyn let her sit in her memories, a pang of pity pulling at her heart. It can't have been easy for Margitte or this Princess Ouna not able to love who they wanted, married off to strangers for the sake of a political alliance. She stirred the tisane and stood to pour it into the delicate china teacup on the doily-laden table between them.

Suddenly Lady Margitte's head snapped up and her eyes were wide with fear. "Who are you?"

The fog had changed its course in her mind. Roslyn would have to take care not to agitate her. She bobbed into a curtsy.

"I've brought you the tea you asked for, milady."

Lady Margitte shrank into the back of her chair, weariness etched into her wrinkles but she nodded. "Very well, set it there."

Roslyn did as she asked, but noticed how the woman stared at the tea like it was poison.

"You may go."

She bobbed again and set the teapot back on the table and stooped to collect her things.

"I said you may go!" Agitation laced the old woman's voice and Roslyn hurried her fingers, shoving everything into the bag and slinging it over her shoulder. As she scurried for the door, Lady Margitte's voice turned shrill. "Charlotta! Charlotta, where are you?"

Roslyn nearly crashed into the buxom maid who bustled through the door. She knelt by her mistress and reached up to stroke her hair. "It's alright, I'm here. I just went to the privy."

Her shushing seemed to still the noblewoman enough for her to place the cup and saucer in her hands. "Drink your tea now and then we'll get you to bed."

Charlotta looked up and caught Roslyn's eye. She suddenly felt like she was intruding on a very intimate moment and her cheeks burnt with shame. She bowed her head and backed silently out of the room.

Chapter 14

Frederik gripped her hand so tightly she saw the white of his knuckles through his flesh. His strength failed and his leg gave way beneath him.

"For the love of Hoff! I never thought walking one length of the apartment would be so hard!" he cursed, trying to smile, but panting too much with effort and pain to make it convincing.

"Lean on me," Roslyn insisted, threading her hand around his waist. "Take a break."

She planted her feet as he transitioned more of his weight onto her shoulders, sighing with visible release. They were pressed against each other closely, his arm resting on the ridge of her shoulders, snaking past the bare skin of her neck where the hairs stood on end at his touch.

Her own shoulder was pressed into the hollow under his arm, soaking in the moisture the exertion had forced from his body. Her nostrils were flooded with his expensive perfume, heady and rich, making her head swim and underneath that, something else, something more primitive—his own natural scent. As she breathed it in, her throat went dry and a heat pulsed between her legs. She tried to swallow as her body betrayed reason; she could not feel this way for the enemy.

He shook a little as he got his breath back and wiped sweat from his brow with a ridiculously flounced sleeve. "I apologise; I am making you wet."

Roslyn nearly choked on her own breath. By the Tree, if he had any idea! She shook her head, her lips pressed into a closed mouthed smile. "Think nothing of it. You need to regain your stamina."

"Aye," Frederik agreed, his hot breath moving stray strands of hair across her forehead.

"When we walk back, remember to use the cane. You were trying to do too much on your own, too soon." Roslyn focused on the task at hand rather than the bead of sweat rolling down his neck that had caught her eye. It left a shiny wet trail on his porcelain skin before disappearing in the vee of his shirt.

"Hoff's hammer! I forgot I had to walk back."

Roslyn laughed, pointing at his couch through the two doorways they had stumbled through. "Well, I can't very well carry you all that way… I suppose I could drag you."

Frederik straightened with a roll of his athletic shoulders and dropped his hand from her back. She felt suddenly cold without it. "No one drags a prince… But it is a fucking long way."

"Use your cane," Roslyn reminded, pleased to see that he shifted his weight on the side of his bad leg over to it. "You just need something to take your mind off it; think of something else."

Frederik grunted as he took his first step. "Like what?"

"Well, you could tell me who Hoff is? You keep talking about him, invoking his name, so… enlighten me.

134

If you are to learn about my people, I suppose I should learn about yours. Who is he?" She clasped her hands behind her back and looked up at him in the poise of the attentive student.

The prince rolled his eyes. "You really want to know?"

"I do."

"Very well then." He took another pained step and then lifted his head from the invisible line he had been following on the floor, cocking it to the side to think. "Well, to know who Hoff is, you need to know about Verketteberg, the Chained Mountain."

His pronunciation of the name of Oderberg's holy mountain made Roslyn's stomach flip. On the lips of the soldiers and servants, the Bergams' clipped accent was harsh, but when Frederik spoke it was soft and enticing, especially as his words were already breathy with the effort of walking.

"I'll tell you the tale exactly as my nursemaid told me." He cleared his throat and assumed the role of a bard, changing his words to suit the tale. "Long ago, Frier, an ice giant sought to hold the land of Bergam in an eternal winter. When the snows should have melted, they remained; when crops should have flourished, the icicles grew longer and the winds howled. By the time of the harvest, when the people should have been living off the fat of the land, they were starving. Something had to be done. One day, a young serf, Olaf, was lost in a snow storm. He was cold, frail and on death's door when he saw a light. Someone had lit a fire in a nearby cave and he could smell the scent of roasting rabbit on the wind. When he stumbled into the cave, he was met by a man and a woman huddled by the fire. They welcomed him, shared their supper with him."

His nursemaid must have told the tale a thousand times the way he recited the story as if reading from a book. Roslyn could almost imagine him sat on the edge of his bed as a chubby cheeked, golden haired child, staring up at the women with wonder.

"Overcome with thanks, Olaf asked what he could do to repay them. The man and the woman looked at each other and then the man pulled out an enormous chain. 'Take this. Not far from here, there is a tall mountain and, in that mountain, there is a deep, dark cave. In that cave, you will find the giant Frier. Use this to bind him. But do not stop there—he is strong and will break free unless you chain him to the very mountain he sleeps in. Wrap it around the peaks, the gullies, the rock faces and clifftops. Wrap it tight.'"

Roslyn couldn't help but snort.

"What!"

"I'm sorry, but one man carried a chain large enough to encircle a mountain and trap a fierce ice giant? Come on!"

Frederik stopped and looked down at her with raised eyebrows. "I listened to you and your stories of living trees and horny gods…"

She pursed her lips and nodded slowly. "Not without interruptions, but continue."

The prince huffed. "Well, needless to say Olaf accomplished his task, which allowed the couple he had met to complete their own task. The man was the god Hoff, and it is with his hammer, forged from the fires in the centre of the earth, that he smashes winter's ice each year. His partner, Veel, takes the water from the ice melt

136

to nourish the land, bringing summer and plenty. But every winter Frier's lover Isapf returns, trying to strengthen his powers and turning the world to winter once again. It's an eternal struggle that never ends, until the end of days where Isapf will free her lover from the chains of Verketteberg and life will be obliterated."

They trudged on in silence for a few steps, the tap of the prince's cane echoing. Roslyn pulled a face.

"Cheerful lot, aren't you? And what of the serf, Olaf? What happened to him?"

Frederik turned to her and grinned, even daring to give his cane a flourish as he flicked it before him. "Oh, he was celebrated as a hero by the people and became their ruler, creating a dynasty unbroken to this day."

She rolled her eyes. "Let me guess, his name was Olaf Oderberg?"

"One and the same."

"Of course it was."

"Just goes to show what a person can achieve, a serf from Fladby becoming king and having a mountain named after him."

"Indeed."

They didn't say anything else as they finished their lap. Frederik was covered by a sheen of sweat by the time he reached the couch and with a final step forward, he stumbled over the cane, swore as he put all his weight on his bad leg and propelled himself into the seat.

"Fuck! Shit! That thing is going to kill me!" He scowled and threw the cane towards the hearth with a clatter. Roslyn winced at his outburst, but walked over to where the piece of carved wood rocked back and forth on the stone flags.

"It's just while you are getting your strength back."

"You don't know that." The prince paused, his voice dipping to a whisper, his eyes wandering, brows furrowed in dread. "What if I'm stuck with it forever?"

Roslyn shook her head. Self-pity was not going to get him on his feet in three days.

"Nonsense. We'll have you dancing the Vallestav in no time."

The prince took a greedy glug of wine before staring at her over the rim of the glass. "Dancing the what now?"

Roslyn swore under her breath. "The Vallestav. It's a traditional Domovnian dance, based on an old man who once cut a branch from Zemya to help him on his travels. The branch was so enraged at being separated from its owner that it fought back, taking the man on the wrong paths, tripping him and sometimes beating him."

Frederik put down his glass, a twinkle in his eyes and a smile on his lips. He laced his fingers together over his stomach and inclined his head towards her.

"Well... what're you waiting for? I have to see it now."

Roslyn gripped the cane in her hands and shook her head, eyes wide. "I... I can't. It's normally performed with many people beating their staves together and besides.... We don't have any music."

Frederik grinned and reached for the cane. Warily, she handed it back to him and watched him wince as he rose. He was still exhausted after his round, but he hobbled over to a sideboard, opened one of its walnut doors and pulled out a fiddle. Roslyn groaned.

"Oh no!"

"Oh yes! Go on, hum the melody." He flopped back onto the couch, threw the cane at Roslyn who had to scrabble to catch it and set the fiddle under his chin,

138

turning the tuning pegs whilst he caressed the strings with the bow.

She cleared her throat, colour rising up her cheeks.Her singing voice had never been exceptional. Croakily, she hummed a slow but lively, upbeat tune.

"Like this?" Frederik played it back to her perfectly. "Well, that seems simple enough. Right, your turn. Ready?"

Roslyn took a deep breath and nodded her head. As the prince began to play, she walked out the steps, tapping the cane on the floor with the rhythm, twirling it around in her hands and holding it high in the air as she spun. At times, the beat was tapped out by her stomping foot, the wooden stick slapping against her hand, her heels, her thighs before the final twirl ended up with the cane giving her a sharp tap on the behind, forcing her to her knees.

"Well, that didn't seem too hard. I could do that tomorrow if you like?" He shrugged up at her unimpressed. Something riled inside her and she narrowed her eyes.

"Oh really? Play it again, but this time faster."

Frederik raised one eyebrow and smirked. "As you wish."

This time the dance was much more fluid, the beats and slaps of the cane on the stone and Roslyn's body adding to the melody. She kept her eyes on the prince and before he finished the final refrain, she smirked.

"Faster."

He obliged, his own smile matching the daring in hers. Her blood was beginning to pump and she was losing herself in the dance.

"Faster!" she cried as the melody began again. By now the cane in her hands was a blur, moving so fast she was having a hard time keeping up with it, but she had done this dance since she was a child, and her body knew what to do. Unbidden, the hoots and cries of 'hey, hey' that often accompanied the dance left her lips. She had the faintest vision of Frederik raising his eyebrows again as she did so, before she spun away again.

"Faster!" The prince shouted over the music, the bangs and claps of the stave and the stomping of his own foot.

"No!" Roslyn cried, laughing, trying to keep up with the now insanely fast dance. "I can't keep up!"

"Of course you can! You are Roslyn Pleveli, you can do anything!" His enthusiasm was intoxicating and even as sweat dripped into her eyes, Roslyn pushed herself to complete the dance. With the final shout of "Hey!" she brought the cane round to tap it on her behind, when her swishing skirts got in the way and she tumbled head over heels over the cane. She rolled into a crumpled heap at the base of the couch, knocking the table over with a crash.

"Oh, shit! Roslyn! Are you alright?" Frederik leapt from his seat and knelt beside her, swearing as his leg slowed him down.

Roslyn lay flat on her back, staring up at his wide blue eyes and began to laugh. Tears formed in her eyes and she panted, wafting her hand in front of her face as she tried to stop.

"You're fine!" The prince shoved her shoulder gently in reproach as she tried to sit, knocking her down again and forcing more hysterical giggles from the pair of them. Their eyes met and the wheezes slowed.

Suddenly the door burst open and in rushed Captain Dietrich, sword drawn, eyes flitting wildly around the room.

"Your highness! I heard shrieks!"

Roslyn caught Frederik's eye and the thought of having to explain what had happened set her off again, laughing so hard she actually snorted. His eyes grew wide and then he was at it again, too.

The guard lowered his weapon and looked down at them reproachfully, pursing his lips so much that his moustache wobbled from side to side as if it were alive.

The prince was the first to regain his breath and heaved himself back up on to the couch, leaving Roslyn a wheezing mess on the floor.

"Dietrich, have you ever heard those kinds of shrieks before and come bounding in here, sword drawn?"

"No, sir. I apologise, sir." He glared down at Roslyn. "I'll leave you to your… activities."

As he swept from the room, slamming the door behind him, Roslyn sat up. "He hates me."

Frederik tutted. "No, he doesn't, he's just very protective of me, that's all. I'll have a word. I know that once he gets to know you, he'll like you just as much as I do."

Roslyn snorted and wiped a stray tear from her cheek. "But you hardly know me. By the Tree, I don't think I've laughed that hard in… well, ever!"

Frederik stood, hobbled over to the sideboard and poured two glasses of wine. "Really, never?"

Roslyn took the glass he offered on his return and shook her head. "Well, one does not have much opportunity for hysterics when foreign soldiers beat, maim and murder your friends and neighbours on a daily basis."

141

As soon as the words were out, she regretted the flippant tone in which she had uttered them. Frederik sat and sipped his wine.

"I am sorry for that." His hand reached out and took hers gently, forcing her eyes up to his. "I mean it. I hate what is happening to your people at the hands of mine, on the orders of my father."

Roslyn slipped her hand from under his and scratched her neck. "He is a monster. How can you stand him?"

"He is my father…" Frederik's voice was croaky. "He was never a monster to us; demanding, but never cruel."

She scoffed. "So, what, he played games with you and was the best father in the world, bought you pretty things and strong horses and because of that, you overlooked the atrocities he committed?"

"No!" he snapped, before lowering his voice. "No. I'd always assumed he was just doing what kings did, to keep order… It wasn't until recently that I learnt the truth."

Roslyn shook her head. "And you still love him?"

Frederik met her fiery gaze. "As difficult as he is to please—as hard as I try to win his favour, his approval and praise—he is still my father."

"Well, it would have been nice to have one. I never knew my parents. They were killed the night of the invasion." She gulped down the rest of the wine, wiped her mouth on the back of her hand and knelt by the broken glasses and bottles that had smashed when she'd knocked the table over. Needing a broom, she walked over to the cupboard in the corner of the room to fetch one when he answered.

"I'm sorry about your parents."

Roslyn nodded, unable to speak for the lump that had clogged her throat. She returned to the mess and as she cleaned, she peeped up at the prince and saw a shadow of melancholy over his beautiful face. As much as she wanted to drop the subject of the king, she knew that talking was sometimes a better medicine that all the herbs in the world. If his father somehow had a hand in his nightmares, then bear it she must. "I am sure he is proud of you," she said softly.

Frederik scoffed. "When I was the infamous party prince you've no doubt heard so much about, I was a slovenly whoremonger; when I said I wanted to study, he accused me of wasting his money as I would not be able to comprehend what my tutors taught. And now, when I have taken an interest in the realm and want to implement change for the better, he calls me a dreamer. I'm always trying to be someone else for him and it's never enough. So, as much as I love him, maybe I just have to learn that he will never be proud of the real me…" He gave a hollow laugh. "After all, why should he? He has his heir; I am just the spare."

He raised his eyes to Roslyn, whose brows had furrowed with pity. Her heart ached for him. He may have had parents, but perhaps that was worse—to have them but not have their love. She reached out and placed a hand on his knee. At her touch, he jolted and tried to smile.

"If only I could be like you. Strong, fierce, not afraid to give anyone a good tongue lashing, royalty or not! Just look how you spoke to my brother, the Crown Prince."

Roslyn cringed. "I think you overestimate me, your highness. I am none of those things, ask anyone back home. I am a Hedgie, the lowest of Domovnians, a wallflower who can't say boo to a goose."

Frederik placed his finger under her chin and tilted her head upwards so that she could look nowhere but his face, framed with those golden curls. His breath smelt of cloves and wine. "And I think you see yourself in the box others have placed you in. I see none of those things, Roslyn. I see someone with powers and passion. Step out of the box and let your true self be free."

Their lips were a finger's breadth apart and Roslyn swallowed, wondering what they would taste like. All she had do so was lean in and… but she couldn't, could she?

Her hands quivered as she placed them on his knees, gently so as to not to disturb the wound. She felt the taught muscle of his thighs through the fabric and closed her eyes as his breath caressed her cheek. She pulled herself up, pressing herself between his legs and raised her lips to his, when a bell sounded. Frederik sighed and sat back, a sad smile on his lips, leaving her feeling exposed and at the same time empty.

"Supper time. Shall we?"

Chapter 15

"This way... turn here..." Frederik called out the directions to Roslyn as she pushed him in a polished wooden chair that had wheels instead of legs. They made their way towards the private dining room of the Oderberg family. The sounds of laughter spilled out into the corridor as they approached and she slowed to a stop.

"What time should I collect you?" she whispered, afraid that if she spoke too loud the king would order her head cut off.

Frederik turned round and furrowed his brow. "What are you talking about? You're coming in, too."

Roslyn put her hands on her hips and scoffed. "I'm what, now? Your highness, there is no way they will allow me in there."

The prince shrugged. "They have to. My manservant is ill and I need an assistant in there. Besides," he shot her a mischievous grin. "Don't you want more inside intel on us despicable Oderbergs?"

He was joking, but Roslyn shuddered. It could indeed prove useful if she was going to figure out how to kill them all. She nodded her head slowly and pushed him inside.

The clatter of cutlery stopped upon their arrival. A mixture of perplexed, enraged and curious stares followed the healer and her patient as she wheeled him to his place at the U-shaped table.

"Must you really bring your savage to dinner, Frederik?" Crown Prince Viktor drawled, finally breaking the silence. "She'll put me off my food."

Roslyn could scarcely breathe as she set the locks on the chair. She bobbed a curtsy before stepping back to the wall where the other manservants or ladies-in-waiting stood. Clasping her trembling hands before her, she finally looked up. Across the table from her she caught the eye of Lady Margitte's maid, Charlotta. The tired woman raised an eyebrow and all Roslyn could do was shrug.

It was a small, intimate space, large enough only to hold the royal family, but even so, there were gaps on all sides of the table. The fragility of the Oderberg dynasty was laid before her. There were no wives a the table, no children. The king and crown prince sat side by side at the centre, the former glaring at her with contempt, the latter with curiosity. On the opposite side of the table from Prince Frederik sat the Lady Margitte, her ruffs holding her ramrod straight, the soup spoon that had been halfway to her lips stuck in midair. Its bright red contents dripped slowly back into her bowl, causing spatters on the white tablecloth. Her eyebrows were raised in confusion, but her mouth was not set in a scowl.

"Ah, Miss Pleveli," she said, as if she had suddenly remembered who she was. "I was not expecting to see you again."

"No, nor should you! Really, Frederik, you are pushing it," King Casimir glowered.

Frederik chuckled and shrugged his shoulders. When he spoke, Roslyn was shocked by the change in his timbre. When they had been in his apartment, his voice had rung clear and honest, but when he spoke now, it was oily with the practised calculation of a courtier. "Come now, father, I don't see the harm in it. Besides, my healer needs to inspect my diet if I am to get better faster. Isn't that so, Miss Pleveli?"

He turned back to her, and gave the slightest of winks. She nodded, and he waved a hand languidly as he turned back to his family. "See?"

"What an excellent idea!" Lady Margitte piped up before the king could reply. "As much as I abhor the magical practices of her people, Miss Pleveli did brew a remarkable tisane that aided my digestion and purged my system whilst travelling."

"Honestly, Grand Tanta!" Crown Prince Viktor groaned, his mouth turning upside down with disgust. "Can we not talk about your bowels at the dinner table? They are a gruesome enough matter at a regular time, but when one is in fact trying to eat..." He shuddered and set his spoon down with a clatter before turning to a servant. "Take this vile, bilge-watery excuse for a soup out of here and bring in some proper food."

Roslyn's stomach growled as the soup tureens were carried out under her nose, all of them more than half full. What were they going to do with it? She swallowed down the saliva lining the inside of her cheeks and hoped at the very least the servants would get to eat it and it wouldn't be wasted.

Lady Margitte shrugged her shoulders at her great nephew's remark and dabbed her lips with her napkin, leaving a red stain on the snow-white linen. Servants entered, bearing steaming platters of vegetables, grains and an enormous roast deer which was set before the king and his heir. Roslyn watched in horror and some degree of jealousy as the plates of the royals were piled so high that the sauce nearly dripped off the gilded edges.

"Mmm, yes…" The king spoke around a full mouth of venison that he had smothered in celeriac puree, "Be that as it may, I do not remember you asking permission to bring a prisoner to my table. It is completely unacceptable." He raised his fork at Roslyn threateningly, about to say something when Frederik laughed.

"Father, Roslyn is not a prisoner. She is here as my guest, and you know that." He shifted onto his elbow, popped a potato in his mouth and continued. "Besides, it's good practice for you all to be waited on by a Domovnian. After all, when the Assimilation Act is passed—"

"Oh, here we go again!" Viktor groaned and tipped his wine down his gullet.

"No… no!" Frederik speared some green beans with so much force that his fork scraped across the plate. Roslyn winced along with the rest of the company, royals and servants alike. "It is time we talked about it, and you promised me, Father, that as soon as I returned from Teadmis, we would enter negotiations and draw up plans."

The king sat back in his seat chewing loudly. "I did, didn't I? Well, that was foolish of me, but now is not the time. Besides, even if I entertain your idea of allowing the heathens more freedom"—Roslyn clenched her jaw and flexed her hands at her side—"they wouldn't be serving us. They would be little more than serfs, would they not, and most certainly not allowed in my presence."

Frederik coughed and rubbed his eyebrow with his finger. "No, of course, Father. It will take time for things to adjust, and we must see that they can handle certain freedoms before granting others."

The blood of Roslyn's beating heart was pounding in her ears. Was that his plan, for her people to be serfs, little more than slaves to a local lord who was still at liberty to treat them however they wanted? Domovnians would still be very much under the Oderberg thumb. She swallowed painfully and tried to steady her breathing. Something white caught her eye and she glanced down at the napkin that had fluttered to her feet.

"Roslyn, my napkin, would you?" Frederik cooed over his shoulder. She glared at him but stooped to pick up the dropped item. Still in her crouch, she handed it back to the prince who looked down at her with wide eyes. What was he trying to wordlessly convey to her—an apology, a reassurance? He gripped her hand hard as she handed the cloth back to him, but she wrenched it away before anyone could see.

Suddenly, there was shouting in the hallway and the door to the dining room burst open.

Viktor was on his feet in a second, sword drawn. Lady Margitte gave a pitiful yelp of fright, holding her napkin up to her lips as if to protect her from the small figure that was dragged before the tables by two guards.

"What is the meaning of this?" the king bellowed, slamming his palm on the tabletop for order.

"My liege," one of the guards started, before clouting the head of the prisoner who was still wriggling and swearing like a troll. "Quiet, you! I apologise, your majesty, but it was of the utmost importance."

Crown Prince Viktor scowled and stalked round the table to confront the soldiers.

"What could possibly be so important that you must interrupt us at table?"

The guard stammered under his gaze. "Please, your highness… this… we thought you'd want to see at once." Without wasting another second, he removed the sack from his captive and the room went still.

Two curled horns spiralled out of a mop of tangled, greying hair. As the owner thrashed, Roslyn spied the tipped points of his ears. He'd been stripped to the waist and beaten, the blood from the lashes dried over his short but muscular frame. But where his waist should have been stood the bucking and scuffing hindquarters and hooves of a goat.

The Oderbergs gasped as one. Viktor lowered his sword just a little while Lady Margitte jumped back from her chair, napkin still clutched at her lips. A piece of meat fell from the king's open mouth. Roslyn couldn't see Frederik's face but she was almost certain it was filled with surprised wonder.

"A satyr? But I thought…" he mumbled.

"Thought we were all dead, did you?" the half-man, half-beast turned his head towards the youngest son of the king and it was Roslyn's turn to gasp. That face, those sneering lips and keen eyes… She'd seen them before and often over the years.

"Silen?" she mouthed, her breath squeezed from her lungs in shock. What was the beggar of Koliba doing here, and how had she never realised—how had any of the town's citizen's never realised—what he was?

The muscles in Frederik's back tensed as she gasped but he took the full force of the satyr's rage calmly.

"Your daddy dearest did try to exterminate us. Set up a grand old hunt for any of us Descendants with hooves or wings, didn't you?" he turned back to the king. "So tell me, you old fool, did we taste good? Did you smother us in berry sauce as you are doing that poor deer now?"

A silence fell after his outburst and even Viktor and Frederik turned opened mouthed to the king.

"Father, please tell me you did not eat—" the crown prince began.

"I did what I had to! I rid this country of these monstrosities. Besides, you enjoyed it." He shot both of his sons a snide grin before turning back to the guard. Both Frederik and Viktor dropped their forks and the scent of the roast venison suddenly made Roslyn's stomach turn.

"What are you even doing here?" Casimir shook as he raised himself to his feet to loom over the prisoner.

Silen laughed and looked around. When his eyes fell on Roslyn, she could have sworn the very corner of his lips lifted in a smile.

"Why, I just wanted a stroll down memory lane. I had a hankering for the past; that comes with old age... doesn't it, my dear?" He turned and bowed towards Lady Margitte who was so startled to be addressed that she gave a small yelp.

"You need not be afraid of me. You know that though, don't you?"

All eyes turned to Lady Margitte as she sat shakily back down in her chair. Her eyes were once again cloudy with memory and suddenly she broke into a smile.

"A satyr? Why, I haven't seen one of these since I was a girl!" She turned to Casimir, her eyes bright with

151

childish delight. "Did you know they used to fill the old courts with laughter—juggling and tumbling, singing songs and setting riddles. Oh tell us a riddle, dear satyr!"

To everyone's surprise she clapped her hands as if she were a girl of no more than six years old.

Silen bowed to her, a grin plastered across his craggy face. "But of course,"

"No, no, no!! I will *not* have this hybrid monster in my court! Kill him!"

"No!" Roslyn and Frederik cried together, shooting a look between them.

Even the satyr's head snapped towards them in the silence which followed. Roslyn felt the prickle of sweat under her arms, the more the king stared at her.

"What… did… you… say?" the monarch growled.

Frederik cleared his throat. "You shouldn't kill him, father."

"And why not?"

Viktor tilted his head over his shoulder, daring his brother to answer.

"Well, the satyrs and fauns and all other such creatures…"

"Centaurs, harpies…" Silen began listing them off on his fingers.

"Yes, yes, all of them are in fact Descendents of the Ancestors and are therefore Domovnians." He looked over his shoulder at Roslyn for confirmation. She couldn't do anything but nod, dumbfounded. "As such, they will also be protected in the Assimilation Act—"

"Ispaf's frozen cunt they will!" the king barked.

"Honestly, Casimir! There is no need for such language!" Lady Margitte quipped as if chastising a child.

"Permit me, father, to include this fellow here…" He lifted his hand and gestured that the satyr tell him his name.

"Silen."

"I propose we include Silen in my experiment, to see if Domovnians and Oderbergs can work together."

Silence fell again as the king picked a morsel of food out of his teeth before laughing. "Why, is he going to heal you too, take you out of your misery with song and dance?"

Frederik laughed to humour him. "Not me, father, but Grand Tanta Margitte." He turned to the old woman. "What do you say, Grand Tanta? Would you like Silen here to fill your days with riddles and music? You have been very much alone since Grand Oncle passed."

The woman pinched her lips together so fiercely, Roslyn thought she was about to bellow in rage, but then realised she was trying not to cry. She placed a hand on her bosom and whispered. "For me? You'd give me a satyr as a companion?" A faint glimmer of hope sparked in her rheumy eyes. "Really?"

Frederik smiled and looked at his father. Viktor groaned, and the king grumbled.

"You can't say no to that now, can you, father?"

Casimir shifted in his seat and cleared his throat. "I can… but I won't. Of course, Tanta, you may have him if you really want him. I would not want to deprive a dear old lady of joy in her final days."

Lady Margitte furrowed her brow in hurt. Then she clapped her papery hands together again and smiled. It was disconcerting to see the old bat actually happy, especially about being gifted a living being as if he were a pet or a toy she could play with. Roslyn clenched her fist in the folds of her skirt.

"Go on then, satyr. Give us a riddle." Crown Prince Viktor shoved another forkful of venison into his mouth.

Roslyn's eyes darted from the king to the satyr, her breath coming out of her nostrils in forceful pants. Frederik looked round at her.

"Roslyn," he whispered, catching her eye. "Are you alright?"

As the satyr bowed, she shook her head. When he rose, he was staring straight into her eyes, freezing her to the spot.

"The seed of an apple is still a tree,
It needs but to know, and so will it be."

A chill ran down Roslyn's spine as Silen bowed in her direction. Her throat was so dry she couldn't swallow, could barely breathe as the heir to the throne booed and threw a gravy-soaked slab of meat at the satyr. It hit him on the cheek and stained his face brown as it slid off, but still he would not take his eyes from her.

"That was rubbish! Call that a riddle!"

"Oh my, what a conundrum…" Lady Margitte waved her great nephew's comment away. "I shall think on this all night. Viktor, dear, there are always hidden meanings to these things."

Only Frederik seemed to sense Roslyn's discomfort. He cleared his throat loudly and clicked his fingers at a servant.

"I find I am easily tired tonight. You, send a full tray up to my apartment. I wish to retire."

He nodded to Roslyn, who wheeled him out of that stifling room as fast as she could. Once they were out of hearing of his family, she let out a breath that sounded

154

more like a strangled cry. He reached back to put a hand on hers, but she snatched it away. She couldn't bear for him to touch her.

"Roslyn, what is it?"

He looked up at her with those large puppy dog eyes of his, which she refused to be drawn into. She shook her head vehemently.

"You... *people*," she spat. They entered his apartment where she pushed the chair away from her, leaving it to freewheel into the back of the sofa.

Frederik pulled it back with a sigh of irritation and glared at her.

"'Us people' what?"

"You liar!" she hissed, finally looking at him, her hair whipping in her eyes. "You said you wanted peace, you said you wanted freedom for my people!"

"And I do!" Frederik hauled himself to his feet with a grunt of pain and, snatching up his stick from where it leaned on the edge of the reading table, stepped towards her.

"You said we would be serfs!" Roslyn threw her pointed finger towards the door and the distant dining room. "Do you have any idea what that means? We'd be even worse off than we are now. At least now, beaten and ostracised as we are, we aren't anyone's property!"

Frederik scratched his chin and shook his head. "No, I don't want that, but how else am I going to even get him to consider it? I have to let him think you will still be under Oderberg control."

Roslyn stepped back and shook her head. "Like Silen and I are?"

"What are you talking about?" Frederik's voice turned cold and he gripped his cane tighter.

155

"Well, we have been taken from our homes, humiliated, forced to work for no reward… all part of your little—what was it you called it—*experiment*? I don't want to be your puppet. I just want to go home! I have no idea how Hedda is, if she is even still alive or if your dogs murdered her on the way out. I've heard from no one since you took me from Koliba! And now you have stolen his freedom, too? Is mine not enough for you?"

Her blood was boiling. In one casual flick of his wrist, Frederik had subjected a centuries old creature into the life of a court jester.

An ugly sneer spread across the prince's face. "You don't understand what I did in there, do you?"

"You humiliated him!" Roslyn stepped forward and yelled up at him. Frederik took another step closer and stared down at her, chest heaving so hard it brushed against hers.

"I saved his life!"

They stood like that in silence, scowling at each other, their faces close enough for a kiss… or a headbutt. Roslyn swallowed as his words hit home and he stepped back, shaking his head.

"You have no idea how much I put on the line to save that fawn."

"Satyr. He is a satyr and his name is Silen," she croaked, the fight having gone out of her.

"I know, and I know you recognised him the moment he was revealed to us. Now, I don't know how and I'm not going to ask, but just be thankful, will you?"

Roslyn shook her head as tears formed. "A life as a slave is no life at all."

Frederik stopped his frantic pacing and stared at her. "You are unbelievable. I literally put not only my neck on

156

the line, but yours and those of all your countrymen to persuade my father to keep the fawn—"

"Satyr!"

"Whatever! He could have killed you and him there and then and quashed the whole possibility of an Act. You may know your people, but you know nothing of diplomacy, and you know nothing of my father. I have to sow the smallest of ideas in the hopes that he will not cut down the bigger ones I will put to him later. Argh!" He threw up his hands in frustration and kicked his cane away from him. It skidded across the grey flagstones and came to a stop in the velvet of the curtains.

For a heartbreaking moment, the pair of them stood, chests heaving, staring at the floor. Then Roslyn bowed her head and walked slowly to retrieve his walking stick. She knew deep down he was right. He had just saved Silen's life. She should thank him, but no matter how hard she tried to say them, the words turned to ash on her tongue.

She held out the carved stick out to him. He took it and pulled her close enough so that he could put a hand on hers.

"I'm asking you to trust me, Roslyn." He placed a hooked finger under her chin and raised it until she could look nowhere but his red-rimmed eyes. "I swear to you I will free your people and right the wrongs, but I need you to trust me with the process."

"Why should I?" Her voice trembled and her lips quivered.

"Because I am trusting you not to kill me. Every day, I put my life in your hands. You are stronger than me right now, you could poison me, smother me in my sleep; there is a myriad of ways to murder me. So every day I put my life in your hands because I don't believe you will. I trust you, so all I am asking is that you do the same."

Damn him. Damn him back to his cursed, Chained Mountain. Roslyn shook, unable to tear her eyes from his. Her traitorous body wanted to lean into his chest, rest her head on his shoulder and feel the embrace of those warm, muscular arms, but she jumped as a knock sounded at the door.

"Your tray, your highness?" a servant called timidly, trying to look anywhere but the prince and his healer squaring up to each other so closely; there was not an inch of daylight between them.

Frederik was the first to step back and turned to the liveried boy. Roslyn pouted and crossed her hands under her chest.

"Thank you. Put it in Miss Pleveli's room, if you would." The servant scurried off through the prince's bedchamber as Frederik turned towards her.

She let her hands drop from her bosom and cocked her head slightly to the side. "You ordered that for me?"

Frederik nodded, and a familiar twinkle sparked in his eyes again. "Your stomach was growling so loudly at dinner. I was worried neither of us would get any sleep tonight." He extended his hand towards her chambers. As the serving boy came out, the prince stopped him. "Get me Dietrich. Tell him to come in his riding leathers, I need him to fetch"—he shot Roslyn a look—"something for me." The boy bowed and ran from the apartments.

"I can administer my draught tonight. I bid you a restful night, Miss Pleveli and that we can both be of better spirits in the morning."

She had no choice but to leave. She began to bob into a curtsy, but then caught herself, sniffed and flounced into her tiny cell, slamming the door so hard it bounced back open.

"Was there something you wanted, Miss Pleveli?" Frederik grinned. Why by the Tree was he so infuriating? Roslyn closed the door again with an enraged grunt before throwing herself on the bed and crying herself to sleep.

Chapter 16

The next morning, Roslyn stayed in bed. Her eyes were swollen and puffy from crying, and her head ached. Her insides were battered and bruised, but nothing could rouse her from her stupor, not even Frederik as he poked his head round the door, looking for his medicine.

"Roslyn? Roslyn, are you alright? Are you sick?"

She didn't move, only squeezed her eyes shut tighter.

"Roslyn, please…" She heard him limp into the room, his cane scuffing on the rushes covering the stone flags. When she didn't answer, she heard him groan and suddenly felt the side of her bed dip as he sat on it.

"Go away." She pulled the scratchy woollen blanket over her head and regretted it instantly. It was stiflingly hot and soon the air in the confined space smelled sour with her morning breath.

She heard a chuckle. "Is that anyway to speak to a prince?"

"Go away, your highness," she grunted. She was in no mood to be mollycoddled by his charm. If he could sulk in bed all day, then she was damn sure she was going to.

"And if you don't go, it will be 'fuck off... your highness.'"

The prince cleared his throat but said nothing for a few moments. She felt the warm solidness of his hand as he placed it on her upper leg, sending a sudden jolt through her. If he'd placed it any higher, it would be on the curve of her buttock. She should tell him to get off, but she didn't. Just the weight of it there soothed her somewhat.

"I'll do my first round of the apartments, then. Perhaps you'll be feeling up to joining me after lunch."

His hand vanished and her leg felt suddenly cool, despite the thick blanket. She dared not speak, fearing her tongue would betray her sulkiness and ask him to stay, so she grunted instead. He stood and walked to the door.

"Is there anything you want? Medicine, food..."

Roslyn choked back a sob. She didn't want to cry again. "I just want to go home."

They both knew that wasn't going to happen, so being alone was the next best thing. After what seemed like an eternity, the prince mumbled, "I'll just leave you alone, then." He left the room, closing the door with a gentle click.

※

The sun was high in the sky when she was woken by the sound of the door scraping open again. Her back was to the door, and she ground her teeth. Hadn't he promised to leave her alone?

"I thought I'd told you to fuck off... your highness!"

"Roslyn Pleveli! I did not raise you to use such foul language!" The familiar, scolding voice made her sit bolt upright, throwing the blankets from her tousled head. It couldn't be, but there she was. Hedda, her own Hedda, was standing above her bed, hands on her hips and a scowl on her wrinkled lips. At the sight of her, Roslyn burst into tears and stretched out her arms. Forgetting her chastisement, the old woman rushed into them and held her, rocking her back and forth with shushing movements as she cried, hiccoughing the words. "H—Hedda! I... thought you were d—dead!"

A smooth hand that smelt of lavender stroked her head. "Now, now, why ever would you think that? I'm alright." She sat back and lifted Roslyn's tear-stained eyes to her own. "I am alright, and so are you."

Mirroring tears were making tracks in the thin layer of dirt that covered Hedda's crinkled cheeks. She pulled her charge into her bosom again and squeezed her tight. Roslyn nestled into it, catching sight of the prince's boot and the tip of his cane leaving the room. "It's me that has been worrying myself sick about you. No word good nor bad... until early this morning, before the sun was even up, that moustachioed soldier was banging on my door. Near dragged me from my bed without time to dress and slung me on a horse."

Roslyn extracted herself from the embrace. "What?"

Hedda didn't seem to hear her. "Rode like the clappers we did, I don't think I'll walk straight for a week. I tell you, if I never have to ride a horse again it will be too soon!" She chuckled.

"But why? Why are you here?" A sudden horror filled Roslyn and she jumped from the bed, pulling Hedda to her feet. "You have to leave, it's not safe for you here!"

Her mother figure and mentor stilled her frantically moving hands, placing them one atop the other and then enclosing them with her own. "I am here because my girl needs me. The Sea itself couldn't stop me from getting to you once I knew. Although that soldier with the silly moustache did strip me of my knife and my satchel." There was a twinkle in her eye. "I guess they thought I might try to slip you something dangerous."

Roslyn crumpled into her arms again, breathing in the familiar scent of her. "I've missed you so much!"

"And I, you…" her voice faltered. "But we haven't much time. As you said, I shouldn't be here, but that nice young prince—"

"Frederik?"

"Yes, well, he has taken every precaution to smuggle me in here for a short time on the pretence you are having… women's troubles. No one would question a midwife coming through the servant's stairs. I must admit, it was rather exciting, like something from a story." The older woman touched up her hair and giggled.

As the smile washed years away from Hedda, it also coaxed one from Roslyn, who finally let her shoulders sink with a sigh.

"Now, you get some food in you, and you can tell me all about life in the castle. I want all the gossip, mind; don't leave anything out!"

And so, they ate and they talked until the sun made hazy orange tracks in the sky. A knock sounded at the door and the prince's voice called through. "It's soon time."

"No!" Roslyn cried, reaching for Hedda's hand. Now she had her here, she didn't want to let her mentor out of her sight again. She was the nearest thing to a mother she had ever had. The thought suddenly struck Roslyn.

"Hedda… before you go. Will you tell me about my mother?"

The old woman had been tying her cloak around her shoulders. She stopped and her eyes flickered sharply to the door.

"Why? Why are you asking this now?" Hedda had lowered her voice to a ragged whisper.

"Lady Margitte, she suffers from the memory fog and she thought I was Princess—well, later Queen I guess—Ouna…"

Too late, Hedda tried to hide the surprise and recognition of that name on her face. She cleared her throat. "Mind fog makes people see many things."

"Hedda! Tell me, how did you come to raise me? I might need to know."

The old woman spun round, dread in her eyes and her voice stern. "The less you know, the better, for your own safety." And with those words, the pieces began to fall into place.

"Am I…?" Roslyn couldn't say it. It couldn't possibly be true.

She was a Hedgie. The Domonovs had all been Botans, able to control all plants, even edibles… hadn't they? The world spun around her and her lungs were as heavy as lead, making the simple act of breathing a feat of strength. All these years she had been made to believe she was nobody, and now…

The words Hedda wouldn't say, Lady Margitte's confusing her for a former Queen—all pointed to the fact that Roslyn was the lost Domonov princess.

She wanted to laugh, a crazed giggle dancing on her lips but Hedda clamped a hand over her mouth, her eyes pleading. "Be silent, Roslyn! Whatever you think you

164

have deduced, say nothing! You are alive today because of what has *not* been said. Let it stay that way."

The door squealed a warning as it opened and the old woman dropped her hand. Frederik shuffled in, apology written across his face. Over his shoulder, Roslyn saw the familiar bottlebrush moustache that would take Hedda home.

Hedda grabbed her face in her hands and kissed her forehead. "You are *my* Roslyn. You are beautiful, brave and strong. You concentrate on healing the prince and then you come home to me, do you hear? You come home."

Roslyn nodded, tears building in her eyes again. "I love you."

"And I love you, sweet girl." Her mentor kissed her once more and squeezed her hand before moving to the door. She looked up at the golden-haired man who towered over her and pointed a finger. "You take care of her, you hear me?"

Frederik nodded, curls bouncing. "Yes ma'am. I will."

The old woman narrowed her eyes but nodded, satisfied. Then she pulled up her hood and followed Captain Dietrich from the room.

"I'll leave you alone again, if you wish." Frederik's voice was low and cautious, but it needn't have been.

"I'd like some company now," she tried to smile, "and a change of scenery. I'll come through in a moment."

He nodded and left the room. In a hurry, Roslyn changed from the dirty dress that she had had on since the day before, and washed herself with the water and cloth resting on the small table by the window. Feeling much refreshed, she made her way to the sitting room where the prince sat on the couch, staring into the fire.

She curtsied before him and kept her eyes lowered. "Thank you, your highness… for fetching Hedda. It was a great kindness."

The prince didn't say anything but patted the fabric of the seat beside him. Then he reached over and poured wine from the decanter that sat on the side table. He handed a glass to her as she sat.

"It wasn't a kindness. It was a necessity. As you rightly pointed out last night, I took you from you home, cutting you off from all you knew, and that hurt you. I am sorry to have been the cause of such pain."

Roslyn sipped the ruby red liquid to cover her shock. "A letter would have sufficed, would it not? Surely it would have been less risky?"

Frederik smiled with his mouth, but his eyes were heavy. "It would, but one never knows what life will throw at us. You have someone you love, who is still here, who you can still touch…" His voice cracked and he took a swig of wine before raising his red-rimmed eyes to hers. "Do you know how much I would give to have my mother's arms around me like that, just one more time?" He wiped a tear away and laughed. "But now look at me, going soft in my old age, clearly."

Roslyn put her hand on his knee and turned towards him, her voice earnest. "Never brush away your compassion. The man who is not ashamed to show his feelings is far stronger than he who lets it fester within, only to release it with the swing of a sword. Your compassion, your empathy prompted you to perform an act of generosity and love."

She raised her hand to his cheek. He nuzzled into her palm, breathing in her scent and his lips brushed her thumb. They were soft and she wondered what they would

166

feel like on her own. Would they taste sweet, or of the wine he had just swallowed? She shook her head slightly; no, she couldn't. He was a prince and she was… perhaps something more than a lowly Hedgie. Why shouldn't she?

He looked up and caught her staring, but then his eyes dipped to her lips. She was frozen, she couldn't move her hand from his face, nor did she want to. He reached up and stroked her cheek. She tried to swallow, but her mouth was suddenly dry. She licked her lips without thinking and left them parted, ever so slightly. Frederik's hand snaked round from her cheek to support her neck, which had gone as weak as her knees and she stared up into his cornflower blue eyes. He sighed and his breath washed over her, lighting a fire in her belly and most alarmingly between her legs. She heard a soft moan and only realised it came from her own mouth as she pressed it to his.

Their lips met in shy unison, brushing against one another, marvelling at the softness of the other. Their breath mingled in the space between skin—sweet, warm and intoxicating. She opened her mouth ever so slightly to take a shallow breath and then pressed harder into the kiss, closing her eyes and losing herself in the breathless excitement. Her tongue met his and she was aware of the wine glass falling from her hand, its crimson contents staining the rug, but she couldn't care less.

Roslyn's chest pounded, her bosom straining against her stays. Her head swam as she inhaled him, kissed him, devoured him. Her hands snaked up to his golden hair, her fingers twisting those silken curls around and around, as a knock sounded at the door. His lips left hers instantly. The sudden rush of air made her gasp and blush to realise the state she was in, leant back against the pillows of the couch, heart pounding, hair trussed and cheeks flushed.

She smoothed herself and hers skirts before turning to the mess the wine had made on the floor as the prince, patting his own hair back into place, opened the door. Roslyn kept her eyes on the task at hand, not wanting anyone to see how her cheeks burned or how her lips were wet and swollen, aching for more.

"Your highness, the king has requested your presence at dinner. I am here to accompany you."

The servant's voice was too loud, too goading, and Roslyn winced.

"Very well." The prince's voice was flat. Roslyn rose and she saw him sit in the wheeled chair. Where only moments ago his eyes had been filled with ravishing hunger, they were now dimmed with disappointment. As he was wheeled away, Roslyn couldn't help but raise her fingers to her lips. The prince in return licked his, sending a pulse shooting through her core... a pulse she soothed with those same wet fingers as soon as the door closed.

Chapter 17

Prince Frederik gripped her hand as she went to open the doors. He was moist with sweat and shaking a little. She turned back and looked up into his brilliant blue eyes, and smiled at the unfounded worry in them.

"Do you think I'm ready? There's a lot riding on this, you know." His voice was as thin as gossamer thread, his nerves gnawing away at him.

"You have worked harder than I asked you to these past days, and it has paid off." Roslyn smiled, trying to put him at ease. "With my cures and your determination, you've done it already. Now, let's go and show your brother what we're worth."

As soon as the door was open, he let go of her hand and smoothed it on his embroidered waistcoat. Then he rolled back his shoulders and, with a nonchalant flick of his walking stick, proceeded out into the castle.

They went at a slow pace, just as Roslyn had told him to, although secretly she doubted if he could go any quicker. The walk they had in mind was a long one, and he would need to pace himself. As they descended the stairs, a feat they hadn't tried until now, Roslyn's heart was in her mouth, her hands secretly ready lest the prince stumble and fall head over heels the rest of the way down.

Eik's words sounded in her head. She could just push him, or trip him enough to make him stumble. She could do that, couldn't she? It would be so easy.

Roslyn stared at Frederik's broad back for an instant, considering it. End him now and claim it was an accident... but then the Act wouldn't be passed. No, she had to wait. She looked down suddenly and saw her hand outstretched, halfway to the broad centre of his back. Horrified at herself, Roslyn swallowed down the bile that rose in her throat and retracted her quivering hand before anyone could see.

Frederik inched his way down the staircase, step after step, using both the wide stone railing and his cane to help him. Halfway down, they noticed Crown Prince Viktor staring up at them, his mouth twisted into a discontented pout. When they reached the bottom, Prince Frederik strode as well as he could up to his brother and gave a half bow. When he arose, that blinding smile of his lit up the room.

"Good day to you, brother," he almost sang in a lilting voice, "and what a fine day it is. Roslyn and I have decided to make the most of the good weather and take a stroll in the Queen's Gardens."

He was talking jovially, not just for the benefit of his brother, but for the other nobles gathered there. Roslyn lowered her head demurely, but could see as she flitted her eyes from side to side that, although they still whispered, they now looked at her with a half measure of actual interest. The hisses were not so vicious as they had been only days before; nevertheless, the smattering of awe was tainted with suspicion. After all, she was still Domovnian.

Crown Prince Viktor scoffed and nodded his head. "The Queen's Gardens? The gardens that have seen no traffic since our dear mother departed this world? Now, why would you be going there?" He looked around at the nobles as if an actor on stage. "Would it be, perhaps, that the Queen's Gardens are the nearest to your bedchamber and therefore require the least amount of walking?"

Roslyn gulped. That was indeed the very reason they had chosen the locale for their first outing, even though it was overgrown and untended. But Prince Frederik laughed and clapped his brother on the arm jovially.

"Well, of course! You just said I had to be on my feet in three days. You didn't say how far those feet had to take me." His eyebrows were raised so high that they disappeared amongst his golden curls. His joke was rewarded by titters from some of the younger ladies present, who were immediately silenced by their fathers, brothers, and above all, the glare that Viktor shot them.

"Well then, enjoy your outing." He turned to Roslyn and gave the smallest of bows. Though it had been a minute physical gesture, the weight of its meaning was incredible, and as Frederik moved them through the crowds, the whispers started up again with an excited buzz. Had the Domovnian just won against the Crown Prince?

They continued walking in silence out of the palace and onto the wide parapet that made up the Queen's Gardens. The Queen had died some years previously of a fever, one that none of her own healers could stop ravaging her frail body. In the wake of that event, the gardens that had brought her so much peace during her lifetime had been left all but abandoned. Despite its neglect, Roslyn looked around in wonder as they walked the length of it.

It had once been astonishingly beautiful. Roses climbed over pergolas and provided shade. Statues of the very people the Domovnians were descended from, the dryads and the naiads, waved to each other from their plinths, some missing hands, some heads, some reaching out of fountains as though perpetually stuck in time since the garden had been closed. The forgotten flowers had claimed the borders and pathways for their own, but the garden was also a haven for numerous weeds. They infiltrated the cracks between the flagstones, crept up the walls and flourished in the shadows. Roslyn suddenly felt at home for the first time since she had arrived in Novlada. By the time they reached the end of the long, narrow garden, Frederik was panting audibly and had started to sweat.

"It's time you had a rest," Roslyn ordered and steered him towards a lichen-covered stone bench underneath a flowing willow tree. She was suddenly grateful for the shade as she stepped out of the blistering heat. The garden had been well planned, making the most of the south-facing sun and vistas of the low-lying hills that smoothed out as the eye travelled, becoming farmland, forests and, far in the distance, the dark smudge of the ocean. She had a sudden urge to bring it to life again. Perhaps she would be allowed to, as her reward for healing the prince… but surely the greatest reward was to go home, wasn't it? Besides, if they did hold on to her, there was no way they would trust her with resurrecting a garden, a haven for plants and possibly Affinity.

172

Frederik sat down with a sigh and loosened his cravat. It took him a while to get his breath back, but Roslyn was quite content to sit in silence and look around the garden. Suddenly the prince nudged her in the ribs.

"Ow!" Roslyn exclaimed, but followed his pointing finger to the corner of the garden where the balcony wall met that of the castle. In the shaded corner, underneath the tree, was a healthy crop of stinging nettles.

"Look, your Affinity plant, I believe." He turned and looked at her pointedly with a half smile on his plump lips. "Do I need to be worried you'll sting me to death?"

Roslyn laughed. While stinging nettles could definitely cause a lot of pain, there was no way that they could sting someone to death. She mentioned this to Frederik and promptly followed it up with, "But I could make a cord from the nettles to strangle you with."

She stood and walked over to the plants in question. They were almost as tall as she was, but bristling with needles, the ones at the base of the thick stems visible to the naked eye from where they sat on the bench. As she approached them Roslyn felt a tingle of her Affinity, and she smiled. She reached for her belt, but as her hand met with its emptiness, she sighed and looked over her shoulder.

"May I borrow your knife?"

Frederik narrowed his eyes, but the corners of his closed mouth were pulled up in a smile, an action which accentuated the dimple in his cheeks. "As long as you promise not to use it on me."

He pulled it from its sheath with a gentle tug, flipped it over in his hand and held out the hilt towards her.

"I will not use the knife on you unless you give me just cause to," she replied haughtily, a grin to match his parting her lips as she tugged it free of his grasp.

She turned, knelt down and cut three of the long stems. Then she rose and, using her bare hands, pulled the length of the stalks through a clenched fist, relieving them of their leaves and needles which fluttered to the ground at her feet.

Frederik looked up at her, brow furrowed and mouth open in amazement. "Did that not hurt you? Show me your hands."

"No!" Roslyn protested and backed away quickly, clenching her fists tight around the nettle stalks. She sat on the bench. The prince, undeterred, took her hands in his, peeling the fingers open to stare at her unblemished palm. She knew he'd been expecting to see it white with the pricks of stings, but she just laughed again.

"Is this part of your power? Are you able to touch them without being stung? What I wouldn't give for that! The number of times I rolled into a nettle heap as a boy when thrown off my horse…"

Roslyn shook her head. "No, no, I've been stung plenty of times. It's just you need to be firm with nettles, show them who's boss. And they'll respect you… most of the time."

The prince grunted in disbelief, but fell silent as he watched her hands. She crushed the stalks, sometimes using the handle of the knife or her teeth on the thicker parts and tearing them open. Then she stripped the outer skin from the bark and, on the edge of the stone in between them, started scraping a thick green paste from them, flicking it onto the ground at his feet.

"What are you doing?"

By this time Roslyn had stripped all three nettles and started to twist them into a thick thread, almost like cordage and was weaving it together in an intricate pattern.

"Most people think nettles are useless or annoying, just a weed they want rid of." Roslyn said this more to herself than to him, even though she could feel the heaviness of his gaze on her face. "But nettles are, in fact, the complete opposite; you can eat the young leaves, in salads or in soups. They are one of the most nutritious plants you could ever come across. Their seeds also are incredibly good for you. You can also make thread, and therefore cloth from nettles. So, they can feed you and clothe you, and, of course, heal you."

Tentatively, she took his hand in hers, ignoring how discoloured her fingers had become with the sap of the nettles, and tied the woven band she had just made around his wrist. She held his hand a little longer than she meant to after she tied the knot on the bracelet, its weight and heat setting her palms tingling far more than any nettle could ever have done.

"And of course, they make beautiful decorations. The more that dries out, the finer it will become. Stronger, too."

Frederik wrenched his hand from hers to stare at the bracelet around his wrist in amazement, leaving her feeling that she had suddenly misplaced something.

"This is fantastic! And the weaving skill here..." The prince blew out his rounded red lips in appreciation, drawing her eyes to them.

Roslyn blushed and shook her head. "I don't have any beads or other threads to wind through it. I've made much better ones before."

But Frederik shook his head and beamed.

"Teach me. I want to learn exactly how to do this, and I'll make one for you to say thank you for putting up with me."

And so the next twenty minutes were taken up in teaching Prince Frederik von Oderberg how to cut, strip and weave nettles into cordage. It was a louder half hour than the previous, based on the amount of swearing he did every time he touched one of the fresh nettles.

"I don't think your Affinity plant likes me very much," he muttered on more than one occasion. When they were halfway through weaving the length, he paused. "Here, hold this."

He passed the cord to Roslyn and fumbled with his shirt sleeve, leaving green stains all over the white silk.

"What're you doing?"

Frederik grinned as he pulled. Roslyn heard the ping of snapping thread and gasped as he held the button aloft. "Here. You said we had no beads, so we'll make do with what we do have."

Roslyn shook her head as he dropped it into her hands and reclaimed his weaving. "I can't. This is…" She peered at it more closely. "And it has your silly Chained Mountain on it. People will think I stole it!"

"Pfft! Nonsense, I lose these all the time. Besides…" he wrapped his fingers around hers, pressing them closed over the button. "I want you to have it. This bracelet is my gift to you, and no one else need know about it."

Roslyn's heart was pounding. She licked her suddenly dry lips and nodded. She took up the work in his lap and as she threaded the button into the cord, she felt her hand brush against the tops of his thighs. Her skin burned as if scalded and her fingers shook making it difficult to ensure

176

it was securely tied. Then she nodded and motioned for him to continue.

By the end, he had made what could be called a bracelet, even if it did look more like a piece of garden twine. With a grin, Frederik took Roslyn's hand in his and wrapped his creation around her wrist.

"There," he said proudly at first and then, as he spied Roslyn's own bracelet next to his creation, his face fell and he muttered pitifully, "Isapf's tits! It's awful, isn't it? Here, give it back."

"No!" Roslyn snatched her hands away and looked at the tangled mess of nettles around her wrist. "I shall wear this with pride, your highness."

They both laughed and fell into a contented silence, their hands side-by-side on the stone bench, covered in green gunk. The tips of their little fingers touched, and they simultaneously looked up from their hands and into each other's eyes.

Roslyn could barely breathe. How could she be so bold as to look at him like this? Then she realised that his breathing was as constricted as her own.

Suddenly, a blaring horn sounded over the garden wall and snapped them out of their trance.

"What's going on?"

Frederik looked over her shoulder and shrugged. "Probably just some mummers come to town. People get giddy about that kind of thing." Roslyn tried to hide the excitement that crept up her face, but it was too late. "Do you want to watch?"

She nodded bashfully and stood up, turning round to help the prince rise unsteadily to his own feet. He leant heavily on the cane, and also on her own forearm, gripping it with more strength than she had expected and she felt her knees buckle. He panted and shook as he hoisted himself off the bench and as he rose, their faces passed an inch away from each other. His ragged breath brushed her cheek and their eyes met for a split second before he stood up to his full height and laughed.

"I think I sat down for too long. I've gone all stiff. They won't be calling me prince limp anymore!"

Roslyn smirked and looked away. She dared not look back and down to see if he meant in more ways than one. They began to walk slowly back up the garden path.

"So," she cleared her throat and changed the subject. "Why does the son of Casimir von Oderberg want peace?"

Frederik sighed and shrugged. As he was formulating the words, every step was punctuated with the tap of the cane on stone.

"The violence," he began, his voice a thin tendril of frustration. "The constant threat of violence has not only damaged the country, but I believe has cursed it. The lands are drying up, food becomes more scarce with each passing year, just like in Bergam. The whole reason father left and brought his people somewhere new, somewhere fertile and verdant, was to get away from that barren and desolate place. Perhaps it's us, perhaps our presence here is what is killing the land, but it can't be, can it?"

Roslyn did not dare to say anything. She didn't even look at him. His people *were* destroying the land, even if it wasn't in the way he thought it was.

"But," Frederik continued. "It's also destroying my father, this curse. It's eating him up from the inside."

He stopped walking and raised his bowed head. Tentatively, he reached out and took Roslyn's hand to stop her from walking away. At his touch, a shiver ran up her arm and down her spine. She gasped as she met his eye.

178

"He is sick, Roslyn. That's why I brought you here, not so much to heal me, but... I want you to heal him, too."

Roslyn couldn't believe it. The world seemed to drop out from beneath her feet and she snatched her hand away, walking to the edge of the parapet. The noise from the streets was loudest here. She was shaking with fury by the time the prince caught up to her.

"I commend your love for your father, but why should I help him?" Frederik tried to take her hands in his again, but she withdrew into herself and stepped away. He had to be joking—he wanted her to heal the man that could quite possibly have murdered her own parents?

"Why? Because deep down, no matter who you think he is, he's a scared man, and he's in pain. I know from what you've told me, from how you have treated me, *your enemy,* that you cannot turn away someone in pain. That's not the healer's way."

Roslyn was about to retort when horns sounded below them and the crowd opened up to reveal a rickety cart. It jolted and rolled on the cracked cobbles of the town, and the Oderberg citizens jeered and threw rotting missiles at the figure riding in the back. It was a young man.

His hands were tied before him and his head was bowed, but even from this distance, they both knew it was a Domovnian. He had a mop of dark hair, his skin was bronzed by the sun and shimmering, but most telling of all, he wore the embroidered shirt displaying his Affinity—lilies.

They followed the track of the cart through the crowds from their crow's nest view. All the while the people were held back by Oderberg soldiers as they lunged at the cart, hissing and hawking up spit at the poor man, who, to his credit, didn't flinch once. The cart rounded into an open square where a scaffold had been erected.

Roslyn couldn't watch anymore. That man was going to his death and she could do nothing to stop it. For once, she did not want to be forced to witness the death of her kind at the hands of the Oderbergs. She sucked in a breath and thought. What would a princess do? She would bargain.

"I will not heal the king." She looked up at Frederik and met his eye, her jaw set squarely. "Until he extends the same love to my people, I will not give him the love of a healer."

Frederik's face froze and then morphed into something she had never seen before. The twinkle in his eyes died and was replaced by a black shadow. His cheeks, normally rounded with smiles, sank as his face elongated with rage. He cocked his head and towered over her.

"Not even if it's an order?"

Roslyn shook her head. How could she have been so naïve? How could she have let herself begin to trust this man, to feel something towards him, when all he was was an arrogant, vicious bully, just like his father and his brother?

"And here I was, thinking that you were different and really wanted peace for this country." She took a step back from him on the wall, still shaking her head. "But I can see now, all you are is a liar."

She turned on her heel and walked as fast as she could out of the garden. She had to get away from him. She couldn't look at him, couldn't even be in his presence lest she strike him or embarrass herself with her emotions.

Perhaps she should have stayed, perhaps she should have done what Eik, the callous bastard, wanted her to. Frederik was still weak, after all. She wouldn't have much time left, the more he recovered his strength. Roslyn sighed as she slipped through the arch that marked the entrance to the garden and leant back on the moss-covered stone. She lifted her head to the sky and breathed out all of her worries and confusion.

Frederik wanted her to heal his father, the man that had brought her country to its knees; the man who had slaughtered not only the Domonovs, the royal family, but so many more; the man who had left most of her generation orphans. How could she even consider it? But, as she thought of her people, she thought of Eik and the rebels, of everything they were fighting for. He was right. It would be so easy. Even if she was caught and put to death, it would make a difference. This could be the Domovnians' chance to fight back, through her. What if, instead of killing Prince Charming, she could go after the big bad wolf himself?

Chapter 18

The day after their walk in the Queen's Garden, King Casimir deemed his son fit enough to attend his duties and Roslyn's dissolved into almost nothing. She still administered the odd pain-relieving draught when she could see the signs of struggle written across the prince's face or when he sent a servant to fetch one. But, being a man, and as is wont of their kind, he rarely admitted to being in pain. However, he did still insist upon the sleeping draught at night, so that was the only time she ever saw him, on her way to bed. When she arose in the mornings, he was already up, dressed and out of the room.

He was back to ignoring her again. Or was it simply that she was no longer needed? He no longer required her services, therefore no longer wished for her company? Either way, it left Roslyn at somewhat of a loss.

No one had said she could go home, but the fact that she was still in the royal apartments and not in a dungeon was a good sign, and she did not want to rock that boat.

Now that the prince needed less medicinal care, she decided to take some of the equipment back down to the apothecary. It was an arduous task, and one that required the help of a servant pushing a trolley. Roslyn herself had helped the poor stablehand who had been commandeered to do it, hoisting the trolley onto her shoulders as they pivoted down the narrow, winding staircase. How they managed not to break anything, she would never know, but she was very grateful they hadn't. That would not have helped her relationship with Apothecary Gruber.

"What are you doing here?" His pompous drawl boomed across the cavern towards her when she entered. A wave of heads lifted from their work and tens of eyes shifted between her and the Head Apothecary uneasily. The clatter of pestles and mortars, the tinkle of glass stirrers all faded away until the only sound was the gentle bubbling of the cauldrons.

"I've come to return these. The prince no longer has need of them."

Gruber sniffed and turned to the stableboy with the trolley.

"You, put them over there against the wall." He turned to a boy wearing the blue robes of an apothecary, a yellow sash tied around his waist to signify he was an apprentice. "And you, wash those beakers, thoroughly. I doubt Miss Pleveli has had time to do it herself."

"Oh, but I have—"

"The boy needs practice. Besides, how could you possibly have got them clean enough up there, where there are no troughs in which to wash them?"

Apothecary Gruber turned to walk away and left Roslyn standing there, taken aback. She had asked the servants to bring up a trough with boiling water and soap with which she cleaned all the instruments, but she thought it best to let that information slide. The tap of Gruber's pernicious footsteps on the stone floor slowed and came to a halt. Then he turned and looked back over his shoulder, raising an eyebrow.

"Why are you still here?"

Roslyn shrugged. "I thought perhaps I could be of assistance; preparing ingredients, washing beakers, visiting some of your patients who live further out in the town?"

Gruber snorted and then threw back his head and laughed until he clutched at his stomach. He stalked back towards Roslyn, his pace quick and menacing, like a snake about to spring.

"Why would I want your help? After that stunt you pulled, getting me near demoted by the crown prince, even though I was only following his orders in the first place! Anyone can see you have talent, girl, but the Oderberg line is discipline and obedience, and if you step outside of that, it's the noose for you. So, I did what I was told, and what I was told nearly got me swinging."

He was breathing heavily, flecks of spittle gathering in the corners of his mouth. "So, you are hereby banished from my apothecary, Roslyn Pleveli. I do not want to see you, I do not want to hear of you. Is that quite clear?"

Roslyn's heart sank. This was the only place she thought she'd actually have anything to do to be useful. She nodded, head bowed, and left the apothecary with her tail between her legs.

✳

After that incident, Roslyn spent her days wandering through the palace. Nobody seemed to notice her anymore. When she first arrived, she'd been the subject of pointed stares and whispers, and the occasional gob of spit. Then she'd graduated to nods of appreciation for what she had done for Frederik, but now it was as if she was a ghost. People looked through her as if she had simply dissolved into the ether. She spent more time than she should have done in the Queen's Garden, acutely aware of how much she missed Hedda, her village and, the Tree be damned, even Eik. She just wanted to go home. No doubt she should have asked someone about that, or tried to find her place in this unfamiliar landscape, but there was no one.

On one such morning, when her spirits were particularly low, she found herself weeding one of the flowerbeds in the garden. She was down on her hands and knees, sleeves rolled up to her elbows, and dirt staining her hands and her forearms. She was lost in the simple act of clearing the earth so that the original plants wouldn't be swamped and had room to grow. Her head was empty, and she thought of nothing but what her hands were doing at that precise moment. She was so absorbed in her task that she didn't hear the footsteps approaching from behind.

"Well, well, well," sang a slimy voice that instantly sent the hairs on the back of her neck reaching for the sky. "If it isn't the little Hedgie, all alone, with nothing to do."

Roslyn sat back on her heels and turned to face the long, golden-haired fop that stood behind her.

"Yannis, isn't it?"

A flash of hatred passed over his face, drawing his thin lips up into an a snarl, but it passed almost immediately

185

and he displayed his sparkling white teeth, like a crocodile enticing its prey.

"It's *Duke* Yannis, to you."

Roslyn bowed her head in humble apology and looked at him expectantly. "How can I help you, Duke Yannis?"

The tall, slim noble sauntered towards her and rested one elbow on the outstretched palm of the statue, placing his weight on his right leg and crossing his left over it. He waved his long-fingered hand in circular motions as he spoke.

"Well, I just wanted to make sure that you are being treated correctly, as a guest of the prince." He looked around theatrically and opened his mouth in a surprised gasp. "But where is he? You are all alone, my dear, and that is simply not right."

He suddenly lurched from his position and bounded yet another step towards her, coming down onto one knee to the gravel beside her. She was relieved to see a grimace of pain flicker across his smug face as the stones dug into his flesh and tore his silken stockings, but that soon passed. He leant into her and let his eyes wander.

He was heavily scented and his breath smelled like mint, none of which was in itself untoward, but on this leering, lecherous fool, it was nauseating.

"How about, Miss Pleveli, you and I take a tour of the town? I can show you many a fine tavern." He reached up and traced a line up her arm with one of his freakishly long fingers. "They do the most splendid luncheons, and then afterwards we could also sample their linens if it pleases you." Roslyn tried to back away, but tripped on the hem of her skirt and found herself flat on her back, staring up at him.

186

"No, no!" She tried to right herself, but he was too quick to take advantage of her mishap.

"Oh, shall we skip the tour then, Miss Pleveli? I didn't know you were that keen."

Roslyn thrust her dirty hands out to stop him from leaning over her. "I said no!"

Yannis grabbed her wrists and wrenched them apart, flinging her back into the soil she had just been tending. His face was a painting of greed and anger at having been denied.

"What, is a Duke not good enough for you, Hedgie? Any girl, let alone a Domovnian would think it is an honour to be bedded by myself or any other of the Oderberg lords, but it's not enough for you, is it? No, you're after the prince himself!" He laughed cruelly, a high-pitched sound, and sneered as he twisted the skin round her wrists, making her cry out. He pressed his weight against her and she felt the hardness of him through her skirts. It made her sick. Hot tears spilled down the sides of her face as she fought with all her might, but couldn't even make him struggle to contain her. He was well practised at this and stronger than he looked.

Frantically, she looked around and saw the young shoot of a nettle poking up from the soil. She called on her Affinity with urgency and the weed coiled up from the rich brown earth and, at her bidding, unfurled itself right across her attacker's face. Yannis swore and yanked the stem away, crushing it and Roslyn's hopes in his hand as easily as if it were straw. What had she been thinking?

"Well, I can definitely show you something that Prince Limp cannot. Now, do be a dear, and shut up."

Roslyn screamed and, finally wrestling an arm free, slapped him round the face with her soil-encrusted hand.

187

As Yannis sat back in consternation, touching his own hand to this spot where she'd hit him, she rolled out from underneath him and scrambled to her feet. She tried to run, but he had stalked her against the wall to block her exit. She was cornered. He was on his feet again and grabbed her by the throat, pressing her up against the lichen-covered wall behind her. Tears poured from her eyes, and as much as she scrabbled and scratched and kicked, she could not get his weight off her. She could not stop his hand squeezing around her throat as his eyes narrowed with hatred.

"No one denies Duke Yannis."

"I do!" a familiar voice shouted from behind her attacker and a whimper escaped her lips.

A thud sounded, and Yannis's eyes widened and went blank. His hands slackened from her throat and he slumped to the ground at her feet.

Roslyn gasped and looked around wildly as she tried to get her breath back.

Never in her life had she been so relieved to see the polished boots and ridiculous moustache smeared across Captain Dietrich's lip. Though flooded with gratitude, it was not for the captain that Roslyn felt indebtedness. Her rescuer stood over Yannis, cane in hand and breathing hard. It was Prince Frederik. She sobbed audibly as he stepped towards her, sweeping her up in his arms.

"Are you alright? Roslyn? Are you hurt?" He gripped her so tightly, running his hands over her face, checking for any injuries and she clung to him until the shaking in her limbs subsided.

"I'm… I'm fine."

Frederik released her, and she gulped at the fire in his eyes. "No, you are not. You were nearly raped by someone

188

I once considered a friend, by someone I knew had their eye on you." He loomed over the unconscious man and gripped the cane, as if he was about to raise it again.

Roslyn lunged forward and took his hand, turning him away from the Duke, forcing his eyes up to hers. She stroked his cheek as his breathing slowed. "Your highness… Look at me. I may be shaken, but I am not physically harmed. I am alright."

She held the prince's hand while the rage drained from his face, leaving it long with sorrow and bitterness.

"I shall have him sent back to Fladby in disgrace for what he has done to you." He nodded to Captain Dietrich, who clanked back towards the palace and hollered for his men to take Duke Yannis away. The prince led her to a bench. They sat, but he did not relinquish her hands. "I am so sorry, Roslyn. This is all my fault."

"How exactly is Yannis being a pig your fault?"

"Because I brought you here, I put you in his line of vision, knowing very well what he is like—"

"And you made it very clear to him not to touch me. This is all on him."

Frederik shook his head and looked down at their joined hands. "But I've been locked up in meetings with my father." It was only now that she noticed the purple smears under his eyes and the gauntness of his cheeks. He was exhausted. "You've been alone, and I failed to place a guard with you… thought you wouldn't want to be treated as a prisoner."

Roslyn smiled and patted his hand. "Well, that's true. I wouldn't have taken kindly to that. You gave me some freedom and I appreciate that."

They fell silent as the palace guards picked the duke up by his arms and legs, lugging him between them like a sack of flour.

"Aren't you going to get in trouble for that?"

Frederik sniffed and straightened his back, finally releasing her hand. "No, I'm the prince; I can do what I like…" He shrugged, the shadow of a smile on his lips. "Well, maybe a little, but he deserved it."

She leant over his shoulder and placed a gentle kiss on his smooth cheek. "Thank you."

The prince looked up at her slowly, his lips grazing hers as she moved backwards. He grinned sheepishly, a pink smear painting his cheeks as Roslyn's own burst into a fiery heat.

"Does that pay off my life debt?"

She smiled and nodded, leaning in to kiss him again. "Close enough."

A cough sounded and a pageboy bobbed before them. "Apologies, your highness, but the recess is over and your presence has been missed. You are wanted back in the council room."

Frederik nodded at the boy who scurried away and shook his head. "I don't want to leave you alone again Roslyn… and I won't." He clicked his fingers and Captain Dietrich appeared. "Until the council is over, Dietrich will watch over you."

Roslyn's sigh was matched by the drooping of the guard's moustache into a frown.

"It won't be for long. Come on, you two. I want you to be friends. You are both dear to me." The prince reached out a hand to both of them. Bashfully, they accepted, but neither could hide their look of horror as Frederik placed Roslyn's hand in the captain's.

"Take good care of her, captain."

With a final grin at their stunned faces, the prince hobbled out of the gardens.

The second he was out of sight, Roslyn and Captain Dietrich dropped their hands.

The Oderberg guard clicked his heels together and bowed his head brusquely. "I am glad you are well. You really shouldn't wander the corridors alone, Miss Pleveli. You are a Domovnian in a strange land."

"This land is my own." More than he knew, Roslyn thought forcefully. Captain Dietrich nodded his apology.

"What I meant to say is, Miss Pleveli, you are an attractive young woman, and it is not safe for you as an indigenous here in the Oderberg stronghold."

Roslyn stopped and put a hand on her hip, cocking her head to the side and looking up at him quizzically. "I don't understand. When first we met, it was you making the threats of assault in front of your soldiers, and now you want to protect me from it?"

Captain Dietrich looked at the ground and sighed. When he looked up again, Roslyn was amazed to see that his countenance had changed. His face had dropped from its poker-straight mask to a softer, more open expression. His eyes, instead of uninterested and unfocused, honed in on her with sincerity.

"When one is approached with a potential threat, and is in front of a group of subordinates, it is necessary to say things one does not mean. I despise it, but that is how one gains respect in this castle. One must be a 'man'." He rolled his eyes. "Or rather, the king's version of what a man should be."

Roslyn nodded, understanding if not entirely condoning his prior behaviour. "Then I would be thankful for your protection and some company." She shrugged her shoulders and gave a lopsided, closed-mouth smile. It was returned with a twitch of that bottlebrush moustache and a twinkle in the captain's eye.

The guard cleared his throat. "Do you ride, Miss Pleveli?"

Roslyn's heart began to pound. Her eyes widened, and she shook her head furiously. Horses terrified her. They were just so enormous.

"Ah, that will delay things…" Captain Dietrich's face fell for an instant. "Nevertheless, meet me in the stable yard after breakfast tomorrow morning. I shall teach you."

He clacked his metal boots together and stomped back down the narrow corridor, not waiting for an answer. Roslyn was left quaking. She didn't know which terrified her more: the prospect of spending a day with Prince Frederik's man-at-arms, or being on the back of a horse.

Chapter 19

The next morning, Roslyn lurked in the archway that led out to the stables and horse yard. She looked about fearfully, seeing no sign of Captain Dietrich. Breathing a sigh of relief, she was about to walk away when a voice called out to her from the shadows of the stables.

"And where do you think you're going, Miss Pleveli?" Captain Dietrich ambled towards her, smiling, holding a small horse by the reins.

Roslyn grunted and walked out of her hiding place. The captain looked her up and down nodded appreciatively. She had thought about this a little. Thankfully, the day she'd been taken from her village, she'd been wearing good sturdy boots, necessary for foraging in the woodlands. She also had on her workday clothes so as not to dirty her best ones, but the skirt only came up to just below her knee. She was slightly worried about how she was going to manage the elegant side-saddle that the Oderberg ladies used when riding, usually with velvet cloth covering their legs and toes, making them appear liked colourful whipped cream swirls on top of their horses.

Roslyn now eyed up the animal Captain Dietrich was holding by the reins. It wasn't overly large, and for that, she was thankful. She noted also the greying of its coat in various places and how easily it let itself be led.

"This is Marble. She is getting on in years, but she's docile and will give you a pleasant ride."

Roslyn grunted again and looked at the saddle and stirrups.

"How does one... ascend?"

The captain laughed a genuine laugh, one that set his eyes twinkling and washed away the worries on his face, making him seem almost friendly.He patted the metal of the stirrup with one hand and the pommel of the saddle with the other. "Put one hand up here, on the saddle. That's what you will used to pull yourself up when your foot is in the stirrup."

Roslyn looked at the instrument in question and the height of it off the ground, and then turned with wide eyes towards her instructor. "How on earth do you expect me to get my foot that high up?"

The captain smiled and shrugged. "We have two options: one, I can get you a stepping stool and you could do it from there. Or—" He grasped her around the waist and hoisted her up so that her buttocks rested on his shoulder. "—I could just give you a leg up."

Roslyn would have shrieked at the indignity had she not been marvelling at the captain's unsuspecting strength, and concentrating so much on holding onto the saddle for dear life. She slipped her left foot into the stirrup they had been discussing and hung there, arse out into the air and knuckles white as she gripped the pommel.

"Now what?"

"Now, you swing your other leg over to the other side of the saddle. Once you're up, you'll find another stirrup there that you put your foot into."

Roslyn nodded and took a deep breath while hurling her other leg over the back of Marble, who wasn't in the least bit bothered about the commotion taking place on her back. There was a frightening moment where Roslyn nearly fell straight off the other side, but she managed to right herself, thanking the core muscles she didn't know she had, and breathed a shaky sigh of relief as she slipped her right foot into the other stirrup.

"That wasn't so bad, was it?" Captain Dietrich smirked as he went round adjusting straps on the saddle and the stirrups, making sure everything was in order.

"Aren't I supposed to ride like the other ladies?"

"Are you a lady?" Dietrich raised an eyebrow but then blew out from behind the strands of his moustache. "I have no experience of that, so cannot instruct you. Besides, from what I hear, it's uncomfortable and awkward. This is the best way to ride."

He waved to a stable hand to bring his own mount over. Roslyn watched with absolute embarrassment at the ease with which he stepped up and swung his leg over, a movement so fluid, he must've been doing it since birth. How he had not laughed at her attempt, she did not know.

Once he was on his own horse, he reached over and showed Roslyn how to hold the reins in her hands, but she noticed he also attached a rope to Marble's bridal.

"Just a precaution, as you're nervous."

Roslyn nodded her thanks and shifted in her seat as the horses began to show their impatience.

"So, where are we going?"

Captain Dietrich made a *tsk* sound and gave his horse the slightest of taps with his foot, and just like that, they were moving.

"I thought we'd get you out of the city for a bit, do some foraging or whatever it is you like to do."

Roslyn had heard his answer, but with the sudden movement of Marble she was concentrating far too much on staying upright to reply. She was also wracked with fear that she would have to ride through the streets of Novlada, a beacon of Oderberg hatred for all to see. But Captain Dietrich led her round to a door she hadn't noticed before.

He nodded at the guards on either side, and as the door swung open, they entered a cool, dark tunnel. This did not put her much more at ease, but the longer they walked through it, the less she heard the noises of the city and the castle behind her. Finally, they reached an iron gate, sunlight streaming through it, a meadow beyond. Again, Captain Dietrich nodded to the man positioned at the exit and suddenly they were out of the castle, out of the capital, and Roslyn could breathe.

A tremendous weight lifted off her shoulders as the sun beamed down on them and she smiled until her cheeks hurt. The sea of grass was dotted with colour; the red of poppies, the yellow of buttercups and the brilliant blue, somewhat like that of Prince Frederik's eyes, of cornflowers. She must have made a noise of joy because Captain Dietrich looked over at her and shared in her delight.

"I thought we could head to the forest and have some lunch by a stream that runs there. Hoff knows, it's too hot in that damned castle in midsummer. Then you can look for your plants, if you wish."

He nodded towards the far end of the meadow where a line of trees was just visible beyond the dip of the hill.

Roslyn narrowed her eyes and said in a soft voice, "Is it safe to leave the castle and go into the woods alone?"

The captain shrugged and looked her in the eye. "You tell me. You're the Domovnian. This is your land. I don't know if anyone is waiting out there. Do you?"

Roslyn shook her head fiercely. Was that what this was about? He wanted to see where her loyalties lay, see if she had been tricking them this whole time? But she wasn't going to throw away the chance of an afternoon of freedom in the summer sun.

"None that I know of. I haven't heard from anyone since I got here and haven't even been able to write to Hedda."

The captain moved the horses on and they crossed the meadow, insects buzzing around them as they ambled slowly, enjoying the landscape.

"Hedda is your mother?"

"No, no. I was orphaned, like many of my generation… on a night we need not speak of." She saw Captain Dietrich bow his head in acknowledgement. "Hedda is the woman who raised me. She is not Descendant, she has no Affinity, but she is a herbalist and a very skilled one. So, I guess it was just as well when I didn't develop much of an Affinity, that I was already under her tutelage. Gave me some sort of purpose."

Her riding companion shifted in his saddle. "And you think a purpose is needed in life, do you?"

Roslyn thought about this for a moment and then shrugged. "Well, it certainly helps to feel useful and needed by your community. Rather than just spending it in dreary existence doing nothing, or worse, exploiting those around you." She bit her lip and changed tack. "Talking of purpose in life, why has the prince, who I was told was a partying whoremonger… why has he suddenly given all that up, after a lifetime of arrogance and privilege? Or so I've heard from the castle gossips."

They were almost at the end of the meadow. Captain Dietrich didn't say anything until they were under the shade of the trees. The heat of the midday sun was fierce now, and they were both grateful for the canopy that stretched over them. He slipped down off his mount and tied the reins around a tree. He did the same to Marble, and then approached the horse's side and looked up at Roslyn. His eyes were heavy and his lips moved, as if he was about to say something. But he only reached out his arms to help her down and then turned away.

Roslyn was suddenly worried she'd crossed some sort of line yet again, and followed the soldier in silence towards the bubbling brook she could hear not far away.

"Frederik and I," Captain Dietrich began in an unsteady voice, questioning his choice of words before speaking them. "We fell in together, as boys. He was playing some sort of prank on his brother, I know not what, but he was about to get the beating of his life down in the old quarter. I was a child fairly used to beatings, and seeing someone smaller than myself about to be pummelled by someone twice his size… I couldn't stand it. He was an angel child, in his rich velvet britches and golden curls bobbing around the place. He was a target not only for his brother, but for every thief or vagabond in the city. So, I challenged Viktor." A wry smile appeared in one corner of his mouth at the memory.

He continued. "Needless to say, I did not come out of that fight very well, but it saved Frederik a nasty black eye. After that, we were inseparable. We'd play for hours, running up and down the streets of Novlada, imagining we were Olaf Oderberg and Hoff. As we got older, our antics turned more mischievous and as one of us would steal apples or hot chestnuts, the other would keep look out crying, 'Isapf comes as the fat man in white', or some such thing, describing whomever had clocked what we were up to…" Dietrich smiled at the memory, his voice thick with reminiscence. "He snuck out the palace so often to play with me in the streets, that his mother decided it would be far more appropriate that they brought me into his service. The master-at-arms trained us together; he as the Lord, me as his squire, and thus we grew up in each other's company."

They had reached the river now, and he lowered the pack from his shoulders, untied the toggle and brought out a blanket which he spread on the ground. He motioned for Roslyn to sit and did so himself, removing his steel boots and the sweat-drenched socks beneath, and stuck his feet into the shallows of the brook with a relieved sigh. He sat there, feet in the water, elbows on his knees, and stared into the forest.

"I know everything about Frederik, and he knows everything about me. We had many firsts together—first arse kicking by the master-at-arms, first drinks together, first visit to a whore house."

Roslyn tried to stifle a shocked gasp.

"The rumours you heard of him were true. Once we were of age and there was no war to be going off to, Prince Viktor having taken on the role of the military commander in his father's stead, we were at a loss as to what to do. We spent many nights in the taverns, in the whorehouses and then he set his sights on the ladies of court whilst I worked my way through the servants." He said it with a little regret in his voice, then turned and met her eye. Roslyn detected a hint of deep sorrow in them. "So, yes he was a rake, but I believe that Frederik didn't use those women, as I did my lovers, for self-satisfaction. You see, he has a tendency to truly love whoever he is with in the moment... but then it passes and his exhilarating love lands on another." His voice dipped to an almost inaudible level, but she heard his heartbreak in the whispered words, "I, of all people, should know."

Roslyn unpacked the hamper to give him time with his thoughts, uncorking a bottle with her teeth and pouring out two glasses of wine, one for herself and one for the captain.

"But it all became stale and all the lovers we thought were exciting were now no longer that. They wanted stability, and that was not what we were looking for. Frederik decided to travel. He wanted to go to see more of the world and to study for a year in Teadmis, at the 'University of Kings'. It is a well-known place of study for all the royals and nobles on the continent. It is surprising that Prince Viktor didn't attend himself, but he insisted there were more important things that needed doing here and—let's be honest—he was gifted more brawn than brains.

"Anyway, as soon as we were out of the palace, Frederik told me of his plan to travel incognito. He wanted to see the land and the world for what it really was, not through the eyes of a prince who had everything laid out before him, but as one of the people. When I asked him why, he said it was because of some comments from the women he'd bedded. Even though they were all Oderbergs, there was something resentful in the way they

200

spoke to him. So, he blackened his hair with charcoal and I grew this moustache." A wry smile lifted the corner of his mouth and Roslyn chuckled.

"What? It's all the rage in the Summerlands for men… in certain circles." He raised the wineglass to his lips and pulled a face as he drank. Then he rose, picked up the bottle and placed it in the flowing water of the brook to cool it down. He knocked back the first glass, wincing, most likely due to the vinegary heat of it, and sighed.

"But our new disguises didn't bring him joy, although they did open his eyes. On the way to the coast, we saw the atrocities the Oderberg soldiers had committed in the name of his father. At first, he didn't want to believe the king had ordered such things. The first time we witnessed a public flogging in a market square he thought it was just one band of rogue soldiers who took their responsibilities too far. But then, as we travelled, we saw the same thing, time and time again. We saw worse than that; we saw soldiers taking women away from their families to be raped, we saw them kicking old men in the dirt, we saw them taking what little food the Domovnians had, leaving them to starve. He wanted to do something, wanted to say something, but when he tried, they set their sights on him as their next victim. He vowed there and then that he would find a way to set this right and so we made all haste to Teadmis."

He walked up and down the stream a little, gathering his thoughts as Roslyn pecked at the bread and fruits in the basket. She was listening, but her rumbling stomach got the better of her and she couldn't help herself any more.

"And that's what he did? He learnt at the University how he can bring peace to Domovnia?" Roslyn mumbled around a mouthful of grapes.

Captain Dietrich laughed coldly and shook his head. "In a way he did, but things only got worse abroad. The other royals disdained his presence. Once they knew he was the son of King Casimir, they said his father was a brute, a dictator. Everything they were doing to Domovnians was all but genocide."

Roslyn raised her eyebrows and sipped her wine. She didn't need to say anything.

"The attack on Domovnia was as much an attack on their lands, they said. When Eluha fell, and the Domonovs killed, the magic powering the Anchors at Yakir and Spiranse also fell, letting in the sea wyrms that ravage the coasts. As much as Frederik tried to defend his father, he couldn't… Just as he couldn't defend himself when those other princes and dukes taught him a lesson."

His face had darkened, and his voice lowered to a croak. His eyes were far away in the past, in an awful moment that etched sorrow and guilt all over his face.

"I should have helped him. That was my job, to protect my prince from anything. But how could I draw a sword on other royals, on other princes? Their men would have strung me up before you could even blink. Frederik knew it, so he forbade me from helping; not that I could have. They held me down. All I could do was watch as they beat my master to the ground and kicked him again and again and again until he was nearly dead. *That* is when he changed, Miss Pleveli."

He met her eyes with a resentful stare. "He changed when he saw what his father had done, not only to the Domovnians, but also to the reputation of the Oderbergs.

202

He has made them a despised peoples across the whole continent. Surrounding kingdoms are bolstering their defences across the borders. *That* is when Frederik changed, when all the joy and carefree exuberance of life was beaten out of him on the shit-stained cobbles of a dockyard. That limp, the one you've been treating, wasn't from any boar attack."

Roslyn was aware that her mouth was hanging open, her brows furrowed in emotion as everything she knew about the prince, everything she had presumed, was swirling around inside her stomach, turning the grapes to acid. "He got it that night."

Captain Dietrich nodded and hissed through his teeth. "When he was all but dead. They stretched out his legs and jumped on them, so that if he lived, he would have to crawl back home." His voice shook with rage. "They left him. They left my best friend to die in the dirt because of what his father had done twenty-five years before, because of what his father continues to do to the Domovnians."

He put his head in his hands and breathed heavily, trying to regain his sense of composure, which had all but dissolved as his tale had progressed. When he looked back up at Roslyn, his eyes were rimmed with the purple of wariness.

"We told him he wasn't fit enough to go after that boar, but I don't think he cared. I think the reason he went after it was because he wanted it to injure him. He didn't want anyone to know that that limp had come from an arse kicking in the Kestian capital, even though he knew it could kill him. He is still a proud man…" Captain Dietrich half chuckled. "But he also didn't want his father's wrath to come down on those who did it to him. How would that help matters? So, regardless of how hard you try, Miss

Pleveli, that limp is here to stay and it will always be a reminder of what the Oderbergs have become."

Roslyn didn't know what to say, so she didn't say anything. She pulled her knees close to her and looked around as she tried to digest the information about the man she'd been tending. She had assumed he was some pampered, arrogant fool whose emotions changed like the winds, but now she saw there was reason to it. There was a reason to the melancholy that had possessed him for several days; a reason he was now sat in negotiations with his father discussing an Assimilation Act between the Domovnians and the Oderbergs.

Dietrich sat down again, pulling the bottle from the brook and taking a large swig. Then he tucked into the food. The conversation was over, or at least, he thought it was. Roslyn rose. Her hands were shaking, her blood boiling inside her veins at the injustice of it all. Not only had that decrepit old bastard Casimir destroyed her country, but he had also got his son near beaten to death, all so he could expand his empire. Right now, Eik's words spoke sense, and she vowed that if she ever got near him, she *would* kill him. But how? The apothecaries had taken anything of any threat, no matter how small, from her satchel.

Captain Dietrich looked up at her as she huffed and fought back tears. She needed to calm down. She set about walking up and down the bank, collecting small, useful plants that she could dry and keep in her satchel. She found some more wild mint and of course dandelion root, which she tucked away with the Lady Margitte in mind. As she went, she reached out to the plants she touched, to the trees above, searching, trying to sense some kind of Affinity with them. If she was the lost princess, she should have Botan powers, shouldn't she? But nothing stirred save her two constants, the nettle and the dandelion. Frustrated, she grumbled. There must be more to it. Perhaps Botans weren't born, but created?

She'd wandered some way by the time her rage had fizzled to a steady resentment, when she saw something that made her stop in her tracks. There, a little way from the bank in the grasses that led back to the meadow, beckoned small white flowers. They were very similar at first glance to the yarrow with which she had saved Frederik's life, but she knew it was something far more dangerous—hemlock.

She glanced over her shoulder, but the soldier was stretched out on the riverbank, his arms folded over his head as he snoozed. She tiptoed off the stones of the bank and fumbled in her satchel. Hurriedly, she pulled out one of the rags that she always carried with her in case her bleeds came in, and wrapped it around the stem of the poisonous plant. With a yank, she pulled up the root, shaking off most of the dirt. The tuber swung by her side, hidden from view by her skirts as she scurried back to the river to wash it. She needed to hide it somewhere safe, but the secret pockets in her satchel were far too small. With shaking hands, she wrapped the root in the rag and shoved it down between her breasts. Behind the stiff fabric of her stays, no one would notice her smuggling in one of the deadliest plants known to man.

When she walked back to the captain, he started at her footsteps and looked around lazily.

"We better be getting back."

Roslyn nodded, and they packed up their belongings and made their way back to the horses. Just before Captain Dietrich helped her to mount Marble, she looked up at him, her hand on the pommel, left leg in the stirrup, but she wouldn't let him hoist her. She looked into his eyes and asked, "This Assimilation Act. Do you think he can do it? Do you think it is possible to change everything, to make the Domovnians and the Oderbergs great again... peaceful?"

Captain Dietrich was misty eyed. "They have inflicted too many wrongs in Domovnia. Only a miracle could bring peace to both parties now."

Roslyn allowed herself to be hoisted onto the back of her horse, her heart heavy and her head full of questions.

They were silent as they rode back to the city, lost in their own thoughts, when suddenly a horde of riders thundered down the dusty road towards them. Messengers. Dietrich only just managed to get them off the path in time.

"Isapf's cunt!" he roared. "Come on—something's happened."

He kicked the horses into as fast a trot as Roslyn could manage, her teeth rattling around her skull as they rode. As they crossed under the portcullis, the noise of uproar met them. A town crier in the square was ringing his bell madly to get attention as the surrounding crowd jostled and called out jeers and jests.

"Hear ye! Hear ye!" After a few rounds of shouting, the crowd finally subdued enough so that the crier's words could be heard over their heads.

"On this day, the sixth of midsummer, His majesty King Casimir von Oderberg has proclaimed an Assimilation Act between the peoples of Domovnia and Bergam." The crowd erupted into confused shouts. Roslyn turned to Captain Dietrich, mouth wide open, and

206

found he was staring tight-lipped at the town crier, his face turning a strange shade of pink.

"From this day forth," the town crier continued, "Domovnians may enter the towns and settlements of the Oderbergs. They may reside within them and trade their wares. They need no longer be restricted to the ghettos or slums. They are to be treated as citizens of Bergam, and will be given a fair trial for any misdemeanours, but their use of magic is still strictly prohibited. Any man, woman or child found aggravating a Domovnian without just cause will be punished. Now is a time for peace and a time for prosperity."

Roslyn didn't hear the rest over the clamour of the crowd. She turned to Dietrich and grabbed his arm excitedly. "He did it… He really did it!"

The captain turned to her and smiled in amazement, shaking his head slightly in awe.

"He did it," he repeated. "How the fuck did he do it?" He swallowed, and a shadow passed over his face. "But will it be enough?"

Chapter 20

It was a hard slog to get back to the castle through the chaos that had erupted in the streets, but Captain Dietrich led her and Marble admirably through it all. Not once was she in fear for her life, even though there were Oderberg citizens protesting her very right to be there, but either they were too swept up in their emotions, or they didn't see her in the crush, so she was left undisturbed.

The palace was in a similar uproar, but one of a more productive nature, punctuated by regular exclamations of disbelief. The kitchens were a hot, steaming factory where scullery maids and kitchen boys ran around carrying baskets, bringing meat and cheeses up from the cellars, and a whole host of chefs were hurriedly preparing a surprise banquet to celebrate the Act.

Again, Captain Dietrich escorted her through the crush, commandeering a tray as they passed that held two bowls of hearty vegetable soup and a whole loaf of bread. He handed these to Roslyn, who he had positioned in an out of the way corner, and returned into the fray, coming back with arms laden full of butter, glasses, plates and a bottle of wine.

"Come on." He looked around furtively, but no one had noticed him. They had far too many other things to be doing. "Let's go to Frederik's apartments. I doubt he will use it tonight."

Roslyn nodded in agreement and followed him as he pushed the kitchen door with his shoulder and moved into the warren of servants' passageways beyond. Roslyn's heart sank at his words; of course Prince Frederik wouldn't be there. He had probably changed for the royal banquet and been seated in the Great Hall before they'd even made it back to the castle. She shook her head to rid herself of the thought and climbed the staircase.

Once seated in the strange calm of the prince's sitting room, Roslyn and Captain Dietrich ate in silence. She found, to her surprise, that she was well used to him by now and settled in his company. It only became uneasy as the night wore on—the food had run out, they'd drunk the bottle of wine that they'd pilfered from the kitchens, leaving Roslyn feeling a tad lightheaded and sleepy, but still no Prince arrived. Finally, the last bell chimed, and Captain Dietrich stood and clicked his heels together, bowing towards Roslyn.

"I do not think any harm will come to you tonight, Miss Pleveli, so, with your permission, I will take my leave and find my bed."

Roslyn nodded, trying as hard as she could to keep her eyelids open. "Thank you, for today."

She expected him to retort with 'only doing my duty' or some other such thing, but the captain paused at the doorway, stroked his moustache thoughtfully and shrugged. "It was my pleasure, Miss Pleveli."

"Please, call me Roslyn."

The small smile spread across his face, opening his lips to reveal a fine set of teeth. "Good night then, Roslyn."

He bowed again and then was out the door. Roslyn sat staring at the fire. She did not know for how long, but her eyes were itchy with tiredness when she decided to make her way to bed. It was at that moment that the door to the apartments swung open.

Frederik loomed at the centre, both leaning on his cane and using the door as a support. He wobbled and looked around with unfocused eyes.He was drunk, but Roslyn's heart beat just that little bit faster at the sight of his rakish grin.

Before he could speak, she ran to his side. He was about to brush her away, protesting that he didn't need any help, when as much to her surprise as his, she found her arms around his neck and she was pulling him into an embrace. He stiffened with shock at her sudden and impromptu rush of emotion, but after a moment he relaxed and she felt one hand sneak around her waist and grip ever so slightly.

"I don't know how you did it," Roslyn said breathlessly. She stepped back, a flush of embarrassment painting her cheeks at the sudden proximity. "But thank you. Thank you from the bottom of my heart, from all of my people. Thank you!"

Prince Frederik smiled sadly and straightened himself, his hand gripping his cane so much that it shook a little. He nodded his head and turned his cobalt eyes towards her own. She couldn't tear her eyes away from him. She tried to, but then found herself staring at his fine cheekbones, his golden curls and the fullness of his lips that were slightly apart and wet with the memory of wine.

Frederik cleared his throat, no hint of joy in his voice at what he had accomplished—simply exhaustion.

"I upheld my end of the bargain, Miss Pleveli." It was then that she noticed the dark circles under his eyes, the tightness in his jaw and the effort it took him to stay upright after days of bargaining with his father—the man that she would have to heal. "Now, it's time for you to do yours."

*

A comely little maid roused Roslyn early the next morning. She was bid to dress in her finest clothes, but the maid held out an apron for her to wear over them.

"Where am I going?" Roslyn asked the girl, who could not have been more than fourteen.

The maid looked at her with a puzzled expression, one eyebrow arched until it disappeared into her fringe.

"Why, to see the king, of course." The girl smiled wryly and rolled her eyes. "It would appear his majesty had too much to drink last night and is in need of some remedies. Prince Frederik suggested you as he went to bed last night, as you were so skilled healing him."

Roslyn sighed and nodded her head. A cover story for why she was seeing the king. So, whatever his illness was, it wasn't common knowledge yet. If it had been, no doubt Eik and the rebels would have attacked before now. A chill ran down her spine as she thought about how ominously silent they had been of late. It was well past the last moon of spring when they had planned to meet, but

211

no rebel attacks had been reported by the Oderberg soldiers.

Instead of descending the steps to the great Hall or the throne room, Roslyn was led through the back passages behind the royal apartments, which were only used by a select few of the staff. These were the hallways that led directly into the chambers of the king and the princes. They stopped in the dusty, dark hallway outside a door where one small torch hung to the side. The young girl knocked three times and then waited. She looked over at Roslyn without moving her head.

"He's not as frightening as he seems," she said jovially, trying to make the healer more at ease, "but then again, I'm not Domovnian, so…"

Roslyn had no time to find out what the maid was going to say because the door swung open and they were blinded by the light from the room beyond. A steward looked her up and down and then turned to the young maid.

"I'll take her from here, Heidi. Off you go."

He didn't give them any further instructions, just turned and walked back into the king's sitting room. Roslyn followed, her palms slick with sweat, making it hard to hold on to her satchel. The steward led her to the fireplace and a high-back chair in which was sat the dishevelled and exhausted form of King Casimir von Oderberg.

Roslyn stifled a gasp. Although he had not seemed well the first time she'd met him, the man before her now seemed to have crumpled in on himself over the space of a few weeks. His hair was thin, almost non-existent, and what remained stuck up in tufts. His cheeks were so gaunt, they seem stretched over his cheekbones like vellum, his skin having taken on a yellowish tinge. He waved a shaking hand at the steward to dismiss him and then motioned to the stool opposite him.

"So, you seem to have done a good job healing my son." He paused and narrowed his eyes, which were still shrewd and cunning, despite the rest of his decaying appearance. "Tell me, Domovnian, will his limp ever heal?"

Roslyn swallowed, finding a lump in her throat. She tried to clear it, but it wouldn't budge.

"It may, your majesty, but then again it may not. As long as he does not push himself too hard and uses his cane whilst he is still healing, then I see no reason he shouldn't have a full recovery." She knew now from her conversation with the prince's man-at-arms that it never would, but looking at the man before her, he didn't have the time to find out for himself.

Casimir nodded and sank deeper into his chair. He placed his elbows on the armrests and steepled his fingers together by his lips. "You know why you have been summoned here?"

Roslyn gave a half nod. "Prince Frederik said that you had been feeling unwell of late."

The king scoffed and snorted so loudly that he made her jump, but his laughter soon subsided into a coughing fit. She jumped from her seat and poured him a glass of water from the table beside him, inwardly cursing Frederik for having read her so well. She had to help the sick, no matter who they were. He took the glass with shaking hands and gulped at the rim, half its contents spilling down his fur-lined morning robe. He waved her away irritably and she sat down again, lowering her eyes as he wiped the spillage away.

"I have been ill for quite some time, yes. Now, I know what is wrong with me, but I want to see if you do. I want to see if you have any other solutions than my brown nosing, stuck-in-their-ways healers…" he paused, and when she looked up into his eyes, she saw fear there, the fear that she had seen many times before and hadn't expected to see in the king. "In essence, Domovnian, you are my second and last opinion."

Roslyn's heart sank and her limbs moved as if made of lead. She rose from her stool and took out some instruments from her satchel. She blew on her hands to warm them and then raised the king's shirt, conducting a full examination of the man, just as if he were the brewer or a beggar in the street.

The first thing she noticed was the large a growth on the lower right side of his abdomen, the skin stretched shiny over the mass. It had taken on a strange purplish hue and throbbed with his pulse. Here was a man who was very ill, indeed. He answered her questions fully and honestly, no matter how invasive.

Casimir groaned when she put her hands to the growth and pressed ever so lightly. She glanced up at him sharply, and saw that his face had drained of blood, the yellowness that had stained his skin suddenly more visible. As his eyes rolled back in his head and he made a sound as if to vomit, Roslyn snatched her hands away. She had seen enough. It was with a heavy sigh that she sat back down and wrung her hands in her apron.

"Your Majesty, I am afraid to tell you that you have the swelling sickness and it is very advanced, most likely it has taken root in the pancreas. There is little I can do for

214

you. All I can do is to make you comfortable… until it runs its course."

"Until I die, you mean?"

She bowed her head and looked him levelly in the eye.

She'd expected ravings, expected him to call for his guards and have her dragged down to the dungeons, but the man before her simply nodded.

"No doubt there are many, yourself included," he gave a wry smile, "that think I've earned this. Comfortable is what I want in the end, and if you can help me hold on a little longer, until my son is wed, then I would be very grateful." Roslyn's heart tightened at his remark. Which son? Frederik? "My son says you have amazing sleeping draughts. In fact, he gave me one of your concoctions last night, and I found it to be most effective."

"I can make you something stronger than that, your majesty. I can make you ones for daytime to chase the pain away, and others for night, to ensure you have a good sleep."

King Casimir stared at her over his gnarled fingers and then laughed again, more gently this time, so as not to induce another coughing fit.

"Well, I would have said before that you'd try to kill me with your potions, and you may very well yet. Go on… have at it. I'm dying anyway, but just leave me enough time to get my affairs in order. You will speak of this to no one, especially not my sons. I will tell them in my own time." He coughed and brought his hand to his throat. He rubbed at the spot, clearing his throat again and again, and as he removed his hand, he brushed away the collar of his nightshirt, revealing a thick, ugly scar that ran across his neck from his left ear to his right shoulder. It was old and had not healed well at the time of injury—the scar tissue was bulbous and swollen.

Roslyn gasped at the sight of it and the king looked down to see what had brought on such a reaction from her.

"Go on, ask away." His voice was etched with weariness but there was the faintest of glints in his eyes.

"How—how did you get that scar? I've never seen one in that place on…"

"On a living man?" the king supplemented. Roslyn nodded, feeling an embarrassed flush rising in her cheeks. The king took little notice of it and stared into the fire.

"I got this twenty-five years ago, on a night that gave me my son's name. Viktor. We were victorious that night when we took this land for our own, but it would appear that all victories have their price."

He touched his hand to the scar again and traced along its length with his spindly fingers. "The Domonov Queen gifted me this." He gave a wry chuckle and the hairs rose of the back of Roslyn's neck.

Her mother. He was talking about her mother.

"She was certainly a sight to see, and a queen unlike any other, even my own wife, Veel, bless her soul. I first saw the Domonov bitch after breaching the inner walls and she was using all of her power, wrenching brambles and briars against my forces to slow them down, to slow me down, as I entered the sacred courtyard at Eluha. At first, I thought she just wanted to live. I thought she was doing it to save her own petty life, but then beyond her, in the flames of destruction, I saw a shadow. A woman was lifting a weeping child up off the ground from the queen's skirts where she clung to them, and carried her into the smoke and away into the night. The Queen was slowing us down to save her child. But we were too many for her.

216

We had machetes; we came prepared for their witchcraft."
The king shifted uncomfortably in his seat. "I ordered men
to find the child, to stop her getting away. I didn't want
any Domonov bastards coming after me in a decade's
time. The Queen knew what I was doing, and in a last-
ditch attempt to stop me, she tore the crown off her head,
a crown of pointed leaves and thorns, and threw it,
spinning through the flames towards me."

He pointed above the fireplace with a crooked finger
and Roslyn, for the first time in her life, saw the fabled
Briar Crown, the crown of the Domonov Queen. The
Queen whose power balanced all flora in the land.

The crown that should have been hers.

A faint whine sounded in her ears as if it was calling
to her.Its beauty, and its harsh ugliness, wrenched a gasp
from her throat. Any woman wearing that would have
been a fearful and empowering sight.

"Impressive, isn't it?" The king growled, "She sliced
my throat with that, so as my life bled out through my
neck, I did the same to her... but I made sure my blade
went all the way through."

He fell silent and Roslyn, not wanting to witness him
in the shadowy dimension of memory, stared up at the
crown, her eyes filled with tears. Now that she had looked
upon it, she could hardly tear her eyes away. It was crafted
of a bronze-coloured metal, leaves and thorns and the
tiniest of flowers all entwined into two pointed horns at
the front. It would have encircled the head and given the
wearer a set of impressive leafy antlers. As she looked up
at it, she felt something blossom within her. She felt the
sudden opposing force to the anger that had ridden within
her so long, the anger that had had no outlet. At the sight
of the Briar Crown, Roslyn was filled with hope.

217

"And the child?" The words left her lips before she knew they'd even moved. Did they have any idea she was still alive?

King Casimir grunted.

"They never found it. Probably died the same night, as the passage where the servant had disappeared soon crumbled in the fire that consumed the palace. Even if it'd been carried out of the rubble alive, there was no way the child would have survived the smoke inhalation... Besides, your rebels have never once proclaimed a pretender to my throne, so she must be dead."

He followed Roslyn's gaze up to the crown on the mantelpiece, the firelight glinting off its copper spikes.

"So, I keep the crown there, and I look at it every day. I look at it as a symbol of lost power, of the night a woman—a mere woman—nearly bested me." He turned to stare coldly at Roslyn, his features twisted in hatred. "I keep it to remind the lot of you that it will never sit on the head of a Domonov again."

✳

She was back in Eluha. The courtyard was no longer bathed in cold, white light, but illuminated by the frantic orange dance of flames. Smoke clouded her vision and snaked down her throat, making her cough. In the obscurity she heard screams, saw people running past her. Tears fell down her cheeks, but she was searching for something. She crawled onwards, her hands turning black and bleeding from the rubble littering the ground. Half of her wanted to sit back and cry, to give up, but then she saw it, the thing she had been searching for. She moved as fast as she could, cursing the long white robe that flowed out behind her and knelt, reaching up for the one person who could stop this nightmare.

The woman was not white or ghostly, but fully fleshed, covered in soot and grime, her cheeks flushed with exertion. The bronze crown on her head reflected the fire, making it a blinding halo atop her dark hair. At the sight of the crown, her ears filled with a high-pitched whining and a piercing dart of pain hit her between her brows. As Roslyn fell into her skirts, the woman stopped her frantic waving; her bellowed orders ceased, and she looked down, abject terror in her eyes.

The woman looked around frantically and screamed at someone, but her words were muffled.

A word was on the tip of Roslyn's tongue, but she couldn't form it; instead, she just reached out with her strangely small, podgy hands.

Suddenly, she was lifted from the ground from behind. She shrieked and wailed, but the look of terror in the woman's eyes dimmed, turning to one of sadness as she planted a hard, shaking kiss on her forehead and pushed her away.

The person carrying her ran from the fire, ran into the smoke and the darkness. A sudden chill made her skin prickle. Where were they? What was happening?

The noise had dimmed and she could hear the frantic breathing of her bearer, the beating of her bosom as she held her close. They stopped at a crossroads in what appeared to be a tunnel. She didn't know which way to go.

"Here!" A voice warbled through the gloaming and a small figure stepped forward. The cloven hooves and haunches of a goat stood beneath the bare chest of a man.

In her dream body, Roslyn clapped her hands. She knew this person but his name wouldn't come.

"This way!" he called, but the woman shook her head.

"I must get the princess to safety. I have to get to the stables."

"It's too late, the tunnel has caved in. You must follow me! It's her only hope."

The woman holding her nodded and they scurried off into the dark, musty labyrinth in the hillside.

The pounding of the woman's heart in her ear and the constant motion as they ran rocked Roslyn to sleep. She was woken by a cool breeze passing over her face. She opened her eyes and gazed up past the horned head of a satyr and the tearstained face of the woman who would raise her as her own, and saw stars scattered across an indigo sky.

Chapter 21

And so began Roslyn's habit of visiting the king in his chambers twice a day, once in the morning and once in the evening. She administered medicines that would ease his pain and send him into oblivion at night. Yet, *she* did not sleep. She had the king in the palm of her hand. She could end all of this now... it was what Eik, the bastard, wanted, and what her people needed.

At least once a day while she was preparing his medicine, her hand would flutter automatically to the hemlock shoved down her bodice. It would be so easy; all she had to do was make him one strong tea...

But every day, something stopped her. She wasn't a killer, but there was more to it than that. She couldn't kill the father Prince Frederik loved.

He was not the one that had committed these crimes; he was not the one who had slaughtered the Domonovs, ridding Domovnia of her rulers, her balance. The sons should not be punished for the sins of the father. And, if she was truly honest with herself, she knew there was another reason too, one that made her blush.

As she made up the batch one evening, her hand resting on her stays, a croaky voice made her spin round from the counter.

"If you are going to do it, just do it."

The king was sat propped up on his pillows, staring at her. She swallowed and shook her head, the lie unconvincing to her own ears.

"I don't know what you mean."

A cold smirk lifted the sagging skin of his cheeks. "Oh, yes you do… Whatever you have shoved down there between your tits will kill me, won't it?" Roslyn was about to shake her head again when his eyes narrowed and he reached for the coverlets. "Don't make me come over there and pull it out myself," he laughed coldly. "It's been a long time since these hands have squeezed a warm, soft teat, so don't think I won't."

Roslyn swallowed down the bile that had clogged her throat and reached in between her breasts, pulling out the linen-wrapped tuber.

"Hemlock." She nodded. "Yes it will kill you—quickly, if I give you any more than a thumbnail of shavings in your tea."

The king nodded and smoothed the blankets back over his knees. "And why haven't you done it yet? End this quickly, be a martyr to your people? Or are you too much of a coward?"

Rage bubbled up inside her and she found herself storming towards the invalid, waving the hemlock angrily under his nose.

"I am no coward!"

The king scoffed and raised an eyebrow. "No? Then let's play a little game." The hairs on her forearms raised.

"You've picked your poison, I have my cancer... Now let's see which kills me first."

Roslyn shook her head.

"No."

"No? Are you refusing me, girl?" His voice dropped and his eyes turned steely.

"Is it an order, your majesty?" *Please say no, please say no.* Her palms were sweating and her stomach churning but she used all her strength to keep herself still and calm in the face of that stare. The old man pursed his cracked lips and then grinned.

"Yes. I order you to put one shaving in my tea a day. Starting now."

She closed her eyes for the briefest of seconds before crossing to the table and picking up the horribly blunt knife they had allowed her to use, and let her fate settle on her shoulders.

"Clever, aren't you?"

"I like to think so, yes, but in this instant, Domovnian, indulge me. Why is my brain so wonderful?"

Slowly she unwrapped the hemlock and held it in her hand, its weight mocking her. "If I refuse you, you will just order them to search me. Your men will find the poison and I'll be executed. If I obey, you will die, possibly sooner than your physicians anticipated so questions will be asked, and they will assume it was me, search me and find the poison. I'm a dead woman either way, aren't I?"

The king brayed his asinine laugh behind her and clapped his hands. "You got me! You are a dead woman, just as I am a dead man!"

Roslyn raised the blade to the tuber and hacked off the thinnest of shavings, her rage giving her the strength to utilise the blunt instrument.

"But why? I thought you wanted to put your affairs in order...I thought you wanted to see your son married?" She dropped the hemlock into the tea and stirred it before turning back to the bed.

The king shrugged, sticking out his bottom lip. "I'm bored..." A grimace of pain flashed over his features, robbing his voice of the mockery it had held seconds before. "And I'm tired. I've had enough of the pain, enough of this country and enough of you people."

"We never asked you to be here! You just came, and you killed and you took, and for what? Just because you could?" Roslyn couldn't help herself. The reminder of what her life should have been hanging above the fireplace, filling her head with that aggravating high-pitched whine. What did it matter how she spoke to the old crackpot king now? She was a dead woman, anyway.

"Wouldn't you like to know," he teased, holding out his hand for the cup, but she held it high out of his reach.

"Well, yes actually, I would. Why? Why did you invade? Why have you terrorised my people, why have you tortured and starved us?" She wanted to claw at his face as she remembered the amount of times she and Hedda had been forced to eat the leaves of her Affinity plants to survive after the Oderberg soldiers had raided their homes and taken anything that resembled food.

"Because you starved us first!" Casimir bellowed back. Roslyn sank to the side of the bed, sitting level with the king, gripping the horn cup in her hands as if for support.

"What?"

224

"Ah, I see they don't teach you that in your rebel history lessons, do they? They don't teach you how the snow and ice in Bergam stayed longer each year, raping our fertile land until we were on our knees with hunger. My father, Hoff bless his soul, was fool enough to love the Domonov bitch that would inherit the throne. Not only did she refuse his proposal after leading him a merry dance, she also refused to send a Botan help speed up our crops in the short window left to us. She could have made an army of Botans with that damn crown of hers, but no, she hoarded your magical powers like a dragon hoards gold and all the while, we starved." He snatched the cup from her hands and chugged it down, rivulets of steaming liquid seeping from the corners of his mouth.

"So, I know hunger, possibly even more than you do, *girl*! I've had it gnaw at my insides longer than you've been alive. My father sat stewing in his hatred until he wasted away. But I did what he could not. I provided my people with food and fertile land and…" He wiped his mouth on the back of his hand. "I got revenge. Now, Miss Pleveli, you may take yours."

Chapter 22

A week had passed since the passing of the Assimilation Act and it was market day.

As part of the Act, Domovnians could now move into the city and trade within city walls. While none had officially moved their place of residence into the Oderberg stronghold of Novlada, that first market day saw a flood of curious but cautious Domovnians rolling in with their carts and wares. Frederik had woken Roslyn early by pounding on her door, as giddy as a boy at Vinterfest.

"Roslyn! Roslyn, get up! It's market day."

Roslyn was unsure why he was so excited, but the sight of him jumping up and down like a puppy lifted her spirits. He'd asked her to wear her best outfit, and he himself dressed in his fine Oderberg clothes. Just before they left the palace gates, he bunched his fist and extended his arm towards her, a glint in his eye.

"Miss Pleveli, may I escort you to the market?" His voice sang with fun and flirtation, and she couldn't help the rush of warmth that flooded her cheeks. She lifted her hand tentatively to his arm and looked up at his smiling face.

"Is this proper?"

Frederik laughed and shook his head. "I highly doubt it, but with you on my arm, the people will see that I have embraced a Domovnian as a friend and equal." Her heart sank a little at his remark. Was that all she was to him? "Therefore, there is no reason for them not to do the same."

His voice was heavy with suggestion and betrayed his anxiety about what was to come. "As a member of the royal family, it is my duty to lead the way, especially when my father cannot."

Roslyn huffed. "What about the crown prince?"

Frederik rolled his eyes and made a *tsk* sound with his teeth. "My brother, it would appear, has been sent away."

Roslyn couldn't help raising her eyebrows in astonishment. "Oh?"

The gates opened, and they walked out into the city, the people giving them a wide berth but staring all the while. Roslyn thought the prince might have shut off their conversation, but it did them good to be seen talking comfortably in one another's presence, as if they truly were friends.

"Yes, my brother has ridden to the coast to investigate the peasant's claims of sea wyrms and then he will return for his wedding to the princess of Pushtet, heiress to the Eredzhi throne. She is a very fine match and will make a suitable Queen in the future…"

There was something unsaid on the tip of his tongue. "But?" Roslyn prompted.

"Well… I have heard that she is not a great beauty."

"How would you even know? Eredzhi women hide their faces behind veils before they are married!" Roslyn shook her head, laughing, and gave his chest a small tap of rebuke, immediately regretting it as the crowd gasped around them. She froze and her eyes widened, but Frederik put his arm around her waist and motioned her forward, whispering in her ear.

"Keep moving, we are only acting as any pair of friends would." He removed his hand and made a show of laughing at her reaction.

The crowd relaxed around them and talked amongst themselves as they watched the couple stride into the marketplace and inspect the stalls of both Oderberg and Domovnian sellers.

The prince nodded politely and engaged in conversation with every store owner, asking about their wares, and calling his steward over to make a note of things he wanted purchased. Roslyn was swept away in a wave of emotion. The smells of the herbs, the spices and the saliva-inducing scent of frying foods mixed with wood smoke took her right back to her village. That it was all here within the stone walls of Novlada, with Bergams and Domovnians—albeit with a large degree of wariness—coexisting and trading together was a little too much. The bridge of her nose prickled and her lip trembled, and she bit the inside of her cheek to stop the tears that were welling up from falling down her cheeks.

After they had passed the bulk of the food stalls, the barrels of open olives, pickles and spices calling to her, they rounded a corner into an aisle filled with stalls made up mainly of homewares and clothing. Alongside the rich velvets the Oderbergs were accustomed to, a few brave Domovnian women had set up their stalls, hawking their beautifully embroidered clothing, handwoven ribbons in bright colours and traditional Domovnian outfits. Roslyn approached one stall and to her surprise, the woman behind the bench bobbed a small curtsy at her. However, her eyes betrayed the suspicion within.

"How may I help you, mistress?"

Roslyn felt Frederik amble up beside her and saw the smile of delight on his face as he saw the woman's wares.

"You make these?" he beamed. As always, his radiance washed over the suspicious woman and she blushed and nodded.

"I... I did your... your... highness."

Frederik held out his hand, and the woman jumped.

"Then I must shake your hand. You are extremely talented. As someone who has no such handicraft skills himself, I am very much in awe. So much so that I would like to purchase something for my friend here as a thank you for healing me."

Roslyn blushed and shook her head. "You really don't need—"

"No, no, Roslyn." He took her hand in his, unaware of the sharp glances of the crowd around them and the stall owner. "I insist."

The stall owner bobbed a grateful nod and cocked her head to the side.

"May I ask the young lady's Affinity?" Her voice was full of trepidation. It was unclear yet whether the Affinity could even be spoken of. It was law that they could not use their powers, but to speak of them and use them as an identifying mark, surely that was permitted?

Roslyn groaned inwardly at the woman's question. It was quite clear what she was. Her clothes, embroidered by herself to a lesser standard than the exquisite wares on the table before them, revealed her Affinity with nettles and dandelions, but she was obliged to answer. The woman smiled wryly, acknowledging her lowly place in Domovnian society. She, of course, was a Bloomer, crocuses and daffodils brightening her sleeves. If only she knew who she really was, Roslyn thought, if only they all knew.

"A Hedgie. Very well. Might I suggest this beautiful ribbon here, for the lady's hair?" She held out a fine ribbon, pulling it through her fingers gently to display its length. The very edges were green, and on a black background wound strands of green thread into the twining vines of ivy. The leaves were delicately highlighted with flecks of white thread, lifting the green from the black and bringing the whole ribbon to life.

Frederik smiled.

"I think that would suit her very well. You have wonderful taste," he directed at the stall owner, who blushed her thanks and wrapped up the ribbon in a paper bag. As with all his other purchases, Frederik left the payment and the removal of the items to his steward and turned back to the centre of the market square. A band had gathered by the fountain and after the short braying of tuning instruments, they kicked up into a lively jig.

An exclamation of glee passed over the Domovnians in the crowd, the Oderbergs looking around suspiciously, wondering what the commotion was about. But when couples took to the open space before the band and began to dance, they relaxed, their shoulders sinking, and some of them even clapped in time with the raucous tune, the prince amongst them.

"This, this is wonderful!" He paused, sadness creeping into his voice. "I wish it could be like this all the

230

time." Roslyn was stunned to silence for a moment but then held out a hand to Prince Frederik, and bobbed a small curtsy.

"Might I have the honour of this dance, your highness?" She looked up, her eyes large and inviting from underneath her fringe, twinkling with daring. Frederik went slightly pale, his smile slipping and then nodded his head.

"If my healer thinks I am up to it, then I will of course accept. However..." He looked around at the other dancers. "I am not familiar with the steps."

Roslyn laughed, grabbed his hand and pulled him into the crowd, teaching him in a very clunky manner around his injured leg and walking stick how to do the basic steps. He was soon red from embarrassment at his inability to perform as easily as the local experts, but he was laughing. Domovnians around him smiled encouragingly. He was trying, and that was more than any Oderberg had done for the past two decades. Besides, who could resist the sheer love of life he exuded?

Suddenly, someone bowed at his side.

"Your highness, might I have the privilege of dancing with your partner?"

As the speaker rose from his bow, he locked eyes with Roslyn and her heart turned to ice. Eik's formidable form towered above her, his eyes narrowed in question. Prince Frederik didn't see anything wrong with it and happily nodded his head.

"Of course, of course, friend I need to rest, anyway." He turned to Roslyn and squeezed her arm gently. "I'll be right over there by that wonderful-looking ale tent."

She could do nothing more. She couldn't protest, couldn't do anything that wouldn't alert the soldiers and disrupt the peace of the day or signify to the man that now swirled around in the jig that she had begun to feel things for the prince limping away from her.

Eik smiled down at her as they danced the first couple of rounds until the Frederik was well out of sight. Roslyn's wrists chafed from where he was gripping her, a feeling she hadn't realised until now that she was all too familiar with, and it was one she loathed. As they swirled and turned, he pushed her away and pulled her back in time to the music so hard she slammed into his chest. He growled down at her.

"What do you think you are doing, dancing with the enemy? Why isn't he dead?"

Roslyn tried to push herself away and join a new partner in the round, but Eik grabbed her upper arm and yanked her back, glaring at the man that should have swept her along in the jig.

"He doesn't need to die," she snarled back up at him, his thick lips and bulbous nose suddenly unsightly to her. What had she seen in him? "He's not the one that caused all the problems, and besides," she gestured around at a scene that would have been impossible but a week ago, Domovnians and Oderbergs dancing, and laughing and eating together. "By healing him, I have done more towards peace than any of the rebellions or murders have. He's the one who initiated this. Just look around, Eik— this is how we move on from here. We have to befriend them, not kill them. It's the only way."

Eik pulled her close in a gesture that was not part of the dance, his plate-sized hands wrapping around the back of her neck and the other pressing the small of her back so that they were pressed up against each other. The heat was overpowering, and she suddenly felt nauseous. His breath stank of garlic and stale ale as he hissed in her ear.

"Yeah, certainly looks like you have been getting friendly with the enemy. Tell me, how long did it take him to open your legs? As long as it took me? What was that, a week? You desperate slut! You are a disgrace to all Domovnians. I'm taking you home before you can embarrass us further."

Roslyn shook her head frantically and pushed against his barrel-like chest with her fists. "No! I'm not going anywhere."

Eik scoffed and snatched her arm, dragging her through the startled dancers. She dug her heels in as much as she could, but her slippers only slid across the cobbles and soon they were heading towards an alley off the marketplace. He was too strong for her, so the only thing to do was use her voice.

"Stop! I will go nowhere with you! My place is here."

As the market crowd parted around them, Eik pulled her into him again and held her neck, squeezing just enough to make her panic with lack of breath, so that she heard every word of his. "Why? Why is your place here with these people? You need to leave this job up to the real Domovnians." Roslyn looked around frantically. They were almost out of the square and she couldn't see Frederik anywhere, but she had a sudden idea.

"Eik… I am now *treating* the king."

He paused and looked like he was about to strike her when she held up a hand and whispered, "They want me to heal him, but I've been spiking his medicine. He *will* die, Eik, that I swear!"

Her former lover looked around nervously and shifted his weight on his feet. "You'd better be serious." He stepped towards her and shoved a sausage sized finger under her nose. "Because if I find out that you…"

Roslyn didn't get to hear the rest of his threat, as a figure stepped in between them.

"Are you in need of some assistance, Miss Pleveli?" Roslyn could have wept for joy at the sound of Frederik's voice, stern as it was. When he had used it on her, it had made her squirm. She thought it had been from fear, but now she realised she liked this harder side to him and she shivered with unexpected pleasure. He turned to Eik and glared up at him, not even flinching as the Domovnian squared up over him, using his height as a shield. "I suggest you unhand the lady, sir," the prince demanded. From the corner of her eye, Roslyn saw Captain Dietrich place his hand on the hilt of his sword and approach the scene.

"She is no lady." Eik hissed and flung Roslyn's hand away from him so forcefully that she barrelled into her rescuer and the pair of them fell backwards into a dung heap that had decorated the corner of the alley.

Roslyn lifted her muck-covered hands out of the pile with a grimace of horror and was suddenly aware of the shocked silence. The music has stopped; the dancers were paused mid-twirl and the rest of the market crowd was staring at herself and the son of King Casimir lying in a pile of pig shit. The Oderberg guards, hands on the hilt of their swords, stalked towards the upset. They had their sights on Eik and he, in turn, was ready to go down fighting. Roslyn looked around, eyes wide. She didn't want to be the reason the Assimilation Act didn't hold. She had to fix this.

Before she could do anything, Prince Frederik laughed and hauled himself out of the shit pile, scrabbling around on hands and knees and stood up, smearing yet more excrement over his fine doublet in a pathetic attempt to clean himself. Once upright, he waved his dung covered hands at the people and laughed merrily.

"Nothing to worry about… nothing to worry about." He glared at the guards, who instantly backed down and, in that moment, Eik disappeared like smoke in the crowd, an impressive feat considering his size. Frederik turned to the muttering crowd again and splayed his arms out before him. "You know what they say, royalty is full of shit… we just don't usually let it show!"

As he laughed, so did those around him. It was a cautious, thin sound, but it was a laugh of relief from both sides.

Roslyn gazed up at him and shook her head, a smile creeping over her lips. He turned round and shrugged before extending his filthy hand.

"Come on! Let's get cleaned up, Lady Muck."

Roslyn took his help, and it was with a few tugs that he eventually extricated her with a squelch. As the dung heap let her go with a pop of sudden release she almost went barrelling into the prince and knocking him over a second time, but he managed to right himself and her in the process, looking down at her as her cheek grazed his soiled chest. She backed away and blushed.

"Ahem. Miss," Prince Frederik gestured to her cheek with a finger. "I think you have a little something…." Roslyn laughed and looked about her for some small piece of clean material with which to wipe her face, but found none.

"So what now, your Royal Highness? They will not let us back into the palace looking or smelling like this." She bobbed her head downwards and crinkled her nose.

Frederik nodded and paced a little before turning to one of his stewards, ordering him back to the stalls they had previously passed to purchase some new clothes in the Domovnian style fit for the prince and his companion. Then he turned to Captain Dietrich, who had finally made his way through the throngs.

The captain raised an eyebrow, trying to keep the smirk under his moustache from erupting into a full-blown snigger.

"The bathhouse, my lord?" he asked with a sense of amusement.

Frederik nodded his head. "The bathhouse. Lead the way."

Chapter 23

They were led down smelly back alleys, out of sight of curious eyes and towards a simple wooden door in the crumbling wall of a building. Steam rose from the myriad of chimneys that dotted its roof.

Captain Dietrich rapped three times on the door, which shook under his blows, and a large woman, face red and shiny from the heat, opened it. She wore a clean dress of blue linen and an apron, which she used to wipe her brow. When she saw who was at the door, she dropped it immediately and bobbed to curtsy.

"Your highness!" Her voice was questioning, and when she rose from her bow, Roslyn saw a twinkle in her eye. The familiarity in her voice was almost brazen. "I haven't seen you in a while…" The woman leant forward and sniffed. "And certainly not in that state. Now I know why you're here. What have you been up to this time?"

She laughed a hearty, raucous laugh and ushered them inside. It was so dark at first that it took Roslyn's eyes a moment to adjust, but when they did, the lavishness of their surroundings amazed her. The walls that she had expected to be cracked like the outside, or perhaps even mouldy from the steam, were whitewashed, clean and scented with lemon, draped in the most luxurious silks, all reds, pinks and purples in hue. She led the group to the main reception area, where a mahogany desk stood squatly in front of a pegboard intended for the heavy brass keys of which only one hung in its place.

The woman shrugged and pointed at the board.

"I'm afraid I've only got the one private bath available right now, your highness. Seems with the market day, there's more traffic than usual. And no doubt the Domovnians have heard of our bathing techniques and want to try them out—not that you can blame 'em, eh?" The woman wrung her hands a little nervously and glanced at Roslyn "Would you like me to escort your lady friend to the communal baths, your highness?"

Frederik laughed and shook his head.

"Oh, for the love of the Mountain, Gertrude, just get us into a bath. We're all friends here. We don't mind sharing, do we, Roslyn?"

Roslyn's cheeks exploded with heat and she shook her head, flabbergasted, unable to form any words. She glanced at Captain Dietrich who, although stood ramrod straight, was trying very hard not to smirk.

"I... I..." Her words failed her.

Gertrude, the proprietress of the bathhouse, seemed to sense her discomfort and called an attendant over to her.

"Brigitta, fetch one of the staff bathrobes for the prince's companion here to protect her modesty."

At this comment Captain Dietrich outright snorted, but stopped when Frederik shot him a look.

"That will do nicely, Brigitta," the prince thanked the servant girl, who rushed off in a hurry to find the garment.

238

Gertrude snatched up the last remaining key from the hooks and made for the passageway beyond the desk.

"Very well. If you'll follow me, then."

"I'll wait here for the new garments, your highness," the captain said with some relief. The rest of the party followed the stout woman into the narrow corridor that was lit with wrapped red lanterns. She opened the door with a rattle, and they found themselves in a large round room, a bathing tub in the centre, which two servant girls scurried to fill from the brass taps at either side.

At the far end of the room, a counter was laden with essential oils, lotions and all sorts of bathing accoutrements that Roslyn had never seen before. To her, a bath was some hot water in the tub in front of the fire and when one person was finished, the next in the household would use the rest of the water. Occasionally, for those recovering from some sort of malaise, Hedda would infuse the waters with herbs, but this was on another scale. Her mouth fell open, and the woman rewarded her with a wide smile.

"They're not all like this." She leant into the Domovnian with a stage whisper. "We keep aside this for more important guests."

Roslyn could see why. She'd thought the drapes in the rest of the bathhouse sumptuous; these were heavenly. Rich velvets and silks were threaded with gold and brass strands that glinted in the lamplight. The lanterns here were dimmed by coloured glass cloches slipped over the tapers, giving off a heady rainbow of flickering light. There were two screens, one on either side of the enormous, polished wooden tub in the centre of the room, each intricately carved from dark mahogany. Although the carvings left plenty of room for holes, again, luxurious

239

satins and silks were draped over them so that the bather could change in peace and privacy.

Prince Frederik wandered off behind one screen, so used to the custom that he left Roslyn standing there gawking in her ignorance. Gertrude tapped her on the hand, as much as she could, considering they were still covered in shit, and pointed her to the other screen.

"Come now, there's a basin of hot water there and some cloths for you to remove the most of"—she looked Roslyn up and down—"the grime before you enter the bath proper."

At that moment, the servant girl Brigitta rushed in with a garment strung over both of her arms.

Gertrude took it and hung it on the edge of the screen. "Once you remove your clothes, place them in that basket there." She motioned to a woven basket at the side of the screen. "They'll be taken and laundered while you bathe. Then, put this on, it will help." She smirked and bobbed a curtsy. "I'll leave you in peace, now. Enjoy your bath", she said, that twinkle in her eye again, and then she left, shutting the door behind her.

Roslyn rid herself of her stinking clothes as fast as she could and then, as the bathing woman had instructed, she washed off most of the muck that was on her skin. It wouldn't do to have a nice clean bath and dirty it with unnecessary grime.

She looked dubiously at the robe Brigitta had hung on the screen. It had two straps that lead down to a bodice, comprising two very obvious breast cups, and then a loose skirt hung from a high waistband. It was made of very thin linen and she was certain that as soon as she stepped in the water, she may as well not have been wearing it at all. But

240

she shrugged it on and called for one of the serving girls who remained to help lace her in.

"By the Tree," she gasped as the final lace was tied. "This is tight."

The serving girl bobbed and smiled. "They are, milady. Once the steam gets at 'em they loosen, so they need to be snug to start with… but they're not usually for women such as yourself. They're for us maids, as we run through the steam in the public rooms. They help us cool down, you see." The girl paused and then looked up at Roslyn. "Would you like me to put some sort of milk in the bath, to obscure the waters a bit more and make you more comfortable?"

Roslyn could have kissed the girl as she listed off the various opaque substances that could be added to the steaming bath beyond.

After she had made her choice of a neutral oat milk, she waited a while and then heard the splash of a body entering the water with a low rumbling groan of pleasure that made the lips between her legs throb. Prince Frederik was in the bath.

"Roslyn, what are you doing behind there? Come and get in the bath before it gets cold. Trust me, you'll feel so much better. It's divine."

Roslyn peeped her head out from the side of the screen and her mouth went dry. Although she had seen the prince shirtless before, that had been on a sickbed, and he had needed care, so her glances had been those of a medical nature. Now, she took in the chiselled frame of a man blessed by the ancient gods. He seemed as if he were one of the statues that lined their halls, sculpted from marble by artisans who knew the beauty of the human form intimately. His head was tilted back on the rim of the basin

241

while his arms, muscles relaxed but still well-defined, spread round its circumference. She followed the line of his neck down his smooth chest, between the slight divide of the pectorals, teasing her eyes lower until they met with the milky white surface of the water. She swallowed and mumbled something incoherent about not wanting to be seen. The prince laughed gently, the lump in this throat bobbing up and down, but he kept his eyes closed.

"Don't worry, I won't look." His voice was silky smooth and relaxed, as if he was almost about to fall asleep. So Roslyn tiptoed out from behind the screen, catching the eye of Brigitta as she slipped from the room with a bob and a wink. She lowered herself into the warm, steamy waters. A rush of clary sage and jasmine wafted up to meet her and she sighed as the water enveloped her calves, then her thighs, the water slicking the thin linen to them almost instantly. It rose over her waist and finally her breasts until she, too, leant her head back on the pillow provided and groaned with relief.

"Nice, isn't it?" His voice was still soft and slow, and all she could do was mumble in response. "Gertrude has the best bathhouse in the entire country, and I'll be damned if anyone says otherwise. She really knows how to take care of her guests."

Roslyn lifted her head and cocked an eyebrow. "Oh really?"

Finally, the prince raised his head and his own brows in return before trying to hide a blush behind his cheeky grin.

"Well, I won't deny she offers some other special services, if one so wishes."

Roslyn nodded, trying to be casual and worldly-wise, but she was suddenly aware of Frederik's gaze on her bare shoulders, on the strand of hair that hung down from her neck and had become wet with the bathwater. It snaked down her shoulders and between her tightly encased breasts that were pushed up by the linen bodice. They were almost separated, and the cut of the cloth amplified their roundness. As predicted, that cloth had become very see-through. The dark circles of her nipples shone through the fabric and she sank lower beneath the water to hide them, suddenly breaking the prince's stare. He shook his head and blushed again, reaching for a glass of wine that stood on a nearby table. He took a large gulp and tried to change the subject.

"So, you want to tell me who that was back there in the marketplace?"

Roslyn sighed and found her own glass of wine waiting. She raised the fine crystal to her lips and took a sip, letting its sweet tang play on her tastebuds while she thought how to answer.

"That was… a friend… from home…"

Frederik cocked his head to the side and looked up at her from under his brows. "Just a friend?" His voice was weaker suddenly, as if he was afraid of her answer.

Roslyn gave him a dry chuckle. "No, he was a bit more of a friend… but he no longer is. So…" She ducked her head to study the water with a sudden intensity as she moved her hands below the surface, making the milk swirl. "I am no virgin, your highness."

The prince was silent for a moment, but when he spoke, his words made her raise her head towards him again. "Does that matter?"

"Well, I thought all you princes wanted was demure virgins you could pluck for the first time."

Her words made him roar with laughter and smack the surface of the water in disbelief.

"Ah, there you have got us all wrong! That seems to be what one is expected to want, especially in a bride. Virginity is overrated. Give me a woman who knows what she wants any day over a simpering and most likely scared innocent."

Roslyn's heart buoyed for a moment that he didn't mind about her previous relations, but then the smile that had been growing on her lips faded. Although Eik had been her lover, she could safely say their relations had been more to his benefit than hers, humping her like a jackrabbit and within seconds, rolling off in a satiated slump, leaving her unfulfilled.

She blushed as she remembered the difference when her kiss with Frederik had lit the fire in her loins, and wondered how different the carnal act would be with the prince. She bit her lip and looked up slowly. "What if she still doesn't know what it is she wants?"

She stretched out her feet under the water and met his. The smoothness of her leg brushed the calf of Frederik's, and she felt the wet golden hairs of his leg waving in the water like silk. She was about to move away when he leant forward and grabbed her thigh. A gasp escaped her but not because of his impropriety; a spark of lightning had shot through her and she knew that she wanted that hand to climb even higher.

His face was closer to hers, his chin just above the surface of the water, causing ripples as he spoke.

"Then she needs someone to help discover her most secret of desires."

Suddenly, he sat back and water sloshed over the side of the tub. Roslyn swallowed painfully, trying to regain a normal rhythm of breath, but the absence of his hand on her thigh was almost painful. She knew now that she wanted it back, gripping her harder than before. So, it was her turn to lean forward in the water, rising so the tips of her rounded breasts broke the translucent surface. "Would you?"

Frederik licked his lips, unable to smile as his eyes were trained on her mouth, on the length of her neck and of the possibility of what lay just beneath the surface of the water. When he spoke, his voice was husky with desire.

"That depends if my healer has approved me for such activity."

The pull of him was magnetic, and Roslyn bent her knees, resting them on the base of the tub. She parted his legs with her hands and felt his thick, sturdy thighs on either side of her waist. She pushed herself up and forwards until her lips were by his ear, her chest pounding hard, just below his chin.

"She does, as long as you don't strain yourself. We wouldn't want all her hard work to go to waste."

The water around them was still swirling with her movement and shifted the thin linen of her bath gown up and away from her thighs. She gave the faintest of gasps as she felt his erection rise between them. It was hard and warm and throbbed against her stomach.

He groaned and grabbed the back of her thighs with two hands, spreading them even further apart until she was straddling him.

"Oh," he panted, "I won't... this is all about you." Before she knew what was happening, he flipped her around so that his cock was now pressed against her lower back and he ran his hands down over her covered breasts, around her waist and then back up again. She moaned at his touch and leant her head on his shoulder. His cheek pressed against hers and she heard his laboured breathing matching her own. Her hips moved of their own accord, as his hands caressed her; first her neck, tracing it delicately with nimble fingers, then sliding down to her shoulders, slipping the straps of the dress from them, then forwards to the centre of her bodice. He took the flimsy fabric of the bathrobe and tore it in two with a sudden ripping sound.

Roslyn gasped as she was suddenly free, able to breathe as hard as she wanted, and she arched her back in ecstasy as his hands squeezed her breasts before travelling down her abdomen again. He spread her legs, teasing her, stroking his fingers up and down her inner thigh. He was so close to where heat radiated from within her, where a yearning overtook her senses. She rocked her hips again, making the prince groan and bite her shoulder. He held her waist with one hand and with the other, finally, let his fingers touch that hot, pulsing spot between her legs.

She leant back into him, feeling every muscle, every dip and crevice of his body as her head began to swim with the steam, the scent, and the sensation of his finger swirling around and around between her legs.

He started slowly, gently. It was comfortable and calmed her, but still her breath was heavy with longing. As he rubbed her clit with one hand, his other moved up towards her exposed breasts, and there he squeezed her nipple between his fingertips. She yelped with delighted surprise and he sped up his swirling finger.

"Do it again," she moaned as his finger went round and round, heat growing in her loins, her toes tingling with anticipation. He gave her right breast a gentle squeeze and then traced his finger around the rose-coloured circle of her areola, making wider and wider circles before tracing it down into the crevice between her tits and up onto the other mound. He swirled his finger up and around, closer to her nipple, where he suddenly squeezed again with intense deliciousness. She couldn't help but cry out.

"Again," she panted, and again his finger sped up. She slipped one hand beneath the water and put it on his working, gyrating finger, pressing it harder into her, showing him exactly where and how hard she wanted it.

The prince's heavy breath in her own ear, the sweat from the steam and the exertion that lay on his skin blended with hers and she wanted every part of him. She wanted more than his finger. As if they had a mind of their own, her hips rocked and as his finger did its work, her pelvis rose to meet it. With every desperate dip of her hips, the water slapped rhythmically against them, teasing her, taunting her over-heightened senses.

She wanted him there and then; wanted to turn around and take him. She started to turn, but he stopped her with a firm hand.

She sighed and let her hand fall away from his, giving him the freedom to make her cum. He knew what he was doing; she didn't have to tell him. He teased her exquisitely well, and he built up the heat that ran through her until she could scarcely breathe. Her breasts were rising with the effort of getting oxygen into her lungs, but she didn't care if she asphyxiated right there. She just wanted him to carry on. She wanted him madly, blindly, her head swimming with passion.

And then there was no more. The tingle that began in her toes rushed up her legs in heated glory and overwhelmed her. The burst of ecstasy that he'd brought forth from his finger made her arch her back with a gargled groan, pushing her hips downward and back over his cock so that he too lurched forward with a groan of his own and held her just above the surface of the water as she came. He cradled her as she panted, kissing her naked spine on each notch as the breath returned to her and the shudders subsided. She was weak with pleasure but still wanted to turn and take him in her arms, sliding his ready, throbbing cock inside her. A knock sounded.

They froze in their huddled, clinging position as a familiar voice sounded from the other side of the door.

"The clothes you ordered are ready, your highness. If you would permit me to enter, I shall have the servant girls make them available to you."

Frederik released Roslyn and guided her to the seat in the bath, where she sank gratefully, her legs unable to support her. He grabbed her neck and held her head in his hands before gently pressing his lips to hers. The world stopped, and she was lost in the delicate passion of his lips. And just as suddenly as it had begun, the kiss stopped, Frederik wrenching himself away from her with a wink and hopping out of the bath.

Chapter 24

When they rode back to the castle to find that Roslyn's things had been moved to a small servant's quarter near the king's apartment, she wondered if the prince was as disappointed as she was. She was no longer Prince Frederik's healer; she was the king's. It was only right that they should move her out of the single and very enigmatic young man's room. However, they still saw plenty of each other in the days that followed.

As part of his mission to unite the Oderbergs and Domovnians, Prince Frederik set about riding to some of the nearby villages. His aim was to befriend the people that lived there, listen to their complaints and take action to improve the infrastructure and, therefore, the lives of those who dwelt beyond Novlada's walls. It was only natural that he should bring his own mascot with him. A shudder ran through her when she wondered if that was how he saw her—a Domovnian toy he could flaunt and play with when it suited him.

It was the height of midsummer, so riding out from the citadel walls and through the countryside was hot, dusty,

249

and sweaty work. Roslyn's riding skill had improved greatly, but every hit of the saddle between her legs made her flush with the memory of what had happened in the bathhouse, awakening an insatiable thirst within her that she knew had nothing to do with the heat of the sun.

She tried not to look as they stopped at streams for water, where the young royal would hop down from his mount and remove his thin cotton shirt, exposing his well-defined torso slick with sweat. Her breath caught in her chest as he bent over to cup cold water in his hands and tip his head to the heavens, dousing himself in it. Oh, what she wouldn't give to be that water, running in rivulets over his chest, his arms and down to the waistband of his britches. She bit her lip and turned away when he suddenly looked up and caught her staring.

Although the prince's company had an escort of guards and the Domovnians looked at them suspiciously at first, it was clear that they were there to protect him from attacks only. They were not to initiate violence of any kind and so eventually the indigenous population relaxed when they saw the golden-haired Prince riding up. However, their faces grew stern as they stared at the young woman by his side. She knew what they were thinking; was she one of them? Or was she simply his whore, having sold out on the promise of sweetmeats and finery? Roslyn's stomach twisted every time they rode into a village, and she tried to persuade them with pleading eyes that she had never stopped being one of them.

Groups hovered on corners, mostly made up of young, angry-looking men, and she knew without a doubt that these were the rebels. She knew that *they* knew why she was in the palace. There was no way Eik would have kept that to himself. On one occasion, as the prince was shaking hands with the village baker, promising extra sacks of wheat for the mill, she turned and caught the eye of one such rebel. He held her stare and nodded slowly, as if reminding her of her task, and then slipped into the shadows of the alleyway.

After that incident, she was sullen and quiet on the journey back to the castle. She didn't speak to any of the soldiers, nor did she laugh at the prince's jokes. She was so quiet and withdrawn that she didn't notice the party had stopped until Frederik grabbed Marble's reins and looked up at her.

"Roslyn?" His eyes were full of questioning, worry. "Is everything alright?"

Roslyn shook her head and tried to smile, but it was a weak performance that deceived no one. "I'm fine. It's just the heat, I swear."

He didn't look convinced and turned to Captain Dietrich at his side.

"Do we have time for a quick break? Some others may need to cool down, too."

It wasn't really a question. The accompanying soldiers took full advantage of the order, sliding down from their mounts and finding refuge in the shade of the pine trees. The prince held out his hands to help Roslyn dismount and she slid into him, her body pressing against his on the way down. When her feet were on the ground, he wrapped his arms around her waist so she couldn't pull away and bent his neck towards her. As she looked up, their lips were only a hand's span apart, and she suddenly forgot the rest of the company around them.

"Roslyn, I can tell something's bothering you. You don't have to tell me, if you don't want, but let's try to make that smile come back, eh?" he cajoled fondly. She smiled, just a little, and nodded.

Frederik took her hand and walked away from the roadside, spreading his arms wide against a backdrop of yellow flowers. "I want you to have some fun, Roslyn."

As soon as she looked up and saw the small round pom-poms of gold, her body tingled with Affinity. The whole meadow was covered in dandelions; barely an inch of green could be seen between them, so thick had they grown. Her lips parted and the corners of her mouth tugged upwards, her eyes widening with sheer joy at the sight. But then she shook her head, the smile disappearing in an instant.

"But… But I can't. It's the law, you know that, you wrote it!"

Frederik shrugged casually."I made the law under duress, I'll admit, and therefore, *I* may grant exceptions." He grabbed Roslyn's hand again, sending a prickle of delight up her arm, and tugged her into the meadow. Then he ran, dragging her behind him, laughing. Roslyn soon found that his laughter was contagious, and she was soon breathless with the wonder of running through a field of living gold.

He stopped, seemingly out of breath, and turned towards her, his eyes earnest and his voice sincere.

"Show me, Roslyn. Show me what you can do."

She bowed her head and shook it a little out of habit. "It's… it's not much, it's silly, really…" He stepped towards her and took her face in his hands, tilting her chin upwards towards his so that their eyes met.

"Nothing you do is ever silly, Roslyn, and I know you are capable of far more than you think. You are the girl who scolds princes and Kings! Go on, I believe in you."

She blushed and finally nodded, stepping back from the prince and closing her eyes.

As she lowered her walls and felt outwards towards the plants, the rush of energy that flowed through her was overpowering, addictive and utterly mesmerising. With all of her Affinity flowers surrounding her, she felt like she was the earth itself, that she was not only one with nature but that she *was* nature. She felt she could do anything, that she could walk on water, that she could fly. She was so buoyed up by their brilliance; she let that feeling wash over her, consume her and seep out through every pore of her being as she stretched out her hands.

She heard a faint gasp and slowly opened her eyes. Frederik was looking around in amazement, and she could see why. The field had been brilliant before she'd called on the power of the plants, but now it was as if they were walking on the surface of the sun, every flower head glowing so brightly that she had to raise a hand to shield her eyes. As she did so, her jaw dropped in amazement. Not only were the flowers glowing, giving off a wondrous, blinding light, but so was she. Where the flowers' luminescence was golden, hers was white—a pure, diamond-white light that she saw reflected on the prince's own skin. She laughed, hesitant, unsure and unbelieving.

"This… this is amazing!" she cried, her own exuberance mirrored on Frederik's face. She cocked her head to one side and placed her teeth on the corner of her lower lip.

"Did you know," she breathed, "that when dandelions go to seed, every single one contains the power to grant a wish? That's why children blow on them, sending their wishes and their hopes out into the universe."

253

She laughed again and flung her arms out at shoulder height.

"Get ready, your highness!"

"For what?"

"To make a wish!"

Then she began to spin on the spot. The more she turned, the more a gentle breeze whipped up around her, batting the heads of the dandelions to follow her motion. She spun faster and faster as the earth's power and the flowers' Affinity took hold of her, hardly able to stop herself when the magic within her changed. Instead of a warming glow, it clashed like symbols in her veins and she cried out in shock at the strength of her power.

"Roslyn! Roslyn, are you alright?"

She heard Frederik's voice from somewhere nearby, but couldn't see him. She slowed her spinning and all she could see was white. For a moment she thought she was blinded by her own glowing skin, but the more she looked, the clearer it became that the white that surrounded her was spinning just as she had done moments ago. It was made up of hundreds, thousands, millions and trillions of soft, fluffy dandelion seeds. They kissed her cheeks as they flew past, and she rotated her outstretched hands, feeling the power of the wishes they held. Her heart was full of wishes, for her people, for peace and she cast these out into the spinning universe, tears in her eyes. As the whirlwind reached its climax and then slowed, each milky white seed head floated gently away on the wind. As they thinned, carried away by the breeze, she finally found Prince Frederik, covered in white fluff. It crowned his golden hair, stuck into every crevice and buttonhole of his clothing, and had even found its way into his nose and mouth, which he was currently trying to dislodge. She laughed and he looked up at her through the haze of fairy fluff.

"You… Are… Incredible," he breathed in wonder.

Roslyn shrugged and felt herself smiling. It was the first time that she agreed with someone about herself, that what she had just done was amazing. It was an unknown and overwhelming feeling, one which she hastily brushed aside. Plucking a seed head from Frederik's hair, she held it in front of his eyes.

"So there you are. I can make dandelions go to seed."

The prince pulled her towards him and stroked her face. He had a strange look in his eye, one that she'd never seen before; it wasn't anger; it wasn't pain nor his usual cheekiness; it was something entirely different and something she was reluctant to put a name to, in case this was all just a happy illusion.

"If *all* you can do is make a whirlwind of wishes, Roslyn, then never change."

✳

It was evening by the time they rode up the long hill towards Novlada, and in the purple light of dusk that fell behind the hilltop castle, stars appeared, small pinpricks of light that twinkled more brightly than the yellow torches and fires illuminating the man-made structure. It had never looked beautiful to Roslyn before. She suddenly saw that it was not just a prison for her, nor the stronghold of a tyrant, but a home, a way of life, and that of the man riding beside her.

He caught her watching him and smiled. They didn't say anything; they didn't need to. Their hearts were full and their heads were light with the promise of the future.

As the party rode up through the streets, people cheered, waving their tankards and calling out to their much-loved prince. Once again, Roslyn saw Frederik through their eyes: the golden-haired child so full of life and vigour, the man who was striving for peace. He gave them hope, too—hope that they could leave the past twenty-five years of hatred and instability behind.

However, the peace disappeared the moment their horses clattered into the stable yard of the castle. A servant ran over to them, scaring the horses and making Marble shy in fear. Roslyn gasped and held on for dear life, squeezing her knees to the side of the horse and gripping the reins as if they were a lifeline. Captain Dietrich jumped from his mount and steadied the horse with shushing noises whilst Frederik lifted her down. Then he rounded on the poor boy.

"What is the meaning of this? Do you not see you could have harmed her?" His voice was raw with protection and Roslyn's heart swelled for an instant before the boy's words cut her off.

"Please, your highness, it's the king!" His eyes were wide and his breath was frantic as he tried to get his message out in one coherent statement. "He needs the healer. He's had an accident. He needs you too, sire!"

Frederik stepped towards the boy and towered over him, taking his shirt in his fist and pulling him ever closer to his face. When he spoke, spittle sprayed across the boy's face.

"Where is he?"

Roslyn placed a hand on Frederik's shoulder to calm him, even though her own heart was pounding. It wasn't the boy's fault.

"In his chambers, sire," squeaked the servant before the prince let him go and he ran up the stairs into the castle two at a time. Roslyn had a hard time keeping up, her satchel banging against her legs. There were some medicinal supplies within the king's chambers, but she preferred to have her own with her. Her heart was in her mouth as they ran through the corridors, servants and nobles parting before them like stalks of corn before a summer storm. Prince Frederik crashed through the king's doors with a clatter and skidded to a kneel at the old man's bedside. He took the wizened, liver-spotted hand in his, pressed it to his lips and looked up at the gaunt, sallow face of King Casimir.

"Father! I'm here, it's Frederik. I'm here." He made shushing noises and grappled with the king's hand.

The invalid pulled free from his son, feebly waving him away. His eyes flickered around the room and fell on Roslyn before he extended a gnarled finger towards her.

"Girl," he croaked. "I need… another… draught."

Roslyn rushed over and held the back of her hand to his head, and checked his pulse at the same time.

"Can you tell me what happened, your majesty?"

The king was so breathless that he could not speak, so instead, his steward stepped forward.

"His majesty was in the throne room, hearing complaints of the people, when he vomited all over the steps and then collapsed. We rushed him up here as soon as we could, and called for the healers, but he would not permit any to see him, but you, Pleveli."

Roslyn looked down at the king and raised her eyebrows, her voice stern.

"Now that was most foolish of you, your Majesty. What would have happened if I hadn't got here?"

She wrenched back the sheets and pressed her hands against his stomach. It was hard. The king groaned, sat up with a sudden judder, and heaved over the side of the bed. Nothing left his lips except a small trail of yellow bile. He was hot to the touch and sweating all over. Roslyn helped the king back onto his pillows, brushing an alarmed Frederik to the side as she rolled up her sleeves, while the steward cleaned up the mess on the floor and around his master's mouth.

"Your majesty," Roslyn spoke loudly and clearly as the man's vision wavered. "I'm going to need to give you a stronger dose of both your medicine and the sleeping draught." Then she rushed off to the counter at the back of the room and began to prepare the medicines for the king. She flipped open her satchel and hurriedly pulled out the ingredients she needed. Her hands shook as they passed over the cloth-wrapped hemlock root; there was no way she would be adding that tonight, no matter what the king's order. Sweat prickled across her brow. She was certain it had caused this sudden bout of illness alongside his cancer.

"Can someone tell me what is happening?" Prince Frederik yelled, his voice wavering with worry. The steward brought him a chair and placed it by his father's bedside. The king finally extended his hand to his son. Frederik snatched it up as his eyes squeezed out tears of confusion.

Casimir turned his grave face towards his son and licked his lips. When he spoke, his breath was ragged, and

258

it forced his chest to heave unnaturally, so much so that it looked as though his ribs were about to rip right through his skin.

"I'm dying, Frederik. Hadn't you noticed?"

The prince shook his head and looked over at Roslyn. "No? No, it can't be. You were so much better!"

The king laughed, or at least tried to, before lapsing into a grating, bubbling splutter.

"Don't look at her, I forbade her from telling you. It is not her fault. I knew I was dying before she even came to me and confirmed it. But, I will admit her medicines are much more effective than those blue-robed buffoons in the basement. She has promised to keep me going as long as she can, so I may see your brother married."

Roslyn winced. Yes, she was cursed with keeping him alive and killing him at the same time. She walked over with the now prepared medicine, and Frederik helped to sit his father up. She poured the draft in slow, steady portions through his cracked lips.

"I can only hope," the king sighed as he leant back into his pillows, "that this Act of yours will keep the country strong when I am gone. But the time for gallivanting is over, Frederik. She," he nodded weakly in Roslyn's direction, "needs to be here with me now, to make me comfortable until the end. And you need to prepare for your marriage."

At these last words, both Frederik and Roslyn blinked and shot a look at each other. The prince sat back in his chair and Roslyn took a minute step back from the bed in alarm. Frederik shook his head, sending his golden curls flying into his eyes.

"My marriage, Father? Has the illness confused you? It is Viktor who is getting married. He will be back any

259

day now and so will his bride. I'm sure you can hold on. You *will* see him married."

King Casimir shook his head as violently as he could and snatched at his son's hand with skeletal claws.

"No! It is time for *you* to do your duty. When I am gone, when your brother is married, you will ride up back to Bergam and you will strengthen the ties I have let slide these past few years as I concentrated on the rebellions. We must not let them think we have forgotten about them."

Roslyn glanced over at Frederik and saw that his face had turned waxen with horror. Her own heart was being squeezed inside her chest as if by an iron clamp that had taken hold and was being tightened by the second. Frederik swallowed, and she watched the slow bob of the lump in his throat and the quiver of his lip.

"You are sending me back to that frozen wasteland?" He swallowed and whispered so quietly she barely heard it. "Who?"

"You are to marry the Dowager Duchess Anita Eitzmer, my cousin. She has been recently widowed, and she is young enough yet to produce an heir, and if not, then you will soon find another, a cousin or something to fill her shoes."

Frederik rose, shaking his head, all the while his eyes widening in disbelief. "You would have me marry your cousin? Your cousin, who is nearly as old as you?"

The king coughed, and a speckle of blood appeared on his hand.

"It is your duty to Bergam, Frederik, to the Oderberg line. Enough of your playboy antics, enough of raking your way through the countryside, enough of your dreams.

You must step up and do what must be done. That is in order. That is my last request…"

Frederik shook with injustice but at the king's words, the fire in his eyes died and his shoulders sank.

After Casimir's expulsion of effort, he tried to suck in breath, but rasped and heaved with such a grating sound that Roslyn was almost convinced he would die right before their eyes. She ran towards him and placed a cup of water to his lips. He gulped at it greedily and eventually calmed down. He rose his watery, tired eyes to Roslyn and nodded.

"Time for the sleeping draught, girl." His voice faded, and his eyes flickered. Roslyn didn't think he needed the sedative, so exhausted was his limp frame, but she followed her order as the prince stormed out of the room to face his.

Chapter 25

It was late by the time Roslyn finally walked away from the king's apartments. He was in a bad way, and guilt wracked her as her feet led her through the quiet, dark halls of the castle.

Had she done this? Was she truly killing the king, or had the swelling sickness got there first? There was no way she could know; the amounts of hemlock she'd added had been so small, but then the king was already being eaten away by the evil inside of him. Small shavings could have done the damage just as easily as if she'd given him a whole tuber. She swore, cursing Eik and his need for vengeance. She cursed the king for making her play his sick game of chance. Both were forcing her into the guise of a killer. That wasn't who she was.

In her confusion and exhaustion, she soon found herself opening the door to Frederik's apartments. She hadn't meant to walk this way. As she opened the door and realised where she was. She turned to leave as quickly as she could, but a sombre voice from the balcony called out to her.

"Roslyn?"

She paused in the doorway, feeling that if she stayed still he wouldn't be able to see her and would believe it a trick of the light.

"Roslyn, please, come here." Although his words were softly spoken, she heard the order in them, heard pleading and the need for company, but not just any company—hers. Even though she could barely face him right now, knowing what she had done, she walked through the lavish apartment, setting her bag down on a couch and out onto the balcony. She found him sitting in a wide, cushioned chair staring out over the dark countryside. She kept her head bowed and wrung her hands before her as she came to a stop at his side, not daring to look at him and bobbed a formal curtsy.

"I'm… I'm sorry for intruding, your highness. I forgot that they'd moved me. I beg your pardon, I'll leave you in peace." She was about to turn when the prince lifted his arm from the chair rest and took her hand ever so gently in his. He didn't squeeze, he didn't grab. He simply held her hand, but the spark that ignited within her stopped her in her tracks.

"Please, Roslyn. I can't be alone right now."

She walked to the edge of the balcony, still not daring to look at his face, and placed her hands on the balustrade, turning her eyes towards the black velvet of the night.

"I must apologise, sire, for not telling you about your father, but he—"

"You know my name is Frederik," the prince interrupted. "Why this formality? Why this coldness, Roslyn?" She heard the creak of the wicker chair as he stood and the gentle tap of his slippers on the stone as he made his way to her side. Then and only then did she turn to look up at him, brows furrowed in sorrow and lips trembling.

"Because now you belong to another… not that you ever belonged to me." A veil of sorrow had been drawn between them, bringing with it distance and fumbled words. "Besides, I was your healer and then you got better. You don't need me anymore. I'm little more than a …."

Frederik moved a step closer. His breath brushed the top of her head as he spoke with vigour. "Please don't say it."

"Conquest."

"Roslyn, you were never that. I swear."

She looked up at him with hard eyes, a sudden ember of anger igniting in her chest. "Says the party prince! That's what everyone called you; they warned me you liked pretty things. Is that all I was to you, a bauble?" She shook her head and wiped away an angry tear on the back of her hand.

Frederik snatched that hand up and kissed the wet silvery trail where the salt water had stained her skin. "Never, Roslyn. Look at me." With his other hand he cupped her cheek and although she tried not to look in his eyes or the way they sparkled in the starlight, her resistance crumbled and streams of argent tears rolled down her cheeks.

He continued, "Do you know what I wished for today, in the meadow? I could have wished for anything in the world. There were thousands, millions of wishes swirling around, but the only thing I wished for was you!"

Roslyn's breath caught in the back of her throat as the hairs on her arms stood up.

"I wished to spend my life with you, and that *we* could be the future of this country. You and I, an example to everyone that Oderberg and Domovnian can live side by side, that they can... can love each other."

Roslyn's breath jarred as she tried to take a breath and shook her head. She extricated herself from Frederik's arms.

"It cannot be, Frederik. You are a Prince, and I—I..." her voice trailed off as she turned her back to him and raised her hand to the bridge of her nose, trying to squeeze the tears back into her eyes. She wanted so badly to tell him who she was, but what would be the point? It wouldn't change anything. She'd only die all the quicker once Casimir found out. "I am a Domovnian Hedgie who is next to worthless. You know as well as I that we cannot be together." Her voice caught as Frederik traced his fingers along her shoulders cautiously. "You know as well as I that as soon as your father dies, the Act will fail, that Viktor will be just as bad as he was, and that you will be sent away to marry and I'll be forgotten, if not killed."

Frederik spun her around and held her close. "No! I will never let that happen, Roslyn. I sent my wish out into the universe today and I know it heard me. We will be together!"

Roslyn couldn't stand it anymore. She wanted him so badly, not just for tonight but forever, and she sank into his chest, tilted her head upwards and their lips met in a crush of tortured passion.

Her head swam with lack of oxygen as he kissed her. Tears streamed down her face at the bittersweet ecstasy of it all. She was finally able to draw breath when his kisses left her mouth and traced their way down her neck to her collarbone, soft as a butterfly's wings. Then, in a sudden rush of movement, he swept her up in his arms. She laced hers around his neck and he lifted her up onto the stone balustrade, spreading her legs as he pressed her towards him.

She groaned as greed coursed through her. She wanted him—body, mind and soul, here beneath the stars. As if reading her mind, Frederik reached his hand up between her legs and stroked the soft skin of her inner thigh. A fire ignited within her at his touch and she burned with frantic tension, running her hands down his chest, the thin fabric of his absurdly flouncy shirt getting in her way.

Her touch prompted him to grasp her thighs, squeezing them as he dipped his head down and kissed her. As the world swam out of focus, she reached up to his collar and gripped it hard, pulling his lips down into hers even harder. When they broke apart, she tore at his shirt and pushed the fabric down off his shoulders. Roslyn looked up from under her fringe and moaned as his finger slid into her hot, wet centre. She writhed with the movement and her hands shot out and down to support herself on the balustrade. He worked his fingers within her, supporting her with his other arm, dipping her back over the edge just enough to make her feel like she was literally on the edge of the world.

Standing there, ripped shirt pushed down to his wrists, the silvery light of the stars and the moon kissing his chest, it was as if an angel graced her presence. Suddenly, he withdrew his fingers, slick with her lust, and scooped her up in his arms to place her gently on the heavily pillowed chair.

Frederik leant down to kiss her and fumbled with the laces on her bodice. He was taking too long. She needed him now. She pushed him back so that he was kneeling at her feet and stood, peeling herself out of her clothes, flinging each item to the ground in her haste; bodice, skirts, stays. She shivered a little as she reached down to lift the hem of her shift and saw the prince swallow. As she pulled it over her head, he sucked in a breath. In the bright light of the moon, there was no doubt of her ancestry—Roslyn's olive skin shone, sparkling as if she'd rolled in the powder of crushed pearls. Frederik wrapped his arms around her bare buttocks, resting his head on her navel and groaning.

"You are…"

What she was, she never found out, because he dived onto her, laying her down on the chair, smothering her mouth with his. She let her hands wander over his shoulders, his torso, down his impeccably sculpted abdominals until she came to the barrier of cloth at his hips. She looked up at him and swallowed, her breathing hard and urgent. She bit her lip and grinned as her hands worked the laces of his britches and freed his cock. She took it in her hands as he slipped the rest of his trousers off over his round, firm arse. He was hot to the touch and so smooth that she couldn't help but rub her hands up and down his length, marvelling.

He stood suddenly and kicked off the rest of his clothes. She was breathless for a moment at the sight of him, standing naked in the moonlight, hard and erect and wanting her. She sat up and slipped her thumbs into the band of her stockings to push them off, but stopped as the prince whispered frantically, "No! Leave them on."

She raised her lips in a smile before placing her hands in between her legs. She spread them, inviting him in. But he just stood there, watching her, unable to move as she gently massaged herself, not breaking eye contact the whole time. She was only mirroring what he had done to her in the bathhouse, but the way she held him helpless as he watched her pleasure herself was spellbinding, and made her feel powerful and in control.

"I'll give the orders now, Frederik," she said pointedly.

He grinned. "There she is… there's my Roslyn."

"I want you," Roslyn licked her lips and scurried further back up the chaise until her head rested on the pillows. "I want all of you… inside me."

The prince leant forwards and crawled towards her, stopping at her toes.

"As you wish, my lady." Roslyn had been expecting him to obey her command immediately, to thrust his cock deep into her like he had his fingers, but he took one of her stockinged feet and kissed the very tips of her toes. Then his mouth worked up to her ankle, calf, decorating it with little butterfly kisses as his hands stroked her other leg, building up tension. Then he followed the tingle up from her toes as if he were planting it there with each tantalising brush of his lips. The kisses turned into nibbles and licks of his hot tongue as he broached the ribbon of her stockings just above her knee. She groaned with both suspense and impatience. Then, grasping his curls in her hand, she forced him to look up at her.

"I said," she moaned, "I want you."

"And you shall have me. Every… which… way, my lady." Frederik grinned, his teeth shining in the moonlight, and suddenly his hands swooped under her buttocks, lifting her hips and his head disappeared between her legs.

She sat up with an unexpected shiver as his tongue traced its way from the bottom of her lips up, searching for that spot he had known so well with his fingers. It didn't take him long to find it and soon she was blindsided

268

by the throb of her clit as he flicked it, sucked it and caressed it with the tip of his tongue. She moaned, and in return he moaned into her, the vibrations making her gasp with pleasure. She felt the rise of climax spreading up her legs, making her head swim, and she clutched the wide armrests of the chair with white-knuckled hands as the explosion burst forth within her. As she came, she shuddered and her hips jerked up and down, but Frederik pushed further into her, still licking, still teasing. When she finally fell still, he stopped and raised his head to peer over her navel.

"Is that what you meant, my lady?"

Roslyn smiled breathlessly and shook her head. "Not in the least."

She stood and pulled him up from the patio, then pushed him roughly in the chest and back into the nest of pillows so that he was on his back. Frederik's cock stood high and proud in the night air, like a flagpole waiting to be dressed. She knelt down, bending over him, and slipped it between her lips, taking it deep within her mouth and coating it with the wetness from her tongue. She heard his muffled cries, and tasted his saltiness on her tongue. When he was wet enough, although not nearly as wet as she was, she gave one final lick from the base of the shaft to the tip, swirling her tongue around its head as she went. Then she rose and stood over him, one leg on either side of his outstretched ones, took his cock in her hand and guided it into her.

The pair groaned simultaneously, and Roslyn lost all sense of order and control. She lost sight of who they were, where they were—everything else in this cursed palace was gone. It was only the two of them, writhing and grinding on each other in their insatiable hunger. She thrust her hips forwards and up, forwards and up, faster and faster and faster. The groans she elicited from the prince were music to her ears. He placed his thumb at the base of his shaft and every time she rocked her hips forwards it hit her in just the right spot, making her want it more, harder, faster. She was sweating with the effort; she was tiring, but she didn't care. She was lightheaded and lost in the heat of the moment. Her eyes had been closed for some time and she opened them to see Frederik's open-mouthed, silent cry of pleasure. When she saw the love in his eyes as he looked up at her naked body, writhing in the movement of passion and the moonlight, she was swept away by exquisite bliss.

She cried out loud as her world exploded into a kaleidoscope of stars and brilliant blond curls. Her cries were joined by an exquisitely tortured series of pants from the man beneath her.

She felt his release burst inside her and then they were still, chests pounding, eyes soft and limbs weak. She slumped into his chest, rolling off him and curling up into the crook of his arm where they lay in a sweet, sweat-drenched stupor.

Frederik held her close as a gentle breeze made her shiver. The coolness of the night and the heat of his body were delicious. With the softest lips in the world, he kissed her forehead, her eyelids, the tip of her nose and finally her willing open mouth. When the kiss was done, he sighed and pulled her tight until the pair of them closed their eyes and slipped into the oblivion of sleep.

Chapter 26

The wispy grey light of dawn was just creeping over the horizon when Roslyn made her way back to her own room. Every step reminded her of the part of Frederik that had filled her so completely during the night and was now lacking. She smiled to herself, letting a little hum dance on her lips. As she passed a window that looked over the courtyard, a sudden commotion caught her eye.

A volley of shouts and the clatter of hooves on cobbles bounced around the walls as a group of riders cantered full pelt into the enclosed space, coming to an abrupt stop that forced their horses to scream. Although she could hear the shouts, Roslyn couldn't make out the words and her pulse rose as she saw one of the horsemen slide from his mount, reach up and pull a limp form from the back of his horse. Her heart stuck in her throat as she saw a mop of blond hair fall over the man's face, obscuring his features. There was no mistaking that golden shade. Servants gathered, shouting for stretchers and healers, and at once she was running through the corridors and down the stairs.

The commotion had awoken others in the palace and before she had even made it into the hallway where they had dragged the unconscious figure, a crowd had gathered. She pushed them aside with her elbows to get to the injured man, but stopped short as she caught her first glimpse of him. It was Crown Prince Viktor. They had laid him out on the floor, and even from this angle, peering around Gruber's arm that shot out like a barrier across her chest at her approach, she knew he was dead. "He will not need our help, Miss Pleveli." The wizened old apothecary dug his fingers into her upper arm and scowled. A chill ran down her spine and the world seemed to slow as his words confirmed what her own eyes refused to believe. "Not even you can raise the dead."

A hush fell abruptly as the news spread. The future of the realm was lying in a crumpled, undignified heap at their feet and no one was quite sure what to do about it. No one knew what this meant, where they would go from here.

A sudden flurry of movement and sound from the back of the hall signalled the arrival of Prince Frederik and the king.

"Sire, I really don't think—" his steward began. But when Casimir saw the strangely waxen figure of his son on the cold stone tiles, limbs flattened and sticking out at odd angles, he stopped. His knees gave way beneath him and his breath was wrenched from his throat by sorrow, twisting it into a gargled cry of agony.

"My son! My son! What have they done?" His cries reverberated around the stone hall, bouncing back onto the members of the crowd, sending shivers down their spines.

Frederik stepped forwards and knelt beside his father with a wince, to hold the old, sick man as he wept gut-wrenching cries of sorrow. He looked from his brother's beaten-up corpse to the men who brought him in with imploring eyes. "What happened?"

The guards had accompanied the crown prince on a trip that should have ended happily, with the arrival of the future king and queen, but instead had ended in disaster and death. They shifted on their feet, trying to get their breath back. Their clothes were spattered with mud, foliage and debris. Their metal armour was horribly bent out of shape, and blood poured down the side of one man's face.

"We were attacked, your highness," the bloodied man rasped.

Prince Frederik stood, allowing his father's steward to take his place by the weeping man. "I can see that. Tell me, right now—what happened?"

The man stood to attention and, through his laboured breathing, gave a report. "We were about a day's ride from the borderlands, your highness, when we had to ride through a wooded area."

"The Borderlands? What were you even doing there? You were supposed to be returning from the coast!" the distraught king shouted.

The man bowed his head and licked his lips nervously. "Yes, your majesty, but his highness Prince Viktor wanted to surprise his bride, welcome her to our country and escort her the rest of the way."

As the king scoffed at the idea, Roslyn felt her own eyebrows raise. She hadn't known Viktor was such a romantic.

"Why were you in the woods? I ordered all roads cleared of trees." The king's voice hovered somewhere between an order and a plea.

The soldier cleared his throat and bowed. "Yes, sire but in the Borderlands, orders are not always so swiftly taken up nor maintained. So, the only way for us to reach Eredzha was to go through this forest. We rode for some time in peace, but then a sense of unease crept up around us and the men reported shadows among the trees. His Royal Highness…" the man gulped and looked at the corpse on the floor. "Prince Viktor, he… he thought they were just silly superstitions, that the men believed in ghosts or something and ordered us to continue. We soon realised that they were not ghosts. There were men running through the forest. Suddenly the trees around us came to life, moving and twisting in demonic creaks, the likes of which you've never heard your majesty." The man's voice was raising with emotion and memory of the attack and a foreboding chill crept up Roslyn's spine.

"They beat us with their branches. They twisted over the road so that we had to force the horses into the woodland proper. But the prince, he urged us on. He told us we could outrun it, and so we did. We kicked the horses as hard as we could, Hoff forgive us, but it was to no avail. Just before we reached the edge of the wood, the largest tree you've ever seen was plucked from the ground and shot the high into the air." The soldier paused, his eyes lost in the memory. His voice petered out. "And then it came crashing down. Right on top of us. Most were fortunate enough to roll out of the way. Many received broken limbs, but the trunk of the tree was aimed at Prince Viktor…"

274

He could say no more. He didn't need to. Everybody could see the mangled limbs, the crushed chest and face that were almost unrecognisable as the strong, stalwart golden Prince. As the courtiers and servants who had gathered wept and the king's howls faded into gurgled hiccoughs, Roslyn closed her eyes and felt her lips quiver.

"What kind of tree was it?" Her voice was so thin that at first, nobody looked around—nobody but Frederik.

His eyes were red-rimmed and his face was twisted in agonising grief that he was trying to hold back for his father, for his people, but was failing. "What does it matter? What does it matter what kind of tree was?"

Roslyn trembled. Her heart sank and her stomach turned into a block of ice. She looked past Prince Frederik at the soldier who had told the tale. "Please, just tell me, what kind of tree?"

All eyes turned to the guard as he shook his head with a perplexed expression. "I… From its size, it could only have been one thing. It was an oak."

That final word was like a death knoll to Roslyn. She sank to her knees and gasped. The oak was Eik's Affinity tree. *Bastard!* She should have known he would do something like this; she should have known and warned Frederik, but how could she? She'd been here the entire time, locked away in her naïve indulgence with the prince, who now looked down at her with calculated horror.

She was level with the king now, and his eyes glowed with fury. "You! You know who did this, don't you? Guards! Take her to the dungeons! No, better yet, run her through! You knew. You set him up, didn't you, you scheming bitch! Guards! Give me that sword and I'll kill her myself!"

He leapt to his feet with a lurch that belied his weakness and snatched the sword from the nearest guard's hands. He raised it above his head, screaming with bitter fury as he wobbled towards Roslyn, who could do nothing but raise her hands above her, pleading for her life.

"I knew nothing! I did nothing!"

Frederik suddenly moved, stepping in front of Roslyn, cutting her off from the king. He reached up and grappled with the liver-spotted hands around the hilt of the sword until the invalid's strength was spent, and then wrenched it from his grasp.

"Father, you are beside yourself. Roslyn has been here the whole time. There was no way she could have informed anyone of Viktor's travels." His voice slowed as a memory flickered across his eyes. "But I do believe she knows who may have been behind the attack…" He turned to Roslyn. "The man who accosted you in the marketplace?"

Roslyn's heart broke in two under his pleading gaze. She could not give up her people, but she was as angry as he was at his brother's mindless death. How could Eik have been so stupid? She couldn't even nod her head, but lowered it to the ground in shame.

"Guards," the king rasped behind Frederik. "Lock her up until she is ready to talk. I will have vengeance for my son, and I will not leave any stone in this miserable country unturned until I find the tree-humping son of a whore who did this!"

This time Frederik didn't stop the guards as they moved towards her. He watched with cold, confused eyes as they bound her hands behind her back with short, sharp movements that burned her wrists and made her grunt with pain and indignation. In the scuffle her satchel was torn

276

from her shoulder and fell to the stone flags with a thud. She tried to reach for it but, it was kicked out of view and was soon lost amongst the forest of legs around her. A cold sweat prickled up her spine and her stomach griped at its loss. She always had it with her and its absence stripped her of all purpose, especially here.

"Easy, men," he ordered, holding out a hand that they were to remain where they were. "She will go willingly, won't you... Miss Pleveli?"

The use of her full name hurt more than the ropes around her wrists, but she bit back her tears and nodded.

The prince looked around at the crowd, at the corpse on the floor and his father's grief-stricken body, supported by his stewards. "For the love of the Chained Mountain, will somebody please lay my brother to rest somewhere more befitting than the hallway!"

The prince swallowed as his gaze met hers, pleading for the truth, but then lowered as if he couldn't stand the sight of her anymore. He turned to the guards. "And what of the princess, what of my brother's bride?"

"We had not yet reached the bride's retinue, your highness. She is safe and well and still en route to her betrothed. There was no time to send a messenger. He wouldn't have got through even if we had...." The guard's voice tapered off as his eyes clouded with memory.

The king was now on his knees, a steward at each elbow as someone ran to fetch a wheeled chair.

"Well, that's as well then." He turned his tear-stained face towards Frederik and said coldly, "Good job I have a spare. We can still keep our alliance with Eredzha. Hoff knows we'll need their forces now. Your Assimilation Act has failed, Frederik. You are now the crown prince, and your bride is coming for you."

He shook his head. "No, there must be a way…" Frederik was still, staring at the space now left on the floor where his brother had been.

The king tipped back his head and laughed, a crazed, injured cackle of a man at the end of his patience. "I thought you would be pleased? Instead of my old cousin, you get to fuck a virgin princess." He shook his head and levelled his gaze. "The only way you could unite the two people now was if you married the lost Domonov princess!"

Casimir turned to Roslyn with a sly smile that made her skin crawl. "You don't happen to know where she is, do you? No? That's because she doesn't exist." He whipped his head back towards his son and growled. "Pull your head out of the clouds Frederik and do your duty to your people." His voice grew louder as his steward started to wheel him away. "As soon as the prince's betrothed arrives, have the marriage performed immediately. We don't have much time. You will no doubt be King before the month is out."

A sudden movement in the crowd forced the discourse to a close. Women gasped and men grumbled as a large figure dressed in blue forced its way through.

"Sires! Oh, save us, sires!" Apothecary Gruber's voice rang loud and clear, echoing off the stone walls. He broke through into the inner circle, one arm held high, the other pointing at her. Roslyn's satchel was slung over his shoulder. Her mouth went dry and she felt the blood leave her face. "This imposter—this harlot, who bewitched our beloved prince into taking her into his home—is a *murderer*!"

A collective gasp rose up from the crowd as every eye turned towards her. She was certain that, had she not already been detained, the guards would have pounced on her now. As it was, they gave her wrists a sharp twist, forcing her words out in a hiss.

"You lie. I have killed no one!"

Gruber took a step closer, thrusting his raised hand forward. "Then what is this?"

She lowered her gaze, already knowing what lay in the folds of cloth at the centre of his palm. She said nothing but stared up at him, her lips quivering with rage. Although his face wore an expression of innocent shock, his eyes twinkled with the malice of victory.

"This," he turned back towards the crowd, "is hemlock…one of the deadliest poisons known to man. It rolled from Miss Pleveli's satchel only moments ago when she was apprehended."

Her chest heaved as she glanced at Frederik. He wasn't looking at her but staring intently at the tuber in Gruber's hand. His skin had turned the colour of old porridge and he looked like he was trying not to vomit.

"And look closer still…" Gruber swung round, his voice booming theatrically, "Shavings have been taken! This whore has been poisoning the king!"

The room erupted into shouts of indignation and surprise. The prince's head snapped up to her, eyes wide and imploring, begging her to deny it. Before she could say anything, a grating, braying sound drowned out the crowd. The king was laughing.

"So, you stuck at it! I did wonder if you had the nerve, even after I ordered you to do it! Didn't think you would; thought you would sack off after that first time, but you proved me wrong. Well done you, Domovnian!"

Frederik turned to his father in stunned silence. "You ordered her to poison you? Are you mad?" His neck whipped round so quickly back at Roslyn, she was amazed it didn't snap. "And you *did* it?"

She shook her head, tears finally breaking through and rolling down her cheeks.

The new crown prince held up a hand as his father cackled madly from the floor. "I cannot believe what I am hearing. This is madness."

"Frederik," she breathed, finally finding her voice. She reached out to touch his arm, clasping the bracelet at his wrist, but he snatched it away from her, the band of nettle cordage snapping and falling to the ground. He nodded to the guards that held her.

"Get my father back to bed. He needs his rest. I'll deal with this." Roslyn's heart was squeezed by an ice-cold grip and she looked towards Frederik, who finally shook off his daze and met her eye.

"Take her away."

* * *

That day was the longest of Roslyn's life. As per the king's command, as much as she tried to stay on her feet and retain some small modicum of dignity, she was dragged, heels scraping on the stone tiles of the floor to the dungeons. The guards sneered as they flung her in the cell; her face slapped against the immovable stone of the far wall, her teeth rattling inside her skull on impact. She slid to the ground as the door slammed behind her and raised a shaking hand to her temple. When she pulled it away, it was wet with her hot and sticky blood.

She remained there all morning and most of the afternoon, listening to the screams of her people as the

280

Oderbergs went after any Domovnian still in Novlada. They were paying the price on Eik's behalf, the feckless coward.

No one brought her food or water, and she was certain she was about to pass out when the door was wrenched open again. The light streamed in and Roslyn flung her hands up to her eyes, shielding herself from the blinding onslaught.

"Get up!" a harsh voice sounded, and she didn't dare disobey. Using the wall behind her for support, she slowly crawled up until she was on her feet, and stared at the enormous guard that filled the doorway. She'd never seen him before, but by the look of him, he knew his business, and that business was death. Was this it? Had her time of execution finally come? She'd known deep down since that day in the woods that she'd been living on borrowed time.

"You and I, and some of my men here, are gonna go for a little ride... at the king's behest, of course." His nasally voice was thick with sarcasm. He didn't even need to take a step into the cell. He merely reached out his ham-fisted hand and grabbed Roslyn's arm, pulling her out into the corridor. She had just enough time, as her eyes adjusted to the light, to look around frantically at the group of assembled soldiers. She knew none of them, save one. Captain Dietrich raised a quick finger to his lips before the world vanished and a hood was pulled down over her head.

Chapter 27

When the cart stopped and Roslyn was dragged kicking and screaming from its splintered wooden boards, she knew it was late by the cool air of evening that raced up her arms. She was hauled to her feet and the hood was removed. She could breathe again, after hours of inhaling her own sour smelling breath and trying to peer through the scratching weave of the sack. She sniffed and smelt burning thatch on the wind.

Clearly the reprisals after the Crown prince's death had spilled over Novlada's walls. She looked around, expecting to see a scaffold, and was amazed to find there was none. At first, she thought they hadn't left the palace, but the more she looked at her surroundings in the dim light, the more her heart sank. A shiver of a new kind spread up the back of her legs. It tripped over her spine and prickled the skin on her arms as she realised where they were. She had seen this place in her dreams.

Eluha.

She twirled around and looked up at the monolith of a guard that was leading the operation. "Why are we here?"

The guard looked down at her with a quizzical expression. "Oh, so you know where we are? Used to coming here, are you, to make all your little schemes and plots with your rebel friends? Is this your headquarters?" He looked around and then, in an obscene theatrical caricature, placed to his hand to his cheek, bent forward slightly and bellowed into the shadows of the ruined palace. "Cooee! Rebels, we've got your little spy here… Come out, come out, wherever you are!"

His men fell about laughing. All save one. She snuck a glance at Captain Dietrich and realised he wasn't wearing his usual livery. Was he in disguise? What was he doing here? She had no time to find out as the giant picked her up by the scruff of her neck and flung her towards the corner of the courtyard. He led her away from the empty pool with its two skeletal trees leaning above in a deathly embrace. It was even more chilling in real life, like a carcass long picked clean by the birds. At least in her dreams, she'd seen the place bathed in a silver light and felt the presence of the castle breathing in its deep slumber, but not now.

Roslyn didn't know whether to be thankful or nervous to be led deeper into the heart of this palace of nightmares. Would the woman be there? Was she real, or was she just a figment of Roslyn's overstretched imagination?

They stopped outside the base of a tower and Roslyn looked up at its smooth, ivory height. It was about the only structure in the whole of Eluha that seemed intact. Only the doorway was crumbling away. She was thrust inside, in much the same manner she had been thrown into the cell at Novlada, but this time she righted herself before she fell over her own feet.

"Welcome to your new home, Domovnian."

283

Roslyn peered into the blackness and saw only the inner walls of the white tower. She looked up and spied the remains of long disintegrated stairs, spiralling up to a platform where one lonely window let in a beam of moonlight.

"What do you mean?"

Panic rose within her as she saw the guards heaving blocks of brick and mortar towards the entrance. They were going to wall her in.

"No! No, you can't do this! I've no food, no water; I'll die!" She cursed herself inwardly at the stupidness of her exclamation.

The giant guard before her sneered. "Well, that's the whole point."

"But why here, why Eluha? Why this way? Wouldn't it have been easier to just execute me?" The guard, who had stepped back to let his men build up the wall that would seal her tomb, paused and tilted his head.

"Well, I recall his majesty saying something along the lines of seeing which one of you died first." He scoffed, and chewed on his thumb as he thought, the clinking of bricks being laid breaking the silence. Roslyn swallowed. She had to admit, the king had outdone himself this time. In a sick sense of irony, he really would kill the last of the Domonovs right where all of this started. "Now, if you ask me, I say we should have just killed you, but the king likes his little games. So, he wanted to see who would die first— him in his palace, or you, locked away in a tower with no one to save you." By this point, he was peering over the wall that had been erected in the doorway. Only a few last bricks needed laying, and then she would be left to die. The huge guard shrugged.

"Goodbye, Domovnian." He turned away as if he had better things to do with his time and left the final bricklaying to one of his guards. Roslyn was beside herself. She clawed up the newly built wall, panic frothing inside her, bubbling up and choking her as she tried to peer out through the minute hole that was left at the top. As her foot scraped on the stone, and the skin on her hands was ripped raw from the fresh mortar, she managed to hoist herself up enough to peer out of it. Her eyes met those of Captain Dietrich.

"Dietrich! Dietrich, what is going on? Can't you stop this? Does Frederik know?"

Captain Dietrich looked over his shoulder quickly. The rest of the guards were already ambling back to the cart, their business seemingly concluded. His voice was hushed and his breathing was quick.

"Frederik does not know about this. This is the king's order. I'll tell him as soon as I'm able—just hold on…" He paused and pulled something out of his dark robes and pushed it through the hole. She snatched it eagerly, hoping it was food to quell her growling stomach, but it was only a tiny slip of folded paper.

One of the guards turned back to Dietrich and shouted, "Are you done yet? Come on, there's a whore with my name on waiting for me!"

Captain Dietrich turned back and waved the last brick in the air. He called back with the voice that Roslyn had first heard in the woodlands near her home when he was putting a show on for the other members of his team, a voice that made her stomach churn with loathing.

"Just got this last one to do." He turned back into the crevice and shouted. "Let's see your weeds save you now!" And with one last sorrowful look, he placed the stone in the hole and blotted out the light.

*

It had rained during the night and Roslyn awoke slumped at the base of the newly bricked in doorway, stiff and cold. Her muscles ached, and as she moved, they screamed at her in protest. Opening her eyes was little different to keeping them shut, as the weak light that filtered down from the window high up in the tower was already dimmed with the grey clouds beyond. She shivered so violently that her teeth chattered, so she stood, brushing her arms vigorously with her hands in a feeble attempt to warm herself.

The clouds were soon chased away by the rising sun, and more light made its way into the base of the spire, allowing Roslyn to make out a few items in the abandoned tower. There was a dusty, bulky table and chair, completely riddled with pockmarks left by woodworm and she was in no doubt that if she tried to sit on said chair, she would soon find herself on the floor in a cloud of dust. A ragged tapestry hung from the wall. She studied the faded depiction.

It was of a man and a woman, or at least that was what she could make out; one larger figure in blue, and one smaller one in white and green. Both had crowns on their heads and they were turned towards each other, the palms of their hands touching, whilst vines wound themselves around their bodies, wrapping them tightly in their shy embrace. A host of figures surrounded them that Roslyn assumed to be people until she looked closer and saw they were melting into the trees and the rivers of the background. They couldn't be the Ancestors, could they? Surely it was just the distortion of the threads by time, soot and decay. She shook her head and returned her gaze to the couple at the centre. She had little doubt who they were, some long-forgotten pair of Domonov rulers... her ancestors. Her gut instinct was confirmed when she spied the crown on the smaller figure's head. The threads that depicted it were of the same copper as the crown that had glinted above Casimir's fireplace. It had the same shape of vines and briars and thorns, twisting round from the back of the head to two tall horns at the front—the Briar Crown.

She shivered again, this time not from the cold. She was hesitant to rip the dusty cloth from its hangings, but if she was to survive, she would need extra warmth. After all, the heat of the day could not penetrate deep enough into the stones of her prison, and she had been wearing only her skirt and cotton blouse when she had been abducted. She draped the musty fabric around her frail shoulders and turned her back to the wall.

There are a few other assortments of items in the room, odd things like a bucket—or had it once been a bowl? It was hard to tell from its damage—that she placed under a drip that ran all the way down from the window, where a small puddle of water had gathered. She scooped some up in her hands greedily, not caring about the dust and mud in the liquid. Food she could go without longer, but water... Water was vital. There was also the hilt of a rusted sword and, to her horror, the remains of a guardsman that she found behind the table. It was all bones by now. The skeleton was encased in elegant,

287

flowing metal armour that would have looked like water running over the body.

After her brief exploration, Roslyn sat back down by the doorway and let misery wash over her. How would she ever get out of here? She wouldn't—it was as simple as that. King Casimir had planned this well. No one ever came to Eluha. It was full of bones and ghosts, and the memory of a former glory that had been snuffed out in one brutal night. No one would hear her cries, so there was no point in trying to call for help. The king must have known about this room; he must have known there was only one entrance and no way out. Whether she liked it or not, this was her tomb. With a sudden cry of fear, she rested her head in her hands and wept.

✳

By the evening of the second day, Roslyn was faint with hunger and almost dehydrated. The bucket she had placed under the window collected just enough water to keep her alive, and she had begun talking to the skeleton that lay on the other side of the room. If she were here much longer, she would have to prop them up into a proper sitting position so they could contemplate the mysteries of death together. Maybe someone would discover them years from now and think them partners in life and death, and think up wild theories of how they died.

"Ancestors, if only this had been a storeroom, there might have been something to eat." Roslyn's stomach rumbled so loudly she could have sworn a wild beast nestled under her rib cage.

"What was your last meal, I wonder?" she called over the table to the empty smile of the guardsman. "They say the Oderbergs attacked in the middle of a feast, the night of the Fall. Just think of it, a feast—spiced rices wrapped in vine leaves, barley, grilled vegetables, cheeses... all dishes that just make your mouth water just thinking about them."

Roslyn actually had to stop herself from doing just that, for she was starting to salivate. "If only Dietrich had tossed me some food before he locked me in here, his last crust of bread or something," she mumbled petulantly. Then she remembered he had given her something, and she cast her eyes about the room.

She looked around the dimly lit space for the tiny packet the prince's guardsman had slipped through the hole before he'd sealed her tomb. She couldn't see it. She began scrabbling around on the dirt floor, frantic that she had lost it, or worse, imagined the whole thing. Then she spied a corner of cream poking out from the tapestry that she'd been using as a blanket.

"Oh, there you are." Her voice croaked with thirst and was tinged with the beginning of madness. "Now, let's see what old Dietrich left for me."

With steadier hands than she thought possible in her weakened state, she gently prised off the smear of wax that sealed the parchment shut and opened its folds as gently as if she were opening a flower bud. The items inside rolled instantly into the creases, forming a square of small green and purple balls—nettle seeds. Nettle seeds?

Suddenly, a delirious smile lit up Roslyn's face. He had given her something useful after all, but she would have to be clever with them. There was little water, and even less earth, but use them she could. She took a few from their bed with her fingertips and set them in the soil that had accumulated inside the stone tower after years of neglect and the seasons' detritus being blown in through the destroyed doorway. Then she rushed over to the bowl of water and dipped the corner of her skirts into it, instantly cussing as a dark patch spread quickly up the cloth. She squeezed it out over the newly planted seeds. Now all she had to do was to encourage them to grow.

At first, the sour taste of fear stung the inside of her cheeks, making her swallow. She closed her eyes and inhaled deeply, steadying her breath. As she did so, an image of a golden field, a whirlwind of dandelion wishes swirling above it, flashed in her mind. Frederik had believed in her. He'd shown her how to use her power, her Affinity to an extent she'd never been able to before. He was right; she needed to harness the confidence she had when she was healing people.

She breathed out again, her breath steady and calm and her focus centred. Then she opened her eyes. She bent lower to the ground over the patch where she had planted the seeds and placed her hands on the wet, stinking earth and reached deep within herself. She poured out her magic, focusing it on those few tiny seeds beneath her fingers. She felt them wriggle and heard their gentle pops and squeaks as they burst into life.

It was as though she had sped up time, pulling the shoots up through the soil until they finally broke the surface. Tiny, serrated-edged leaves unfolded from stems that reached for the distant light, , lengthening and thickening with each passing second. More leaves sprouted until Roslyn was satisfied with their height and amount of plumage. Then she withdrew her Affinity from the plants and felt it fizzle back into her veins to lay dormant once again.

Her head was light with such concentrated effort and she sat back on her heels, a foolish grin on her face as she waited for the world to stop swirling.

"Hello friends," she panted with utter joy. The patch of nettles only rose to her waist when kneeling, but they waved at her and turned their smaller leaves towards her. Roslyn flushed and bowed her head gratefully as she reached out, not caring about any stings, and plucked the young leaves from the stems.

"Thank you. I will never forget this kindness. I will return your borrowed strength one day." She looked down at the small collection of leaves in her hands and breathed a sigh of relief. She had food, and not only would it fill her belly once she had made it into the thinnest soup imaginable, but it would replenish her body with a cornucopia of vitamins and nutrients. Now she just needed to make a fire.

She was about to head over to her skeleton friend and search its belongings when she heard a voice. No... multiple voices.

Roslyn shook her head and laughed. "Now I'm hearing things, I'm that hungry!" But as she stood to make her way over to her dead companion, she heard the voices again, stronger this time. There were people in Eluha and the harder she listened, the more she recognised one voice in particular.

Although distorted, Roslyn knew it was Eik. It seemed a lifetime ago that she had seen him address the crowd of would-be rebels back in her village, yet it was the same tone he used now.

"The caravan of the prince's fiancée will pass not far from here, just after dusk. We only have one chance to intercept them."

Roslyn beat on the bricks in the doorway, screaming at the top of her lungs. "Eik! Eik! Anybody? I'm in here! Let me out!"

But nobody heard her, nobody came, and it was then that she realised the voices came from much further away and echoed around the courtyard. She could hear them, but they could not hear her.

"This is our last chance," Eik continued, his voice rising in an impassioned crescendo, "to stop the Oderberg line once and for all. If he marries that Princess and spawns an heir, the Domovnians are finished. Eredzha has the largest military in the whole of Zemkoska! Oderberg after Oderberg after Oderberg will sit on that throne!" Roslyn could hear the mumbled sounds of agreement. "And, to make matters worse, to really rub salt in our wound, the king on his deathbed decrees that the new foreign Princess shall wear the Briar Crown!"

Roslyn couldn't help but gasp with the other rebels. The Briar Crown, her crown by rights, on the head of a foreigner? King Casimir had sworn to her it would never sit on the head of the Domonovs again, but she thought he meant the royal family of Domovnia, the ones he had all wiped out. She didn't even think, naïve as it was, that he meant it should not sit on the head of any Domovnian ever again. It was sacrilege—blasphemous—to give such an iconic item, the symbol of a people, a place, a way of life, to… who knew who?

The talking started again, Eik's condescending drawl making her crinkle her nose in disgust. "Now, we know the caravan will pass by here, and we also know that the royal women of Eredzha are bound to wear veils, hiding their faces from the world until they are married. So, nobody knows what this princess looks like. Tonight, we waylay her caravan, and we ride to Novlada in their stead."

Roslyn's gut twisted. Eik's voice grew fainter and she could only presume he had turned to someone in the crowd.

"Ladies, you will take the places of the maids, take their clothes. And you, Rose…" His voice was heavy with affection, the sort that Roslyn had once hoped for and had been drip fed, keeping her on his line for when he wanted her. She felt suddenly sick and could almost see the smug smile that would be spreading across the bitch's painted lips. Of course, he would have made things official with Rose Troyand as soon as she'd been carted off by the Oderbergs!

"Rose will take the place of the princess. She will go through with the wedding ceremony and once the Briar Crown is on her head"—Roselyn gritted her teeth at the thought—"she will kill the prince. That is the signal for the rest of us to attack. We will wipe out the Oderbergs in their own stronghold, just as they did to us in ours! Look, look at where we stand…" Roslyn swallowed hard, not caring for the rest of his impassioned speech. They were going to kill Frederik.

"No," she breathed soundlessly. "No!"

She had to get out; she had to warn him, but how? Again, she flung herself at the brick wall, pounding it with her fists, hoping to dislodge some of the mortar, screaming, pleading with those in the courtyard to let her out. It was all for naught. The voices faded. They had left Eluha, and she was still trapped inside. Her cries turned

293

hysterical and she could barely breathe, her hand shaking before her chest as if that would get more air in somehow. Her cries blended with her deprived gasps, leaving her hoarse and shaking.

Something silenced her. An icy chill enveloped her, and Roslyn had the unsettling feeling she was being watched. As she sank to her knees, she found herself staring at the shimmering white hem of a gown. Her heart stopped and so did her crying as fear sucked them both dry. Slowly, she raised her head and nearly choked with terror as the woman from her dreams stood before her. The ghostly slit on her neck shimmered more than ever, a bluish stain dripping from the wound down her decolletage and over the white of her dress.

"M… mother?"

The spectre said nothing, but tilted her head to the side and her lips rose in a fraction of a smile.

"But how…" Roslyn whispered "I'm not a Botan; I'm just a Hedgie."

The spectre made as if to touch her cheek but then moved her hand and pointed to something lying on the floor. Roslyn was afraid to tear her gaze away from the ghost, lest she attacked her from behind, but the pull of the pointing finger was too much for her. Her eyes followed its trajectory, and she spotted the parchment with the nettle seeds lying on the floor. She turned suddenly, but the strange woman had vanished, a cool eddy of air all that remained where she had stood.

Roslyn's hands were shaking as she picked up the parchment. If nettles could feed her, they could also help her out. As fear and rage coursed through her veins again, she threw the seeds on the floor, closed her eyes and spread her arms wide. She clenched her fists and power

294

overwhelmed her. Fuelled by her desperation to save the man she loved, her Affinity burst through like never before.

It was so powerful, she found it a struggle to stay in the moment, blackness threatening the edges of her vision, but she had to save Frederik. So she steadied herself and poured all of her strength, all of her feelings down through the ground and up into the seeds of the nettles so that they grew and flowered and seeded, grew and flowered and seeded until the whole base of the tower was covered in nettles. She opened her eyes, but the nettles didn't stop.

They reached higher and higher into the air, growing thicker and stronger with each breath, each pulse of power that she expelled from her with anguished cries. Within minutes they were as thick as small tree trunks and just as high, brushing the bottom step of the desiccated wooden stairs high above her that led up to the platform and the window beyond.

In the split second she took to marvel at what her power had done, it ebbed and rushed back into her like a coiled spring. Roslyn was thrown back onto the ground, heaving with exertion.

But she couldn't stop, she couldn't rest. Frederik was in danger, and she was the only one could save him. She grabbed at the nettles and began to work them, crushing the stems and peeling the skins from them, twisting them and weaving them into cordage, over and over again until she had a long thick piece of rope that would support her from the window down to the ground. Or at least, she thought it would, if she could even get up to the window, but the nettles had given her the solution to that problem as well.

They had grown to monstrous, barbaric proportions. The usually fine, almost invisible needles stuck out like spears from the side of their trunk-like stems. She swallowed, a little fearful at the thought of being stung by one of them now, but as she gazed up, she realised they had created a ladder. Wrapping the tapestry around her like a cloak, tying it around her neck, she took a deep breath, picked up her rope, and climbed.

It was heavy, difficult and dangerous, and she was sweating after only a few steps up the needles, but she couldn't give up now, even though her drained, starving and dehydrated body begged her to. She raised her hands again and took the next thick needle in her arms and pulled herself up. She did this again and again, all the while dodging other needles that stuck out and tried to ensnare her.

Finally, she made it. She was level with the last step of the staircase. She clung to the stem of the giant nettle as she assessed the stair. It was almost paper-thin and she could see the ground below through various holes that dotted the plank. The next two or three up were not much better, and she doubted any of them would hold. She panted as disappointment and frustration threatened to quell the anger that had driven her this far. Her lip quivered and as she was about to cry, she flung her head upward and pressed her lips together. But as she did so, she noticed a large iron hook in the centre of the ceiling. A dusty lantern hung there, but there was plenty of space for a rope to sit beside it.

Roslyn gritted her teeth and made a loop at the end of her thick cordage. With a calculating glance, she swung the rope round in her hands and then thrust it upwards in her first attempt to land on the hook. It didn't work.

Neither did the second nor the third, but just when she thought she was about to give up, just when all hope was about to leave her, she pulsed with Affinity and on the last throw the rope in her hands stretched itself taught and found its mark. She laughed out loud, a hysterical, almost frantic laugh and gave the rope the tug. The iron was secure in the stone and it would hold. Wrapping the cord around her waist, she readied herself and leapt onto the crumbling staircase.

The first few steps, as predicted, vanished underneath her feet, turning to dust as soon as she touched them. She scrabbled up the remaining steps. They, too disappeared just as her foot pressed up and off them, thrusting her onto the next one, onwards and upwards in a frantic dash until she reached the platform and flung herself onto it, the staircase crashing to the ground behind her.

The condition of the platform was not much better, the wood creaking under her weight, but it held. She lay there panting and sweating, her heart hammering in her chest so hard she could hear nothing else.

When she could breathe again, she glanced around and spied not one but three skeletons, just like the one below, sitting around a table. Although these showed no signs of injury, they had still died here, most likely from starvation. As cautiously as she could, she crawled towards them. They looked at her with their empty eyes and gormless grins, and Roslyn half expected them to greet her. Cautiously, fearing that any sudden movement would bring the platform crashing back to earth, she raised herself to her feet, holding her arms out wide to spread her balance. The wood groaned.

She paused, staring up from her crouched position at the three comrades in death. The one nearest to her had a blade attached to its hip, and it was that she was reaching for. The rebels were armed, and she knew what she was about to do was dangerous and so she, too, needed a weapon. Painstakingly slowly, she stretched her arm out and, one by one, wrapped her fingers around the hilt of the dagger. She tried to slide it out of the sheath, but it wouldn't budge. It hadn't been used in so long that it was stuck. She gave it a little jiggle, and it moved a fraction, displaying shiny bright steel. The blade was good. It just needed more force—but she could not exert it up here. She would have to take the whole knife belt. She groaned inwardly, then edged herself inch by perilous inch towards the skeleton sat in the wooden chair.

"I'm sorry," she whispered as she wrapped her arms around its waist and undid the clasp of the belt. She slipped it round the body and slowly rose to her feet. She paused again, not daring to move too quickly, her heart pounding and sweat dripping down her brow. Slowly, she wrapped the belt around her own waist and tied the buckle tight. Suddenly, the wood beneath her feet groaned loudly and began to crack.

There was no time for caution. She had to get out now and with a sudden burst of panicked energy, ran across the platform and flung herself at the window. Her arms grasped at the ledge as the wood disappeared beneath her feet, crashing—skeletons and all—down into the forest of nettles below. Roslyn screamed as her feet slipped and slid on the wall of the tower, not able to find any purchase.

"Please, somebody help me!" Her voice was pitiful. She knew there was nobody that could answer her. Just when she thought her sweat-slicked hands could no longer hold on to the ledge, a pale white hand reached out and grasped her round the wrist. She looked up and saw her mother's ghost. This time, the woman had determination and anger written across her face and with a sudden tug, Roslyn found herself dragged upwards. Using the momentum, she hoisted herself into a seated position on the ledge of the window. The spectral woman took Roslyn's face in her ice-cold hands and turned it out towards the horizon. The sea to the east glittered in the dying light, but the woman pointed instead at a shape in the distance—Novlada, the stronghold of the Oderbergs.

Roslyn looked back at those pale, orb-like eyes, feeling all the emotions within them: hurt, loss, anguish and rage and nodded. They were her feelings, too. "How do I make it right?" She was barely aware of her voice as it slipped through her open lips.

"The crown," an unearthly rattle sounded, ghostly blood bubbling at the slit on the woman's throat. "The crown is the key!" The pale woman gagged on the phantom blood choking her and tried to smile, but the darker shimmer that spurted from her lips made it more of a chilling grimace. The ghost of the last Domonov queen began to fade, her image juddering in and out of sight in the dying light. With her last ounce of power, she lowered her hand from Roslyn's face to her chest, and pushed her out the window.

299

Chapter 28

Roslyn was going to die. As her body fell through the air, the breath was sucked from her lungs, preventing her from even screaming. She suddenly remembered the cordage around her waist. At that precise moment, she stopped falling. The pain around her middle was unbearable, leaving her winded and choking. Her body swung on the end of the nettle rope and slammed into the smooth white surface of the tower and then back out again. She looked up from where she had fallen, but unsurprisingly, the woman was gone. Had she even been there? Roslyn had no time to hang there and ponder—Frederik's life was in danger.

She looked down in the dying light and realised she wasn't too far from the top of a parapet wall. Carefully, she untied the cordage around her waist. It rolled out to its full length and she spun, dropped, and landed like a cat on the cracked and blackened stones. She breathed a sigh of relief to have solid ground beneath her feet again, but then scampered down the staircase and out of the ruins of Eluha.

It wasn't hard to find the trail of the rebels. There were so many of them that they left tracks all over the place, something Roslyn had imagined they should be better at hiding. But for now, she was relieved at their lack of caution. The trail led down the hill from the old castle, through bramble-choked woodlands that clawed at Roslyn as she tried to make her way through, down towards the road.

From her slightly heightened position, she could make out figures squatting along both sides of the road. She crouched low and crept towards the figure nearest to her. It was a rebel about her size, no doubt stronger and better trained, but Roslyn had the element of surprise. She looked around her, searching silently in the forest refuse for something to use as a weapon. The knife at her belt was for last resorts only; she knew now she didn't ever want to kill anyone.

Her hand touched upon something thick and heavy and she raised it from its leafy bed with some difficulty. It was a large oak log, thinner at one end—a perfect handle. Roslyn raised the club high above her head, whispering her plea of forgiveness to the Ancestors before bringing it crashing down on the woman's head. She slumped instantly and rolled to the side, Roslyn swooping in to catch her before her crash made too much noise. She stripped her and shed her own clothes, pulling on the stranger's with a shiver of unease. They smelt wrong. The woman had chosen to obscure her face with a wide-brimmed hat, and Roslyn rammed this onto her head before using the last bit of cordage she had, tying the unconscious woman to a tree and gagging her. Cautiously, she stepped forward and took her place in the line.

Bird calls sounded in the near darkness, a signal of the rebels, as the sound of a carriage echoed down the deserted roadside.

It passed by Roslyn's position first and though it was nearly dark, she could make out the fine golden filigree of a royal carriage. Silken curtains waved from the windows and light streamed out of them, illuminating the dust of the road with patches of flickering purple. High-spirited voices came from within, but she couldn't make out any of their words. Then chaos erupted from the treeline.

Men and women burst from the hedgerows, weapons drawn and screaming. Their cries of war were joined with shrieks of terror from the women inside the carriage and on the wagon behind. The bewildered guards scrambled for their weapons but found them already wrenched from their hands, their attackers upon them. Roslyn ran down to the roadside, her knife raised as she had seen the others do, but it was already over.

The rebels pulled everyone from the wagon and carriage and lined them up on the roadside.

A nervous silence fell as a colossal figure paraded before the captives, swinging a huge wooden club in his hands. Though the brim of his hat obscured his eyes, Roslyn knew it was Eik.

"I'm so sorry to have caused such a fright, your highness." He turned to the quivering veiled figure at the centre of a protective bubble of equally frightened maidservants. "But it seems there has been a misunderstanding. You see, there will be no wedding... not for you, at least."

He and the other members of the crew laughed in a low rumble.

"What is the meaning of this?" One of the princess's guardsmen dared step forward and received a club to the face for his trouble. He dropped like a stone with half of his face caved in, his blood flooding the dust of the roadside. Eik inspected the mess on the end of the wooden weapon and casually wiped it on the soft, striped fabric of the fallen guard's pantaloons.

Roslyn gagged as the captives whimpered, not even daring to scream this time, lest that be their fate too.

Suddenly, the young woman at the centre pushed her servants aside and stepped forwards, squaring up to Eik as much as she could.

"You have killed one of my guards." It was not a question.

"Yes." Eik looked at the corpse on the ground as if he had merely dropped a glove. "It would appear I have."

"Why? Why do you do this?" The princess's accent was thick and laced with anger, but her courtly breeding kept her defiant in the face of danger.

"It's nothing personal, no, indeed quite the opposite. You see, we are doing this to protect you. You don't want to marry that Oderberg prince."

The young woman stepped forwards, her lilac veil waving softly, the rounded bells of her trousers swooshing together. "And why not? He is an advantageous match and the marriage would cement peace between the Oderbergs and the Eredzhi."

The rebels that surrounded her almost growled, making the princess look around and hesitantly take a step backwards towards the safety of her women.

"There you have it, Princess. We don't want anyone to have peace with the Oderbergs. We want to destroy them. So, if you value your life, I suggest you and your

303

servants take off your fancy clothes, give them to us, and be on your way back to wherever it is you came from."

A gasp rose from the foreigners and another guard stepped forwards.

"You dishonour the princess!"

Eik raised his club again, and the man shrank backwards, making the Domovnian chuckle. "Don't worry, she ain't got anything I haven't seen before. Now strip!"

Roslyn didn't want to watch. Her cheeks flamed with rage and indignity at the whole situation as each rebel picked out a servant, the beautiful black-haired Rose approaching the princess, and overseeing their shedding of clothes. They tied the captives' hands before their naked forms and hustled them onto rough wooden carts pulled from the woodlands. As Roslyn escorted her own prisoner, she pulled her close, pressed her knife in its sheath into the woman's hands and whispered.

"Take this. Do not use it to free yourselves until we are well out of sight. Trust me, they will kill you all if they see."

The stunned woman turned to look at her with wide, imploring eyes, but playing the part, Roslyn pushed her head down. "There is a village four miles southwest of here and not far from the border. Follow the road and it will take you there. In the meantime…" She hoisted the woman up onto the back of the cart and untied the tapestry from her neck. "Take this. Cover your princess."

She closed the wooden flap on the cart with a clatter and an imploring look. "Remember, wait until we are out of sight."

304

The maidservant nodded and translated Roslyn's words to the rest of her party, who nodded their wide-eyed thanks. She turned and was about to make her way back to the pile of clothes she was to change into, when a soft voice called out to her. It was the princess.

She was still majestic in her nudity; the tapestry was draped around her like the tattered sail of a shipwreck, her long black hair falling over her coffee-coloured shoulder. "Thank you, stranger. May the Djinn keep you safe and reward you for your kindness…?"

"Roslyn," she whispered, as low as a breath of wind.

"May we meet again, Roslyn," the princess replied just as quietly.

The flea-ridden nag attached to the cart was hit firmly on the rump and the cart rumbled away, knocking the princess off her feet.

Roslyn swooped down to pick up her disguise and ducked behind a tree, changing before anyone could recognise her. She felt safer behind the purple cloth of the veil that hid her face as Eik rounded jovially on the women in the group.

"Ladies," he intoned playfully as he bowed and held open the gilded carriage door. "We've got a wedding to get to."

✳

They travelled in silence to Novlada and with each roll of the carriage's wheels, Roslyn's gut clenched. This was madness. Surely, they were all going to get caught and she would be lumped in with the traitors. The atmosphere

305

inside the carriage was so tense, it crackled like the air just before a summer storm.

They trundled up towards the gate. Muffled voices could be heard outside between the Oderberg guardsmen and the rebels disguised as Eredzhi, but it ended on a cheerful crescendo and the carriage was waved on. Roslyn shrank back behind the safety of her veil every time they passed a group of soldiers, or nobles, or anyone she might have crossed paths with during her stay at the palace. The streets were loud and raucous, drinkers well into their cups, rolling out into the streets as their establishments closed their doors for the night.

Rose, the fake princess, let out a loud luxurious squeal. "Well, I don't know about you all, but I am most looking forward to sleeping on a featherbed tonight."

The others laughed, blowing the fabric of the veils with their breath. Roslyn forced herself to smile, even though no one could see it. As they rolled into the palace courtyard, a sudden blaze of lights almost blinded them. She peeped through the window and was met with the sight of a full welcome retinue of servants and stewards. Roslyn's heart stopped beating for a few seconds when she saw Prince Frederik—now Crown Prince Frederik—in full regalia.

As the 'princess' was escorted from her carriage and led up the red velvet carpet to the awaiting Prince, Roslyn snuck a glance at his face. It was long, drawn, and the twinkle in his eyes that he was known for was alarmingly absent. She had to stop herself from gasping out loud. This was not the man she knew. As Rose stood before him, dropping into a curtsy that jangled with the decorations of her outfit, Frederik inclined his head and bowed stiffly.

"Your highness." His voice was low and dull. "We had been expecting you before now. I am glad you have arrived safely."

Rose stood from her curtsy and nodded her head. When she spoke, she mimicked the accent of the Eredzhi perfectly, as if she had been practising, which no doubt all of this rebel band had. "We broke a wheel, sire. We had to stop to fix it, but we are here now and I must admit I am ready to retire. It has been a long journey."

Frederik inclined his head formally, and Roslyn could see the purple bags under his eyes. He hadn't been sleeping and looked like he had spent much of the past two days weeping. "Of course. I will see that you are taken straight to your room. Food shall be brought up if you wish it and your groomsmen and guards suitably housed. I shall bid you good night and will see you tomorrow at the ceremony."

"Thank you," Rose lilted and Roslyn could tell the smile behind her veil was snide and calculating. "I very much look forward to it, your highness."

With that, Frederik stepped back from the carpet, head still slightly lowered as Rose passed. He straightened as the rest of her retinue followed. Roslyn ached to rip off her veil, to explain everything, to at the very least touch his hand as she passed, but he looked right through her.

Chapter 29

Although the beds of the future queen and her handmaidens were far more comfortable than anything Roslyn had ever slept on, and the apartment was filled with luxury and sweet things to eat, Roslyn couldn't sleep. She had to come up with a plan. How was she going to save Frederik? If she saved him, she would be dooming Domovnians to a life of servitude under the Oderbergs, but she couldn't let him die. He had believed in peace between the two peoples; he had believed in a better future, but did he still? Eik had murdered his brother and even she had poisoned his father. What reason did he have for trusting Domovnians, now?

She must have fallen asleep at some point, but she rose early before most of the others and dressed, making sure that none saw her face. At that moment, the crowing of a cockerel sounded somewhere in the castle grounds. The fake Princess stirred with an air of arrogance, as if she really had been royalty all her life. She propped herself up on her elbows, hugging the satin pillow underneath her, and squinted around, taking in the sleepers around her and then noticing the dressed figure standing in the middle of the room.

"Is that you, Isabel?" Roslyn barely had time to nod before the next 'royal decree' came. "Make us some tea, would you? Something to give us strength for this day. After all, it is not every day one marries and then murders her husband."

The blood pulsed through Roslyn's veins in a sudden frenzy. She clenched her hands at her side to stop them from striking the self-important Bloomer that had elevated herself above the rest of them. Just because she was playing a princess did not mean she was one, not unless…

Eik was the last noble of the Domovnians, the last oak Arbor which made him royalty in the eyes of their people. Had he promised Rose queenship? Was Eik thinking of becoming king of Domovnia? Could he even reinstate the royal house of Domonov without one of their bloodline? Or was he simply planning to build a new royal line, the house of Devero?

No, she couldn't allow it. If anyone was going to wear the Briar Crown, it was damned well going to be her, the rightful heir, not some boyfriend-stealing Bloomer! After all, her mother had said the crown was the key, not only to saving Frederik, but Domovnia, too. She had to get Rose out of the way, but how?

"Isabel?" Rose's voice snapped her out of her thoughts. "What are you still doing here? Tea! Chop, chop!"

✳

Roslyn's feet led her automatically down to the kitchens, where the hustle and bustle of preparing a wedding feast came to an abrupt halt at her entrance.

Wide eyes stared at her, in curiosity more than anything else, and she looked down at her foreign garments. She wore low-waisted trousers that ballooned out before being cinched in again around her ankles, and a pair of delicate, pointed and beaded slippers. A section of her midriff was bare, exposing her olive skin. She hoped none of the servants would notice it was several shades lighter than that of a true Eredzhi. Her top, although one of a maidservant, was much more ornate than any the Oderberg servants might wear. It was decorated with fringes and tassels and clinking metal decorations, not to mention she was also wearing the purple veil across her face.

She hesitated on the threshold, listening to the bubble of pots, the scream of kettles and the withdrawn breaths of the household.

"I…" she started, before remembering she was supposed to have an accent. She'd never even attempted an Eredzhi accent and had almost never heard one. But she gave it her best shot, hoping that few of the Oderbergs had either. "My lady requires tea, strong tea that will fortify her for her wedding day."

The head chef nodded to the rest of his staff, who reluctantly returned to their work and approached the strange figure in the doorway. He half bowed, before realising that she too was a servant, but then again, foreign countries sometimes used minor nobles as servants to their lords and ladies, so he was cautious with his words.

"Of course, of course… And would your lady require some fresh spiced roles for breakfast, too?"

Roslyn inclined her head slowly. "A hearty breakfast would be most agreeable, sir. There are also the other ladies-in-waiting in the rooms who will need refreshments. It is going to be a long day."

The chef bobbed and nodded eagerly. "Yes, yes indeed, it will be." He stood and looked around before extending his hand to a small doorway, just off the corridor that led to the kitchen. "If you wouldn't mind waiting in here, I will have someone prepare trays for you. I'm afraid I cannot spare any staff to take the trays to the room, but you must be accustomed to serving on your lady yourself?"

Roslyn inclined her head again respectfully. "Of course, Sir, I am but a servant to my lady. I will gladly wait."

With that, the cook nodded again to the room where she was to wait and returned into the steaming, noisy chaos that was his realm. Roslyn's heart was in her mouth as she pushed open the doorway to the small cell where she had sat and eaten lunch that first day before she'd met Prince Frederik. The same table and chair sat neatly, waiting to be filled. This was obviously the room's purpose, to service visiting servants, rather than let them mix with those of the Oderbergs.

As she waited, she decided not to take a seat and instead paced the tiny space. She had to shut the door to do so, and when she did, her jaw dropped. Shoved behind the doorway, out of sight and completely forgotten, abandoned like a sole dirty sock, was her satchel. Her shoulders sank and tears pricked her eyes at the sight of it and she dived to her knees, checking the doorway the whole time and unclipped its fastenings. Everything was there. Some things were a little damaged, but nothing had leaked or spoiled.

Now she had a means of stopping Rose from making it to the wedding. She looked at the dried plants, at the pre-made medicines and poultices, trying to decide what to use when she heard footsteps and the chatter of two servants coming down the corridor towards her.

"Urgh, have you ever smelt anything so disgusting?"

"Well, if you find that bad, whatever you do, do not look under the cloth!"

Roslyn peeped round the door and watched as two servant girls carried a chamber pot and a tray down the staircase from the royal apartments, trying not to gag. She recognised them as Lady Margitte's maids.

"I mean, what is wrong with her? The old woman must be rotting on the inside!"

Indeed, the smell that wafted from the cloth-covered chamber pot forced bile up her own throat as they passed the open door, but it was one that she recognised and one that gave her an idea.

With lightning speed, she plucked two items from the paper packets and shoved them into the waistband of her trousers. Just as the door swung open, Roslyn returned to her seat, crossed her legs and picked at her nails nonchalantly, sighing when the kitchen maids entered.

They placed the tea trays on the table, stacking them one atop the other, so that Roslyn could make her way back up the staircase to serve her mistress. They didn't say anything, but giggled at her strange clothes and she could hear them whispering all down the corridor after they'd left. She didn't have long to work. Rose and the other rebels would be expecting her back at any moment, so hastily she lifted the lid of the teapot and inserted the

312

crushed-up nettle leaves and shaved dandelion root. She gave the mixture a quick stir before touching her finger to the teapot and zapping it with a quick blast of Affinity to speed its infusion as she made her way back up to the fake princess's rooms. She hoped it would be enough to stop them.

✳

"Oh, curse the Ancestors!"

A distraught growl, followed by a disgusting squelching sound, came from beyond the wooden door to the privy. Similar sounds were coming from other corners around the room, screens hastily placed around pots and bowls and anything that could catch the sudden explosive diarrhoea that the foreign princess's retinue had come down with... all but Roslyn. She placed her head on the wood of the door and knocked gently.

"Rose? Are you alright?"

"Does it sound like I am alright?" came the snapped reply from beyond. Another grunt and splash followed. Roslyn backed her head slightly away from the door, although that did nothing to ease the smell that had pervaded the entire room from the other afflicted. Her nostrils burned and her eyes watered. "Isabel, who else is sick?"

"Everyone. Everyone is shitting their guts out. What are we going to do?" Roslyn played into the ruse. If Rose could pretend to be a princess, then she could pretend to be this Isabel.

"But not you. You don't seem to have been affected."

"No," Roslyn called back. "I think it must have been something in the spiced bread. I didn't have any. I was given some plain while I was waiting in the kitchen." A pause followed, a pause that stretched on just a little too long for Roslyn's liking, and her palms crawled with sweat.

"You sound different, Isabel."

Roslyn almost stopped breathing, but licked her lips and fumbled a reply, "I—Oh, I'm coming down with a cold, these silly garments with the bare waist... It's unhealthy, not to say improper." A wry laugh came from the other side of the door.

"And when did you care about being improper? Anyway, that's just as well you ate in the kitchen." Roslyn could hear the fatigue in Rose's voice from the sudden sickness that had overcome her. "I cannot perform the wedding ceremony like this. I cannot complete the task. And it would appear no one else can. It's up to you Isabel, you have to go through with the ceremony. You have to kill the prince."

Roslyn gulped. Although her aim had been to prevent Rose and the other rebels from going ahead with the wedding, the reality of what she was about to do hit her hard. In order to get the crown she had to pretend to be the princess of Eredzha...and marry the prince. The room spun. The Oderberg retinue would knock on the door soon, to collect the bride and take her to the chapel to be wed.

"I... I don't know if I can," she stammered. From the other side of the privy door, Rose slammed her hand on the stone wall and groaned.

"You have to, Isabel! They will come any minute to collect the princess of Eredzha and if they do not find her, they will realise that something is up. We will have our heads on pikes before the morning is out, so you have to do this. For Domovnia. Now, get that wedding dress out of the chest, make sure your face is veiled and for the love of the Tree, do not forget the dagger!"

Roslyn nodded breathlessly; Rose certainly did have a commanding aura about her. And every word she said was true. If the Oderbergs thought anything was amiss, the rebels would be rounded up and slaughtered, ensuring yet more violence against her people in the years to come. Roslyn rushed to the chest and somehow made her way into the strange bridal garments of the Eredzhi. There were several gowns in the trunk, and she cursed as she called back over her shoulder. "Which one?"

A strained groan sounded before one of the other rebels poked her head out from behind a screen. "The top one, remember? The second is for the dinner and the third for dancing before the negligee for the wedding night. All these funny customs they have, these foreigners, and each outfit could feed a family for a year!" She tutted weakly before diving back behind the screen with a curse and a splosh. Roslyn grimaced and pulled on the ceremonial gown.

The dagger Rose spoke of lay on the table beside her bed. It was a plain brutish thing, perfect for the ugly task it was intended for. Roslyn's hand shook as she reached for it. It was cold in her hand and she shivered at its touch. No, she wouldn't be taking that. Glancing round the room, she saw all the rebels too occupied in their misery to notice her. She snatched up the veil, white silk for the wedding and made her way into the reception area. She closed the door as softly as she could and then thrust the common blade through the looped handles to the bedchamber, locking the inflicted rebels inside. Just as she slipped the veil over her head, a knock sounded at the door to the apartment.

"We request the presence of her highness Princess Aylin of Eredzha at her wedding to Crown Prince Frederik von Oderberg," the Herald announced through the doorway. "If it pleases you, your highness, we are ready."

Roslyn smoothed her hands on the white lace of her bridal gown, took a deep breath and opened the door.

She held her head high, but the Oderberg herald and stewards paused, craning their necks to see through the gap in the door to the empty room beyond before she shut it.

"I apologise, your highness…. but is it custom in your country that the bride should go to church alone?"

Roslyn didn't know what to do. Should she tell them that the rest of the party was indisposed, or should she play along with his unfamiliarity with foreign customs? She swallowed and nodded.

"It is so. Normally, one would have a mother or father to give the bride away, but never handmaidens. Therefore, I shall take my first steps as Queen myself."

Without saying another word, she swept past the herald and, head held high, walked proudly down the corridor and away towards her impending wedding.

Chapter 30

The corridors of the palace opened up into the formal courtyard. The space was lined with guards in their best livery, standing to attention, lances tipped together to form the arch under which Roslyn now walked.

Her slippers were so thin she could feel the bulge of the cobbles through the red carpet that led her to her groom. Her breath caught in her throat when she saw him in his wedding attire. As she was swathed in white with clanking ornamentation of gold, Frederik stood gleaming in the morning sunlight, his well-tailored suit cut from golden cloth. He was a beacon of royalty, the richness of the cloth making his normally yellow hair appear white and luminous. She could have been walking towards a servant of the sun, not a prince, had she not known every single line of his perfect face. She had mostly seen it lifted in a perpetual smile, but she had also seen how misery and grief altered it, making it no less beautiful.

That was the face she stared at now as she forced her feet onwards. His mouth was a tight line above his chin, pinched white. The dimples on his merry cheeks had been ironed out to gauntness and his blue eyes were dull, the colour of the ocean before a storm. A vice clamped itself around her heart at the sight of him, willingly giving his life over to misery and everything he had fought so hard to change. If only there was some way she could tell him who hid behind the veil, but she couldn't reveal herself before the ceremony was over. He raised his head as his bride approached and his golden brows knitted together. He closed his eyes and drew a deep breath.

He opened them as Roslyn stepped from the archway of swords and fixed a strained smile on his face.

"Good morning, Princess. A fine day for a wedding, is it not?"

Roslyn barely dared speak and nodded her head. When she didn't reply, Frederik sighed and extended his arm towards her, fist balled.

"Shall we to chapel then?"

Roslyn nodded again and set her shaking hand upon his arm. At the sight of it, his expression softened just enough to give her hope, but as she gazed up at it, a sight over his shoulder made her blood run cold. Eik was dressed as one of the princess's guardsmen and was standing to attention along the route the betrothed would take. His face was black with fury and the knuckles of the hands that gripped his pike were white. He'd noticed the lack of attendants. He knew something was wrong, something had happened to his perfectly planned assassination.

Roslyn turned her veiled face towards Frederik's and nodded. "Yes, sire."

And with that, the procession made its way along the parapeted wall and through the neat and orderly gardens of lawn and box hedges that decorated it to the small, squat building sat on the very edge, lording over the city below.

As they walked, Roslyn racked her brain for ways to let Frederik know she was there. With Eik and half the court watching, she couldn't just tell him. They'd drag her away and execute her immediately. She had, after all, poisoned their king. She tried squeezing his arm, but he simply placed a hand over her shaking one, sending a jolt of lightning down her spine and bent his head ever so slightly to whisper.

"I too am nervous, Princess. I do not doubt you had your own hopes and dreams of who your intended would be and that it was not me... but I hope we can make the best life we can together."

Behind her veil, Roslyn closed her eyes to stop the tears that accompanied the breaking of her heart. Was he so loyal to his father, to the Oderbergs, that he would marry a complete stranger?

They walked a little further in silence, listening to the chapel bells clanging a discordant jangle at their approach, and Roslyn cast her eyes to the ground. Suddenly she stopped and gasped, "Oh!"

The procession skipped to an unprepared halt, and Prince Frederik looked down at her, worried.

"What is it? Are you alright?"

Roslyn smiled and bent down to the base of one of the box hedges. She plucked the stem of a plant, its milky white sap running over her fingers.

"A dandelion?" The crown prince frowned. "I'd told the gardener to make sure the paths were clean. I must apologise, your highness." A grimace passed over his already strained face and caused Roslyn to choke back tears.

"It's quite alright," she said, forcing a smile to her lips so that her voice would mirror it. She took deliberate care to insert the slightly dishevelled flower into the middle of the bouquet of roses she had been handed in the courtyard. "Where I come from, this plant is a portent of good fortune within a marriage…"

She raised her head to his, but he looked away and raised his hand for her to take again and scoffed. "Someone once told me their seeds were wishes, but she is gone now, along with her wishes. Don't believe all the folk tales you hear, princess." His voice softened suddenly. "But if it pleases you, you shall have it."

"Thank you, your highness." Roslyn sniffed as tears ran down her cheeks. He hadn't picked up on her clue, but someone else had. Eik's eyes bore into her so hard from the lineup that she couldn't help but turn her head towards his as the prince pulled her forwards. An ugly snarl was smeared across his face and his hands were now shaking. For the moment, she was safe. It would be after the wedding that he would come for her. She had no doubt in her mind that before the consummation ceremony where the princess's veil would finally be lifted, he would find a way to swap Rose back in and she would be at his mercy. She had to tell him.

Roslyn gripped Frederik's arm.

"Sire… I fear you are in danger."

The prince clenched his jaw and swallowed. Then, with a forced smile, he looked down at his bride to be. "Princess, I understand you are nervous, the events of the past week have been most unsettling. But I can assure you, after my brother's death, we have taken every precaution against the rebels. We are perfectly safe."

Roslyn wanted to protest, but they had arrived and were ushered in silence into the tiny stone chapel. Her only hope now was to go through with the wedding and reveal the danger afterwards. She threw up a prayer to the Ancestors. Perhaps, if she was already his wife, they wouldn't kill her straight away.

She was relieved the chapel was only large enough to hold a handful of witnesses. The guards, including the princess's retinue, were stationed around the perimeter, for which she was thankful. Eik would not be inside to watch.

She looked around nervously as they walked down the aisle from the door to the altar, curious of the Oderbergs' preference for dead stone in a place of worship. Although Roslyn had never particularly wished to marry, on the odd occasion she had indulged the fantasy, she'd always seen herself binding her life to another's in the living willow halls of the Domovnians, their joined hands wrapped by the very vines that ran through the structure, joyous blooms exploding from the walls when the union was made.

Instead, she walked solemnly on cold flagstones, her path lit by the sparse flash of colour from the stained-glass windows that perforated the shadows engulfing the room. Long tapering candles added an eeriness to the darkness, but they also drew her attention to the two crowns placed on the stone bench at the far end of the room.

One was the crown she had last seen on Casimir's head. Although he sat in the foremost pew, looking back at his son with a smug sneer of one who has won, she knew his neck was no longer strong enough to support its weight. She peered at the king more closely through her veil as they approached. His face was grey and his cheeks hollow. His eyes bulged out of his head and any remaining hair had vanished, revealing the spotted and veined skull beneath. The crown would belong to Frederik in days, regardless.

The other crown made her swallow painfully, the the bridge of her nose fizzing with tears—the Briar Crown. Her crown. Its warm metal was enhanced in the flickering light of the candles, and it stood towering over the gaudy, bejewelled Oderberg crown in muted resplendence, the very tips of its thorny horns winking in the candlelight. The closer she walked, the less she could take her eyes from it, the symbol of her ancestors calling to her. She shook her head slightly as a tinny buzz pierced her ears, but with each step she took towards the crown, it grew in intensity.

"The crown is the key..." her mother's ghastly voice echoed in her mind and sounded like chairs scraping across stone. The key to what?

Before she knew it, they were stood before the altar, and a priest stepped forward, blocking her view of the crown.

"We are gathered here today to join this man and this woman in matrimony," he began, his voice as dry as skeleton leaves. "It is not every day we also bring together two great nations. We pray that not only will they bear many heirs, but also the fruits of a prosperous alliance; peace, wealth and strength."

The priest, near smothered in his official robes, peeked his head out of the wide brimmed collar and grinned, making him look like a turtle extending his neck from his shell. He spoke the words of the ceremony in a monotone voice that soon made Roslyn's mind wander,

322

but not her eyes; those she couldn't tear away from the crown by the official's elbow.

Suddenly the man's monologue ceased, and she snapped back to the present only to find the priest, king and all the congregation staring at her expectantly. She gasped and looked around. Shit, what was she supposed to have done, or said?

"I'm sorry," she said in her atrocious excuse for an Eredzhi accent. "Nerves... could you repeat, please?"

The king wheezed a laugh behind her. "It is only right for a virgin to be nervous on her wedding day. Go on, Brother, repeat." He waved a liver-spotted hand at the priest, who bowed to him but glared at the veiled princess before him. The Lady Margitte, who was sat beside the king, swatted his thigh with her hand reproachfully. The movement caught Roslyn's attention and it was then that she saw Silen sat at her feet, a collar around his neck. His mistress held the bejewelled leash in one hand and stroked his curly hair with the other. He looked up and as if he could see through the veil, raised an eyebrow and very slowly nodded, the shadow of a knowing smile on his lips.

"Man, face your woman. Woman," the priest leered at Roslyn, forcing her to snap back to the ceremony. "Face your man."

At his behest, the betrothed turned to face one another.

"Do you, son of the Chained Mountain, offer up your life to your betrothed, swear to protect and love her until Hoff the Almighty, calls you home?"

Frederik held out both hands, palms up. "I do." His voice was steady but dull, dead.

The Priest turned to Roslyn.

"And do you, daughter of the Djinn, place your life in the hands of your betrothed, promising to honour and

323

obey, fulfilling your duties as wife and mother, until the Hoff the Almighty calls you home?"

Roslyn grimaced inwardly at the inequality of the vows, but she swallowed and raised her own quivering hands, placing them in the prince's.

"I… I do." His skin was soft and warm, giving her the sudden urge to squeeze his hands, but she looked up at his face instead. He wasn't looking at her, only at their hands with alarming intensity. He was beyond pale, his face taking on a waxy sheen as the priest wrapped a link of cold metal chains around their joined hands. She stared down at the clanking metal, a symbol of their union that was final and absolute, her stomach turning.

"The Almighty Hoff has now joined your souls in matrimony." The priest beamed and from the corner of her eye, Roslyn was aware of King Casimir's shoulders relaxing as he sighed. "But there is one more task demanded of you."

The official turned to the altar and picked up the glittering bauble that was the Oderberg crown. He held it aloft, as high as he could considering his age and its weight, booming, "From this day forth, Frederik von Oderberg shall be known as King Expectant, first of his name! All hail!"

A chorus of "Hail" reverberated around the stone walls of the chapel as the priest lowered the crown to Frederik's brow. As soon as it was placed on those beautiful curls, Roslyn saw the pressure of its office press down onto his shoulders. He didn't look at her. He simply stared at the floor, his jaw clenched.

The priest turned back to the altar and took up the Briar Crown. Its lightness surprised him and he nearly dropped it as he swung to Roslyn, raising it above her own head. The buzzing intensified to a high-pitched whine, and she squinted, barely able to hear his words.

"The crown is the key!" Again, that grating voice filled her head.

"From this day forth, you, life partner of the King Expectant, as witnessed by Hoff and Veel, shall be known as Queen Expectant. All hail!"

The whining in her ears reached such a piercing timbre that, as the priest lowered the Briar Crown towards her, she couldn't hear the chorus of hails that followed. She couldn't hear anything, couldn't see anything, so excruciating was the pain that she had squeezed her eyes shut and was gripping Frederik's hands with such force that he finally raised his eyes to her. She pressed a hand to her temple to try and ward off some of the pain, dislodging the veil and baring the skin on the left side of her forehead. She grappled with it as the Priest finally set the crown her mother and grandmother had both worn on her head.

As the cool metal of the crown pressed against her exposed brow and she felt its circlet slip down her hair, the world before her vanished. Instead, her eyes met with the darkness of warm earth, her ears deafened with the cracking and crackling of roots as they moved and stretched through the soil. Her body was filled with an immense rush of power as she felt every single tree, bush, blade of grass, and weed on Domovnian soil pulse through her. The rush of Botanic powers overwhelmed her and she couldn't breathe. The plants, the roots, the sunlight that fed them, all swirled before her eyes in a sickening kaleidoscope as her body pitched forward.

She could only have been out a second, but when she came to, Frederik was cradling her, concern etched in rills across his brow.

"Are you alright?" he whispered as she opened her eyes and took a deep breath, gulping in air.

She raised a hand to her forehead as the spinning slowed and nodded. "Just a little overcome," she mumbled, unsure if she had used an accent or not.

Other faces peered down at her from above, but her new husband waved them away. "Please give her some space."

King Casimir cackled in the background, muttering something about the weaknesses of women, but she ignored him and slipped her hand into Frederik's extended one.

As he pulled her up into a standing position, he slipped a hand around her waist and his other grabbed her wrist for more support, but as it did so, he stopped and peered into Roslyn's veil questioningly. She went still and cold as the King Expectant gripped her wrist, feeling around with his fingers. A flash of hope marred with confusion flickered in his eyes. She lowered her eyes to glance at what had sparked such a reaction and found him stroking the nettle bracelet he had made for her, the silver button he'd ripped from his doublet that day glinting in the candlelight.

"Where did you get this?" he breathed, eyes imploring, as a much louder voice filled the room.

"Come now!" bellowed the king. "They are wed. Let's get them fed and then to bed!"

An approving roar sounded from the congregation and the newlyweds were swept up in a frenzied crowd of merrymakers and out into the arms of the new Queen's waiting attendants.

Chapter 31

Roslyn found her hand slipped from Frederik's arm and she was pulled away into the mass of handmaidens by a pair of strong, rough arms.

"As is our custom," a high clear voice rang out from one of the veiled maids, "We must now wash and cleanse the princess, stripping her of her former life as princess of the Eredzhi to queen of the Oderbergs, making her ready for her… husband!"

The rebel was good; Roslyn had to give her that. She stirred up the crowd and put such a rising inflection on her last word that no one could mistake her meaning. A rowdy cheer went up, drowning out Roslyn's protests.

Frederik bowed and allowed her to be bundled away by her giddy, giggling servants back towards the palace.

"Well, well, well, Roslyn, I wasn't expecting to see you here." Eik hissed in her ear as soon as they were away from the major crowd. She spun round, eyes wide with panic, and found herself surrounded by the now recovered ladies-in-waiting of the foreign princess, or rather the rebels that she had indisposed. She couldn't see behind the veils, but the hatred in their stares pierced her, forcing her to swallow down a wave of nausea.

They said no more until they lifted the flap of the golden tent on the lawn, set up for this traditional garment change. The bride would emerge from this tent unveiled, allowing her new husband to lay eyes on her face for the very first time. She could hear the crowd gathering for the spectacle outside, but she couldn't tear her eyes away from the woman that rose from a chair to greet her.

She was tall, poised, and wearing an even more lavish and revealing gold gown. Her black hair was twisted in curled braids atop her head, and her beautiful, unveiled face was contorted with rage. Rose strode forward, snatched the crown from Roslyn's head and placed it on her own, before landing a slap on her cheek. She gasped in shock and struggled against the arms that bound her to retaliate.

"Think you could get away with this, did you, you little bitch? Did you really think you could save your little princeling, put his life above those of our people?"

Roslyn's mouth twisted with rage. "You wanted to kill the only person who ever tried to create peace in this country!"

Rose adjusted the Briar Crown on her head so that it sat proudly on the fabric that had been pulled back to expose her face and rolled her shoulders back to stand regally, her ladies-in-waiting hovering round her like a swarm of bees.

"Now we will never know if he could." She patted the sash around her waist and Roslyn's heart turned to ice as she made out the faint outline of the dagger just behind the folds of delicate fabric that would soon be plunged into Frederik's heart.

"Come on, ladies, we've got a king to kill." She cast a last glance over at Roslyn, whose arms were stretched back behind her by Eik and snatched the bouquet of roses that dangled from her hand. Roslyn struggled and tried to scream, but her captor clamped his enormous hand over her nose and mouth, suffocating her. As the curtain was pulled back and the crowd applauded the beauty of their new Queen, she saw Rose slither her way towards the prince, linking arms with him, brazenly, showing none of the timidness Roslyn had in the chapel. He looked down at her with a raised eyebrow.

"You are most lovely, my Queen. It is an honour to finally know your face."

Rose gave a simpering laugh and pointed to her now assembled ladies' maids.

"You are too kind. Shall we to luncheon… husband?" She bowed her head in mock humility at the freshness of her words and caught sight of the single yellow flower amidst a sea of red roses. Without a second thought, Rose plucked the dandelion from the bouquet and threw it to the ground, trampling it on her way up the stairs and into the palace. Roslyn's last glance of Frederik, before she was dragged out the back of the tent into the deserted stable yard, was of him peering down at the crushed bloom with an unreadable expression.

Eik didn't release his grip on her, even though they were out of sight behind the golden tent. He tightened it instead, squeezing out what little air was left in her lungs. His thick, sweaty hand was preventing more from coming in, and soon Roslyn found her head swimming with lack of air. The surrounding shadows deepened as he hauled her inside. The scent of hay, horse, leather and muck stung her nostrils. He threw her into a stall with a smile of someone who knew they were about to eradicate their enemy as easily as stepping on a bug. She bounced on the piled hay in the stall and fell forward onto her knees, tearing the lace of her dress and scraping her knees on the cobbles below. As her blood stained the bridal gown, Eik towered over her.

"I never thought that you, of all people, Ros—a stunted Hedgie who can barely make weeds blow in the breeze—would almost foil our plan. Do you know how long we have worked for this, how long we have wanted the chance to get our revenge on the fucking Oderberg scum who obliterated our people?"

Every Domovnian harboured and lived in the hatred and resentment against the overlords who oppressed them, stole their food, beat, whipped and murdered them for no apparent reason. But she still knew what they were doing was wrong.

She tilted her head up towards him as he ripped the veil from her head, revealing her tear-stained cheeks.

"Of course I do! All I have ever wanted was peace for Domovnia, but this is not the way, Eik. Frederik is a good man, I promise you!"

Eik took a step back and looked down at her, realisation breaking over his face.

"You love the bastard." Then he laughed and shook his head. "You really are an Oderberg's whore, aren't you? Well then, there's nothing else I can do for you, Ros, other than to send you the same place your precious prince is going." His eyes glittered with menace as he pulled the sword strapped to his back from its sheath and swung it

330

before him, making the air hiss and sing as the blade sliced through it. Roslyn stared at it, eyes wide, the acidic taste of fear clawing up her throat. She tried to scramble away, only to find herself cornered against the solid stable wall.

"Oh, you're not going anywhere this time." Eik took a step towards her. "Ros... petal." It seemed a lifetime ago that she had craved to hear him use the customary term of endearment. Now, it was a final slap in the face. "It was fun, for a while, until you turned coat and opened your cunt for that whore's son. Now it's time for you to pay for your treason."

In a flash, Eik lunged and grabbed Roslyn by the hair, dragging her kicking and screaming out of the stall and into the courtyard, where several of the other rebels had gathered. She swung her hands up and swatted his wrists in a frail attempt to make him let go, but he just pulled harder, shaking her so much she thought her scalp would rip off. She cried pitifully as he kicked the back of her knees and threw her to the ground. He wrenched her head upwards, so she was looking up and backwards at him and his hideous, leering smile.

"That's right, whore, down on your knees where you belong!" The other rebels laughed and made grunts of approval as he pushed her head back down so she was staring at the straw strewn cobbles and placed the blade of his sword parallel to her exposed neck.

"Eik... please," her voice was feeble and seemed so foreign on her tongue. "Don't do this."

The brute wrenched at her hair again, causing another yelp to escape her lips.

"Why? What are you going to do about it, you pathetic little Hedgie?" Being a man of flair and dramatics, Eik raised his sword high above his head, planning to bring it down in a sweeping arc and sever her head from her body in one swift blow—the death of a traitor. But in that very moment, Roslyn's anger spilled over. Her hands shook, her eyes narrowed, and she reached out to the power vibrating all around her.

Through the stone of the cobbles, Roslyn felt the tingling anticipation that lay dormant in the earth. She suddenly knew it was waiting for her, eager to do her bidding. She closed her eyes and in the split second before the blade was brought down on the nape of her neck, she drank it from the very core of the earth and unleashed the power instilled in her by the crown.

The cobbles beneath her vibrated, clinking together as they freed themselves from their muddy bed and spread outwards like a wave from the prone, crouched figure.

"Ros…" Eik's voice was suddenly wary. "What are you doing?"

She turned and glared over her shoulder, hatred fuelling her words. "Something I should have done a long time ago."

Without warning, a long, slender vine of ivy burst through the cobbles with a clatter and snaked around Eik's wrist, freezing him in the executioner's stance.

"What the…" He barely had time to think, let alone comment, as more vines exploded from the earth, sending the cobbles flying like iron pellets from a cannon into the other howling rebels. As her rage fuelled the plants, some grew thick and tall, snapping against the towers of the palace, sending masonry crashing down around them. A chunk fell a few steps from her with a dull thud.

"Shit!" Roslyn cried as she grappled with her new unlocked power. She had to get it under control. She took a deep breath and centred herself. The vines halted, awaiting their next instruction. She flexed her new power again carefully, centring it on tripping up the rebels who were trying to escape. The vines did her bidding. Roslyn needed only to think about it and the ivy obeyed her every whim, snaking around Eik until he could no longer move, wrapped tight as if he were a baby bird coiled between the scales of a viper. They dragged him back towards the cold stone of the courtyard wall and fastened him in place. Roslyn stood slowly, dusted herself off, and turned towards him.

"Pathetic, am I?" She took a step towards him, her clothes hanging in tatters.

"What are you just standing there for? Get her!" He yelled at his troop.

The rebels turned towards her, swords at the ready. Roslyn gave a grunt of frustration, cupped her hands and then released the vibrating pressure that pulsated between her fingers. The floor of the courtyard erupted. Brambles and briars, thick wooden stems adorned with razor sharp thorns rose up, knocking the weapons from the men's hands. They creaked and groaned as they grew and swirled around the unfortunate rebels, paying no heed to their cries as the thorns scraped across flesh and left trails of blood in their wake. As the din died down, the petrified men found themselves trapped in an impassable barbed cage. Then she turned back to Eik.

"What in the name of the Ancestors?"

Roslyn's lip quivered as years of Eik's emotional manipulation battered against her newfound sense of pride.

"You have only ever seen me as you wanted to, as someone weak, someone who struggled, someone who could only be of use to you by sucking your cock while you took up with that bitch Rose behind my back…" Hot tears rolled down her cheeks. She took a step towards the strung-up man and nodded slowly. He flinched, and hit the back of his head on the stone, unable to get away.

"You say all I can do is make my Affinity plants bend in the wind, but there's something you don't know about weeds, Eik. They are survivors, and so am I. You beat me down, made me think I was worthless, that I had to depend on you for protection, affection, love… but I know better now. I know what love is…" Her voice cracked as she thought of Frederik, and her monologue stilled. At this very moment, he could have a knife to his throat. She narrowed her eyes, her hands shaking with fury as she turned her back on the Arbor who'd once controlled her.

"I've wasted enough time on you," she whispered before running from the stable yard and up the palace steps.

Chapter 32

Roslyn ran up the steps into the palace, knocking aside any guard that tried to stop her with a flick of her vines, or a gust of razor-sharp leaves. She didn't have time for questions. She didn't have time to explain herself. As she swung round the corner, a large cohort of Oderberg soldiers, alerted by the commotion, stood before the doorway to the banqueting hall, pikes and swords raised, their backs to the towering oak doors.

"Stand back! I order you, stand back!" One of the militiamen shouted. Roslyn shook her head furiously.

"Get out of the way! The prince is in danger!"

"The only danger I see is standing right before me, you witch!" the guard retorted, grasping the hilt of his sword tighter and readying his stance as if to pounce. Roslyn sighed, still shaking her head, and closed her eyes before raising her hands, palms outstretched, fingers wide up towards the oak doors behind them.

When it had lived the tree they had come from had been ancient, watching the rise of the Ancestors, birthing many of the dryads whose blood ran through her veins. It

335

had been dead a long time, felled alongside Eluha and carved into the hideous doors that now blocked her path. It may be dead, but she could feel the residue of anger within its corpse, and borrowing the power of the enraged earth that flowed through her veins once more, she sped up its decay, the wood crumbling so quickly the doors exploded in a shower of dust. The air was filled with glittering dust particles, some wood, some gilded paint that attacked the lungs of those who stood nearby. Most of the guards had been blown off their feet and were scrambling about in the obscurity of destruction as Roslyn walked through the dust, causing swirls behind her as she entered the banquet hall.

All faces turned towards her as she stepped from the dust cloud. But she only paid heed to one.

Frederik stood warily, his mouth slack with astonishment and his eyebrows furrowed. "Roslyn? They told me you were dead?" He turned to his father, sat at his right hand, his voice changing, turning brittle and bitter. "You told me she was dead!"

Captain Dietrich, who stood behind the King Expectant's chair, placed a hand on the hilt of his sword but remained as the old king ignored his son and shouted to his guards, "Stop her! Stop the Domovnian witch!"

Roslyn strode down the aisle, past the tables of merrymakers and wedding guests whose forks, spoons and goblets hung halfway to their mouths as they watched the scene unfurl before them. The guards that dared approach her were prevented either by a curling vine wrapping itself round an ankle that dragged them backwards or a bushel of thorns and briar that caged them where they stood.

The gasps and shrieks within were mirrored by the wide eyes of all who sat on the top table, including Frederik.

"Roslyn? What are you doing?"

"I am saving your life!" Roslyn panted. She barely had time to think as the woman at Frederik's side stood. Roslyn locked eyes with Captain Dietrich and bellowed, "Isapf comes in the form of the false bride!" just as Rose reached to her waistband and pulled out a glittering knife, which she thrust into the air behind the crown prince's back.

Roslyn shot out a hand and from her very fingertips, thin tendrils of flora whipped towards the top table, but she couldn't sustain holding back the guards and saving the prince. The magic was draining her. A flash of fear crossed Frederik's face as he turned, slack-jawed at her proclamation, to see the knife intended for his heart an inch away from his eye. It quivered and hung there, vibrating as the woman who held it grunted and strained against the hand that held her fast. Captain Dietrich had his own knife to her throat as he bent her wrist back with terrifying strength. There was a crunch, a scream, and the clatter of a blade on the stone floor. For a moment, all was silent.

Then the hall erupted as the rebel ladies-in-waiting leapt into action. Cascades of whizzing petals and leaves sliced through the air and the flesh of anyone in their way. Tables were overturned, sending dishes, platters and goblets scattering across the floor as the wedding guests screamed and tried to protect themselves. Silen slipped his leash and ran into the fray, an ululating war cry on his tongue, ramming guards and rebels alike with his horns, or bucking them with his hooves.

"Free my men!" Dietrich bellowed at Roslyn as he fought a violent struggle with Rose; she was wrapping his arms in rose stems, thorns leaving bloody lines across his skin, but he wouldn't let go. She wafted her hand in the direction of the Oderberg soldiers and the vines and briars that held them shrivelled.

"There are more in the courtyard!" she yelled and was aware of Dietrich barking orders to a group of men already running out the door. It was costing her energy to keep Eik and his men trapped and she needed to use her efforts on the rebels who were engaged in battle with the soldiers, baffling them with their supernatural powers.

One was staring at the balcony, hands outstretched. Suddenly, Roslyn heard the thump of footsteps and her heart stuck in her throat as she saw an enormous willow tree walking towards them. It waved its tendril like branches up over its crown, bending down to whip and slice any Oderberg who approached. It clambered up over the edge of the balcony, the stone crumbling under its mass of roots, and shot a branch straight towards Frederik.

Roslyn screamed and ran headlong into the rebel, knocking her off her feet and causing her hold on the tree to waver. It groaned and listed over the cowering nobles, threatening to come crashing down on them. She had to do something; she had to get hold of that tree, but was that even possible?

She looked up and glanced around, searching for an answer. She caught sight of Silen who yelled through the commotion.

"The seed of an apple is still a tree, it needs but to know, and so will it be. Know the power is in you, girl! Be the tree!"

She nodded. She knew the power of a Botan flowed within her, the power of the lost royals who had the ability to give but also to take away. Roslyn reached out with her power and in a sickening lurch, a moment where she and the Arbor were both inside the tree and each other, she ripped the Affinity from the woman and righted the tree, stilling its branches.

The rebel sank to her knees, her hands shaking, her mouth open with shock, as the guards swarmed around her. Roslyn felt the woman's power squirming inside her and wanted to be sick. This was unnatural, this was wrong, like her soul was spliced and rotting; what was she doing?

She turned to the willow, placed her hand on its bark and released the Affinity back into the wood. Suddenly she could breathe again and even though she shook with fatigue, she had a shocking realisation. She knew what she had to do. She had to disable the rebels.

One by one, she wrenched their powers from them, each time with the same sickening feeling of invasion, forcing tears to spill down her cheeks, before she gave the plants their own power back, severing any connection the rebels ever had with them.

She left Rose until last. She had stopped struggling with Dietrich and stared at her in horror.

"No! No, please! Don't take my Affinity!"

Roslyn shook her head, her words wheezing out in strained exertion. "What the Ancestors gifted to us can also be taken back. You have dishonoured them and no longer deserve to call yourself a Descendant!"

"Who gives you the right? This kind of punishment is for treason to the crown! Who gave you that power?" Rose's voice was shrill with panic and hatred.

Roslyn was exhausted. She could barely lift her arm to point at the shining bronze antlers poking out of the destruction of the high table. "The crown itself!"

With a last thrust of energy, she sapped Rose of her power. The rebel slumped in Captain Dietrich's arms, sobbing loudly as her Affinity was severed. As she let the power go back into the roses from which they came, she felt her ties on the rebels in the courtyard loosen. They had been detained. She would disable them as soon as she was able.

Black was tinting her vision. She had used too much of herself too quickly. As her knees give way, a pair of hands caught her, breaking her fall.

A cup was pressed to her lips and although half its contents spilled down her chin, she gulped at the sweet wine gratefully. She looked up past its rim and saw eyes like sapphires gazing down at her. As the wine restored her strength, she raised a shaking hand to Frederik's cheek. Worry crinkled his brow and tainted his eyes, but the hint of the grateful smile danced on the corners of his lips.

"Guards," he called over his shoulder, motioning to Rose. "Bind this woman." He swallowed somewhat painfully, a flash of shame creeping up from his collar and onto his cheeks. "Take my... wife and her ladies to the dungeons to await her trial."

At a nod from Dietrich, the soldiers shook themselves off and did the King Expectant's bidding, dragging the now malleable and distraught women from the room. Only Rose still had fire in her eyes and as she was carried

340

through the doorway, she yelled, "What have you done? What have you done?"

There was a scuffle of movement to the side and King Casimir, with the help of his stewards, rose from under the upturned table to his feet.

"Yes, girl, do you know what you have done? I'll tell you. You have ruined our alliance with Eredzha and in doing so you have sealed Domovnia's fate, that every single one of you magic-wielding sons of whores will be obliterated!"

Roslyn began to chuckle at the sight of the enraged, red-faced man, held up by his men bellowing as if he hadn't just witnessed the scene everyone else had.

"What?" the king spat. Everyone turned to Roslyn, who could not contain the somewhat hysterical laugh that bubbled up from her chest. It echoed round the room as the courtiers and servants gazed on in confusion. "What is so funny?"

Roslyn gripped Frederik's arm and looked up at King Casimir. "Is that anyway to speak to your daughter-in-law?"

The room erupted into a fizz of exclamations, questions and hissing gossip that ran the length of the room. When it died down, the first word uttered in the tentative stillness came from Frederik's lips, drawing Roslyn's eyes to them. "What?"

"*I* was the one in the church. *I* was the woman who said those vows, not Rose. The rebels came to Eluha, where your father had imprisoned me and I overheard their plan." Frederik shot his father, who had now returned to his seat and was gasping for air, a look of utter disgust. "I used my Affinity to escape. I integrated myself in with the rebel crew. I gave the real Princess and her retinue the

341

means to escape once they were out of our sight and…"
She paused and gave a somewhat apologetic smile. "I also
used my Affinity to ensure that Rose and the other rebels
could not take part in the ceremony. They were going to
kill you; I had to warn you somehow. I just didn't intend
that I would be the one saying those vows alongside you.
I'm sorry, Frederik, but I just wanted to keep you safe!"

As her voice faded away, the silence deepened, their
affair exposed. Frederik stood and walked to the detritus
of the banquet table. He remained motionless, staring at a
spot of spilled wine on the silk tablecloth. Roslyn's palms
grew sweaty as the soldiers looked around in agitation and
tightened their grips on their weapons again.

Finally, Frederik looked up, tears in his eyes. "So that
means that *you* are my wife…"

Roslyn nodded, trembling slightly.

"I have a Domovnian wife, who tried to kill my father,
albeit on his own orders…" He tilted his head over his
shoulder and smiled, a familiar twinkle in his eye. "That
has just been crowned Queen Expectant with none other
than the Briar Crown."

"Preposterous!" King Casimir screamed, slamming
his hand onto the table, making the smashed glasses clink
and clatter. "You have no proof that this is the woman that
was in the chapel with you. You just wish it so, as you
prefer the taste of her cunny! The woman was veiled. We
have no idea which woman it was."

"But I do, father." Frederik wheeled around to the old
man. "When the woman in the chapel fainted, I caught her
and when I helped her up I noticed that on her wrist was a
band woven from plant fibres. Hung on that cord was a
silver button, bearing the Oderberg emblem. A band I

342

wove myself for the woman I love…" he turned to Roslyn. "Do you have such an item on your person?"

Roslyn swallowed and lifted her right arm into the air, allowing the lace sleeve of the bridal gown to slip down to her elbow, exposing the bracelet wrapped around her shimmering olive skin. She showed the button, the Chained Mountain glinting in the light..

Frederik rushed to her and knelt at her feet, snatching up her left hand in his and kissing it. "I knew, I knew you couldn't be dead, but…" He looked round and the destruction her entrance had caused, and the foliage that she had produced to entrap those who'd got in her way. "You said you were barely even a Hedgie, but here you are showing all the powers of a Botan, powers only the royal house of Domonov used to possess." He stood and held both her hands in his as a collective gasp ran around the room. "Are you the lost princess?"

Roslyn's head swam as the piece of gossip reverberated around the stone walls, dread snaking its way down her spine, numbing her fingers and toes. She looked up into Frederik's blue eyes, her voice a breathless whisper.

"I think so… but I can't be entirely certain. I never knew who my parents were, but Lady Margitte mistook me for Queen Ouna. Hedda saved my life from the ruins of Eluha that night. When the crown was placed on my head, I felt something. The whole world moved within me; that's why I fainted. It was too much power, all at once." She released her hands from Frederik's, stood shakily and walked to the high table where the Briar Crown lay on its side. Roslyn picked it up and pulled the tablecloth from it, plucking the fabric from its thorns and leaves before holding it before her in both hands.

Frederik followed and put his hands around hers, so they both held the crown between them. He licked his lips and stammered, "Maybe you are the lost princess, maybe not. It doesn't matter to me because I fell in love with Roslyn Pleveli... but I do know one thing. The moment we were married, you became royalty. You became the Queen Expectant, but not just any queen. When the Briar Crown touched your head, you also became Queen of Domovnia."

The room was still. Everyone, noble and guard alike, stared open-mouthed at the Oderberg King Expectant and the new Domonov Queen. Frederik gently eased the crown from Roslyn's fingers, raised it high, and placed it on her head. Then he took her hand and turned her around so they stood side-by-side, hands clasped together facing the court. He cleared his throat and addressed them in a loud, clear voice.

"Today, a Domovnian married an Oderberg. Through this marriage, Domovnia and Bergam have been united. Let that be an end to the strife between our nations. Let us work together to restore both peoples and this land to their former beauty and glory." He looked round at the guards. "Cast down your weapons. Set aside your hatred, and learn to love one another, as my Queen and I do."

"No!" screamed Casimir, gasping for air with the effort of his objection. "I am the king and I order you to—"

"Father." Frederik turned and addressed him kindly but with firmness. "You have named me King Expectant and in doing so have declared yourself unfit to rule. I suggest you get some rest." He turned to the stewards. "Please take my father to his rooms. This has all been too much for him."

The stewards bobbed their heads and wheeled the protesting old king away, dodging his kicks and the swipes of his cane. As his caterwauling dimmed the farther they wheeled him from the hall, the Oderbergs, soldiers, courtiers and servants stood and looked around, unsure what to do next.

A rustling sounded from the side of the room and a figure stepped forward, brushing debris from her dark velvet skirts and straightening her ruff, which had come askew. Her footsteps echoed as she made her way to the couple on the steps of the platform.

She sniffed and looked up at Roslyn with the same haughty expression that had greeted her in the carriage so long ago.

Her voice was brittle and reprimanding as she spoke. "Standing there in that hideous crown, I have never seen you look more like your grandmother, girl!" Roslyn gasped as Lady Margitte's face broke into a genuine smile, a teasing glint in her eye as she waved at her torn and bloodied Eredzhi gown. "Not that she would ever have worn anything so… unbefitting of a Domonov, of course."

She lowered herself painfully to the ground, batting off Charlotta who had run forward to help her ancient knees, and bowed her head. "Allow me to be the first to pledge my allegiance, my Queen."

At the old woman's words, the people fell to their knees in waves. Roslyn was stunned. She could barely breathe and tears pricked the corners of her eye. As she looked around at her new subjects, a few stray dandelion seeds blew in through a window on the breeze.

Frederik stretched out his hand and let them land on his palm. He turned to Roslyn over his shoulder and whispered, "It looks like my wish came true, after all."

Epilogue

The late summer sun shone down on the Queen's gardens as Roslyn took in the surrounding splendour, stretching with blissful contentment. Where only one year prior the beds had been almost barren and smothered by weeds, now they were a riot of colour and scent, packed with so many different types of flowers and herbs, she couldn't even count them all. She could, however, feel the thrum from each one of them in her veins and the love with which they were planted.

As the gates of Novlada were thrown open, Domovnians streamed into the palace grounds to pay thanks to the woman who had given them their freedom, filling her gardens with their Affinity plants. They were filled with life and were soon overflowing, instigating a much-needed seasonal change. Every three months the doors were opened to those who wished to bless the gardens with their plant, keeping the grounds beautiful and functional all year round.

The cold stone chapel had been torn down and a Living Church of willow and blossom sprung up in its

347

place, protecting the stone altar of the Oderbergs. It quickly became a symbol of their union and a place of pilgrimage.

She yawned. The sun was making her drowsy, and she looked down at the long since forgotten letter in her lap and smiled. Princess Aylin of Eredzha's latest missive was as entertaining as usual. The pair had become firm friends after Roslyn's daring rescue, freeing not only Frederik but also the princess from an unwanted marriage.

She was soon woken from her haze by the familiar tapping of a walking stick and a cheerful voice making its way along the path, its owner greeting everyone it passed as a long-lost friend.

"There's my girl!" The voice was suddenly filled with love as it rung out just behind her. Roslyn smiled as she turned her head, squinting in the sunlight to see a halo of blond curls duck down in her direction. She raised her lips to await Frederik's kiss, but was left sadly wanting as her husband bent down to the bundle on the grass at her feet. But she wasn't angry. There was only one person who could command that look of love in his eyes other than her, and she couldn't blame him.

She watched as Frederik lowered himself onto the grass, so that his eyes were level with the large, wide ones of the babe who gurgled and gave a toothless grin when she saw him. Roslyn's heart filled with warmth at the sight of her daughter's podgy little hand playfully slapping the beaming cheeks of her father. He cooed back to her babbles, turning them into a conversation.

"Well, yes, I had a lovely day, and... you'll never guess what?"

348

The baby, who was on her back, swung her toes up, catching them in her chubby fingers, and raised her eyebrows with a stunted squeal.

"The restoration is almost finished! We'll be moving back to Eluha before the winter is here!"

The babe clapped her hands at her father's excitement and giggled.

"Well, yes! You should be excited, because your room is going to be the biggest of them all!"

He laughed and looked up at Roslyn, love of a different kind making him serious. She smiled, thrilled at the news, and lowered herself to the ground beside them. She, too, looked down at her daughter and spoke in a sing-song voice.

"And are you going to show Pappa what you did today?"

"What did you do, my clever girl?" The babe laughed as Frederik sat back up, the suspense widening his grin.

Roslyn pushed him back gently with the her hand, giving the child more room. She picked her up and placed her on her stomach. Her head wobbled adorably as she looked up at her parents and grinned. Then Roslyn she patted the grass an arm's length away. "Go on then, show him." Her voice was soft and encouraging.

Her eyes met Frederik's for a brief second and she smiled conspiratorially before nodding towards the now straining child that was rocking on the grass. She veered onto her side, sticking an arm out under her large head.

"Go on, sweetheart!" Frederik flung his hands over his mouth as his exclamation diverted her attention from her task.

With a final, somewhat frustrated grunt and a kick of her chubby legs, the baby let the weight of her head pull her over onto her back.

"She rolled over!" The king exclaimed. In his joy, he swooped down upon the baby girl and scooped her up in his arms, smothering her with kisses. "Such a clever, clever girl. Yes, you are."

Roslyn smiled and touched him gently on the arm, redirecting his attention to the patch of grass where the infant had just rolled. "But look what else she did, Frederik."

Where only moments before there had been plain grass, the space now was filled with white flowers, their golden centres shining like a thousand tiny suns.

"Does this mean… we can finally name her?"

Roslyn finally let go of the joyful tears she had been holding in all day. "Yes! Our daughter has an Affinity. We can finally give her a name!"

Frederik snuggled into the excited little creature and pressed his forehead against Roslyn's, wrapping the small family together in the joy of the moment. "And I can think of nothing better than her Affinity plant." He rose suddenly and held the babe up in the air.

"Ladies and gentlemen, citizens of Domovnia and Bergam…" he called joyfully over the gardens, turning the heads of those who tended the plants or were simply walking its beautiful paths. "May I present to you the now named Crown Princess—Deyzi Domonov."

A roar of applause rang out not just from the gardens, but from the town below where his words had also carried.

"May she wear the Briar Crown as beautifully as her mother and rule this land with grace and patience,

350

strengthening the peace we now enjoy. All hail, the crown princess."

Another bellow of jubilation sounded and Roslyn laughed as she thought of the panic that would take place in the kitchens at the unexpected news and public feast that would follow. No doubt nine months from this night, many more Domovnians would be born, Deyzi's future subjects and friends and possibly a future king. Her heart sank a little at the thought that there would only ever be Queens and King Consorts from now on, the head piece of the Domonov king still missing. Many had seen her father wearing it the night of the Fall, many had seen him struck by an arrow, but then according to many more, he had simply vanished, the helm with him. His body was never found.

Frederik saw her change of mood and placed Deyzi in her lap. As their daughter reached up to touch the lower leaves of her crown, unafraid of its thorns, he rubbed Roslyn's back.

"We'll keep looking. We'll find it, don't worry."

Roslyn nodded and shook her worry to the back of her mind, just as a familiar sight rolled into the garden.

"What's this I hear about my granddaughter? She finally has a name?" Hedda's voice rang loud and clear over the cheers as she pushed Lady Margitte towards them. The old woman smiled and clapped her hands.

"What a beautiful baby!" Her voice croaked with age and she raised her rheumy eyes to Roslyn's. "Is she yours?"

Roslyn nodded with a sad smile on her face, but Hedda wasted no time in prising Deyzi from her mother's hands, smothering her in kisses and placing her in Margitte's lap.

"Come on then, clever girl. Show Nanny and Grand Tanta what you can do!"

The babe gurgled and reached up to stroke Margitte's wrinkled cheek with wonder. As her podgy fingers slapped back down into the crushed velvets of her skirts, a spray of daisy heads rolled over the fabric. A cheer of adoration and pride sounded from the small, happy family.

Restoring the balance could wait. For now, there was peace and a named heir to the throne. Roslyn leaned over and kissed Frederik gently on the lips, listening to the sounds of celebration in a land united by love.

Thank you for reading The Briar Crown!

If you enjoyed it, don't forget to leave a review on your site of choice.
Reviews not only allow authors to become more visible, but they also help readers find the perfect books for them.

Be the first to learn about
Helen Rygh-Pedersen's
news and future releases!

Sign up for my newsletter at:
www.helenryghpedersen.com
Or follow me on Instagram
@ryghpedersenwrites

Notes

The Briar Crown is a fairy tale retelling of one of the lesser-known tales by the Brothers Grimm, Maid Maleen. I first came across it in the Usborne Forgotten Fairy Tales of Brave and Brilliant Girls as 'The Nettle Princess' written by Rob Lloyd Jones.

Now, I am a bit of a nerd and prior to finding this story; I had already fallen down the rabbit hole of the wonderful world of nettles and was amazed at all of their uses, including, as mentioned in the book, being able to make cloth from it. I had even collected, retted and processed some nettles, ending up with a handful of wispy white fibres.

If you are at all interested, I highly recommend you visit the Facebook group, *Nettles for Textiles,* and watch Sally Pointer's instructional videos on YouTube for how to make your very own cordage from the common stinging nettle.

I took some artistic license with the process, but stuck to it as closely as I could whilst moving the scene along.

Acknowledgements

The first thank you goes to my husband, who kept the children entertained during CampNanowrimo so that I could talk to myself and my dictaphone and get this book written. If you hadn't done that, I would probably still be writing it.

Thank you to my wonderful critique partner, Abbey Fox, who did an amazing job of keeping up with the pace and instructing me in the finer arts of fantasy romance. Your comments made me learn and laugh, and gave me the confidence to carry on.

Next, my thanks go to my team of Beta Readers; Victoria Seidal, Rosie Walters, Jacqui Dobor, Laura Testa-Reyes, Azulina, Victoria Butler, Kris Marchesi, Charis Negley and April Samore. You all read quickly and replied promptly and in depth with both things you loved and changes to implement, which I am sure has made it a better book.

Heartfelt thanks go to my editor, Rachel Marchesi, who worked incredibly hard to beat this book into shape.

Julia Scott, my last minute formatting marvel, thank you for being so patient with all my silly questions!

To my cover designer, Angela, thank you for designing the *perfect* cover for this book. You brought the Briar Crown to life before my very eyes!

Thank you to my family, who encouraged my love of reading and writing from a young age. Thank you to my sister, Amy. You are without a doubt my greatest cheerleader.

Thank you to everyone who follows and supports me on all the social media sites. Thank you for sharing my announcements, posting reviews, and spreading the word. I really couldn't do this without you.

And last, but by no means least, thank you, dear reader, for picking up this book and making it this far. I really hope you will join me for the next instalment of The Zemkoska Chronicles.

Printed in the USA
CPSIA information can be obtained
at www.ICGtesting.com
LVHW031453251023
762116LV00001B/60

9 788293 831112